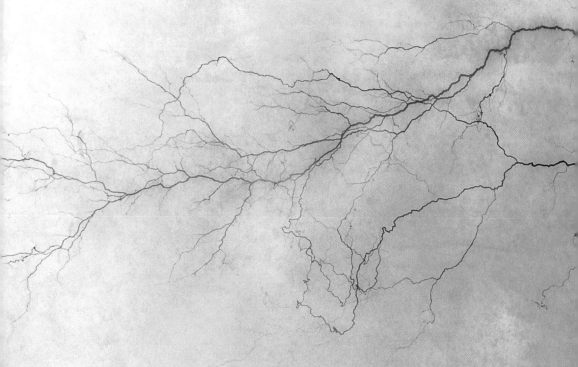

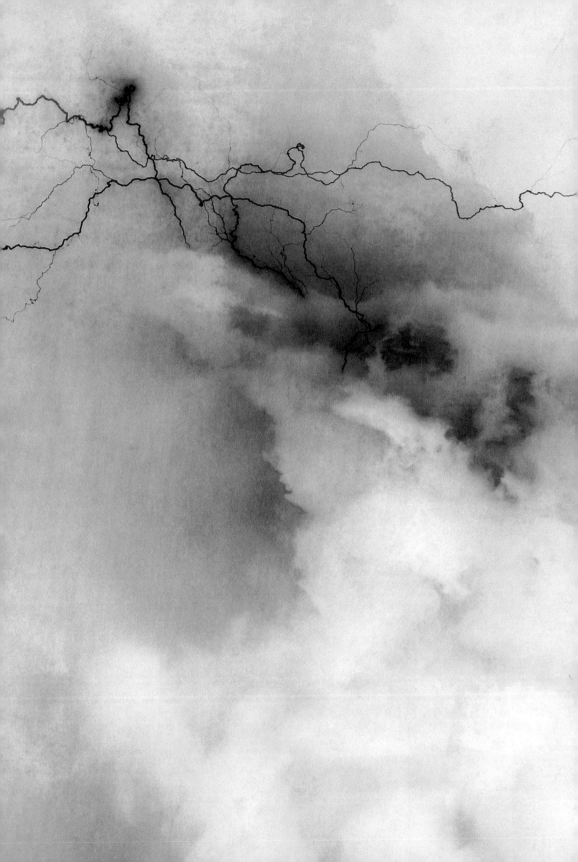

FRANKENSTEIN
OR, THE MODERN PROMETHEUS

MARY SHELLEY

....

ANNOTATED FOR SCIENTISTS, ENGINEERS, AND CREATORS OF ALL KINDS

EDITED BY

DAVID H. GUSTON, ED FINN, AND JASON SCOTT ROBERT

MANAGING EDITORS

JOEY ESCHRICH AND MARY DRAGO

THE MIT PRESS
CAMBRIDGE, MASSACHUSETTS
LONDON, ENGLAND

Title Page of the First Edition of *Frankenstein*, 1818 (litho), English School (19th century)/
New York Public Library, USA/Bridgeman Images

This book was set in Century Schoolbook Pro and PF DIN Pro by The MIT Press. Book design by Marge Encomienda. Printed and bound in the United States of America.

Library of Congress Cataloging-in-Publication Data

Names: Shelley, Mary Wollstonecraft, 1797–1851, author. | Guston, David H., 1965- editor. |
   Finn, Ed, 1980- editor. | Robert, Jason Scott, 1972- editor.
Title: Frankenstein : annotated for scientists, engineers, and creators of
   all kinds / Mary Shelley ; edited by David H. Guston, Ed Finn, and Jason Scott Robert.
Description: Cambridge, MA : The MIT Press, 2017. | Includes bibliographical references.
Identifiers: LCCN 2016041014 | ISBN 9780262533287 (pbk. : alk. paper)
Subjects: LCSH: Frankenstein, Victor (Fictitious character)--Fiction. |
   Frankenstein's Monster (Fictitious character)--Fiction. |
   Scientists--Fiction. | Monsters--Fiction. | Horror fiction. | Science
   fiction. | Shelley, Mary Wollstonecraft, 1797-1851. Frankenstein. |
   Science in literature.
Classification: LCC PR5397 .F7 2017 | DDC 823/.7--dc23 LC record available at https://lccn.loc.
gov/2016041014

10   9   8   7   6

For Sam and his enthusiasm and patience—Dave Guston

For Anna and our beloved monsters, Nora and Declan—Ed Finn

For three very well-parented creatures: Annika, Astrid, and Alexandra—Jason Robert

And to the memory of our friend and colleague Charles E. Robinson.

Charlie's scholarship and generosity were crucial to this volume,
as to so much of the prior study of *Frankenstein*. We hope through his work
presented here, among the last of his completed before his death,
that his knowledge, wisdom, and gentility will reach a new generation
of readers.

CONTENTS

....

FRANKENSTEIN
OR, THE MODERN PROMETHEUS

ESSAYS

APPENDIXES

EDITORS' PREFACE
DAVID H. GUSTON, ED FINN, AND JASON SCOTT ROBERT

No work of literature has done more to shape the way humans imagine science and its moral consequences than *Frankenstein; or The Modern Prometheus*, Mary Shelley's remarkably enduring tale of creation and responsibility. *Frankenstein* is the literary offspring of an eighteen-year-old girl ensconced in a romantic yet fraught summer getaway on the shores of Lake Geneva in response to a "dare" to come up with a ghost story. That dare was issued a little more than two hundred years ago. In writing *Frankenstein*, Mary produced both in the creature and in its creator tropes that continue to resonate deeply with contemporary audiences. Moreover, these tropes and the imaginations they engender actually influence the way we confront emerging science and technology, conceptualize the process of scientific research, imagine the motivations and ethical struggles of scientists, and weigh the benefits of scientific research against its anticipated and unforeseen pitfalls.

The world will celebrate the bicentennial of *Frankenstein*'s publication on 1 January 2018. Arizona State University (ASU) will be the epicenter of this celebration of the power of literature, science, art, imagination, and ingenuity. ASU's Frankenstein Bicentennial Project is a constructive, intellectual, and public endeavor meant to celebrate *Frankenstein*'s pervasive influence on contemporary culture and scientific research. With funding from the US National Science Foundation (NSF Award no. 1516684), we are producing a citizen-curated, digital narrative experience of *Frankenstein* and Frankensteiniana in collaboration with dozens of museums and other partners. Our goal is to understand the galvanizing power of *Frankenstein* to stoke the public imagination and to harness that energy to ignite new conversations about creativity and responsibility among science and technology researchers, students, and the public. We hope these conversations will inspire a deeper understanding of how to govern science and technology responsibly. We believe *Frankenstein* is a book that can encourage us to be both thoughtful and hopeful: having these conversations can help all of us make better decisions about how to shape and understand scientific research and technical innovation in ways that support our well-considered values and ambitions.

Mary Shelley's landmark fusion of science, ethics, and literary expression provides an opportunity both to reflect on how science is framed and understood by the public and to contextualize new scientific and technological innovations, especially in an era of synthetic biology, genome editing, robotics, machine learning, and regenerative medicine. Although *Frankenstein* is infused with the exhilaration of seemingly unbounded human creativity, it also prompts serious reflection about our individual and collective responsibility for nurturing the products of our creativity and imposing constraints on our capacities to change the world around us. Engaging with *Frankenstein* allows a broad public and especially future scientists and engineers to consider the history of our scientific progress together with our expanding abilities in the future and to reflect on evolving understandings of the responsibilities such abilities entail.

...

This critical edition of *Frankenstein* for scientists and engineers is—like the creature himself—the first of its kind and just as monstrous in its composition and development. Originally proposed by our colleague Cajsa Baldini in ASU's Department of English, the skeleton of the critical edition was fleshed out at a workshop at ASU in the spring of 2014, hosted by two of us (Guston and Finn) and funded by the NSF (NSF Award no. 1354287) to explore science-and-society projects that might be built around *Frankenstein*). Robert served as scribe in breakout sessions dedicated to fleshing out the critical edition, which also included Baldini, historian Catherine O'Donnell, and representatives from the ASU Libraries, a local high school, and the larger community. We then sent copies of *Frankenstein* to professors and students in science, technology, engineering, and mathematics (STEM) fields and asked them to identify key terms and passages requiring elucidation and elaboration for STEM students from high school to graduate school. We received almost one thousand suggestions! And so the editorial work began in earnest.

In the spring of 2015, still working with NSF funding, we brought together a small group of advisers to discuss both a print version and an immersive digital version of an annotated *Frankenstein*. One key contributor was Charles E. Robinson, emeritus professor at the University of Delaware and one of the world's leading scholars of *Frankenstein*. Robinson graciously offered us the opportunity to use his painstakingly line-edited and amended version of the original manuscript published in 1818 as our core text. The workshop yielded a strong sense of what distinguishes our critical edition from previous ones, which have dwelt on the novel's literary or historical importance, addressing it as representative of romanticism or the gothic. Other volumes have focused on the science or ethics of *Frankenstein* or both, but they have been either critical anthologies or otherwise engaged with the novel in a secondary fashion. We wanted our version to be unique in bringing together the primary text and annotations and short essays by a diverse group of experts. This juxtaposition will allow STEM readers to explore critical understandings of the ethical and societal dimensions of scientific inquiry in the immediate company of Victor Frankenstein, his creature, and a gripping narrative of creativity and responsibility.[1] Rather than focusing on the specifics of the science and what Mary Shelley got or did not get right,[2] our version (although including some such discussion) emphasizes broader questions of the scientific endeavor, the roles of scientists, and the relationship between scientific creativity and responsibility.

With the serial and at times massively parallel assistance of Valerye Milleson, Mary Drago, and Joey Eschrich, we vetted the lengthy list of suggested annotations and then solicited, assigned, collected, edited, amplified, truncated, massaged, and merged the annotations into the far-ranging critical conversation composing this volume. We also identified key themes to be highlighted in longer essays—including creativity, imagination, monstrosity, angst, responsibility, and the roles of gender in *Frankenstein* and in science and engineering—and commissioned essays from leading scholars and writers at ASU, across the United States, and around the world. The end result, we believe, is an edition of *Frankenstein* that incites a deeply engaging cross-disciplinary exploration of the complexities of the development of personal and professional identity and of the rightful place of science and scientists in our rapidly changing world.

...

In organizing and editing this material, we were faced with innumerable decisions about style and content. Upon reflection, perhaps the most consequential are the naming conventions we have adopted. First, we have decided to refer to the author and her main protagonist simply as Mary and Victor wherever possible. We do not wish to diminish them with this familiarity, but we do wish precisely to render them more familiar. Mary was eighteen years old when she began to set her ideas to paper. Victor was a young man, still very much a student. Both of them are more like you, the reader, in that sense than like us. We want you to see them more as colleagues, classmates, and maybe even as friends rather than as a distant contributor to the literary canon and the maniacal character she devised.

Recognizing—as many have before us, from the author of Genesis to Mary herself—that to name something is to assert some measure of creative power over it, we have decided to attempt to consistently identify Victor's creation as "the creature." We do this for several reasons, foremost among them to allow readers to determine for themselves whether the appellations *daemon* (frequently used in the text) and *monster* (most often used in posterity) are appropriate. For us, *creature* is a more neutral, descriptive, and pedagogically appropriate denomination.

It is worth pointing out that the way we now use the word *creature* ignores a richer etymology. Today, we refer to birds and bees as creatures. Living things are creatures by virtue of their living-ness. When we call something a creature today, we rarely think in terms of something that has been created, and thus we erase the idea of a creator behind the creature. We have likewise lost the social connotation of the term *creature*, for creatures are made not just biologically (or magically) but also socially. In the contemporary film *Victor Frankenstein* (2015), for example, *Harry Potter*'s Daniel Radcliffe plays Igor—Victor's hunchback assistant not present in Mary's novel but invented for stage and screen—who is rescued from a circus, cured of his malformation, and embraced by Victor first as assistant and then as partner in his laboratory. Victor raises him from a subhuman existence, even giving him the name "Igor" because the freak-show hunchback has no name, and makes him an English gentleman worthy of invitations to clubs and balls and even the affection of a beautiful woman. Igor understands that he is Victor's creature in this regard, just as surely as if his life were created from nonlife. So to recognize both the biological and the social aspects of creation—as well as the failure of Mary's Victor to name his creation, thus rejecting the creature's social creation—we have decided on "the creature." So Mary, Victor, and the creature constitute the trinity of our text.

We also want to reflect on the fact that we are a trio of roughly middle-aged guys potentially appropriating Mary's work. Although changing the biological aspects of our identities for the purposes of this volume is not really an option, we can consider what it was like for us to confront issues of gender in *Frankenstein* and raise these issues for ourselves and for our readers. First, we must emphasize again that although the idea for the Frankenstein Bicentennial Project came from one of us, the idea for this volume came from our colleague Cajsa Baldini. As a lecturer in English at ASU, Cajsa is in a more vulnerable academic position than we are (two of us are tenured, one is on the tenure track). She had the further burden, familiar to many women, of family medical challenges that ultimately caused her to pass the project to us. Without her creative spark, this project would never have existed, and we are grateful for her blessing and her willingness to allow us to pursue the work in her stead.

It may be difficult for some readers, especially those accustomed to living the relatively privileged life of the white male, to recognize how hard it was for Mary to write and publish this book as a young woman without money or the support of her family (with the exception of her husband, the poet Percy Bysshe Shelley, who was just as much an outcast as she was).

When the first edition appeared in 1818, it listed no author, and some reviewers and readers assumed Percy was the real architect of the narrative. Several reviewers who knew the truth found it deeply alarming: the *British Critic* blamed the flaws it perceived in the text on the gender of its author, brutally ending its review by saying, "The writer of it is, we understand, a female; this is an aggravation of that which is the prevailing fault of the novel; but if our authoress can forget the gentleness of her sex, it is no reason why we should; and we shall therefore dismiss the novel without further comment" ("Review of *Frankenstein*" 1818). It was only one of the many times Mary was excluded from consideration because of her gender and her unconventional choices.

We can also speak of what it was like to learn from Mary because any failure on our part to acknowledge the sheer brilliance of her composition, its heritage and its progeny, its intricacies and its clarion vision, would be a failure as colossal as Victor's failure to acknowledge the intelligence of his creature—except that we are Mary's creatures and not the other way around. As university teachers, we know—but we do not always show— that our students have things to teach us. We do not labor under the misapprehension that we are bringing very much at all to Mary; rather, our hope is to bring Mary more clearly and powerfully to you. This endeavor requires, as we hope we have done through the invited essays and annotations, the recognition that Mary was not just an interesting writer but also a powerful thinker. Her parents—the feminist philosopher Mary Wollstonecraft, who died as a consequence of Mary's birth, and the similarly radical political philosopher William Godwin—provided her with the raw material. Tales of her intensive tutoring bring to mind that imposed by other nineteenth-century tiger fathers such as James Mill, who in educating John Stuart Mill produced a nervous breakdown in his son before producing a political theorist who surpassed him. Turning gender roles around, Mary did not turn inward and anxious but instead turned outward and rebellious. Sixteen-year-old Mary ran off with Percy from England to continental Europe, returning shortly after only to run off again on the jaunt that led to her to imagine *Frankenstein*. Mary was doing drugs (laudanum, a powdered opiate) and became pregnant by a man who was at the time married to someone else: if she had turned up at ASU or any other school, she would have been labeled an "at-risk student" and targeted for intervention.

And the risks she faced were significant. By the time Mary began writing *Frankenstein*, she had already become a mother and lost a child. Little Clara arrived two months early in February 1815, only to die two weeks later, to Mary's harrowing sorrow. Mary wrote later of a "waking dream" that inspired *Frankenstein* in which she managed to revive baby Clara by moving her closer to the fire and nursing her to health. Mary would give birth to four children in all and bury three of them. Throughout Mary's life, birth and death were intimately connected. The themes of parenthood and responsibility in *Frankenstein*, of lost creatures and dead children, were visceral experiences for Mary. Among its many faces, *Frankenstein* was a very personal ghost story for its author.

After *Frankenstein* was published, Mary's life was perhaps even more challenging. She lost two other children, largely because of traveling with them across Europe in precarious conditions for the sake of her beloved Percy, and then she lost him, too, when he drowned in Italy at the age of twenty-nine. A less-resilient heroine of novels of Mary's time might have followed Percy to the grave by her own hand. Mary persisted. And just as we are in the thrall of her intellectual power, we are in awe of her resilience and emotional strength.[3]

The questions of gender and marginality come to the fore in several of the essays we have collected in this volume, specifically in the contributions by scholar Anne K. Mellor and fiction writer Elizabeth Bear. We subscribe to the idea that only Mary, with her bodily experience and embodied wisdom, could have written *Frankenstein* with such profundity. Indeed, questions about Mary's authorship persisted even after her name as author was first revealed; later critics supposed that it was really Percy's work, as if Mary could not have done it. To be sure, Percy contributed a great deal. But if you have visited the manuscript and fair copy at the Bodleian Library at the University of Oxford and been given a brilliant tour of its revelatory details by Bruce Barker-Benfield (as one of us has), you can see exactly how she did it—the dynamics of love and creativity played out in the looping flow of Mary's authorial hand and the angular interjections of Percy's editorial additions. This book by a young woman who would spend hours reading literature, philosophy, and history by her mother's grave, who was cut off by her father when she fled to Europe with Percy, and who lost a child of her own at seventeen is singular. No one else before or since could have written *Frankenstein* with the same combination of intellectual breadth, moral depth, and intense personal experience.

...

We also feel it is important to make the case for bringing Mary, Victor, and the creature into the heart of conversations about contemporary science and technology. Of course, it is a privilege to engage with one of the most influential and widely assigned (if not as widely read) novels in the

English language and one that has inspired so many high and low cultural expressions. That fecundity reveals something important about this story: *Frankenstein* is unequivocally not an antiscience screed, and scientists and engineers should not be afraid of it. The target of Mary's literary insight is not so much the content of Victor's science as the way he pursues it. This target is the same in much of science fiction—a genre that Mary certainly helped to invent—especially the kind that takes a dystopian turn.[4] We can choose to focus on the cautionary nature of the tale or on the part that continues to inspire students who believe that they can do better—as creative and responsible thinkers, makers, researchers, and citizens.

Since Mary's day, science and technology have become more pervasive in society. (We will demur from saying which society was changing faster, Mary's under steam power or ours under solar, nuclear, and computational power.) As we anticipate the third century beyond Mary's vision, we open the door to what may be the most pervasive scientific and technical endeavors yet: the creation and design of living organisms through techniques of synthetic biology, the creation and design of planetary-scale systems through climate engineering, and the integration of computational power and processes into nearly every sector of global society and even the fibers of our being. These technologies, radically different from each other in scale and materials, share a Promethean perspective. Each fuses natural processes with updated human ingenuity and purpose to offer much-needed benefits, but at the same time each presents real and even existential risks that have roots in the long stream of previous iterations of human ingenuity and purpose. Yet this framing of synthetic biology, climate engineering, and ubiquitous computation in terms of risk and benefit conceals crucial questions of values and politics: Who gets to decide on the agenda for scientific research and development? Who gets to say what problems or grand challenges we try to solve? Who gets to say how we solve them (or resolve them or muddle through them)? Who gets to partake in those benefits, and are they the same people put at risk by our attempts to solve the problems at stake?

These and many other questions are part of the enduring legacy of Mary Shelley's *Frankenstein*, here brought to you in a new critical edition designed to enhance our collective understandings and to invent—intentionally—a world in which we all want to live and, indeed, a world in which we all can thrive.

NOTES

1. By "critical," we mean being engaged in a detailed way with the text so that we are dealing not with superficial appearances but rather with deeper meanings and understandings. Scholars in the humanities often call this approach "close reading." We do not mean "critical" in the sense of "demeaning" or "disparaging." In fact, for the style of critical engagement you will encounter in this volume, simply attacking the novel or highlighting its flaws would not be nearly so revealing or fun.

2. One contemporary source for this perspective is an episode of the cable television series *Prophets of Science Fiction* (2011), dedicated to Mary Shelley and *Frankenstein*. The series was conceived, hosted, and executive-produced by blockbuster science fiction film director Ridley Scott.

3. The challenges of understanding Mary Shelley across the centuries have been brought to life brilliantly by a monologue commissioned and performed at the Bakken Museum. Located in Minneapolis, the Bakken is a small museum dedicated to the history of research into electricity and magnetism inspired by Earl Bakken, inventor of that most Frankensteinian technology, the transistorized pacemaker. At the workshop in May 2014, we were treated to a performance of this monologue by Dawn Krzykowski Brodey.

4. The relationship between science fiction and society's broader relationship to the future is central to the work that one of us (Finn) pursues at the Center for Science and the Imagination at ASU. The center was founded to explore and expand our collective capacity to imagine a broad range of possible futures, especially in terms of creativity and responsibility.

ACKNOWLEDGMENTS

This volume would not have been possible without the tireless efforts, wise counsel, and formidable intellect of our friends and colleagues.

We thank the following readers, who painstakingly identified passages in the text for annotation: Cristi Coursen, Mary Feeney, Steve Helms Tillery, Gary Marchant, and Clark Miller of Arizona State University as well as Stephanie Naufel of Northwestern University.

We also thank all of the participants in the "Multi-disciplinary Workshop on Scientific Creativity and Societal Responsibility" at Arizona State University in April 2014, where we first discussed plans for this volume, as well as Al DeSena, the program officer at the National Science Foundation who supported the workshop with a generous grant and more generous wisdom. We especially thank Cajsa Baldini, who originally conceived of the idea for this edition (you can learn more about Cajsa's invaluable contributions to the project in the "Editors' Preface"), and all of the members of the Critical Edition Working Group: Joshua Abbott, Brad Allenby, Joe Buenker, Jenefer Husman, Jane Maienschein, Catherine O'Donnell, and Jameson Wetmore of Arizona State University as well as Deedee Falls of the Bioscience High School in Phoenix.

In May 2015, we held a second advisory board workshop at ASU to make critical decisions about the goals for this project and the structure of the book. The conversations at that workshop were truly formative and immensely helpful. We thank all of our advisory board members for their intellectual generosity, good vibes, and keen insights: Torie Bosch of *Slate* magazine, Elizabeth Denlinger of the New York Public Library, Karin Ellison and Erika Gronek of Arizona State University, Kate Kiehl and Corey Pressman of Neologic, and Charles E. Robinson of the University of Delaware.

Special thanks to Valerye Milleson, a former postdoctoral fellow at the Lincoln Center for Applied Ethics and an incisive thinker in the field of clinical ethics, for shepherding this project through its earliest stages with careful attention and brio.

At ASU, institutional support was provided by Patrick Kenney, dean of the College of Liberal Arts and Sciences, and Sethuraman "Panch" Panchanathan, executive vice president for research and director of ASU's Knowledge Enterprise Development. We thank them profusely, as well as the many who provided other kinds of support, including Sally Kitch, George Justice, and Jim O'Donnell.

We are immeasurably grateful to all of our collaborators, including anyone we have failed to mention here. Any errors that remain are ours alone.

INTRODUCTION
CHARLES E. ROBINSON

In this novel written by Mary Wollstonecraft Shelley (1797–1851), Victor Frankenstein (never called "Dr." Frankenstein) leaves behind his idyllic childhood and Edenic Geneva, goes to university, studies the latest technologies and medical procedures, creates an unnamed monster,[1] and suffers the dangerous consequences of his pursuit of knowledge when his creature destroys his brother William; his wife, Elizabeth; and his best friend, Henry Clerval. In short, *Frankenstein* is a cautionary tale. And it is now for the first time published by an institute of technology for the purposes of educating students who are pursuing science, technology, engineering, and mathematics (STEM). (Some readers may wish or need to substitute *medicine* for *mathematics* in this acronym.) Up until this edition, *Frankenstein* has been primarily edited and published for and read by humanities students, students equally in need of reading this cautionary tale about forbidden knowledge and playing God. And to embrace the largest audience, we are publishing what may also be defined as a "STEAM edition" of Frankenstein, the A edited in for the arts, design, and humanities.

STEAM provides us a launching point for an analysis of *Frankenstein*, for its action takes place in the 1790s, by which time James Watt (1736–1819) had radically improved the steam engine and in effect started the Industrial Revolution, which accelerated the development of science and technology as well as medicine and machines in the nineteenth century.[2] The new steam engine powered paper mills, printed newspapers, and further developed commerce through steamboats and then trains. These same years were charged by the French Revolution, and anyone wishing to do a chronology of the action in *Frankenstein* will discover that Victor went off to the University of Ingolstadt in 1789, the year of the Fall of the Bastille, and he developed his creature in 1793, the year of the Reign of Terror in France.[3] Terror (as well as error) was the child of both revolutions, and Mary's novel records the terrorizing effects of the birth of the new revolutionary age, in the shadows of which we still live.

Frankenstein presents us with a world full of shadows and darkness and terror: we frequently read these three words and their variants in the text of *Frankenstein*; we encounter the visuals of these three words in the many hundreds of stage and screen adaptations of this novel, often figured by the Boris Karloff neck-bolted monster; and we experience the shadows and darkness and terror when we read the many news reports about cloning, genetic engineering, Frankenfoods, and the most recently unearthed Frankenvirus announced in September 2015. All of these references derive their metaphoric origin from a teenager named Mary Godwin, who eloped to the Continent with the already married poet Percy Bysshe Shelley

(1792–1822) in late July 1814, when she was sixteen; began writing her novel about Victor and his creature in Geneva in mid-June 1816, when she was eighteen; married Percy in London in late December 1816 after his first wife, Harriet, committed suicide; finished her novel in April or May 1817, when she was nineteen; and published it on 1 January 1818, when she was twenty years old. And this STEAM edition of the novel is being prepared exactly two hundred years later in commemoration of the bicentennial of this young woman's achievements.

It needs to be firmly stated here that Mary was not a Luddite opposed to new technologies. In fact, she was very interested in scientific matters, probably as a consequence of her parents, Mary Wollstonecraft (1759–1797) and William Godwin (1756–1836). Wollstonecraft was a famous political philosopher and feminist who died eleven days after her daughter was born as Mary Godwin, but the daughter was nurtured by reading her mother's works, including *Thoughts on the Education of Daughters* (1787) and the more famous *Vindication of the Rights of Woman* (1792), in which she argued that elementary school girls of the period should perform the simple experiments in "natural philosophy" or science that boys of the same age performed. Mary also received a scientific education indirectly from her father, a famous novelist and political philosopher who was visited at home by many famous writers and intellectuals, including the scientist and inventor William Nicholson (1753–1815). As a young girl, Mary almost certainly met Nicholson during his many visits to Godwin up through February 1810, and she likely knew of his publications, which included *The First Principles of Chemistry* (1790; third edition, 1796) and his earlier student textbook *Introduction to Natural Philosophy* (2 vols., 1782; fifth edition, 1805). As William St. Clair has remarked in his authoritative biography of the Godwins and the Shelleys, William Godwin turned to Nicholson "for information on the latest theories in chemistry, physics, optics, biology, and the other natural sciences" and for "his advice on scientific method" ([1989] 1991, 61).

When Mary met Percy Shelley, she learned that he had been encouraged in his scientific studies at Eton by Dr. James Lind (1736–1812), who was a member of the Lunar Society, a club that included scientists such as James Watt; the physician and poet and natural philosopher Erasmus Darwin (1731–1802), who published *Zoonomia* (1794–1801), a medical-philosophical treatise dealing with such matters as reproduction, development, sensation, and disease; and the dissenting minister and political activist Joseph Priestley (1733–1804), who knew Benjamin Franklin and published *The History and Present State of Electricity, with Original*

Experiments (1767).[4] Mary also must have known that at Oxford in 1810–1811 Percy had constructed his own electrical kite, made sparks by an electrical apparatus, and stored the "fluid" of electricity in Leyden jars: these actions provide the basis for the electrical experiments by Victor's father, Alphonse, in *Frankenstein*. The two Shelleys attended at least one of the many lectures in London on chemistry and electricity at this time, Mary recording on 28 December 1814 that they attended the "Theatre of Grand Philosophical Recreations" at the Great Room, Spring Gardens, where the famous balloon ascender and parachute descender "Professor Garnerin" gave a lecture titled "Electricity, Gas, Aerostation, Phantasmagoria, and Hydraulic Sports."[5] In Geneva in June 1816, during the coldest summer on record, Mary listened to conversations between Lord Byron and Percy about possibly discovering "the nature of the principle of life" (pp. 191–192), about galvanism and the experiments of Erasmus Darwin, and about the possible reanimation of a corpse.[6] And in early August 1816, she made Percy a balloon and purchased a telescope for his birthday.[7] Within a few months, by 28 October, she recorded her familiarity with the science of Sir Humphry Davy (1778–1829), whose book *Elements of Chemical Philosophy* (1812)[8] she read while she was drafting the first chapters of *Frankenstein* in the fall of 1816.

During the two-year period before Mary began to write *Frankenstein*, she was almost certainly aware, by way of Percy, of the famous vitalist controversy on the definition of life between two prominent scientists, John Abernethy (1764–1831) and his pupil, William Lawrence (1783–1867), the two professors of anatomy and surgery at London's Royal College of Surgeons.[9] Percy had attended some of Abernethy's lectures in 1811, and Lawrence was Percy's personal physician.[10] Moreover, Mary had met Lawrence at least twice when she accompanied her father to tea on 1 June 1812 and 5 March 1813 at the home of John Frank Newton, known for his vegetarianism.[11] Lawrence and Abernethy had become opponents by 1814: the former argued for a materialist explanation of life and against Abernethy's theory of vitalism, which explained life in terms of "some 'superadded' force … , some 'subtile, mobile, invisible substance,'" analogous on the one hand to soul and on the other to electricity."[12] This debate between Lawrence and Abernethy may have inspired Mary's depiction of Victor's relationships with his two different professors at the University of Ingolstadt (1472–1800), an actual Bavarian institution that had faculties of science, humanities, and medicine.[13] Victor first encountered and rejected "M. Krempe, professor of natural philosophy" (p. 28), who ridiculed him for his concentration on the alchemical philosophers Albertus Magnus

(c. 1193–1280) and Paracelsus (1493–1541) and who recommended the latest books on natural philosophy. Victor was not naive, but his negative reaction to Krempe was dictated by the professor's physiognomy (appearance is a thematic motif in this novel: witness the horrified reactions to the deformed creature). As Victor himself explains, "I had long considered those authors useless whom the professor had so strongly reprobated; but I did not feel much inclined to study the books which I procured at his recommendation. M. Krempe was a little squat man, with a gruff voice and repulsive countenance; the teacher, therefore, did not prepossess me in favour of his doctrine. Besides, I had a contempt for the uses of modern natural philosophy" (p. 29).

Victor changed his opinion about modern science once he heard M. Waldman (also modeled on Percy Shelley's kindly Etonian professor, Dr. Lind) deliver a lecture about the history of science, a lecture that most STEM students need to hear today:

> M. Waldman entered shortly after. This professor was very unlike his colleague. He appeared about fifty years of age, but with an aspect expressive of the greatest benevolence. ... He began his lecture by a recapitulation of the history of chemistry and the various improvements made by different men of learning, pronouncing with fervour the names of the most distinguished discoverers. He then took a cursory view of the present state of the science, and explained many of its elementary terms. After having made a few preparatory experiments, he concluded with a panegyric upon modern chemistry, the terms of which I shall never forget:—
>
> "The ancient teachers of this science," said he, "promised impossibilities, and performed nothing. The modern masters promise very little; they know that metals cannot be transmuted, and that the elixir of life is a chimera. But these philosophers, whose hands seem only made to dabble in dirt, and their eyes to pore over the microscope or crucible, have indeed performed miracles. They penetrate into the recesses of nature, and shew how she works in her hiding places. They ascend into the heavens; they have discovered how the blood circulates, and the nature of the air we breathe. They have acquired new and almost unlimited powers; they can command the thunders of heaven, mimic the earthquake, and even mock the invisible world with its own shadows." (p. 30)

That same evening Victor seeks out Waldman in his own house and discovers that his new mentor is exceptionally kind and affable:

He heard with attention my little narration concerning my studies, and smiled at the names of Cornelius Agrippa, and Paracelsus, but without the contempt that M. Krempe had exhibited. He said, that "these were men to whose indefatigable zeal modern philosophers were indebted for most of the foundations of their knowledge. They had left to us, as an easier task, to give new names, and arrange in connected classifications, the facts which they in a great degree had been the instruments of bringing to light. The labours of men of genius, however erroneously directed, scarcely ever fail in ultimately turning to the solid advantage of mankind." ... [I] added, that his lecture had removed my prejudices against modern chemists; and I, at the same time, requested his advice concerning the books I ought to procure. (pp. 30–31)

Before inviting Victor to use the machines in his laboratory, Waldman gives him a message that speaks across the decades to the STEM students of the twenty-first century:

"Chemistry is that branch of natural philosophy in which the greatest improvements have been and may be made; it is on that account that I have made it my peculiar study; but at the same time I have not neglected the other branches of science. A man would make but a very sorry chemist, if he attended to that department of human knowledge alone. If your wish is to become really a man of science, and not merely a petty experimentalist, I should advise you to apply to every branch of natural philosophy, including mathematics." (p. 30)

Despite these endorsements of chemistry and natural philosophy in her novel, Mary realized that science could be abused, as is certainly evident in Victor's reckless and selfish experiments, which do not account for their consequences. Even Victor is aware of the distinction between his selfish actions and his selfless actions. In his initial conversation with the scientific explorer Robert Walton, the narrator of this frame-tale novel,[14] he refuses to share his secret knowledge: "I will not lead you on, unguarded and ardent as I then was, to your destruction and infallible misery." Victor continues: "Learn from me, if not by my precepts, at least by my example, how dangerous is the acquirement of knowledge, and how much happier that man is who believes his native town to be the world, than he who aspires to become greater than his nature will allow" (p. 35). On his death bed at the end of the novel, Victor addresses a similar warning to Walton: "Seek happiness in tranquillity, and avoid ambition, even if it be only the apparently innocent one of distinguishing yourself in science and discoveries. Yet why do I say this? I have myself been blasted in these hopes, yet another may succeed" (p. 182).

Although Mary seems to be leaving the door open here for a future when selflessness and science will mutually serve each other, the novel's basic argument is that science can be as destructive as it is constructive. That argument about the dangers of knowledge is emphasized when the creature "found a *fire* which had been left by some wandering beggars, and was overcome with delight at the warmth I experienced from it. In my joy I thrust my hand into the live embers, but quickly drew it out again with a cry of pain. How strange, I thought, that the *same cause should produce such opposite effects!*" (p. 84, my italics).[15] By her subtitle *The Modern Prometheus*, Mary is asking her reader to recall the Promethean myth, in which the Titan Prometheus steals fire (representing knowledge) from the Olympian Zeus to give to primal and prerational man, only to suffer the consequences of his actions. Zeus chains Prometheus, the creator of rational man, to a rock, where he is visited daily by a vulture/eagle that devours his liver/heart, only to have the same punishment repeated each day. So knowledge does cause sorrow, and fire does cause pain; and the etymology of the name "Prometheus" (Forethought) is ironic: Victor, "the modern Prometheus," lacks forethought and fails to understand the destructive consequences of his actions in constructing his creature. Although Mary did not make the corollary myth explicit in her narrative, Prometheus's brother Epimetheus (Afterthought) is associated with all the evils released from Pandora's box: fulfilling that myth have been the technocratic decisions leading to the pesticide DDT, the atom bomb, Three Mile Island, Chernobyl, and the British government's permission, reported in the British newspapers on 1 February 2016, that a stem cell scientist could perform genome editing despite objections that ethical issues were being ignored.

Prometheus is not the only myth that Mary used to develop her theme. Even more noticeable are her many references to the Book of Genesis, with its Garden of Eden and the Tree of the Knowledge of Good and Evil. The epigraph on the title page of the first edition of *Frankenstein* in 1818 is taken from John Milton's famous epic poem *Paradise Lost*, one of the books from which the creature learns to read. He is a "quick study" when he reads that Adam and Eve, tempted by Satan to be like God in knowing good and evil, ate of the tree and were exiled from paradise. Knowledge led to sorrow and the fall of humankind from the sin of pride or hubris. The attentive reader will notice that Victor's Edenic childhood in Geneva is lost when he goes off to university to study science: he laments the loss of his "native town" (p. 53) in the same way that the creature laments his loss after he learns the "godlike science" of speech (p. 91) and "the science of letters [reading]" (p. 97): "sorrow only increased with knowledge. Oh, that I had for ever remained in my native wood, nor known or felt beyond the sensations of hunger, thirst, and heat!" (p. 99).[16]

The parallels between Victor's and the creature's statements about the dangers of knowledge draw our attention to the doppelgänger or double theme of this novel in which the physical ugliness of the creature reflects the psychological ugliness of his creator, Victor. As Victor himself expresses that relationship, "I considered the being whom I had cast among mankind, and endowed with the will and power to effect purposes of horror, such as the deed which he had now done, nearly in the light of my own vampire, my own spirit let loose from the grave, and forced to destroy all that was dear to me" (p. 59). If man was made in God's image, it is only appropriate that the creature would be made in the image of his psychologically disfigured creator, one whose head or reason has destroyed his heart or emotions in the persons of Elizabeth and Clerval: in the 1831 edition, Victor identifies his Elizabeth as the "living spirit of love" that he needs for psychic completion; and in both the 1818 and 1831 editions, Victor "saw the image of [his] former [and better] self" in Clerval (p. 134). A diagram helps to demonstrate the symbolic relations among all of the major characters as they externalize Victor's internal conflict:

HEAD	Robert Walton	Victor Frankenstein	the creature
HEART	Margaret Walton Saville	Elizabeth Lavenza and Henry Clerval	the female creature

Once Victor destroys the female creature, it is inevitable that the creature himself will destroy Elizabeth and Clerval; in effect, the novel "ends" the night that Victor constructs his creature, and the rest of the plot merely literalizes and externalizes Victor's self-destructive acts when he rules love out of his heart and, in the form of his monstrous self, kills Elizabeth and Clerval in what may be read as an act of suicide.

This reading of *Frankenstein* is but one among the many that this novel allows. Victor constructing his monstrous creature may also be read as political science or political philosophers creating the destructive French Revolution or the science of natural philosophy creating the dehumanizing Industrial Revolution. Yet another reading of the novel is that it is about the creating of the novel itself: just as Victor assembles bones and muscles and sinews and other body parts of his creature, so also Mary assembled the words and images and symbols and punctuation of her novel. To make this point, she used birthing metaphors in her introduction to the 1831 edition: she did "*dilate* upon, so very hideous an idea": "I bid my hideous *progeny* go forth and prosper. I have an affection for it, for it was the *offspring* of happy days" (pp. 189, 193, my italics).[17]

Those happy days involved collaboration with Percy Shelley in 1816 and 1817, when the novel was written—and there is a lesson to STEM students in the facts of that collaboration, which is often essential for most scientific discovery. As I have outlined in other publications,[18] Percy edited Mary's novel, suggesting that she expand a shorter version of it into the novel we now read, in the margins of the draft manuscript advising about some of the plot, rewriting parts of the concluding pages as he fair copied the draft into the pages that would be submitted to the publisher, advising her about transforming her thirty-three-chapter draft into a twenty-three-chapter "fair copy," and writing at least five thousand of the seventy-two thousand words of this novel. In general, Mary relied on Percy for some of her accomplishments in the first edition of the novel she published on 1 January 1818.[19] In doing so, she implicitly honored the character of Clerval, who, as a social scientist and linguist staying in Geneva to honor his father's wishes and leaving there with the hopes of pursuing his own education, only to end up nursing Victor, offers an example to the reader: Clerval, whose "science" involves other people, does not isolate himself as Victor does in his pursuit of knowledge. As Victor describes him later, "Clerval! beloved friend! … He was a being formed in the 'very poetry of nature.' His wild and enthusiastic imagination was chastened by the sensibility of his heart" (p. 132). It is likely that Percy wrote these words in a late addition to the proofs of the novel, and the reference to "imagination" (the head or reason chastened or directed by the heart) will help bring this introduction to what I hope is an illuminating end.

The chastened or creative imagination is at the heart of English romanticism, and its various definitions somehow involve or evolve from the famous and short thirteenth chapter of *Biographia literaria* (1817) by Samuel Taylor Coleridge (1772–1834), in which he simply states that the "primary imagination [is] the living power and prime agent of all human perception, and … a repetition in the finite mind of the eternal act of creation in the infinite I am" ([1817] 1907, 202). Just as God ontologically created or fashioned this universe from chaotic matter, so also does the human mind or imagination epistemologically creates its own universe from the chaotic sensory data that a person receives from the external world. Man is not God (although Victor tries to be); rather, man is like unto

God in each and every one of the creative perceptions that take place every second of a human being's existence. What this means is that we never know the thing in itself—we know only our creative constructs of a thing. Percy Shelley put it most bluntly: "nothing exists but as it is perceived," and "All things exist as they are perceived."[20] These statements mean that for Percy Shelley, rather than an ontology (or theory of being) determining what our epistemology (or theory of knowledge) might be, epistemology is primary or privileged in all human experience. If creative perception determines existence, then it is fair to say that a novel is just as real or true as a scientific theory—both are constructs by the human imagination to give form to the chaos of our experiences. Such reasoning puts the A back into STEM and demonstrates that there really are not Two Cultures, science and the humanities[21]—there is only one unified theory of being created by us as a means to give form to a reality that we never fully know in itself. The Shelleys are attempting to tell us that the humanities, including in this case *Frankenstein*, offer a representation of the world that is just as valid as an engineer's blueprint.

Thus, *Frankenstein* and this introduction encourage STEM students to respect the humanities as offering a valid means of defining and even improving the world, much as science hopes to do. *Frankenstein* is certainly not the only work of art that addresses these issues, but it has become a metaphor for science that ignores human consequences and values. Every day some blog or newspaper or magazine or book or movie or television show alludes to *Frankenstein* in order to describe science gone bad. But these allusions to the evils of science can teach us much about our human condition. In fact, some recent Frankenstein-inspired "moving pictures" (the first *Frankenstein* film was produced in 1910 by the inventor Thomas Edison) actually show a nonhuman being gaining respect for human life and human values. Ignoring the usual suspects among the many "Frankenstein" movies, including Mel Brooks's wonderful *Young Frankenstein* (1974),[22] I conclude here by mentioning two of my favorite allusive works of art: James Cameron's film *Terminator 2: Judgment Day* (1991) and the CBS television series *Person of Interest* (2011–2016), which centers on an artificial intelligence (AI) machine.

Most people do not realize that *T-2* is an homage to Mary and her novel, but the viewer is reminded of *Frankenstein* by the opening electric flashes as the nonhuman android Arnold Schwarzenegger materializes, comes back from the future, and reveals that he has apparently developed the equivalent of a heart that can feel for humanity. Even more allusive is his selfless destruction of the computer chip that conveniently saves Los Angeles and the world from the thermonuclear destruction that would occur on August 29, 1997, the day before Mary's two hundredth birthday—so that we could celebrate her bicentennial without holding her responsible for starting the scientific revolution that eventually led to the computer chip that led to the microprocessor that led to Skynet that led to the destruction of billions of lives.

Less allusive but equally compelling is the plot of *Person of Interest*, in which computer programmer, engineering genius, and tech billionaire Harold Finch (he also goes by other bird names) creates an AI machine for the government to prevent terrorist attacks. At the same time that the government abuses the power of this all-seeing and all-hearing AI machine, Finch and his associates use it to predict and prevent local murders and other acts of nonterrorist violence. The amoral Machine, which electronically monitors every cell phone and email message and surveillance camera in the world to detect terrorism, teaches itself and apparently develops, as the Terminator did, compassion for the local victims of violence. As it is pursued by various antagonists and attacked by a competitor machine called Samaritan, it hides itself in the national power grid. At the end of season 4, as Samaritan shuts down the power grid starting on the West Coast, the Machine retreats to a large electrical substation in Brooklyn until Finch and associates download enough of the computer code into a hard drive that will be carried away in a suitcase—in hopes of saving the world from Samaritan's machinations (as it were). Electricity, technology, and the "Frankenstein" myth seem to come full circle at this moment of the plot: from Benjamin Franklin's kites and electrical storms to Joseph Priestley's history of electricity that led to late eighteenth-century and early nineteenth-century scientific experiments, to *Frankenstein*, to Hollywood adaptations of *Frankenstein* that use lightning to power the electrical machines that generate the creature, and to the most recent adaptations that feature computers and codes and algorithms and hard drives and a final apocalyptic machine on which the fate of the world depends.[23]

University of Delaware

NOTES

1. In my previous publications on *Frankenstein*, I referred to Victor Frankenstein's unnamed creation as "the monster," what I deemed the most appropriate of the names given to him in the novel (he is also denominated "creature," "Being," "wretch," "devil," and "dæmon"). In this introduction, I follow the editors' use of the word *creature* to denominate the unnamed "Being," despite the fact that some who use the word *creature* tend to excuse his actions, whereas some who use the word *monster* tend to hold him accountable for the murders he commits. Mary certainly wanted to force the reader to morally judge the "creature" by not giving him a name.

For example, were we to call him a "dæmon," we would not necessarily demonize him, for "dæmon" to Mary meant not a devil (and not a program running in a Unix system) but, as in Greek mythology, a runner between heaven and earth, a superhuman being less than a god. By having no single name, the monster has a universality that embraces all of humankind; indeed, when Mary saw in the playbill of the first theatrical performance of her novel in 1823 that the "_____" was being played by "Mr T. Cooke," she remarked in a letter to Leigh Hunt that "this nameless mode of naming the un[n]ameable is rather good" (M. Shelley 1980, 1:378). The reader is also reminded that "naming" is a symbolic act in which the namer is greater than the named; that Victor does not name his "creature" tells us much about their relationship.

2. Watt's many legacies include the name of the unit of power that we now call the "watt."

3. See Robinson 2016b, 1:lxv–lxvi and especially lxxv n. 46, where Anne K. Mellor and Leonard Wolf are also cited, and Robinson 2016a. See also Crook 1996, 1:51 n.

4. Readers of this edition who wish to pursue these various antecedents to *Frankenstein* are encouraged to seek information on these and other eighteenth-century scientists in the *Oxford Dictionary of National Biography* (available online in most university library databases) and to read their works and others online at Google Books and hathitrust.org.

5. See M. Shelley 1987, I:56 and n., and an advertisement in the *Morning Post* for 8 November 1814, p. 2, col. 1. The "Professor Garnerin" referred to is probably the aeronaut André-Jacques Garnerin (1769–1823), but it also might possibly be his brother Jean-Baptiste-Olivier Garnerin (1766–1849). Because of a misreading of Mary's journal entry, the lecturer is incorrectly identified as Andrew Crosse in scores of websites and a number of books—see, for example, Prior 2015. (Note that difficult-to-correct error creeps into literary as well as scientific papers.) It is also possible that the lectures to which Godwin took Mary in early 1812 (January 2, 9, 13, 16, 20, and 27), as recorded in his diary, dealt with anatomy and chemistry—see Godwin 2012 and http://godwindiary.bodleian.ox.ac.uk/diary/1812.html.

6. That cold summer resulted from the Indonesian volcano Tambora erupting in 1815 and blanketing the atmosphere with gas and ash (see "Frankenstein's Summer" and "Ice Tsunami in the Alps" in D'Arcy Wood 2014, 1–11, 150–170). Assembled during the telling of ghost stories at Byron's Villa Diodati were Mary and Percy, the twenty-eight-year-old poet Lord Byron (1788–1824); Mary's eighteen-year-old and slightly younger stepsister Clara Mary Jane (Claire) Clairmont (1798–1879), pregnant with Byron's child; and Byron's young personal physician, John William Polidori (1795–1821).

7. See M. Shelley 1987, 121–122, journal entries for 1–4 August 1816.

8. Garrett 2002, 24–25. Shelley read Davy's *Elements of Chemical Philosophy* (1812) on September 28–31, 1816, while drafting *Frankenstein*. The clever reader may wish to find echoes of Davy's works in *Frankenstein*.

9. For more on materialism and vitalism, see Jane Maienschein and Kate MacCord's essay "Changing Conceptions of Human Nature" in this volume.

10. See Bieri 2008, 135, 266, 313, 383–384.

11. Newton had recently published *The Return to Nature, or, A Defense of the Vegetable Regimen; with Some Account of an Experiment Made during the Last Three or Four Years in the Author's Family* ([1811] 2015). Note that the creature is a vegetarian who survives on "acorns and berries" (p. 121).

12. M. Butler 1993a, 12–14, quoting John Abernathy. See also "The Shelleys and Radical Science," Marilyn Butler's introduction to *Frankenstein; or, The Modern Prometheus: The 1818 Text* (Butler 1993b, xv–xx), which was reprinted and reissued in an Oxford World's Classics edition of *Frankenstein* (M. Shelley 2008). For more on this matter, see Mellor 1987 and Mellor's essay in this volume. See also Rushton 2016.

13. The University of Ingolstadt was also defined by the Illuminati, a secret and revolutionary society founded there in 1776.

14. The frame tale is essentially a didactic device: from the outside in, the reader is to Walton just as Walton is to Victor just as Victor is to the creature just as the creature is to the De Laceys. From the inside out, the De Laceys teach the creature, who teaches Victor, who teaches Walton, who teaches his sister, Margaret Walton Saville (note the initials MWS), and thereby teaches the reader about the dangerous consequences of the pursuit of knowledge.

15. Mary makes the same symbolic point when the creature delivers firewood to assist the De Lacey family with their chores but then later burns down the De Lacey cottage after the family rejects him.

16. The third Western myth about the dangerous consequences of the pursuit of knowledge can be found in Plato's *Symposium* (Plato 1999), in which Aristophanes, in attempting to define love, tells the story of the circular and sexually complete (four arms and four legs) primal being who rolls halfway up Mount Olympus and with the extra appendages scales the remaining heights and intrudes on the dominion of the gods. In response to that being's presumption and pride, the gods split the being down the middle. Aristophanes concludes that love is the desire to make whole, complete, and entire what once had been whole, complete, and entire. Mary does not allude to this myth until her 1831 edition, in which Victor tells Walton that "we are unfashioned creatures, but half made up, if one wiser, better, dearer than ourselves—such a friend ought to be—do not lend his aid to perfectionate our weak and faulty natures. I once had a friend [Clerval], the most noble of human creatures, and am entitled, therefore, to judge respecting friendship" ([1831] 2000, 38). Mary became aware of this myth when she, as amanuensis, transcribed Percy's translation of the *Symposium* in 1818.

17. For one of the many birthing metaphors in the novel proper, consider that Frankenstein's "cheek had grown pale with study, and [his] person had become emaciated with confinement" (p. 38) during the period he constructs his creature, "confinement" denoting the period shortly before the birth of a child. For another reference to this metaphor, consider that Walton's narrative takes place over 276 days—that is, the nine-month gestation period.

18. See my "Frankenstein Chronology" (Robinson 2016a, 1:lxxvi–cx), especially the entries between 15 June 1816 and 28 October 1817; this chronology can be consulted online in the Shelley–Godwin Archive at http://shelleygodwinarchive.org. This archive also makes available digital images of all the manuscript pages of the Shelleys' draft and fair copy of the novel, but the reader is cautioned that the facing transcription pages lack the lineation of the hardbound edition and also lack the extensive footnotes to each manuscript page. For my more recent essay on this collaboration, see Robinson 2015. For a visual representation of Percy's words in Mary's draft, see M. Shelley 2008, 39–254.

19. The first edition was published in three volumes in 500 copies by Lackington, Hughes, Harding, Mavor, & Jones. A second edition in two volumes was published on 11 August 1823 in 500 copies by G. and W. B. Whittaker. A revised and third edition in one volume with an added chapter was published on Halloween, 31 October 1831, in 4,020 copies by Henry Colburn and Richard Bentley.

20. For these two quotations, see Percy Shelley's essays "On Life" and "A Defence of Poetry" in P. Shelley 2002.

21. I here allude to the famous lecture "The Two Cultures" delivered by the chemist, physicist, and novelist C. P. Snow (1905–1980), published under the title *The Two Cultures and the Scientific Revolution* ([1959] 2013).

22. See my "'Frankenstein Filmography" in Robinson 2013. For other lists of *Frankenstein* films, see http://knarf.english.upenn.edu/Pop/filmlist.html; see also the catalog of all things *Frankenstein* in Glut 1984.

23. In the final episode of season 5 of *Person of Interest*, which aired on CBS on 21 June 2016, we encounter an Ice-9 computer virus that eventually destroys Samaritan and nearly destroys the Machine; a "cyber apocalypse" survived by the Machine and Finch and some of his associates; and two universal lessons voiced by the Machine that Finch created: "everyone dies alone," but "maybe you never really die." Although *Frankenstein* is never directly invoked in any of the 103 episodes, *Person of Interest* testifies to the life of Mary Shelley and of her creature during the past two hundred years.

FRANKENSTEIN;

OR,

THE MODERN PROMETHEUS.

IN THREE VOLUMES.

Did I request thee, Maker, from my clay
To mould me man? Did I solicit thee
From darkness to promote me?——
PARADISE LOST.

VOL. I.

London:
PRINTED FOR
LACKINGTON, HUGHES, HARDING, MAVOR, & JONES,
FINSBURY SQUARE.

1818.

VOL.

PREFACE

The event on which this fiction is founded has been supposed, by Dr. Darwin,[1] and some of the physiological writers of Germany, as not of impossible occurrence. I shall not be supposed as according the remotest degree of serious faith to such an imagination; yet, in assuming it as the basis of a work of fancy, I have not considered myself as merely weaving a series of supernatural terrors. The event on which the interest of the story depends is exempt from the disadvantages of a mere tale of spectres or enchantment. It was recommended by the novelty of the situations which it developes; and, however impossible as a physical fact, affords a point of view to the imagination for the delineating of human passions more comprehensive and commanding than any which the ordinary relations of existing events can yield.

I have thus endeavoured to preserve the truth of the elementary principles of human nature, while I have not scrupled to innovate upon their combinations. The *Iliad,* the tragic poetry of Greece,—Shakespeare, in the *Tempest* and *Midsummer Night's Dream,*—and most especially Milton, in *Paradise Lost,* conform to this rule; and the most humble novelist, who seeks to confer or receive amusement from his labours, may, without presumption, apply to prose fiction a licence, or rather a rule, from the adoption of which so many exquisite combinations of human feeling have resulted in the highest specimens of poetry.

The circumstance on which my story rests was suggested in casual conversation. It was commenced, partly as a source of amusement, and partly as an expedient for exercising any untried resources of mind. Other motives were mingled with these, as the work proceeded. I am by no means indifferent to the manner in which whatever moral tendencies exist in the sentiments or characters it contains shall affect the reader; yet my chief concern in this respect has been limited to the avoiding the enervating effects of the novels of the present day, and to the exhibition of the amiableness of domestic affection, and the excellence of universal virtue. The opinions which naturally spring from the character and situation of the hero are by no means to be conceived as existing always in my own conviction; nor is any inference justly to be drawn from the following pages as prejudicing any philosophical doctrine of whatever kind.

1. Erasmus Darwin (1731–1802), a friend of Mary's father, William Godwin, was a physician, naturalist, philosopher, and poet. He contributed an early formulation of a single origin for all life, which undergirded what came to be known as the theory of evolution as elaborated by his grandson, Charles Darwin.

Jason Scott Robert.

It is a subject also of additional interest to the author, that this story was begun in the majestic region where the scene is principally laid, and in society which cannot cease to be regretted. I passed the summer of 1816 in the environs of Geneva. The season was cold and rainy, and in the evenings we crowded around a blazing wood fire, and occasionally amused ourselves with some German stories of ghosts, which happened to fall into our hands. These tales excited in us a playful desire of imitation. Two other friends (a tale from the pen of one of whom would be far more acceptable to the public than any thing I can ever hope to produce) and myself agreed to write each a story, founded on some supernatural occurrence.

The weather, however, suddenly became serene; and my two friends left me on a journey among the Alps, and lost, in the magnificent scenes which they present, all memory of their ghostly visions. The following tale is the only one which has been completed.[2]

LETTER I.

To Mrs. SAVILLE, *England.*
St. Petersburgh, Dec. 11th, 17—.

You will rejoice to hear that no disaster has accompanied the commencement of an enterprise which you have regarded with such evil forebodings. I arrived here yesterday; and my first task is to assure my dear sister of my welfare, and increasing confidence in the success of my undertaking.

I am already far north of London; and as I walk in the streets of Petersburgh, I feel a cold northern breeze play upon my cheeks, which braces my nerves, and fills me with delight. Do you understand this feeling? This breeze, which has travelled from the regions towards which I am advancing, gives me a foretaste of those icy climes. Inspirited by this wind of promise, my day dreams become more fervent and vivid. I try in vain to be persuaded that the pole is the seat of frost and desolation; it ever presents itself to my imagination as the region of beauty and delight. There, Margaret, the sun is for ever visible; its broad disk just skirting the horizon, and diffusing a perpetual splendour. There—for with your leave, my sister,

---

2. Lord George Gordon Byron (1788–1824) answered his own challenge that evening by writing the first paragraph of a vampire story inspired by the German ghost stories. John Polidori (1795–1821) later extended that beginning into "The Vampyre" (1819), a short story that went on to inspire Bram Stoker's tremendously successful novel *Dracula* in 1897.
Ed Finn.

I will put some trust in preceding navigators—there snow and frost are banished; and, sailing over a calm sea, we may be wafted to a land surpassing in wonders and in beauty every region hitherto discovered on the habitable globe. Its productions and features may be without example, as the phænomena of the heavenly bodies undoubtedly are in those undiscovered solitudes. What may not be expected in a country of eternal light? I may there discover the wondrous power which attracts the needle;[3] and may regulate a thousand celestial observations, that require only this voyage to render their seeming eccentricities consistent for ever. I shall satiate my ardent curiosity[4] with the sight of a part of the world never

3. When Captain Walton talks about the "wondrous power [of] the needle," he talks about magnetism and its very first application in a compass. For centuries, people ascribed magical powers to magnetite and lodestones, until William Gilbert (1540–1603) first discovered the basic features of magnetism and the fact that Earth itself is a weak magnet. The links between electricity and magnetism were a major subject of scientific investigation during Mary's lifetime, and a number of expeditions departed for the North and South Poles in the hopes of discovering the secrets of the planet's magnetic field.
Nicole Herbots.

4. For moderns, this comment may seem self-evident, if a little florid. But such Promethean ambition does not characterize all historical periods or all cultures or all individuals; rather, it reflects the interesting combination of curiosity, ambition, and historical perspective that coevolved with the European exploration of science and a profoundly multicultural world. Mary was writing at the close of the Age of Discovery, during which Europeans rounded the southern tip of Africa, "discovered" and colonized the New World, and circumnavigated the globe. Polar exploration was one remaining feat. It was also the age of romanticism, the paintings of Caspar David Friedrich (1774–1840) and Eugène Delacroix (1798–1863), as well as the music of Ludwig van Beethoven (1770–1827) and Hector Berlioz (1803–1869). This eagerness for exploration is express in "Ulysses," the poem written in 1833 by Alfred, Lord Tennyson (1809–1892):

> I cannot rest from travel: I will drink
> Life to the lees: All times I have enjoy'd
> Greatly, have suffer'd greatly, both with those
> That loved me, and alone, on shore, and when
> Thro' scudding drifts the rainy Hyades
> Vext the dim sea: I am become a name;
> For always roaming with a hungry heart.
> . . . .
> I am a part of all that I have met;
> Yet all experience is an arch wherethro'
> Gleams that untravell'd world whose margin fades
> For ever and forever when I move. (Tennyson 2004, 49)

The irony, at least to modern sensibilities, is that this romantic language befits the pursuit of art, not the rational pursuit of science.
Braden Allenby.

before visited, and may tread a land never before imprinted by the foot of man.[5] These are my enticements, and they are sufficient to conquer all fear of danger or death, and to induce me to commence this laborious voyage with the joy a child feels when he embarks in a little boat, with his holiday mates, on an expedition of discovery up his native river. But, supposing all these conjectures to be false, you cannot contest the inestimable benefit which I shall confer on all mankind to the last generation, by discovering a passage near the pole to those countries, to reach which at present so many months are requisite; or by ascertaining the secret of the magnet, which, if at all possible, can only be effected by an undertaking such as mine.

These reflections have dispelled the agitation with which I began my letter, and I feel my heart glow with an enthusiasm which elevates me to heaven; for nothing contributes so much to tranquillize the mind as a steady purpose,—a point on which the soul may fix its intellectual eye. This expedition has been the favourite dream of my early years. I have read with ardour the accounts of the various voyages which have been made in the prospect of arriving at the North Pacific Ocean through the seas which surround the pole. You may remember, that a history of all the voyages made for purposes of discovery composed the whole of our good uncle Thomas's library. My education was neglected, yet I was passionately fond of reading. These volumes were my study day and night, and my familiarity with them increased that regret which I had felt, as a child, on learning that my father's dying injunction had forbidden my uncle to allow me to embark in a sea-faring life.

5. The phrase *manifest destiny* emerged in nineteenth-century America. It described the notion that the expansion of the American people, culture, and institutions across North America was a mission of divine Providence, not merely one driven by practical need for more land and resources. But the concept is much more deeply rooted and widespread, appearing in the earliest Western writings in the form of the Promised Land of Abraham and his Israelite descendants. Robert Walton invokes the concept implicitly in his exploration, which seems to need no justification other than that it might help him to "accomplish some great purpose" (p. 5). By the nineteenth century, the development of science and industry not only facilitated such explorations but also made the conquest of knowledge itself into a frontier that began to rival the conquest of land in importance—and that was similarly justified in terms of a manifest destiny. The story of *Frankenstein* mirrors this transformation as Walton's determination to visit that which has never before been visited is juxtaposed alongside Victor's determination to do that which has never before been done. We often use the metaphor of the frontier—for example, "frontiers of research"—in describing the reach of scientific inquiry. Worried that the American westward expansion and the manifest destiny that fueled it had run its course, MIT engineer and presidential adviser Vannevar Bush (1945) coined the phrase *the endless frontier* for the title of a report issued to President Harry Truman toward the end of World War II. The report advocated for continued strong support of scientific research by the federal government after the war ended because scientific research could provide the inspiration and economic benefits that westward expansion had previously provided.
Ariel Anbar.

These visions faded when I perused, for the first time, those poets whose effusions entranced my soul, and lifted it to heaven. I also became a poet, and for one year lived in a Paradise of my own creation; I imagined that I also might obtain a niche in the temple where the names of Homer and Shakespeare are consecrated. You are well acquainted with my failure, and how heavily I bore the disappointment. But just at that time I inherited the fortune of my cousin, and my thoughts were turned into the channel of their earlier bent.

Six years have passed since I resolved on my present undertaking. I can, even now, remember the hour from which I dedicated myself to this great enterprise. I commenced by inuring my body to hardship. I accompanied the whale-fishers on several expeditions to the North Sea; I voluntarily endured cold, famine, thirst, and want of sleep; I often worked harder than the common sailors during the day, and devoted my nights to the study of mathematics, the theory of medicine, and those branches of physical science from which a naval adventurer might derive the greatest practical advantage. Twice I actually hired myself as an under-mate in a Greenland whaler, and acquitted myself to admiration. I must own I felt a little proud, when my captain offered me the second dignity in the vessel, and entreated me to remain with the greatest earnestness; so valuable did he consider my services.

And now, dear Margaret, do I not deserve to accomplish some great purpose. My life might have been passed in ease and luxury; but I preferred glory to every enticement that wealth placed in my path. Oh, that some encouraging voice would answer in the affirmative! My courage and my resolution is firm; but my hopes fluctuate, and my spirits are often depressed. I am about to proceed on a long and difficult voyage; the emergencies of which will demand all my fortitude: I am required not only to raise the spirits of others, but sometimes to sustain my own, when their's are failing.

This is the most favourable period for travelling in Russia. They fly quickly over the snow in their sledges; the motion is pleasant, and, in my opinion, far more agreeable than that of an English stage-coach. The cold is not excessive, if you are wrapt in furs, a dress which I have already adopted; for there is a great difference between walking the deck and remaining seated motionless for hours, when no exercise prevents the blood from actually freezing in your veins. I have no ambition to lose my life on the post-road between St. Petersburgh and Archangel.

I shall depart for the latter town in a fortnight or three weeks; and my intention is to hire a ship there, which can easily be done by paying the insurance for the owner, and to engage as many sailors as I think necessary among those who are accustomed to the whale-fishing. I do not intend to sail until the month of June: and when shall I return? Ah, dear sister, how can I answer this question? If I succeed, many, many months, perhaps years, will pass before you and I may meet. If I fail, you will see me again soon, or never.

Farewell, my dear, excellent, Margaret. Heaven shower down blessings on you, and save me, that I may again and again testify my gratitude for all your love and kindness.

Your affectionate brother,
R. WALTON.

LETTER II.

To Mrs. SAVILLE, *England.*
Archangel, 28th March, 17—.

How slowly the time passes here, encompassed as I am by frost and snow; yet a second step is taken towards my enterprise. I have hired a vessel, and am occupied in collecting my sailors; those whom I have already engaged appear to be men on whom I can depend, and are certainly possessed of dauntless courage.

But I have one want which I have never yet been able to satisfy; and the absence of the object of which I now feel as a most severe evil. I have no friend,[6] Margaret: when I am glowing with the enthusiasm of success, there will be none to participate my joy; if I am assailed by disappointment, no one will endeavour to sustain me in dejection. I shall commit my thoughts to paper, it is true; but that is a poor medium for the communication of feeling. I desire the company of a man who could sympathize

---

6. Throughout the novel, the problem of companionship recurs for Walton, for Victor, and for Victor's creature. Friendship is one of the foundations for community because it connects the individual to a larger human endeavor—be it society, government, or scientific exploration. The novel explores the value of trust and camaraderie wherein one can divulge deep concerns, passions, and ambitions with another and so gain another's insight into one's own perspective. Throughout the novel, the failure to connect with a friend becomes a problem with serious consequences. Mary rarely has such companionship except, perhaps, with Percy Shelley. Percy's friendship with Lord Byron is well documented and acclaimed as an example of romantic poets and thinkers who shared ideas and artistic passion.
Ron Broglio.

with me; whose eyes would reply to mine. You may deem me romantic, my dear sister, but I bitterly feel the want of a friend. I have no one near me, gentle yet courageous, possessed of a cultivated as well as of a capacious mind, whose tastes are like my own, to approve or amend my plans. How would such a friend repair the faults of your poor brother! I am too ardent in execution, and too impatient of difficulties. But it is a still greater evil to me that I am self-educated: for the first fourteen years of my life I ran wild on a common, and read nothing but our uncle Thomas's books of voyages. At that age I became acquainted with the celebrated poets of our own country; but it was only when it had ceased to be in my power to derive its most important benefits from such a conviction, that I perceived the necessity of becoming acquainted with more languages than that of my native country. Now I am twenty-eight, and am in reality more illiterate than many school-boys of fifteen. It is true that I have thought more, and that my day dreams are more extended and magnificent; but they want (as the painters call it) *keeping*; and I greatly need a friend who would have sense enough not to despise me as romantic, and affection enough for me to endeavour to regulate my mind.

Well, these are useless complaints; I shall certainly find no friend on the wide ocean, nor even here in Archangel, among merchants and seamen. Yet some feelings, unallied to the dross of human nature, beat even in these rugged bosoms. My lieutenant, for instance, is a man of wonderful courage and enterprise; he is madly desirous of glory. He is an Englishman, and in the midst of national and professional prejudices, unsoftened by cultivation, retains some of the noblest endowments of humanity. I first became acquainted with him on board a whale vessel: finding that he was unemployed in this city, I easily engaged him to assist in my enterprise.

The master is a person of an excellent disposition, and is remarkable in the ship for his gentleness, and the mildness of his discipline. He is, indeed, of so amiable a nature, that he will not hunt (a favourite, and almost the only amusement here), because he cannot endure to spill blood. He is, moreover, heroically generous. Some years ago he loved a young Russian lady, of moderate fortune; and having amassed a considerable sum in prize-money, the father of the girl consented to the match. He saw his mistress once before the destined ceremony; but she was bathed in tears, and, throwing herself at his feet, entreated him to spare her, confessing at the same time that she loved another, but that he was poor, and that her father would never consent to the union. My generous friend reassured the suppliant, and on being informed of the name of her lover instantly abandoned his pursuit. He had already bought a farm with his money, on which he had designed to pass the remainder of his life; but he bestowed the whole on his rival, together with the remains of his prize-money to purchase stock, and then himself solicited the young woman's father to consent to her marriage with her lover. But the old man decidedly refused, thinking himself bound in honour to my friend; who, when he found the father inexorable, quitted his country, nor returned until he heard that his former mistress was married according to her inclinations. "What a noble fellow!"[7] you will exclaim. He is so; but then he has passed all his life on board a vessel, and has scarcely an idea beyond the rope and the shroud.

But do not suppose that, because I complain a little, or because I can conceive a consolation for my toils which I may never know, that I am wavering in my resolutions. Those are as fixed as fate; and my voyage is only now delayed until the weather shall permit my embarkation. The winter has been dreadfully severe; but the spring promises well, and it is considered as a remarkably early season; so that, perhaps, I may sail sooner than I expected. I shall do nothing rashly; you know me sufficiently to confide in my prudence and considerateness whenever the safety of others is committed to my care.

I cannot describe to you my sensations on the near prospect of my undertaking. It is impossible to communicate to you a conception of the trembling sensation, half pleasurable and half fearful, with which I am preparing to depart. I am going to unexplored regions, to "the land of mist and snow"; but I shall kill no albatross,[8] therefore do not be alarmed for my safety.

---

7. There are two meanings to the word *nobility*, and they are often conflated. The first refers to possessing a character with the highest qualities found in human beings, such as integrity, decency, honor, and goodness. But these qualities are often attributed to persons of the highest social rank in society—the second meaning of the word. The lieutenant, who gives up the woman he is engaged to when she says she loves another and generously provides her lover with the financial means to gain the acceptance of her family, goes well beyond what is expected. Perhaps this behavior earns him the exclamation point? Mary gives these noble qualities to Walton's second in command, perhaps challenging the taken-for-granted hierarchy that typically ascribed these qualities to individuals at the top. Yet she qualifies this choice by stating that the lieutenant didn't know any better, given that he spent so much time aboard a ship, further hinting that in the end his sacrifice was no great loss to him. In real life, Mary marries into a noble family that opposes her union with their son because of her father's indebtedness.

Mary Margaret Fonow.

8. Mary has Captain Walton allude to the poem *The Rime of the Ancient Mariner* (1798), written by Samuel Taylor Coleridge (1772–1834). In the poem, which Mary heard Coleridge reading during his many visits to the Godwin house, the title character kills an albatross that has been following his boat, turning a good luck sign into an ill omen.

David H. Guston.

Shall I meet you again, after having traversed immense seas, and returned by the most southern cape of Africa or America? I dare not expect such success, yet I cannot bear to look on the reverse of the picture. Continue to write to me by every opportunity: I may receive your letters (though the chance is very doubtful) on some occasions when I need them most to support my spirits. I love you very tenderly. Remember me with affection should you never hear from me again.

Your affectionate brother,
ROBERT WALTON.

LETTER III.

To Mrs. SAVILLE, *England.*
July 7th, 17—.

MY DEAR SISTER,
I write a few lines in haste, to say that I am safe, and well advanced on my voyage. This letter will reach England by a merchant-man now on its homeward voyage from Archangel; more fortunate than I, who may not see my native land, perhaps, for many years. I am, however, in good spirits: my men are bold, and apparently firm of purpose; nor do the floating sheets of ice that continually pass us, indicating the dangers of the region towards which we are advancing, appear to dismay them. We have already reached a very high latitude; but it is the height of summer, and although not so warm as in England, the southern gales, which blow us speedily towards those shores which I so ardently desire to attain, breathe a degree of renovating warmth which I had not expected.

No incidents have hitherto befallen us, that would make a figure in a letter. One or two stiff gales, and the breaking of a mast, are accidents which experienced navigators scarcely remember to record; and I shall be well content, if nothing worse happen to us during our voyage.

Adieu, my dear Margaret. Be assured, that for my own sake, as well as your's, I will not rashly encounter danger. I will be cool, persevering, and prudent.

Remember me to all my English friends.[9]

Most affectionately yours,
R. W.

9. Throughout *Frankenstein*, Mary utilizes an epistolary structure: significant sections of the novel are made up of letters exchanged among the characters. These letters are often long and tender, and they contain a wealth of personal details and endearments that do little to move the plot forward.

LETTER IV.

To Mrs. SAVILLE, *England.*
August 5th, 17—.

So strange an accident has happened to us, that I cannot forbear recording it, although it is very probable that you will see me before these papers can come into your possession.

Last Monday (July 31st), we were nearly surrounded by ice, which closed in the ship on all sides, scarcely leaving her the sea room in which she floated. Our situation was somewhat dangerous, especially as we were compassed round by a very thick fog. We accordingly lay to, hoping that some change would take place in the atmosphere and weather.

About two o'clock the mist cleared away, and we beheld, stretched out in every direction, vast and irregular plains of ice, which seemed to have no end. Some of my comrades groaned, and my own mind began to grow watchful with anxious thoughts, when a strange sight suddenly attracted our attention, and diverted our solicitude from our own situation. We perceived a low carriage, fixed on a sledge and drawn by dogs, pass on towards the north, at the distance of half a mile: a being which had the shape of a man, but apparently of gigantic stature, sat in the sledge, and guided the dogs. We watched the rapid progress of the traveller with our telescopes, until he was lost among the distant inequalities of the ice.

This appearance excited our unqualified wonder. We were, as we believed, many hundred miles from any land; but this apparition seemed to denote that it was not, in reality, so distant as we had supposed. Shut in, however,

---

This approach might seem like an inefficient storytelling strategy, but it is quite the opposite. Mary uses these letters strategically to emphasize the importance of the social bonds that give characters such as Victor and Captain Walton emotional sustenance during incredibly stressful times. The letters are tangible artifacts of emotional labor—the investments of time, wit, and emotional energy that make human relationships functional and rewarding. They contrast with the creature's life and reveal precisely what he is missing. He has no one with whom to share his experiences and frustrations, so his life becomes unbearable, and he lashes out violently.

Language is an important way that we show love and understanding as well as receive it. The laborious, solitary way that the creature acquires language, through scavenging books and eavesdropping, demonstrates just how removed he is from any form of nurturing social interaction.

Walton narrowly avoids making the same mistake as Victor, pursuing scientific discovery without considering the safety and well-being of the people around him. Walton is luckily in continuous written contact with his sister, Margaret, who lovingly discourages him from going through with his expedition to the North Pole. Their conversation, conducted through a series of letters, might be what saves his life and the lives of his crew.

Joey Eschrich.

by ice, it was impossible to follow his track, which we had observed with the greatest attention.

About two hours after this occurrence, we heard the ground sea; and before night the ice broke, and freed our ship. We, however, lay to until the morning, fearing to encounter in the dark those large loose masses which float about after the breaking up of the ice. I profited of this time to rest for a few hours.

In the morning, however, as soon as it was light, I went upon deck, and found all the sailors busy on one side of the vessel, apparently talking to some one in the sea. It was, in fact, a sledge, like that we had seen before, which had drifted towards us in the night, on a large fragment of ice. Only one dog remained alive; but there was a human being within it, whom the sailors were persuading to enter the vessel. He was not, as the other traveller seemed to be, a savage inhabitant of some undiscovered island, but an European. When I appeared on deck, the master said, "Here is our captain, and he will not allow you to perish on the open sea."

On perceiving me, the stranger addressed me in English, although with a foreign accent. "Before I come on board your vessel," said he, "will you have the kindness to inform me whither you are bound?"

You may conceive my astonishment on hearing such a question addressed to me from a man on the brink of destruction, and to whom I should have supposed that my vessel would have been a resource which he would not have exchanged for the most precious wealth the earth can afford. I replied, however, that we were on a voyage of discovery towards the northern pole.

Upon hearing this he appeared satisfied, and consented to come on board. Good God! Margaret, if you had seen the man who thus capitulated for his safety, your surprise would have been boundless. His limbs were nearly frozen, and his body dreadfully emaciated by fatigue and suffering. I never saw a man in so wretched a condition. We attempted to carry him into the cabin; but as soon as he had quitted the fresh air, he fainted. We accordingly brought him back to the deck, and restored him to animation by rubbing him with brandy, and forcing him to swallow a small quantity. As soon as he shewed signs of life, we wrapped him up in blankets, and placed him near the chimney of the kitchen-stove. By slow degrees he recovered, and ate a little soup, which restored him wonderfully.

Two days passed in this manner before he was able to speak; and I often feared that his sufferings had deprived him of understanding. When he had in some measure recovered, I removed him to my own cabin, and attended on him as much as my duty would permit. I never saw a more interesting creature: his eyes have generally an expression of wildness, and even madness; but there are moments when, if any one performs an act of kindness towards him, or does him any the most trifling service, his whole countenance is lighted up, as it were, with a beam of benevolence and sweetness that I never saw equalled. But he is generally melancholy and despairing; and sometimes he gnashes his teeth, as if impatient of the weight of woes that oppresses him.

When my guest was a little recovered, I had great trouble to keep off the men, who wished to ask him a thousand questions; but I would not allow him to be tormented by their idle curiosity, in a state of body and mind whose restoration evidently depended upon entire repose. Once, however, the lieutenant asked, Why he had come so far upon the ice in so strange a vehicle?

His countenance instantly assumed an aspect of the deepest gloom; and he replied, "To seek one who fled from me."

"And did the man whom you pursued travel in the same fashion?"

"Yes."

"Then I fancy we have seen him; for, the day before we picked you up, we saw some dogs drawing a sledge, with a man in it, across the ice."

This aroused the stranger's attention; and he asked a multitude of questions concerning the route which the dæmon, as he called him, had pursued. Soon after, when he was alone with me, he said, "I have, doubtless, excited your curiosity, as well as that of these good people; but you are too considerate to make inquiries."

"Certainly; it would indeed be very impertinent and inhuman in me to trouble you with any inquisitiveness of mine."

"And yet you rescued me from a strange and perilous situation; you have benevolently restored me to life."

Soon after this he inquired, if I thought that the breaking up of the ice had destroyed the other sledge? I replied, that I could not answer with any degree of certainty; for the ice had not broken until near midnight, and the traveller might have arrived at a place of safety before that time; but of this I could not judge.

From this time the stranger seemed very eager to be upon deck, to watch for the sledge which had before appeared; but I have persuaded him to remain in the cabin, for he is far too weak to sustain the rawness of the atmosphere. But I have promised that some one should watch for him, and give him instant notice if any new object should appear in sight.

Such is my journal of what relates to this strange occurrence up to the present day. The stranger has gradually improved in health, but is very silent, and appears uneasy when any one except myself enters his cabin. Yet his manners are so conciliating and gentle, that the sailors are all interested in him, although they have had very little communication with him. For my own part, I begin to love him as a brother; and his constant and deep grief fills me with sympathy and compassion. He must have been a noble creature in his better days, being even now in wreck so attractive and amiable.[10]

I said in one of my letters, my dear Margaret, that I should find no friend on the wide ocean; yet I have found a man who, before his spirit had been broken by misery, I should have been happy to have possessed as the brother of my heart.

I shall continue my journal concerning the stranger at intervals, should I have any fresh incidents to record.

August 13th, 17—.

My affection for my guest increases every day. He excites at once my admiration and my pity to an astonishing degree. How can I see so noble a creature destroyed by misery without feeling the most poignant grief? He is so gentle, yet so wise; his mind is so cultivated; and when he speaks, although his words are culled with the choicest art, yet they flow with rapidity and unparalleled eloquence.

He is now much recovered from his illness, and is continually on the deck, apparently watching for the sledge that preceded his own. Yet, although unhappy, he is not so utterly occupied by his own misery, but that he interests himself deeply in the employments of others. He has asked me many questions concerning my design; and I have related my little history frankly to him. He appeared pleased with the confidence, and suggested several alterations in my plan, which I shall find exceedingly useful. There is no pedantry in his manner; but all he does appears to spring solely from the interest he instinctively takes in the welfare of those who surround him. He is often overcome by gloom, and then he sits by himself, and tries to overcome all that is sullen or unsocial in his humour.

---

10. This is how Victor appears to the leader of the rescuing ship, Captain Robert Walton, though Walton knows only that Victor is European and not comparable to the seemingly "savage" (p. 11) creature he is chasing. Even in his much diminished state, Victor's noble qualities are apparent. Victor might become the noble friend Walton so longs for, someone of equal status who understands him and can provide wise counsel. Mary attributes both noble and not-so-noble qualities to Victor, but Walton will need to hear the full story before the complexities of Victor's character are revealed.

Mary Margaret Fonow.

These paroxysms pass from him like a cloud from before the sun, though his dejection never leaves him. I have endeavoured to win his confidence; and I trust that I have succeeded. One day I mentioned to him the desire I had always felt of finding a friend who might sympathize with me, and direct me by his counsel. I said, I did not belong to that class of men who are offended by advice. "I am self-educated, and perhaps I hardly rely sufficiently upon my own powers. I wish therefore that my companion should be wiser and more experienced than myself, to confirm and support me; nor have I believed it impossible to find a true friend."[11]

"I agree with you," replied the stranger, "in believing that friendship is not only a desirable, but a possible acquisition. I once had a friend, the most noble of human creatures, and am entitled, therefore, to judge respecting friendship. You have hope, and the world before you, and have no cause for despair. But I——I have lost every thing, and cannot begin life anew."

As he said this, his countenance became expressive of a calm settled grief, that touched me to the heart. But he was silent, and presently retired to his cabin.

Even broken in spirit as he is, no one can feel more deeply than he does the beauties of nature. The starry sky, the sea, and every sight afforded by these wonderful regions, seems still to have the power of elevating his

11. Robert Walton, in letters to his sister, Mrs. Saville, revisits the conditions of his own early life: "[my] education was neglected, yet I was passionately fond of reading ... [and I] inherited the fortune of my cousin" (p. 4). The knowledge gained from understanding his own initial conditions may have inspired Walton's decision to set challenging goals for himself. He seems to have worked hard at addressing some of his educational shortcomings as well as his limited perspective on hard work and hardship. Albert Bandura reminds us that "people motivate and guide their actions by setting themselves challenging goals and then mobilizing their skills and effort to reach them. After people attain the goal they have been pursuing, those with a strong sense of efficacy set higher goals for themselves" (1994, 265). Walton does not appear to be an exception. His intellectual isolation grows during this fateful voyage, with the need for finding a wiser, highly experienced, caring "companion" becoming of paramount importance. His cry for intellectual companionship, a mentor or mentors, is rewarded in two ways, with approval and intimacy. The value that Walton places on approval is rather telling: "I must own I felt a little proud, when my captain offered me the second dignity in the vessel, and entreated me to remain with the greatest earnestness; so valuable did he consider my services" (p. 5). However, it is the arrival of an educated, enigmatic stranger that brings forward the excitement that Walton places on intellectual companionship (mentor–mentee dynamics): he worries that he "should find no friend on the wide ocean; yet I have found a man ... so gentle, yet so wise; his mind is so cultivated; and when he speaks, although his words are culled with the choicest art, yet they flow with rapidity and unparalleled eloquence" (p. 13). Walton finds a "true friend," an intellectual companion, a great mentor, a divine wanderer "a celestial spirit, that has a halo around him" (p. 15).

Carlos Castillo-Chavez.

soul from earth. Such a man has a double existence: he may suffer misery, and be overwhelmed by disappointments; yet when he has retired into himself, he will be like a celestial spirit, that has a halo around him, within whose circle no grief or folly ventures.

Will you laugh at the enthusiasm I express concerning this divine wanderer? If you do, you must have certainly lost that simplicity which was once your characteristic charm. Yet, if you will, smile at the warmth of my expressions, while I find every day new causes for repeating them.

August 19th, 17—.

Yesterday the stranger said to me, "You may easily perceive, Captain Walton, that I have suffered great and unparalleled misfortunes. I had determined, once, that the memory of these evils should die with me; but you have won me to alter my determination. You seek for knowledge and wisdom, as I once did; and I ardently hope that the gratification of your wishes may not be a serpent to sting you, as mine has been.[12] I do not know that the relation of my misfortunes will be useful to you, yet, if you are inclined, listen to my tale. I believe that the strange incidents connected with it will afford a view of nature, which may enlarge your faculties and understanding. You will hear of powers and occurrences, such as you have been accustomed to believe impossible: but I do not doubt that my tale conveys in its series internal evidence of the truth of the events of which it is composed."

You may easily conceive that I was much gratified by the offered communication; yet I could not endure that he should renew his grief by a recital of his misfortunes. I felt the greatest eagerness to hear the promised narrative, partly from curiosity, and partly from a strong desire to ameliorate his fate, if it were in my power. I expressed these feelings in my answer.

"I thank you," he replied, "for your sympathy, but it is useless; my fate is nearly fulfilled. I wait but for one event, and then I shall repose in peace. I understand your feeling," continued he, perceiving that I wished to interrupt him; "but you are mistaken, my friend, if thus you will allow me to name you; nothing can alter my destiny: listen to my history, and you will perceive how irrevocably it is determined."

12. "How sharper than a serpent's tooth it is / To have a thankless child!" Perhaps Mary has Victor make this apparent reference to Shakespeare's play *King Lear* (I.iv.288–289) to show that he recognizes his paternity of the creature, but, like Lear, he still does not recognize his own full measure of culpability and responsibility.
David H. Guston.

He then told me, that he would commence his narrative the next day when I should be at leisure. This promise drew from me the warmest thanks. I have resolved every night, when I am not engaged, to record, as nearly as possible in his own words, what he has related during the day. If I should be engaged, I will at least make notes. This manuscript will doubtless afford you the greatest pleasure: but to me, who know him, and who hear it from his own lips, with what interest and sympathy shall I read it in some future day!

....

FRANKENSTEIN;

OR, THE MODERN PROMETHEUS.

CHAPTER I.

I am by birth a Genevese; and my family is one of the most distinguished of that republic.[13] My ancestors had been for many years counsellors and syndics; and my father had filled several public situations with honour and reputation. He was respected by all who knew him for his integrity and indefatigable attention to public business. He passed his younger days perpetually occupied by the affairs of his country; and it was not until the decline of life that he thought of marrying, and bestowing on the state sons who might carry his virtues and his name down to posterity.

13. The setting for the story is Geneva, Switzerland, one of the oldest major capitals of Europe, and Victor is from one of its noblest families. He uses his scientific training to create a new life but then fails to take responsibility for loving and caring for that life. He is shocked and disgusted when his creation doesn't turn out as he planned. Yet he is also mostly unaware that his failure to take care of his creation in turn has created the creature he fears and rejects. Mary and her family traveled in more liberal and even radical circles, and she abhorred and flaunted the conventional mores of high society. In *Frankenstein*, is she calling attention to the propensity of those at the top to ignore the consequences of their actions? Social status cannot fully protect individuals from unintended consequences. Scientists and engineers who are often at the highest ranks of the academy need to be more mindful of the unintended consequences of their discoveries.
Mary Margaret Fonow.

As the circumstances of his marriage illustrate his character, I cannot refrain from relating them. One of his most intimate friends was a merchant, who, from a flourishing state, fell, through numerous mischances, into poverty. This man, whose name was Beaufort, was of a proud and unbending disposition, and could not bear to live in poverty and oblivion in the same country where he had formerly been distinguished for his rank and magnificence. Having paid his debts, therefore, in the most honourable manner, he retreated with his daughter to the town of Lucerne, where he lived unknown and in wretchedness. My father loved Beaufort with the truest friendship, and was deeply grieved by his retreat in these unfortunate circumstances. He grieved also for the loss of his society, and resolved to seek him out and endeavour to persuade him to begin the world again through his credit and assistance.

Beaufort had taken effectual measures to conceal himself; and it was ten months before my father discovered his abode. Overjoyed at this discovery, he hastened to the house, which was situated in a mean street, near the Reuss. But when he entered, misery and despair alone welcomed him. Beaufort had saved but a very small sum of money from the wreck of his fortunes; but it was sufficient to provide him with sustenance for some months, and in the mean time he hoped to procure some respectable employment in a merchant's house. The interval was consequently spent in inaction; his grief only became more deep and rankling, when he had leisure for reflection; and at length it took so fast hold of his mind, that at the end of three months he lay on a bed of sickness, incapable of any exertion.

His daughter attended him with the greatest tenderness; but she saw with despair that their little fund was rapidly decreasing, and that there was no other prospect of support. But Caroline Beaufort possessed a mind of an uncommon mould; and her courage rose to support her in her adversity. She procured plain work; she plaited straw; and by various means contrived to earn a pittance scarcely sufficient to support life.

Several months passed in this manner. Her father grew worse; her time was more entirely occupied in attending him; her means of subsistence decreased; and in the tenth month her father died in her arms, leaving her an orphan and a beggar. This last blow overcame her; and she knelt by Beaufort's coffin, weeping bitterly, when my father entered the chamber. He came like a protecting spirit to the poor girl, who committed herself to his care, and after the interment of his friend he conducted her to Geneva, and placed her under the protection of a relation. Two years after this event Caroline became his wife.

When my father became a husband and a parent, he found his time so occupied by the duties of his new situation, that he relinquished many of his public employments, and devoted himself to the education of his children. Of these I was the eldest, and the destined successor to all his labours and utility. No creature could have more tender parents than mine. My improvement and health were their constant care, especially as I remained for several years their only child. But before I continue my narrative, I must record an incident which took place when I was four years of age.

My father had a sister, whom he tenderly loved, and who had married early in life an Italian gentleman. Soon after her marriage, she had accompanied her husband into his native country, and for some years my father had very little communication with her. About the time I mentioned she died; and a few months afterwards he received a letter from her husband, acquainting him with his intention of marrying an Italian lady, and requesting my father to take charge of the infant Elizabeth, the only child of his deceased sister. "It is my wish," he said, "that you should consider her as your own daughter, and educate her thus. Her mother's fortune is secured to her, the documents of which I will commit to your keeping. Reflect upon this proposition; and decide whether you would prefer educating your niece yourself to her being brought up by a stepmother."

My father did not hesitate, and immediately went to Italy, that he might accompany the little Elizabeth to her future home. I have often heard my mother say, that she was at that time the most beautiful child she had ever seen, and shewed signs even then of a gentle and affectionate disposition. These indications, and a desire to bind as closely as possible the ties of domestic love, determined my mother to consider Elizabeth as my future wife; a design which she never found reason to repent.

From this time Elizabeth Lavenza became my playfellow, and, as we grew older, my friend. She was docile and good tempered, yet gay and playful as a summer insect. Although she was lively and animated, her feelings were strong and deep, and her disposition uncommonly affectionate. No one could better enjoy liberty, yet no one could submit with more grace than she did to constraint and caprice. Her imagination was luxuriant, yet her capability of application was great. Her person was the image of her mind; her hazel eyes, although as lively as a bird's, possessed an attractive softness. Her figure was light and airy; and, though capable of enduring great fatigue, she appeared the most fragile creature in the world. While I admired her understanding and fancy, I loved to tend on her, as I should on a favourite animal; and I never saw so much grace both of person and mind united to so little pretension.

Every one adored Elizabeth. If the servants had any request to make, it was always through her intercession. We were strangers to any species of disunion and dispute; for although there was a great dissimilitude in our characters, there was an harmony in that very dissimilitude. I was more calm and philosophical than my companion; yet my temper was not so yielding. My application was of longer endurance; but it was not so severe whilst it endured. I delighted in investigating the facts relative to the actual world; she busied herself in following the aërial creations of the poets. The world was to me a secret, which I desired to discover; to her it was a vacancy, which she sought to people with imaginations of her own.

My brothers were considerably younger than myself; but I had a friend in one of my schoolfellows, who compensated for this deficiency. Henry Clerval was the son of a merchant of Geneva, an intimate friend of my father. He was a boy of singular talent and fancy. I remember, when he was nine years old, he wrote a fairy tale, which was the delight and amazement of all his companions. His favourite study consisted in books of chivalry and romance; and when very young, I can remember, that we used to act plays composed by him out of these favourite books, the principal characters of which were Orlando, Robin Hood, Amadis, and St. George.

No youth could have passed more happily than mine. My parents were indulgent, and my companions amiable. Our studies were never forced; and by some means we always had an end placed in view, which excited us to ardour in the prosecution of them. It was by this method, and not by emulation, that we were urged to application. Elizabeth was not incited to apply herself to drawing, that her companions might not outstrip her; but through the desire of pleasing her aunt, by the representation of some favourite scene done by her own hand. We learned Latin and English, that we might read the writings in those languages; and so far from study being made odious to us through punishment, we loved application, and our amusements would have been the labours of other children. Perhaps we did not read so many books, or learn languages so quickly, as those who are disciplined according to the ordinary methods; but what we learned was impressed the more deeply on our memories.

In this description of our domestic circle I include Henry Clerval; for he was constantly with us. He went to school with me, and generally passed the afternoon at our house; for being an only child, and destitute of companions at home, his father was well pleased that he should find associates at our house; and we were never completely happy when Clerval was absent.

I feel pleasure in dwelling on the recollections of childhood, before misfortune had tainted my mind, and changed its bright visions of extensive usefulness into gloomy and narrow reflections upon self. But, in drawing the picture of my early days, I must not omit to record those events which led, by insensible steps to my after tale of misery: for when I would account to myself for the birth of that passion, which afterwards ruled my destiny, I find it arise, like a mountain river, from ignoble and almost forgotten sources; but, swelling as it proceeded, it became the torrent which, in its course, has swept away all my hopes and joys.[14]

Natural philosophy[15] is the genius that has regulated my fate; I desire therefore, in this narration, to state those facts which led to my predilection for that science. When I was thirteen years of age, we all went on a party of pleasure to the baths near Thonon: the inclemency of the weather obliged us to remain a day confined to the inn. In this house I chanced to find a volume of the works of Cornelius Agrippa. I opened it with apathy; the theory which he attempts to demonstrate, and the wonderful facts which he relates, soon changed this feeling into enthusiasm. A new light seemed to dawn upon my mind; and, bounding with joy, I communicated my discovery to my father. I cannot help remarking here the many opportunities instructors possess of directing the attention of their pupils to useful knowledge, which they utterly neglect. My father looked carelessly at the

14. This passage is about perceived momentum: the past reconstructed from the viewpoint of the present always appears to have a structure, a momentum, and an obvious path. It is this deep misconception in part that leads to optimism regarding the ability to predict the future and to manipulate the present in such a way as to achieve desired future states. But the challenges of technology and governance in an increasingly complex world mean that such optimism is both hubristic and dysfunctional. It is hubristic because it dramatically overestimates the ability of anyone, technologist or policy maker, to predict future paths of sociotechnological systems, and it is dysfunctional because it leads to becoming lost in a haze of whimsical fantasy rather than to putting effort into the difficult and constantly changing challenge of dealing ethically, responsibly, and rationally with an ever-morphing, fundamentally unpredictable, real world. You can reach back and claim there is a clear stream from your deep past to your present situation, but what you are really doing is building an entirely normative reconstruction, an arbitrary and partial one at best.

Braden Allenby.

15. *Natural philosophy* and *natural philosopher* were broadly encompassing terms for the theoretical and empirical inquiry into the natural world and those who conducted such inquiries. The latter was used prior to the rise of the term *scientist*, which was not coined until 1834, although Mary does use the word *scientifical*: "our family was not scientifical," says Victor in describing the Frankensteins (p. 22).

A biography of Humphry Davy (Golinksi 2016, 1) that focuses on how Davy, who was acquainted with Mary's father William Godwin and whose work was read by Mary, became "a scientist before there was such a thing," uses quotations from Mary's novel as the epigraphs to each chapter, as if to suggest that Davy's difficulty in forging a scientific career is associated with and can be communicated by Mary's portrayal of Victor's similar difficulties.

David H. Guston.

title-page of my book, and said, "Ah! Cornelius Agrippa! My dear Victor, do not waste your time upon this; it is sad trash."

If, instead of this remark, my father had taken the pains to explain to me, that the principles of Agrippa had been entirely exploded, and that a modern system of science had been introduced, which possessed much greater powers than the ancient, because the powers of the latter were chimerical, while those of the former were real and practical; under such circumstances, I should certainly have thrown Agrippa aside, and, with my imagination warmed as it was, should probably have applied myself to the more rational theory of chemistry[16] which has resulted from modern discoveries. It is even possible, that the train of my ideas would never have received the fatal impulse that led to my ruin. But the cursory glance my father had taken of my volume by no means assured me that he was acquainted with its contents; and I continued to read with the greatest avidity.

When I returned home, my first care was to procure the whole works of this author, and afterwards of Paracelsus and Albertus Magnus.[17] I read and studied the wild fancies of these writers with delight; they appeared to me treasures known to few beside myself; and although I often wished to communicate these secret stores of knowledge to my father, yet his

16. Alchemy has roots in the ancient world, although the word itself comes from Arabic. It was concerned primarily with the transformation of materials, notably the transmutation of base metals such as lead and tin into gold and silver. Much historical alchemy can usefully be conceived as protochemistry and included such practices as metallurgy and the making of dyes and imitation gems. Alchemy also had a strong connection with medicine, and for some in the Renaissance it came to be associated with astrology, mysticism, and even magic. During the eighteenth and nineteenth centuries, alchemy was increasingly viewed as a pseudoscience and the domain of charlatans. Both Victor's father and Professor Krempe reflect this view and strongly distinguish between the modern science of chemistry and irrational, premodern alchemy.
Joel A. Klein.

17. Many European alchemists in the Middle Ages and Renaissance believed that it was possible to produce an "elixir" or medicine that could prolong life or even heal all diseases. Some, including Cornelius Agrippa (Heinrich Cornelius Agrippa von Nettesheim, 1486–1535), associated such elixirs or medicines with the philosopher's stone: a substance of alchemical legend that could turn metals such as lead into gold. The medieval theologian Albertus Magnus (c. 1200–1280) did not officially support such views, but a text called the *Little Book on Alchemy* that falsely purported—but was widely believed—to be by Albertus did. The texts whose ideas on alchemy and life were most influential, however, were attributed to—although likely not penned by—the Renaissance physician and iconoclast Paracelsus (1493–1541). In one of these, a work titled *On the Nature of Things*, the author describes the artificial creation of a little human called a "homunculus" in a process vaguely similar to Victor's animation of "lifeless matter" (pp. 34, 37). Heating a sealed flask containing putrefying semen would produce a human form after forty days, and the fully formed homunculus—which would have marvelous powers and knowledge—would be complete after forty weeks of feeding with a preparation of human blood.
Joel A. Klein.

indefinite censure of my favourite Agrippa always withheld me. I disclosed my discoveries to Elizabeth, therefore, under a promise of strict secrecy; but she did not interest herself in the subject, and I was left by her to pursue my studies alone.

It may appear very strange, that a disciple of Albertus Magnus should arise in the eighteenth century; but our family was not scientifical, and I had not attended any of the lectures given at the schools of Geneva.[18] My dreams were therefore undisturbed by reality; and I entered with the greatest diligence into the search of the philosopher's stone and the elixir of life.[19]

18. This passage implies that formal education is superior to being self-educated. Further, there is a sentiment that formal schooling can ground someone in truth and that a person trying to learn on his or her own may not be able to separate fiction from fact because he or she hasn't been taught what is right by someone else. This is a particularly interesting way to view schooling because all schooling is biased in some way: by the curriculum developed, by the instructor's views on that curriculum, and even by what questions the instructor entertains in the classroom. There is an assumed unbiased truth associated with formal schooling, but this assumption is flawed.

Sara Brownell.

19. Cornelius Agrippa remains among the most intellectually compelling magical theologians and natural philosophers of his time. His magnum opus, *De occulta philosophia libri tres* (Three books of occult philosophy), occupied the majority of his life, starting with a juvenile manuscript dedicated to his teacher, Abbot Trithemius of Sponheim; it began to circulate in 1509–1510 and had a first printed edition in 1531 and a final edited edition in 1533. The book attained wide print circulation, appearing in German, Latin, and French editions before 1535 as well as in reprints and in English throughout the seventeenth and eighteenth centuries. Agrippa's reputation as a dark magician also grew, despite the lack of evidence to support it, and a fourth book spuriously attributed to him was in fact a book of dark magic, appearing in English in the seventeenth century and outselling the original work through the nineteenth century.

It is not clear whether Victor Frankenstein read *De occulta philosophia*, but his appreciation for the "theory he [Agrippa] attempts to demonstrate" (p. 20) suggests he might have encountered the magical cosmology it contained. Agrippa embeds magic in the Creation, contending that God placed magic in the world as a system of connections, sympathies, and antipathies by which adepts could transcend the natural sphere and influence the superior realms. Although *De occulta philosophia* clearly engages with Neoplatonic philosophy and sees a clear path by which the study of God's work improves the adept, it is unique in that Agrippa also includes the possibility for the living adept to transcend the natural sphere through magical work and to re-enter the godhead. Through the spiritual improvement (requiring the adept to shed human desires and ambitions) required to attain such magical skills, Agrippa believes the adept would use his magical skills to continue the world order conceived by God—perhaps seeing the adept as an important source of defense in the case of an apocalypse. It is not clear, however, what would happen if a disciplined but evil adept achieved the godhead—perhaps he could derail the order of the world. At any rate, Victor's sense that he can equal God might have come from this text because he read it outside the context of Renaissance theology and without understanding the tremendous discipline required of a magical adept. His creature serves as an object lesson about the threats posed by undisciplined, ambition-fueled, and ego-driven science. It does not operate as a corrective to the problems of Renaissance natural philosophy solved by modern science but instead serves as evidence for the importance of the increasingly common peer-reviewed and institutionally defined investigations that came to be known as science in the early nineteenth century.

Allison Kavey.

But the latter obtained my most undivided attention: wealth was an inferior object; but what glory would attend the discovery, if I could banish disease from the human frame, and render man invulnerable to any but a violent death![20]

Nor were these my only visions. The raising of ghosts or devils was a promise liberally accorded by my favourite authors, the fulfilment of which I most eagerly sought; and if my incantations were always unsuccessful, I attributed the failure rather to my own inexperience and mistake, than to a want of skill or fidelity in my instructors.[21]

The natural phænomena that take place every day before our eyes did not escape my examinations. Distillation, and the wonderful effects of steam, processes of which my favourite authors were utterly ignorant, excited my astonishment; but my utmost wonder was engaged by some experiments on an air-pump, which I saw employed by a gentleman whom we were in the habit of visiting.

The ignorance of the early philosophers on these and several other points served to decrease their credit with me: but I could not entirely throw them aside, before some other system should occupy their place in my mind.

When I was about fifteen years old, we had retired to our house near Belrive, when we witnessed a most violent and terrible thunder-storm. It advanced from behind the mountains of Jura; and the thunder burst at once with frightful loudness from various quarters of the heavens. I remained, while the storm lasted, watching its progress with curiosity and delight. As I stood at the door, on a sudden I beheld a stream of fire issue from an old and beautiful oak, which stood about twenty yards from our house; and so soon as the dazzling light vanished, the oak had disappeared, and nothing remained but a blasted stump. When we visited it the next morning,

20. The young, rebellious, intelligent, and ambitious Victor is motivated by the search for glory and public renown. He wants to make a name for himself. He wants not just to be successful but to be brilliantly, notoriously successful. And he seeks that glorious reputation through modern natural philosophy, what we now call experimental science, the "genius that ... regulate[s his] fate" (p. 20). Victor's stated goal, to create a kind of immortality, is just the kind of thing that could bring him the renown he desperately seeks.

JJ LaTourelle.

21. Accepting the failure to learn as the student's responsibility can be described as a student-deficit model of instruction, where any gap in learning is the student's fault and instructors are presumed to be faultless in their teaching. This perspective also represents an instructor-centered approach to teaching, where it is the student's responsibility to listen to and learn from the instructor. It stands in stark contrast to how many view education today as a constructivist activity that should be student centered, where students are creating their own learning.

Sara Brownell.

we found the tree shattered in a singular manner. It was not splintered by the shock, but entirely reduced to thin ribbands of wood. I never beheld any thing so utterly destroyed.

The catastrophe of this tree excited my extreme astonishment; and I eagerly inquired of my father the nature and origin of thunder and lightning. He replied, "Electricity"; describing at the same time the various effects of that power. He constructed a small electrical machine, and exhibited a few experiments; he made also a kite, with a wire and string, which drew down that fluid from the clouds.[22]

This last stroke completed the overthrow of Cornelius Agrippa, Albertus Magnus, and Paracelsus, who had so long reigned the lords of my imagination. But by some fatality I did not feel inclined to commence the study of any modern system; and this disinclination was influenced by the following circumstance.

My father expressed a wish that I should attend a course of lectures upon natural philosophy, to which I cheerfully consented. Some accident prevented my attending these lectures until the course was nearly finished. The lecture, being therefore one of the last, was entirely incomprehensible to me. The professor discoursed with the greatest fluency of potassium and boron, of sulphates and oxyds, terms to which I could affix no idea; and I became disgusted with the science of natural philosophy, although I still read Pliny[23] and Buffon[24] with delight, authors, in my estimation, of nearly equal interest and utility.

22. Dramatic encounters with natural phenomena are inspirations for scientific as well as literary imagination. This passage reconstructs the way that the philosopher Francis Bacon (1561–1626) thought that scientists come to understand natural phenomena and, in turn, use their understanding to construct technologies that make use of the same underlying processes. In describing how Victor's father translates the mechanisms of thunder and lightning into various technologies— a small electrical machine (perhaps a galvanic pile and Leyden jar) and a kite that attracts and conducts electricity (after Benjamin Franklin's experiment), both of which were part of Percy Shelley's education—the passage foreshadows Victor's eventual use of electricity to animate the creature he creates. The sense of wonder the narrator describes at witnessing the storm is important: delight, curiosity, awe, and other emotions motivate scientific inquiry by captivating the imagination and emotions. Mary likely shared some of her protagonist's emotions as she endured the relentless rains and thunderstorms that plagued Geneva in the summer of 1816.
Dehlia Hannah.

23. Pliny the Elder (23–79 CE) was a Roman naturalist and natural philosopher who published the encyclopedic text *Naturalis historia* (Natural history). He died in the explosion of Mount Vesuvius while attempting to help friends escape.
David H. Guston.

24. Georges-Louis Leclerc, Comte de Buffon (1707–1788), was a French naturalist whose multivolume work *Histoire naturelle* (Natural history) echoed Pliny the Elder's. In a century in which natural historians were still attempting to understand whether and how species changed,

My occupations at this age were principally the mathematics, and most of the branches of study appertaining to that science. I was busily employed in learning languages; Latin was already familiar to me, and I began to read some of the easiest Greek authors without the help of a lexicon. I also perfectly understood English and German. This is the list of my accomplishments at the age of seventeen; and you may conceive that my hours were fully employed in acquiring and maintaining a knowledge of this various literature.

Another task also devolved upon me, when I became the instructor of my brothers. Ernest was six years younger than myself, and was my principal pupil. He had been afflicted with ill health from his infancy, through which Elizabeth and I had been his constant nurses: his disposition was gentle, but he was incapable of any severe application. William, the youngest of our family, was yet an infant, and the most beautiful little fellow in the world; his lively blue eyes, dimpled cheeks, and endearing manners, inspired the tenderest affection.

Such was our domestic circle, from which care and pain seemed for ever banished. My father directed our studies, and my mother partook of our enjoyments. Neither of us possessed the slightest pre-eminence over the other; the voice of command was never heard amongst us; but mutual affection engaged us all to comply with and obey the slightest desire of each other.

CHAPTER II.

When I had attained the age of seventeen, my parents resolved that I should become a student at the university of Ingolstadt. I had hitherto attended the schools of Geneva; but my father thought it necessary, for the completion of my education, that I should be made acquainted with other customs than those of my native country. My departure was therefore fixed at an early date; but, before the day resolved upon could arrive, the first misfortune of my life occurred—an omen, as it were, of my future misery.

Elizabeth had caught the scarlet fever; but her illness was not severe, and she quickly recovered. During her confinement, many arguments had been urged to persuade my mother to refrain from attending upon her.

Buffon proposed a theory that New World species, including humans, were degenerate compared to Old World species. His theory led to a heated correspondence with Thomas Jefferson, who sent samples of robust North American wildlife—including a stuffed moose—across the Atlantic to him. David H. Guston.

She had, at first, yielded to our entreaties; but when she heard that her favourite was recovering, she could no longer debar herself from her society, and entered her chamber long before the danger of infection was past. The consequences of this imprudence were fatal. On the third day my mother sickened; her fever was very malignant, and the looks of her attendants prognosticated the worst event. On her death-bed the fortitude and benignity of this admirable woman did not desert her. She joined the hands of Elizabeth and myself: "My children," she said, "my firmest hopes of future happiness were placed on the prospect of your union. This expectation will now be the consolation of your father. Elizabeth, my love, you must supply my place to your younger cousins. Alas! I regret that I am taken from you; and, happy and beloved as I have been, is it not hard to quit you all? But these are not thoughts befitting me; I will endeavour to resign myself cheerfully to death, and will indulge a hope of meeting you in another world."

She died calmly; and her countenance expressed affection even in death. I need not describe the feelings of those whose dearest ties are rent by that most irreparable evil,[25] the void that presents itself to the soul, and the despair that is exhibited on the countenance. It is so long before the mind can persuade itself that she, whom we saw every day, and whose very existence appeared a part of our own, can have departed for ever—that the brightness of a beloved eye can have been extinguished, and the sound of a voice so familiar, and dear to the ear, can be hushed, never more to be heard. These are the reflections of the first days; but when the lapse of time proves the reality of the evil, then the actual bitterness of grief commences.[26] Yet from whom has not that rude hand rent away some dear connexion;

25. The death of the mother is seen as evil, indeed as an "irreparable evil." As a child, Mary would sit by her mother's grave and read; this is a special form of grief that the created feel when they lose those who created them. Much of Victor's effort in making the creature is driven by his thoughts about the evil of death, the finitude of human life. The passage here then goes on to correlate the perception of an evil as evil with its emotional impact, in this case grief. Ironically, when he succeeds in making the creature, he makes a motherless one.
Joel Gereboff.

26. When Victor describes his grief at the death of his mother, he focuses on its impact on him. He grieves her absence rather than feeling sorrow for the pain she experienced in dying or for the experiences of life she will now miss. Victor's grief at his mother's death plays a central role in shaping his character going forward. It is the mirror of the creature's experience in the novel. Victor grieves the presence of an absence—that is, his mother. The creature grieves the presence of an absence—that is, a friend, fellow, and mate. Given all that Victor knows of grief and loss, we would expect him to be more sympathetic to the creature's plight. He seems blind to the many things he has in common with his creation. Perhaps he is willfully blind because he must continue to dehumanize his creation in order to distance himself from it and from his responsibility for it.

and why should I describe a sorrow which all have felt, and must feel? The time at length arrives, when grief is rather an indulgence than a necessity; and the smile that plays upon the lips, although it may be deemed a sacrilege, is not banished. My mother was dead, but we had still duties which we ought to perform; we must continue our course with the rest, and learn to think ourselves fortunate, whilst one remains whom the spoiler has not seized.

My journey to Ingolstadt, which had been deferred by these events, was now again determined upon. I obtained from my father a respite of some weeks. This period was spent sadly; my mother's death, and my speedy departure, depressed our spirits; but Elizabeth endeavoured to renew the spirit of cheerfulness in our little society. Since the death of her aunt, her mind had acquired new firmness and vigour. She determined to fulfil her duties with the greatest exactness; and she felt that that most imperious duty, of rendering her uncle and cousins happy, had devolved upon her. She consoled me, amused her uncle, instructed my brothers; and I never beheld her so enchanting as at this time, when she was continually endeavouring to contribute to the happiness of others, entirely forgetful of herself.

The day of my departure at length arrived. I had taken leave of all my friends, excepting Clerval, who spent the last evening with us. He bitterly lamented that he was unable to accompany me: but his father could not be persuaded to part with him, intending that he should become a part-ner with him in business, in compliance with his favourite theory, that learning was superfluous in the commerce of ordinary life.[27] Henry had a refined mind; he had no desire to be idle, and was well pleased to become his father's partner, but he believed that a man might be a very good trader, and yet possess a cultivated understanding.

We sat late, listening to his complaints, and making many little arrange-ments for the future. The next morning early I departed. Tears gushed from the eyes of Elizabeth; they proceeded partly from sorrow at my depar-ture, and partly because she reflected that the same journey was to have taken place three months before, when a mother's blessing would have accompanied me.

It remains to be seen whether scientists and engineers, as creators, can afford to recognize them-selves in their work or can afford not to.

Sean A. Hays.

27. Much of education now is focused on applied learning, in particular technical degrees, and is intended to prepare a skilled workforce. This view was not the dominant one in Mary's time, when learning was thought to be for the privileged and not all that useful for everyday life.

Sara Brownell.

I threw myself into the chaise that was to convey me away, and indulged in the most melancholy reflections. I, who had ever been surrounded by amiable companions, continually engaged in endeavouring to bestow mutual pleasure, I was now alone. In the university, whither I was going, I must form my own friends, and be my own protector. My life had hitherto been remarkably secluded and domestic; and this had given me invincible repugnance to new countenances. I loved my brothers, Elizabeth, and Clerval; these were "old familiar faces"; but I believed myself totally unfitted for the company of strangers. Such were my reflections as I commenced my journey; but as I proceeded, my spirits and hopes rose. I ardently desired the acquisition of knowledge. I had often, when at home, thought it hard to remain during my youth cooped up in one place, and had longed to enter the world, and take my station among other human beings. Now my desires were complied with, and it would, indeed, have been folly to repent.

I had sufficient leisure for these and many other reflections during my journey to Ingolstadt, which was long and fatiguing. At length the high white steeple of the town met my eyes. I alighted, and was conducted to my solitary apartment, to spend the evening as I pleased.

The next morning I delivered my letters of introduction, and paid a visit to some of the principal professors, and among others to M. Krempe, professor of natural philosophy. He received me with politeness, and asked me several questions concerning my progress in the different branches of science appertaining to natural philosophy. I mentioned, it is true, with fear and trembling, the only authors I had ever read upon those subjects. The professor stared: "Have you," he said, "really spent your time in studying such nonsense?"

I replied in the affirmative. "Every minute," continued M. Krempe with warmth, "every instant that you have wasted on those books is utterly and entirely lost. You have burdened your memory with exploded systems, and useless names. Good God! in what desert land have you lived, where no one was kind enough to inform you that these fancies, which you have so greedily imbibed, are a thousand years old, and as musty as they are ancient? I little expected in this enlightened and scientific age to find a disciple of Albertus Magnus and Paracelsus. My dear Sir, you must begin your studies entirely anew."[28]

28. This passage is meant to illustrate a problem with self-learning: the autodidact (someone who teaches himself or herself) may not know the appropriate texts to read or the appropriate way to evaluate them. But the passage also raises the question of whether there is any benefit to be had in reading about ways of thinking that are considered inaccurate in the current time. Are we so certain in the dominant viewpoint of the time that previous ways of thinking do not hold any use? Sara Brownell.

So saying, he stept aside, and wrote down a list of several books treating of natural philosophy, which he desired me to procure, and dismissed me, after mentioning that in the beginning of the following week he intended to commence a course of lectures upon natural philosophy in its general relations, and that M. Waldman, a fellow-professor, would lecture upon chemistry the alternate days that he missed.

I returned home, not disappointed, for I had long considered those authors useless whom the professor had so strongly reprobated; but I did not feel much inclined to study the books which I procured at his recommendation. M. Krempe was a little squat man, with a gruff voice and repulsive countenance; the teacher, therefore, did not prepossess me in favour of his doctrine. Besides, I had a contempt for the uses of modern natural philosophy. It was very different, when the masters of the science sought immortality and power;[29] such views, although futile, were grand: but now the scene was changed. The ambition of the inquirer seemed to limit itself to the annihilation of those visions on which my interest in science was chiefly founded. I was required to exchange chimeras of boundless grandeur for realities of little worth.[30]

29. Many scholars argue that science and technology, especially as practiced in the West, have always been about achieving "immortality and power" (see, e.g., *The Religion of Technology* [1997], where David Noble notes that from the early Middle Ages "technology came to be identified more closely with both lost perfection and the possibility of renewed perfection, and the advance of the arts took on new significance, not only as evidence of grace, but as a means of preparation for, and a sure sign of, imminent salvation" [12]). The Enlightenment in some ways was a profound assertion of a humanistic perspective, and the end goals of that assertion, often not stated as clearly as in this passage of the novel, have not changed that much. But before we challenge the obvious hubris, it bears remembering that the opposite has also not changed: those who do not seek immortality and power too often suffer, die young, and serve under another's yoke.
Braden Allenby.

30. Victor suggests a change in the ways that natural philosophy is currently employed as compared to the past. The history he creates suggest that scientists of the past held higher aspirations than his contemporaries, who, according to him, are interested in what science can show is *not* possible rather than pressing the human imagination forward. Because this comparison was made two centuries ago, it raises questions for modern readers about the common idea that the sciences of the past had more scope for imagination ("boundless grandeur," as Victor puts it) than the sciences of today.
Despite his conviction about the impossibility of the quest of the masters of science for "immortality and power," Victor finds himself drawn to the "chimeras of boundless grandeur." The term *chimera* has two potential meanings captured here: the mythological Greek fire-breathing monster with a lion's head, a goat's body, and a serpent's tail or an illusory or impossible goal. Mary's careful word selection allows readers to see both definitions in her usage. The concept of the chimera in modern biology (which of course would not have been known to Mary) is a single organism composed of different zygotes, which is the merger of multiple fertilized eggs; this multiple composition may happen through tissue transplant or mutation.
Hannah Rogers.

Such were my reflections during the first two or three days spent almost in solitude. But as the ensuing week commenced, I thought of the information which M. Krempe had given me concerning the lectures. And although I could not consent to go and hear that little conceited fellow deliver sentences out of a pulpit, I recollected what he had said of M. Waldman, whom I had never seen, as he had hitherto been out of town.

Partly from curiosity, and partly from idleness, I went into the lecturing room, which M. Waldman entered shortly after. This professor was very unlike his colleague. He appeared about fifty years of age, but with an aspect expressive of the greatest benevolence; a few gray hairs covered his temples, but those at the back of his head were nearly black. His person was short, but remarkably erect; and his voice the sweetest I had ever heard. He began his lecture by a recapitulation of the history of chemistry and the various improvements made by different men of learning, pronouncing with fervour the names of the most distinguished discoverers. He then took a cursory view of the present state of the science, and explained many of its elementary terms. After having made a few preparatory experiments, he concluded with a panegyric upon modern chemistry, the terms of which I shall never forget:—

"The ancient teachers of this science," said he, "promised impossibilities, and performed nothing. The modern masters promise very little; they know that metals cannot be transmuted, and that the elixir of life is a chimera. But these philosophers, whose hands seem only made to dabble in dirt, and their eyes to pore over the microscope or crucible, have indeed performed miracles. They penetrate into the recesses of nature, and shew how she works in her hiding places. They ascend into the heavens; they have discovered how the blood circulates, and the nature of the air we breathe. They have acquired new and almost unlimited powers; they can command the thunders of heaven, mimic the earthquake, and even mock the invisible world with its own shadows."

I departed highly pleased with the professor and his lecture, and paid him a visit the same evening. His manners in private were even more mild and attractive than in public; for there was a certain dignity in his mien during his lecture, which in his own house was replaced by the greatest affability and kindness. He heard with attention my little narration concerning my studies, and smiled at the names of Cornelius Agrippa, and Paracelsus, but without the contempt that M. Krempe had exhibited. He said, that "these were men to whose indefatigable zeal modern philosophers were indebted for most of the foundations of their knowledge. They had left to us, as an easier task, to give new names, and arrange in connected classifications, the facts which they in a great degree had been the instruments of bringing to light. The labours of men of genius, however erroneously directed, scarcely ever fail in ultimately turning to the solid advantage of mankind."[31] I listened to his statement, which was delivered without any presumption or affectation; and then added, that his lecture had removed my prejudices against modern chemists; and I, at the same time, requested his advice concerning the books I ought to procure.

"I am happy," said M. Waldman, "to have gained a disciple; and if your application equals your ability, I have no doubt of your success. Chemistry is that branch of natural philosophy in which the greatest improvements have been and may be made; it is on that account that I have made it my peculiar study; but at the same time I have not neglected the other branches of science. A man would make but a very sorry chemist, if he attended to that department of human knowledge alone. If your wish is to become really a man of science, and not merely a petty experimentalist, I should advise you to apply to every branch of natural philosophy, including mathematics."

He then took me into his laboratory, and explained to me the uses of his various machines; instructing me as to what I ought to procure, and promising me the use of his own, when I should have advanced far enough in the science not to derange their mechanism. He also gave me the list of books which I had requested; and I took my leave.

Thus ended a day memorable to me; it decided my future destiny.

CHAPTER III.

From this day natural philosophy, and particularly chemistry, in the most comprehensive sense of the term, became nearly my sole occupation. I read with ardour those works, so full of genius and discrimination, which modern inquirers have written on these subjects. I attended the lectures, and cultivated the acquaintance, of the men of science of the university; and I found even in M. Krempe a great deal of sound sense and real information, combined, it is true, with a repulsive physiognomy and manners, but not on that account the less valuable. In M. Waldman I found a true friend.

31. A major rationale for the autonomy of science and scientists—that is, their ability to make their own choices free from interference by governments or lay people—in their pursuit of knowledge is the presumed certainty of the superior instrumental outcome of that pursuit, regardless of the potential presence of error or bias. According to chemist and philosopher of science Michael Polanyi, the ideal organization is "scientists, freely making their own choice of problems and pursuing them in the light of their own personal judgment" (1962, 54).
David H. Guston.

His gentleness was never tinged by dogmatism; and his instructions were given with an air of frankness and good nature, that banished every idea of pedantry. It was, perhaps, the amiable character of this man that inclined me more to that branch of natural philosophy which he professed, than an intrinsic love for the science itself. But this state of mind had place only in the first steps towards knowledge: the more fully I entered into the science, the more exclusively I pursued it for its own sake.[32] That application, which at first had been a matter of duty and resolution, now became so ardent and eager, that the stars often disappeared in the light of morning whilst I was yet engaged in my laboratory.

As I applied so closely, it may be easily conceived that I improved rapidly. My ardour was indeed the astonishment of the students; and my proficiency, that of the masters. Professor Krempe often asked me, with a sly smile, how Cornelius Agrippa went on? whilst M. Waldman expressed the most heartfelt exultation in my progress. Two years passed in this manner, during which I paid no visit to Geneva, but was engaged, heart and soul, in the pursuit of some discoveries, which I hoped to make. None but those who have experienced them can conceive of the enticements of science. In other studies you go as far as others have gone before you, and there is nothing more to know; but in a scientific pursuit there is continual food for discovery and wonder. A mind of moderate capacity, which closely pursues one study,

---

32. The idea of a having a single scientific mentor is not ideal, and Victor knows this well. He is mentored by two complementary, imperfect, and valuable individuals—namely, M. Krempe and M. Waldman. We see that scientific mentoring does not take place in a vacuum. Developmental psychologist Jean Piaget described the process of intellectual development with the words "intelligence organizes the world by organizing itself" (quoted in Chess and Hassibi 1978, 63). One reading of Piaget suggests that he models learning as a complex adaptive system, and so as the human body experiences stimuli, it begins to organize and anticipate stimuli, creating complex systems of mental actions and anticipated results in an effort to predict and control stimuli to generate more favorable results. As a result, collaborative interactions among individuals with different perspectives and experiences (mentor and mentee) provide conversational stimuli for developing new understandings. L. S. Vygotsky, citing Piaget, describes a similar process: "Such observations [of child argumentation] prompted Piaget to conclude that communication produces the need for checking and confirming thoughts, a process that is characteristic of adult thought" (1978, 90). Mentor–mentee dynamics create the stimuli that drive Victor's curiosity, creativity, and learning. M. Waldman, who loves chemistry, notes that "I have not neglected the other branches of science" (p. 31), impressing the importance of interdisciplinary learning on Victor. As this passage shows, passion for learning is also the outcome of dual mentorship: "natural philosophy, and particularly chemistry, in the most comprehensive sense of the term, became nearly my sole occupation." Finally, the search for knowledge, regardless of direction, drives Victor's research. Discipline, passion, focus, and effective diverse mentorship philosophies characterize Victor's status at this time.

Carlos Castillo-Chavez.

must infallibly arrive at great proficiency in that study; and I, who continually sought the attainment of one object of pursuit, and was solely wrapt up in this, improved so rapidly, that, at the end of two years, I made some discoveries in the improvement of some chemical instruments, which procured me great esteem and admiration at the university. When I had arrived at this point, and had become as well acquainted with the theory and practice of natural philosophy as depended on the lessons of any of the professors at Ingolstadt, my residence there being no longer conducive to my improvements, I thought of returning to my friends and my native town, when an incident happened that protracted my stay.

One of the phænomena which had peculiarly attracted my attention was the structure of the human frame, and, indeed, any animal endued with life. Whence, I often asked myself, did the principle of life proceed? It was a bold question, and one which has ever been considered as a mystery; yet with how many things are we upon the brink of becoming acquainted, if cowardice or carelessness did not restrain our inquiries. I revolved these circumstances in my mind, and determined thenceforth to apply myself more particularly to those branches of natural philosophy which relate to physiology. Unless I had been animated by an almost supernatural enthusiasm, my application to this study would have been irksome, and almost intolerable. To examine the causes of life, we must first have recourse to death. I became acquainted with the science of anatomy: but this was not sufficient; I must also observe the natural decay and corruption of the human body. In my education my father had taken the greatest precautions that my mind should be impressed with no supernatural horrors. I do not ever remember to have trembled at a tale of superstition, or to have feared the apparition of a spirit. Darkness had no effect upon my fancy; and a church-yard was to me merely the receptacle of bodies deprived of life, which, from being the seat of beauty and strength, had become food for the worm. Now I was led to examine the cause and progress of this decay, and forced to spend days and nights in vaults and charnel houses. My attention was fixed upon every object the most insupportable to the delicacy of the human feelings. I saw how the fine form of man was degraded and wasted; I beheld the corruption of death succeed to the blooming cheek of life; I saw how the worm inherited the wonders of the eye and brain. I paused, examining and analysing all the minutiæ of causation, as exemplified in the change from life to death, and death to life, until from the midst of this darkness a sudden light broke in upon me—a light so brilliant and wondrous, yet so simple, that while I became dizzy with the immensity of the prospect which it illustrated, I was surprised that among so many men of genius, who had directed their inquiries towards the same science, that I alone should be reserved to discover so astonishing a secret.[33]

Remember, I am not recording the vision of a madman. The sun does not more certainly shine in the heavens, than that which I now affirm is true. Some miracle might have produced it, yet the stages of the discovery were distinct and probable. After days and nights of incredible labour and fatigue, I succeeded in discovering the cause of generation and life; nay, more, I became myself capable of bestowing animation upon lifeless matter.[34]

The astonishment which I had at first experienced on this discovery soon gave place to delight and rapture. After so much time spent in painful labour, to arrive at once at the summit of my desires, was the most gratifying consummation of my toils. But this discovery was so great and overwhelming, that all the steps by which I had been progressively led to it were obliterated, and I beheld only the result. What had been the study and desire of the wisest men since the creation of the world, was now within my grasp. Not that, like a magic scene, it all opened upon me at once: the information I had obtained was of a nature rather to direct my endeavours so soon as I should point them towards the object of my search, than to exhibit that object already accomplished. I was like the Arabian who had been buried with the dead, and found a passage to life aided only by one glimmering, and seemingly ineffectual, light.

I see by your eagerness, and the wonder and hope which your eyes express, my friend, that you expect to be informed of the secret with which I am acquainted; that cannot be: listen patiently until the end of my story,

---

33. Biologists can seem godlike in their laboratory research, making decisions pertaining to animal and human life while having little immediate need to answer to anyone save their conscience. What kind of ethics does practicing applied biological science require? A personal ethics of individual morality pertaining to, for example, dishonesty and irresponsibility in observing humane practice? A research ethics pertaining to, for example, what specific "raw" material is used, what the source of the "raw" material is, and what the individual researcher or group of researchers is doing with the "raw" material? Or a social ethics pertaining to the positive and negative social impacts the biological research might have at present and in the future? Because the gradations between personal research and social ethics are rarely so distinct, how should biologists relate to them? How does Victor relate to his raw "materials" (p. 36)?

Miguel Astor-Aguilera.

34. Victor here claims to have invented a way to instill life. The narrative does not delve into questions of ownership or patenting, but future narratives building on Frankenstein do, in novels (e.g., *Next* by Michael Crichton [2006]), film (*Blade Runner* [Ridley Scott, 1986]), and television (*Orphan Black* [BBC, 2013–]). Patenting adds the motivation of financial reward to scientific fame and glory, and it can provide motivations for both holding something secret, until rights are secured, and publicizing it after rights are granted.

Robert Cook-Deegan.

and you will easily perceive why I am reserved upon that subject. I will not lead you on, unguarded and ardent as I then was, to your destruction and infallible misery. Learn from me, if not by my precepts, at least by my example, how dangerous is the acquirement of knowledge, and how much happier that man is who believes his native town to be the world, than he who aspires to become greater than his nature will allow.

When I found so astonishing a power placed within my hands,[35] I hesitated a long time concerning the manner in which I should employ it. Although I possessed the capacity of bestowing animation, yet to prepare a frame for the reception of it, with all its intricacies of fibres, muscles, and veins, still remained a work of inconceivable difficulty and labour.[36]

35. Victor engages materiality in a much different manner than his not-so-distant pre-Enlightenment European brethren. He equates "life" with animate human bodies; however, animated life is found throughout Earth in a variety of organic forms. Do not simple cells move and have life? Plants also move, though most of them quite slowly, and have frames composed of "fibres, muscles, and veins" conceptually analogous to those of animals. What of plants' visible animation, seeming to indicate volition: vines creeping along the sides of buildings toward where there is more light, sunflowers' "faces" following the path of the sun, predatory Venus flytraps moving quite quickly to ensnare their victims, and the *Mimosa pudica*, the "sleepy plant" in Mesoamerica (also found in Melanesia and Africa), shying away when touched and then recomposing itself after apparent danger has subsided? When do we, if we do, grant plants, nonhuman animals, and human animals volition and at what stage of life? Do only human animals have emotions and volition? Do simple cells shy away if they are nudged or pricked and move away if they bump into another mobile simple cell?

Miguel Astor-Aguilera.

36. Victor finds himself chasing a "frame" of flesh and its union with life. His ambition reflects several forms of mechanistic thought current at the time Mary wrote *Frankenstein*: an understanding of biological systems as physical machines controlled solely by physical laws. Nineteenth-century biology and physiology embraced and developed mechanistic perspectives while at the same time discarding earlier kindred understandings of the body. In the seventeenth century, the conceptualization of the human body by René Descartes (1596–1650) was similarly mechanistic, but he explained the transition from physical machine to a living, thinking entity as an act of God. The deity endowed otherwise idle material with consciousness. By Mary's time, the latter part of Decartes's argument had lost favor, but mechanistic ideas had gained scientific prominence.

Victor's "frame" is a product of part-by-part fabrication and lacks "animation"—then a term for the state of being alive. His power makes the idle machine something living. In a sense, the story presents a separation between body and consciousness similar to the one championed by Descartes. And yet no deity is at work. Victor installs life into his constructed "frame" using only his scientific prowess.

Mechanistic thought remains an important part of the life sciences, and the ambition to build frames for life is found in twenty-first-century efforts to produce so-called protocells or, in the language of some synthetic biologists, the "chassis." The structures, built with basic chemicals "from the ground up," are envelopes for biological phenomena. Although present-day research is unlikely to deliver anything like Mary's creature, it holds to a similar concept of life as machine. Descartes long ago lost his place in the natural sciences, and Victor's power has yet to be realized, but mechanistic thinking persists.

Pablo Schyfter.

I doubted at first whether I should attempt the creation of a being like myself or one of simpler organization; but my imagination was too much exalted by my first success to permit me to doubt of my ability to give life to an animal as complex and wonderful as man.[37] The materials at present within my command hardly appeared adequate to so arduous an undertaking; but I doubted not that I should ultimately succeed. I prepared myself for a multitude of reverses; my operations might be incessantly baffled, and at last my work be imperfect: yet, when I considered the improvement which every day takes place in science and mechanics, I was encouraged to hope my present attempts would at least lay the foundations of future success. Nor could I consider the magnitude and complexity of my plan as any argument of its impracticability. It was with these feelings that I began the creation of a human being.[38] As the minuteness of the parts formed a great

37. Although Victor begins this passage hesitant of his ability to create a creature like himself, he says that his imagination overtakes his questions. He pictures his imagination as an element of his personality motivated by its own success. The idea of imagination as internal to the self might remind the modern reader of the concept of the ego as developed by psychologist Sigmund Freud more than one hundred years after Mary wrote *Frankenstein* (*The Ego and the Id* [(1923) 1960]). Freud's ego is that part of the human psyche modified by external forces. The success of his initial work leaves Victor unable to doubt this ability to create a human life. In a cyclical fashion, detached from material realities, this type of imagination is empowered by its own interplay internally. The ability to act based on imagination and the changing of the imagination itself in relation to those actions are fundamental to Victor's understanding of the concept.

Hannah Rogers.

38. With "creation," Mary draws on some of the widest possible literary themes, and the biblical resonances are emphasized by the creature himself. But creativity and the labor of one's hands had multiple significances within wider nineteenth-century society, as they do today. It is not often recognized, for instance, that creativity and labor play a crucial role in legitimizing the idea of "property." How do we justify establishing ownership over something? One important argument, most directly associated with the political philosophy of John Locke (1632–1704), stated that applying one's labor to nature through writing, crafting, and so on made that creation one's property (see Locke 1821). For example, earthen clay, once owned by everyone, through a transformative act of labor and creativity (so the argument goes) becomes a single person's property.

Through *Frankenstein*, we can therefore question scientific work and its ownership. Although we might arbitrarily decide that humans are exempt from being classed as property—a decision not yet achieved in Mary's time—what of the creature? Is it right to think of the term *creation* as implying ownership? Or what of the ownership of children created by parents? Or what of the ownership of any nonhuman organism for that matter? Should it be the case that merely the act of laboring on something makes it property? The existence of Victor's potential proprietary rights in his work and his (irresponsible?) refusal to acknowledge those rights allow us to generalize the significance of his creative act. Perhaps it is not in the creation of a human that he errs but in the conceptualization of his labors.

Dominic Berry.

hindrance to my speed, I resolved, contrary to my first intention, to make the being of a gigantic stature; that is to say, about eight feet in height, and proportionably large. After having formed this determination, and having spent some months in successfully collecting and arranging my materials, I began.

No one can conceive the variety of feelings which bore me onwards, like a hurricane, in the first enthusiasm of success. Life and death appeared to me ideal bounds, which I should first break through, and pour a torrent of light into our dark world. A new species would bless me as its creator and source;[39] many happy and excellent natures would owe their being to me.[40] No father could claim the gratitude of his child so completely as I should deserve their's. Pursuing these reflections, I thought, that if I could bestow animation upon lifeless matter, I might in process of time (although I now

---

39. The religious language of this passage connects Victor's ambitions to a long tradition of humans playing god. In Jewish folklore, for instance, several great rabbis are said to have made clay animate, much as Adam was formed from clay according to biblical legend. These animated clay creatures are known as golems, and they resemble men except for the fact that they are mindlessly obedient. Following orders literally, they inevitably become destructive, revealing their creators' arrogance by showing those creators' limited foresight and the perils of hubris. Similar patterns play out in many cautionary tales about technology, such as *R.U.R.* by Karel Čapek and Josef Čapek (1920), a play in which robots confound the expectations of their builders by becoming violently rebellious. And yet although we are philosophically attuned to our arrogance, and although hubris is a persistent theme in mythology and literature (including *Frankenstein*), the temptation to play god seems only to increase with the increasing power of science and technology. This phenomenon is especially evident in two fields of active research: synthetic biology and artificial intelligence (AI). Central to the agenda of synthetic biology is a literal desire to create new species: for example, bespoke organisms such as *Mycoplasma mycoides* JCVI-syn1.0, which the J. Craig Venter Institute made in 2010 by inserting a lab-assembled genome into a bacterium. The promise of synthetic biology is total genetic control of organisms that can bless us with new foods, drugs, and fuels. The peril is that the future behavior of such bespoke organisms, like that of the Čapeks' robots, cannot be completely predicted. AI is arguably even more hubristic—and perilous— because of the potential for machine intelligence to exceed—or be incomprehensible by—human intelligence. From a superhuman AI's perspective, arrogant *Homo sapiens* might be deemed as dangerously irrational as Victor's creature or golems.

Jonathon Keats.

40. There is a notion that scientists become so engrossed in their own pursuits that they forget that they are "standing on the shoulders of giants," as Sir Isaac Newton (1642–1726) put it, and instead feel overweening pride of ownership in the science they are studying and in the results of their research. Such an attitude, occurring time and again in the history of science, impedes scientific progress. In science, knowledge cannot be owned by anyone. Knowledge must be shared, must be questioned, must be built upon. Here Victor gets lost in his own ability as a scientist. He forgets that although he may create something new (be it knowledge or life), he is not truly the owner of those creations.

Melissa Wilson Sayres.

found it impossible) renew life[41] where death had apparently devoted the body to corruption.[42]

These thoughts supported my spirits, while I pursued my undertaking with unremitting ardour. My cheek had grown pale with study, and my person had become emaciated with confinement. Sometimes, on the very brink of certainty, I failed; yet still I clung to the hope which the next day or the next hour might realize. One secret which I alone possessed was the hope to which I had dedicated myself; and the moon gazed on my midnight labours, while, with unrelaxed and breathless eagerness, I pursued nature to her hiding places.[43] Who shall conceive the horrors of my secret toil,

41. Victor here implies flesh-and-blood immortality because the universe inherently and automatically renews life from death. All life on Earth depends on things cyclically dying as other things, including humans, procreate, live, flourish, and eventually die as the cycle continues. Victor, due to the very emotional personal experience of having a person he loves pass unto death, desires that humans need not have to die and hence is driven to seek the "secret" to life regeneration. Life renewing from death is present in biblical scripture (Genesis 3:19, 18:27; Job 30:19; Ecclesiastes 3:20) as well as in the Anglican Christian Book of Common Prayer (Burial Rite 1:485, 2:501) and is a topic highly present, though different ontologically from Judeo-Christian-Muslim views, in indigenous cosmologies (Astor-Aguilera 2010). Some of the world's societies have been known to practice infanticide or care for their elderly only up until they become too much of a burden on the younger population, which needs a certain amount of resources to survive. How old is old enough for a human to live and at what cost to Earth's resources? Should humans not die at all and be perpetually regenerated through scientific breakthroughs?

Miguel Astor-Aguilera.

42. Victor articulates a set of hypothesized or imagined consequences for his research should it succeed, including the conquering of death and the creation of a race of beings who would worship him. These "imaginaries" are fictions that follow, reasonably but not necessarily, from success in his research. Perhaps at this point, Victor might have explored what fictions might reasonably but not necessarily follow from failure or from a different or incomplete kind of success.

David H. Guston.

43. Victor chooses to conduct his experiments with life in secret; he isolates himself from friends, family, and colleagues at his university. The isolation is both geographical and social. During the period of feverish research and creation, he doesn't exchange correspondence or share his ideas with anyone.

Isolation makes it possible for Victor to undertake his grisly and socially unacceptable project. Certainly, his colleagues and family would have intervened to stop him. But Victor's self-imposed isolation also makes it impossible for the creature to gain access to the social resources he needs to construct a livable life (J. Butler 2010). He is cut off from the possibility of family, friends, and membership in society. He removes himself from the structured and institutionalized relationships that we depend on for sustenance, fellowship, and relief, such as education, health care, and a humane justice system.

An individual depends in countless ways on being recognized as a social being—as a person with feelings and rights, enjoying fellowship in social groups, relying on institutions to provide support, to safeguard our rights, and to care for us when we are in need. Victor's decision to conduct his work in isolation and his abandonment of the creature at birth makes it impossible for the creature ever to achieve this social legibility and to participate functionally in society.

as I dabbled among the unhallowed damps of the grave, or tortured the living animal to animate the lifeless clay?[44] My limbs now tremble, and my eyes swim with the remembrance; but then a resistless, and almost frantic impulse, urged me forward; I seemed to have lost all soul or sensation but for this one pursuit. It was indeed but a passing trance, that only made me feel with renewed acuteness so soon as, the unnatural stimulus ceasing to operate, I had returned to my old habits. I collected bones from charnel houses; and disturbed, with profane fingers, the tremendous secrets of the human frame. In a solitary chamber, or rather cell, at the top of the house, and separated from all the other apartments by a gallery and staircase, I kept my workshop of filthy creation; my eyeballs were starting from their sockets in attending to the details of my employment. The dissecting room and the slaughter-house furnished many of my materials; and often did my human nature turn with loathing from my occupation, whilst, still urged on by an eagerness which perpetually increased, I brought my work near to a conclusion.[45]

As a result, we see the creature as a vagrant, an outlaw, and a vigilante throughout the novel. All of these identities are built on a foundation of social exclusion. Victor's isolation means that the creature has little choice but to become a monster. He is left with no pathways into a peaceful life inside of human society.

Joey Eschrich.

44. Victor's grave robbing and torture of animals raise the following questions: Do the ends ever justify the means in research or in other areas? If useful data can be gathered through unethical means, should they be? And if such data are so gathered, ought they to form part of the evidence base of science? Analysis of the history of human experimentation in the twentieth century comes solidly down on the negative answer, based on experiences like those of concentration camp inmates experimented on by Nazi doctors during World War II and of African Americans and Guatemalans experimented on by US Public Health Service researchers in the decades following the war. The principles of bioethics hold that human beings may never be used solely as experimental means to a scientific end, but human autonomy can also create an affirmative role for self-sacrifice, allowing people ethically to volunteer for dangerous experiments. Some bioethicists also argue that if a practice is physically or viscerally repugnant—"the horrors of my secret toil," in Victor's words (p. 38)—then the practice is at least suspect of being morally repugnant. For a time, the ethical debate about human embryonic stem cell research focused on whether medical science should be permitted to progress based on research that was putatively unethical in its destruction of human embryos to derive human pluripotent stem cells. Is such research always spoiled as the fruit of evil exploits?

David H. Guston and Jason Scott Robert.

45. Victor here expresses pangs of conscience as he reflects on his singular goal of animating life. To what extent he sees his conscience as a reliable guide is not clear, for in the end he continues his activities despite these reservations. A sharp emotional reaction of loathing cannot overcome his intense drive, his eagerness, to complete his task of animating life. Here the novel gives expression to the tension between emotional, morally significant reactions and human desire and drive.

Joel Gereboff.

The summer months passed while I was thus engaged, heart and soul, in one pursuit. It was a most beautiful season; never did the fields bestow a more plentiful harvest, or the vines yield a more luxuriant vintage: but my eyes were insensible to the charms of nature. And the same feelings which made me neglect the scenes around me caused me also to forget those friends who were so many miles absent, and whom I had not seen for so long a time. I knew my silence disquieted them; and I well remembered the words of my father: "I know that while you are pleased with yourself, you will think of us with affection, and we shall hear regularly from you. You must pardon me, if I regard any interruption in your correspondence as a proof that your other duties are equally neglected."

I knew well therefore what would be my father's feelings; but I could not tear my thoughts from my employment, loathsome in itself, but which had taken an irresistible hold of my imagination.[46] I wished, as it were, to procrastinate all that related to my feelings of affection until the great object, which swallowed up every habit of my nature, should be completed.

I then thought that my father would be unjust if he ascribed my neglect to vice, or faultiness on my part; but I am now convinced that he was justified in conceiving that I should not be altogether free from blame. A human being in perfection ought always to preserve a calm and peaceful mind, and never to allow passion or a transitory desire to disturb his tranquillity. I do not think that the pursuit of knowledge is an exception to this rule. If the study to which you apply yourself has a tendency to weaken your affections, and to destroy your taste for those simple pleasures in which no alloy can possibly mix, then that study is certainly unlawful, that is to say, not befitting the human mind. If this rule were always observed; if no man allowed any pursuit whatsoever to interfere with the tranquillity of his domestic affections, Greece had not been enslaved; Cæsar would have spared his country; America would have been discovered more gradually; and the empires of Mexico and Peru had not been destroyed.

But I forget that I am moralizing in the most interesting part of my tale; and your looks remind me to proceed.

My father made no reproach in his letters; and only took notice of my silence by inquiring into my occupations more particularly than before.

---

46. Victor's unease at dealing with body parts from the dead is overpowered by the force of his imagination propelling him to complete his work. The relationship between imagination, creativity, and conventional views expressed in this case as strongly negative emotions recurs throughout the novel. And in sticking with his project, Victor overcomes his own feelings and dismisses his father's. At hand is the question of to what extent feelings express with accuracy what ought to be done morally.

Joel Gereboff.

Winter, spring, and summer, passed away during my labours; but I did not watch the blossom or the expanding leaves—sights which before always yielded me supreme delight, so deeply was I engrossed in my occupation. The leaves of that year had withered before my work drew near to a close; and now every day shewed me more plainly how well I had succeeded. But my enthusiasm was checked by my anxiety, and I appeared rather like one doomed by slavery to toil in the mines, or any other unwholesome trade, than an artist occupied by his favourite employment. Every night I was oppressed by a slow fever, and I became nervous to a most painful degree; a disease that I regretted the more because I had hitherto enjoyed most excellent health, and had always boasted of the firmness of my nerves. But I believed that exercise and amusement would soon drive away such symptoms; and I promised myself both of these, when my creation should be complete.

CHAPTER IV.

It was on a dreary night of November, that I beheld the accomplishment of my toils. With an anxiety that almost amounted to agony, I collected the instruments of life around me, that I might infuse a spark of being into the lifeless thing [47] that lay at my feet. It was already one in the morning; the rain pattered dismally against the panes, and my candle was nearly burnt out, when, by the glimmer of the half-extinguished light, I saw the dull yellow eye of the creature open; it breathed hard, and a convulsive motion agitated its limbs.

How can I describe my emotions at this catastrophe, or how delineate the wretch whom with such infinite pains and care I had endeavoured to form? [48]

---

47. Mary refers to a "spark" that animates Victor's creature and brings him to life. This reference alludes to the use of electricity to reanimate a body, a relatively new idea at the time of this novel's publication. Toward the end of the eighteenth century, Luigi Galvani (1737–1798) had demonstrated the use of electrical current to activate muscle, a discovery he made on dissected frog legs. Mary was well aware of these experiments, and Galvani's work was one of her main influences in generating the idea for her novel. Furthermore, these principles have endured in medicine. Today, electric stimulation is used to aid millions of human bodies with everything from defibrillators and pacemakers to partial treatments for paralysis and systems that link prosthetic limbs and cameras to the brain.

Stephanie Naufel.

48. Emotions again serve to express assessments. On the surface, they are assumed to be correct moral judgments, though in the end their accuracy is questioned implicitly when Victor's rejection and horror drive the creature away and lead over time to the creature's loneliness. The experience of isolation and deprivation of basic social relations turn the creature from a natural disposition toward goodness to a disposition toward evil that impels him to engage in horrific and destructive acts.

Joel Gereboff.

His limbs were in proportion, and I had selected his features as beautiful. Beautiful!—Great God! His yellow skin scarcely covered the work of muscles and arteries beneath; his hair was of a lustrous black, and flowing; his teeth of a pearly whiteness; but these luxuriances only formed a more horrid contrast with his watery eyes, that seemed almost of the same colour as the dun white sockets in which they were set, his shrivelled complexion, and straight black lips.[49]

The different accidents of life are not so changeable as the feelings of human nature. I had worked hard for nearly two years, for the sole purpose of infusing life into an inanimate body.[50] For this I had deprived myself of rest and health. I had desired it with an ardour that far exceeded moderation; but now that I had finished, the beauty of the dream vanished, and breathless horror and disgust filled my heart. Unable to endure the aspect of the being I had created, I rushed out of the room, and continued a long time traversing my bed-chamber, unable to compose my mind to sleep. At length lassitude succeeded to the tumult I had before endured; and I threw myself on the bed in my clothes, endeavouring to seek a few moments of forgetfulness. But it was in vain: I slept indeed, but I was disturbed

49. Victor characterizes the moment he succeeds in bringing his creation to life—when the creation opens his eyes and gazes back—as a "catastrophe." Contrast this scene with the same moment of creation of intelligence noted in Genesis 1:32: "God saw all that he had made, and it was very good." An enduring conversation in the philosophy of beauty asks whether beauty is more an innate property of the "thing" being considered or resides instead in the eye of the beholder. Conflations of beauty and goodness are also quite common in both popular culture and philosophical inquiry. In many ways, this entire novel explores the relationship between beauty, goodness, and perceptions. In the end, Victor's characterization of his creature depends more on Victor himself than on the creature's identity. Outward perceptions of beauty or the lack thereof influence how others understand the creature and whether they perceive his actions as "good" or "evil." Imagine how the story would unfold if Victor were instead to have looked upon his creature at this very moment and felt that it "was good." In the scene as given in the novel, Victor looks for himself in the creature's eyes and finds someone else.
Stephani Etheridge Woodson.

50. Victor constantly equates "life" with animation. Does animacy provide life, or is that function served by the metaphysical soul purportedly found within active human bodies? Within Judeo-Christian-Muslim religions, it is the sacred soul placed within the human body during fetal development by a divine God that makes life different in humans from other animals. Nonhuman animals are treated differently from humans in Western society, whereas many non-Western societies do not make a striking difference from human to animal to plant (Astor-Aguilera 2010). For Western humans, the divine soul is what makes life sacrosanct, but nonhuman animal life is typically not as important. Is Victor playing God in his laboratory research, trying to infuse life or the spark of a soul within a human body composed of inactive tissue? When is the "soul" present in humans, if at all? Is soul matter inherent to human tissue at conception and therefore present in stem cells?
Miguel Astor-Aguilera.

by the wildest dreams. I thought I saw Elizabeth, in the bloom of health, walking in the streets of Ingolstadt. Delighted and surprised, I embraced her; but as I imprinted the first kiss on her lips, they became lurid with the hue of death; her features appeared to change, and I thought that I held the corpse of my dead mother in my arms; a shroud enveloped her form, and I saw the grave-worms crawling in the folds of the flannel. I started from my sleep with horror; a cold dew covered my forehead, my teeth chattered, and every limb became convulsed; when, by the dim and yellow light of the moon, as it forced its way through the window-shutters, I beheld the wretch—the miserable monster whom I had created. He held up the curtain of the bed; and his eyes, if eyes they may be called, were fixed on me. His jaws opened, and he muttered some inarticulate sounds, while a grin wrinkled his cheeks. He might have spoken, but I did not hear; one hand was stretched out, seemingly to detain me, but I escaped, and rushed down stairs. I took refuge in the court-yard belonging to the house which I inhabited; where I remained during the rest of the night, walking up and down in the greatest agitation, listening attentively, catching and fearing each sound as if it were to announce the approach of the demoniacal corpse to which I had so miserably given life.

Oh! no mortal could support the horror of that countenance. A mummy again endued with animation could not be so hideous as that wretch.[51] I had gazed on him while unfinished; he was ugly then; but when those muscles and joints were rendered capable of motion, it became a thing such as even Dante could not have conceived.

51. Egyptian mummies were present in the British Museum since the mid-1750s, donated by private antiquity collectors. British attention to ancient Egypt broadened during Napoleon's campaign of 1798–1801; his inclusion of scholars with his army was mocked in England as wartime propaganda, but the French documented and exported antiquities that were later transferred to London after their defeat. Probably more important than these events to the interpretation of Mary's text, however, is the use of the purported curative powder "mummia" or "mummy," which had been available throughout Europe since the twelfth century. Referred to as both medicine and pigment by early English writers including Edmund Spenser, William Shakespeare, and John Donne, mummia was either the bituminous substance used in mummification to dry out body cavities after the removal of organs or the ground-up body parts of mummies themselves when this bituminous substance was in short supply. Mary's reference to mummies here and later in Walton's characterization of the texture and color of the creature's hand (p. 183) may serve several purposes: (1) Ancient mummification enabled the preserved body to be available for use by the spirit in the afterlife—another kind of reanimation of a dead body. (2) The creature's mummylike hand would have exhibited the characteristic darkened skin produced by the drying material, whereas the creature's facial skin is elsewhere described as yellow, further highlighting his patchwork nature. (3) In light of the mutilation of mummified bodies for questionable medicinal treatments, is it possible that Mary used the term *mummy* to enhance her ethical critique?
Judith Guston.

I passed the night wretchedly. Sometimes my pulse beat so quickly and hardly, that I felt the palpitation of every artery; at others, I nearly sank to the ground through languor and extreme weakness. Mingled with this horror, I felt the bitterness of disappointment: dreams that had been my food and pleasant rest for so long a space, were now become a hell to me; and the change was so rapid, the overthrow so complete!

Morning, dismal and wet, at length dawned, and discovered to my sleepless and aching eyes the church of Ingolstadt, its white steeple and clock, which indicated the sixth hour. The porter opened the gates of the court, which had that night been my asylum, and I issued into the streets, pacing them with quick steps, as if I sought to avoid the wretch whom I feared every turning of the street would present to my view.[52] I did not dare return to the apartment which I inhabited, but felt impelled to hurry on, although wetted by the rain, which poured from a black and comfortless sky.

I continued walking in this manner for some time, endeavouring, by bodily exercise, to ease the load that weighed upon my mind. I traversed the streets, without any clear conception of where I was, or what I was doing. My heart palpitated in the sickness of fear; and I hurried on with irregular steps, not daring to look about me:

> Like one who, on a lonely road,
>   Doth walk in fear and dread,
> And, having once turn'd round, walks on,
>   And turns no more his head;
> Because he knows a frightful fiend
>   Doth close behind him tread.[53]

Continuing thus, I came at length opposite to the inn at which the various diligences and carriages usually stopped. Here I paused, I knew not why; but I remained some minutes with my eyes fixed on a coach that was coming towards me from the other end of the street. As it drew nearer, I observed that it was the Swiss diligence: it stopped just where I was standing; and, on the door being opened, I perceived Henry Clerval, who, on seeing me, instantly sprung out. "My dear Frankenstein," exclaimed he,

---

52. It is understandable that Victor would experience feelings of fear and awe after realizing he successfully created life, especially given the strength and power of his creation. However, abandoning and then "avoid[ing] the wretch" because of this fear means he also avoids taking responsibility for his creature's life and suffering. Victor's avoidance does not lead to the protection of himself and his loved ones, and it intensifies the creature's anguish and destructive behavior.
Nicole Piemonte.

53. Coleridge's "Ancient Mariner." [Mary's note]

"how glad I am to see you! how fortunate that you should be here at the very moment of my alighting!"

Nothing could equal my delight on seeing Clerval; his presence brought back to my thoughts my father, Elizabeth, and all those scenes of home so dear to my recollection. I grasped his hand, and in a moment forgot my horror and misfortune; I felt suddenly, and for the first time during many months, calm and serene joy. I welcomed my friend, therefore, in the most cordial manner, and we walked towards my college. Clerval continued talking for some time about our mutual friends, and his own good fortune in being permitted to come to Ingolstadt. "You may easily believe," said he, "how great was the difficulty to persuade my father that it was not absolutely necessary for a merchant not to understand any thing except book-keeping; and, indeed, I believe I left him incredulous to the last, for his constant answer to my unwearied entreaties was the same as that of the Dutch school-master in the Vicar of Wakefield: 'I have ten thousand florins a year without Greek, I eat heartily without Greek.' But his affection for me at length overcame his dislike of learning, and he has permitted me to undertake a voyage of discovery to the land of knowledge."

"It gives me the greatest delight to see you; but tell me how you left my father, brothers, and Elizabeth."

"Very well, and very happy, only a little uneasy that they hear from you so seldom. By the bye, I mean to lecture you a little upon their account myself.—But, my dear Frankenstein," continued he, stopping short, and gazing full in my face, "I did not before remark how very ill you appear; so thin and pale; you look as if you had been watching for several nights."

"You have guessed right; I have lately been so deeply engaged in one occupation, that I have not allowed myself sufficient rest, as you see: but I hope, I sincerely hope, that all these employments are now at an end, and that I am at length free."

I trembled excessively; I could not endure to think of, and far less to allude to the occurrences of the preceding night. I walked with a quick pace, and we soon arrived at my college. I then reflected, and the thought made me shiver, that the creature whom I had left in my apartment might still be there, alive, and walking about. I dreaded to behold this monster; but I feared still more that Henry should see him. Entreating him therefore to remain a few minutes at the bottom of the stairs, I darted up towards my own room. My hand was already on the lock of the door before I recollected myself. I then paused; and a cold shivering came over me. I threw the door forcibly open, as children are accustomed to do when they expect a spectre to stand in waiting for them on the other side; but nothing appeared. I stepped fearfully in: the apartment was empty; and my bed-room was also freed from its hideous guest. I could hardly believe that so great a good-fortune could have befallen me; but when I became assured that my enemy had indeed fled, I clapped my hands for joy, and ran down to Clerval.

We ascended into my room, and the servant presently brought breakfast; but I was unable to contain myself. It was not joy only that possessed me; I felt my flesh tingle with excess of sensitiveness, and my pulse beat rapidly. I was unable to remain for a single instant in the same place; I jumped over the chairs, clapped my hands, and laughed aloud. Clerval at first attributed my unusual spirits to joy on his arrival; but when he observed me more attentively, he saw a wildness in my eyes for which he could not account; and my loud, unrestrained, heartless laughter, frightened and astonished him.

"My dear Victor," cried he, "what, for God's sake, is the matter? Do not laugh in that manner. How ill you are! What is the cause of all this?"

"Do not ask me," cried I, putting my hands before my eyes, for I thought I saw the dreaded spectre glide into the room; "*he* can tell.—Oh, save me! save me!" I imagined that the monster seized me; I struggled furiously, and fell down in a fit.

Poor Clerval! what must have been his feelings? A meeting, which he anticipated with such joy, so strangely turned to bitterness. But I was not the witness of his grief; for I was lifeless, and did not recover my senses for a long, long time.

This was the commencement of a nervous fever, which confined me for several months. During all that time Henry was my only nurse. I afterwards learned that, knowing my father's advanced age, and unfitness for so long a journey, and how wretched my sickness would make Elizabeth, he spared them this grief by concealing the extent of my disorder. He knew that I could not have a more kind and attentive nurse than himself; and, firm in the hope he felt of my recovery, he did not doubt that, instead of doing harm, he performed the kindest action that he could towards them.

But I was in reality very ill; and surely nothing but the unbounded and unremitting attentions of my friend could have restored me to life. The form of the monster on whom I had bestowed existence was for ever before my eyes, and I raved incessantly concerning him. Doubtless my words surprised Henry: he at first believed them to be the wanderings of my disturbed imagination; but the pertinacity with which I continually recurred to the same subject persuaded him that my disorder indeed owed its origin to some uncommon and terrible event.

By very slow degrees, and with frequent relapses, that alarmed and grieved my friend, I recovered. I remember the first time I became capable of observing outward objects with any kind of pleasure, I perceived that the fallen leaves had disappeared, and that the young buds were shooting forth from the trees that shaded my window. It was a divine spring; and the season contributed greatly to my convalescence. I felt also sentiments of joy and affection revive in my bosom; my gloom disappeared, and in a short time I became as cheerful as before I was attacked by the fatal passion.

"Dearest Clerval," exclaimed I, "how kind, how very good you are to me. This whole winter, instead of being spent in study, as you promised yourself, has been consumed in my sick room. How shall I ever repay you? I feel the greatest remorse for the disappointment of which I have been the occasion; but you will forgive me."

"You will repay me entirely, if you do not discompose yourself, but get well as fast as you can; and since you appear in such good spirits, I may speak to you on one subject, may I not?"

I trembled. One subject! what could it be? Could he allude to an object on whom I dared not even think?

"Compose yourself," said Clerval, who observed my change of colour, "I will not mention it, if it agitates you; but your father and cousin would be very happy if they received a letter from you in your own hand-writing. They hardly know how ill you have been, and are uneasy at your long silence."

"Is that all? my dear Henry. How could you suppose that my first thought would not fly towards those dear, dear friends whom I love, and who are so deserving of my love."

"If this is your present temper, my friend, you will perhaps be glad to see a letter that has been lying here some days for you: it is from your cousin, I believe."

CHAPTER V.

Clerval then put the following letter into my hands.

"*To* V. FRANKENSTEIN.
"MY DEAR COUSIN,

"I cannot describe to you the uneasiness we have all felt concerning your health. We cannot help imagining that your friend Clerval conceals the extent of your disorder: for it is now several months since we have seen your hand-writing; and all this time you have been obliged to dictate your letters to Henry. Surely, Victor, you must have been exceedingly ill; and this makes us all very wretched, as much so nearly as after the death of your dear mother. My uncle was almost persuaded that you were indeed dangerously ill, and could hardly be restrained from undertaking a journey to Ingolstadt. Clerval always writes that you are getting better; I eagerly hope that you will confirm this intelligence soon in your own hand-writing; for indeed, indeed, Victor, we are all very miserable on this account. Relieve us from this fear, and we shall be the happiest creatures in the world. Your father's health is now so vigorous, that he appears ten years younger since last winter. Ernest also is so much improved, that you would hardly know him: he is now nearly sixteen, and has lost that sickly appearance which he had some years ago; he is grown quite robust and active.

"My uncle and I conversed a long time last night about what profession Ernest should follow. His constant illness when young has deprived him of the habits of application; and now that he enjoys good health, he is continually in the open air, climbing the hills, or rowing on the lake. I therefore proposed that he should be a farmer; which you know, Cousin, is a favourite scheme of mine. A farmer's is a very healthy happy life; and the least hurtful, or rather the most beneficial profession of any. My uncle had an idea of his being educated as an advocate, that through his interest he might become a judge. But, besides that he is not at all fitted for such an occupation, it is certainly more creditable to cultivate the earth for the sustenance of man, than to be the confidant, and sometimes the accomplice, of his vices; which is the profession of a lawyer. I said, that the employments of a prosperous farmer, if they were not a more honourable, they were at least a happier species of occupation than that of a judge, whose misfortune it was always to meddle with the dark side of human nature. My uncle smiled, and said, that I ought to be an advocate myself, which put an end to the conversation on that subject.

"And now I must tell you a little story that will please, and perhaps amuse you. Do you not remember Justine Moritz? Probably you do not; I will relate her history, therefore, in a few words. Madame Moritz, her mother, was a widow with four children, of whom Justine was the third. This girl had always been the favourite of her father; but, through a strange perversity, her mother could not endure her, and, after the death of M. Moritz, treated her very ill. My aunt observed this; and, when Justine was twelve years of age, prevailed on her mother to allow her to live at our house. The republican institutions of our country have produced simpler and happier manners than those which prevail in the great monarchies that surround it. Hence there is less distinction between the several classes of its inhabitants; and the lower orders being neither so poor nor so despised, their manners are more refined and moral. A servant in Geneva does not mean the same thing as a servant in France and England. Justine, thus received in our family, learned the duties of a servant; a condition which, in our fortunate country, does not include the idea of ignorance, and a sacrifice of the dignity of a human being.

"After what I have said, I dare say you well remember the heroine of my little tale: for Justine was a great favourite of your's; and I recollect you once remarked, that if you were in an ill humour, one glance from Justine could dissipate it, for the same reason that Ariosto gives concerning the beauty of Angelica—she looked so frank-hearted and happy. My aunt conceived a great attachment for her, by which she was induced to give her an education superior to that which she had at first intended. This benefit was fully repaid; Justine was the most grateful little creature in the world: I do not mean that she made any professions, I never heard one pass her lips; but you could see by her eyes that she almost adored her protectress. Although her disposition was gay, and in many respects inconsiderate, yet she paid the greatest attention to every gesture of my aunt. She thought her the model of all excellence, and endeavoured to imitate her phraseology and manners, so that even now she often reminds me of her.

"When my dearest aunt died, every one was too much occupied in their own grief to notice poor Justine, who had attended her during her illness with the most anxious affection. Poor Justine was very ill; but other trials were reserved for her.

"One by one, her brothers and sister died; and her mother, with the exception of her neglected daughter, was left childless. The conscience of the woman was troubled; she began to think that the deaths of her favourites was a judgment from heaven to chastise her partiality. She was a Roman Catholic; and I believe her confessor confirmed the idea which she had conceived. Accordingly, a few months after your departure for Ingolstadt, Justine was called home by her repentant mother. Poor girl! she wept when she quitted our house: she was much altered since the death of my aunt; grief had given softness and a winning mildness to her manners, which had before been remarkable for vivacity. Nor was her residence at her mother's house of a nature to restore her gaiety. The poor woman was very vacillating in her repentance. She sometimes begged Justine to forgive her unkindness, but much oftener accused her of having caused the deaths of her brothers and sister. Perpetual fretting at length threw Madame Moritz into a decline, which at first increased her irritability, but she is now at peace for ever. She died on the first approach of cold weather, at the beginning of this last winter. Justine has returned to us; and I assure you I love her tenderly. She is very clever and gentle, and extremely pretty; as I mentioned before, her mien and her expressions continually remind me of my dear aunt.

"I must say also a few words to you, my dear cousin, of little darling William. I wish you could see him; he is very tall of his age, with sweet laughing blue eyes, dark eye-lashes, and curling hair. When he smiles, two little dimples appear on each cheek, which are rosy with health. He has already had one or two little *wives*, but Louisa Biron is his favourite, a pretty little girl of five years of age.

"Now, dear Victor, I dare say you wish to be indulged in a little gossip concerning the good people of Geneva. The pretty Miss Mansfield has already received the congratulatory visits on her approaching marriage with a young Englishman, John Melbourne, Esq. Her ugly sister, Manon, married M. Duvillard, the rich banker, last autumn. Your favourite schoolfellow, Louis Manoir, has suffered several misfortunes since the departure of Clerval from Geneva. But he has already recovered his spirits, and is reported to be on the point of marrying a very lively pretty Frenchwoman, Madame Tavernier. She is a widow, and much older than Manoir; but she is very much admired, and a favourite with every body.

"I have written myself into good spirits, dear cousin;[54] yet I cannot conclude without again anxiously inquiring concerning your health. Dear Victor, if you are not very ill, write yourself, and make your father and all of us happy; or——I cannot bear to think of the other side of the question; my tears already flow. Adieu, my dearest cousin.

"ELIZABETH LAVENZA.
"Geneva, March 18th, 17—."

"Dear, dear Elizabeth!" I exclaimed when I had read her letter, "I will write instantly, and relieve them from the anxiety they must feel." I wrote, and this exertion greatly fatigued me; but my convalescence had commenced, and proceeded regularly. In another fortnight I was able to leave my chamber.

---

54. Narrative reflection has transformative power—the process of writing one's story can actually change one's understanding of the story. Because reflecting on and writing about an experience can influence how a person feels about the experience, it is possible for Victor to "write himself" into better spirits. Note in this regard that Mary does not at this point describe Victor as having made any notes on his experiments, even for his private use, if not for publication. For more on reflective writing, see Bolton 2014.
Nicole Piemonte.

One of my first duties on my recovery was to introduce Clerval to the several professors of the university. In doing this, I underwent a kind of rough usage, ill befitting the wounds that my mind had sustained. Ever since the fatal night, the end of my labours, and the beginning of my misfortunes, I had conceived a violent antipathy even to the name of natural philosophy.[55] When I was otherwise quite restored to health, the sight of a chemical instrument would renew all the agony of my nervous symptoms. Henry saw this, and had removed all my apparatus from my view. He had also changed my apartment; for he perceived that I had acquired a dislike for the room which had previously been my laboratory. But these cares of Clerval were made of no avail when I visited the professors. M. Waldman inflicted torture when he praised, with kindness and warmth, the astonishing progress I had made in the sciences. He soon perceived that I disliked the subject; but, not guessing the real cause, he attributed my feelings to modesty, and changed the subject from my improvement to the science itself, with a desire, as I evidently saw, of drawing me out. What could I do? He meant to please, and he tormented me. I felt as if he had placed carefully, one by one, in my view those instruments which were to be afterwards used in putting me to a slow and cruel death. I writhed under his words, yet dared not exhibit the pain I felt.[56] Clerval, whose eyes and feelings were always quick in discerning the sensations of others, declined the subject, alleging, in excuse, his total ignorance; and the conversation took a more general turn. I thanked my friend from my heart, but I did not speak. I saw plainly that he was surprised, but he never attempted to draw my secret from me; and although I loved him with a mixture of affection and reverence that knew no bounds, yet I could never persuade myself to confide to him that event which was so often present to my recollection, but which I feared the detail to another would only impress more deeply.

55. It is only in hindsight that Victor recognizes the consequences of engaging in unreflective "natural philosophy" or scientific study. Had he seriously considered the ethical consequences of making his creature, and had these considerations outweighed his hubris and desire for personal success, it is unlikely he would have proceeded. This healthy fear of unchecked scientific progress (that Victor develops too late) highlights the need for attention to the scientist's personal and professional development as well as the need for scientists to engage in self-reflection to consider ethical issues before they commence scientific studies.

Nicole Piemonte.

56. Maintaining his secret and keeping positive human interactions cause Victor distress, but his failure to have positive interactions with the creature causes the creature distress as well. The challenge not to allow feelings to be visible in normal bodily reactions is immense. Cultural systems see emotions as embodied. From shortly after birth, infants are able to read approval and disapproval on their parents' faces.

Joel Gereboff.

M. Krempe was not equally docile; and in my condition at that time, of almost insupportable sensitiveness, his harsh blunt encomiums gave me even more pain than the benevolent approbation of M. Waldman. "D—n the fellow!" cried he; "why, M. Clerval, I assure you he has outstript us all. Aye, stare if you please; but it is nevertheless true. A youngster who, but a few years ago, believed Cornelius Agrippa as firmly as the gospel, has now set himself at the head of the university; and if he is not soon pulled down, we shall all be out of countenance.—Aye, aye," continued he, observing my face expressive of suffering, "M. Frankenstein is modest; an excellent quality in a young man. Young men should be diffident of themselves, you know, M. Clerval; I was myself when young: but that wears out in a very short time."

M. Krempe had now commenced an eulogy on himself, which happily turned the conversation from a subject that was so annoying to me.

Clerval was no natural philosopher. His imagination was too vivid for the minutiæ of science.[57] Languages were his principal study; and he sought, by acquiring their elements, to open a field for self-instruction on his return to Geneva. Persian, Arabic, and Hebrew, gained his attention, after he had made himself perfectly master of Greek and Latin. For my own part, idleness had ever been irksome to me; and now that I wished to fly from reflection, and hated my former studies, I felt great relief in being the fellow-pupil with my friend, and found not only instruction but consolation in the works of the orientalists. Their melancholy is soothing, and their joy elevating to a degree I never experienced in studying the authors of any other country. When you read their writings, life appears to consist in a warm sun and garden of roses,—in the smiles and frowns of a fair enemy, and the fire that consumes your own heart. How different from the manly and heroical poetry of Greece and Rome.

Summer passed away in these occupations, and my return to Geneva was fixed for the latter end of autumn; but being delayed by several accidents,

---

57. Victor's observation about Clerval underscores the romantic interest in the problem of the degree of imaginative power necessary to the arts versus the sciences. In *Biographia literaria* (1817), Samuel Taylor Coleridge, for example, defines a difference between the active "imaginative" act and the "fancy," the recounting of a memory that may be altered or extended but that is always passive. Clerval is described as having too much imagination for science because imagination is defined in opposition to details. Yet earlier Victor has detailed his belief that his attraction to science comes in part from its visionary quality (see p. 29). This apparent contradiction in Victor's position, which may be Mary's way of showing the character's limitations, remains unresolved. However, it is notable that by the 1831 edition, this point about the imagination being too vivid for science had been omitted (see "Introduction to *Frankenstein* [1831]," pp. 189–193).
Hannah Rogers.

winter and snow arrived, the roads were deemed impassable, and my journey was retarded until the ensuing spring. I felt this delay very bitterly; for I longed to see my native town, and my beloved friends. My return had only been delayed so long from an unwillingness to leave Clerval in a strange place, before he had become acquainted with any of its inhabitants. The winter, however, was spent cheerfully; and although the spring was uncommonly late, when it came, its beauty compensated for its dilatoriness.

The month of May had already commenced, and I expected the letter daily which was to fix the date of my departure, when Henry proposed a pedestrian tour in the environs of Ingolstadt that I might bid a personal farewell to the country I had so long inhabited. I acceded with pleasure to this proposition: I was fond of exercise, and Clerval had always been my favourite companion in the rambles of this nature that I had taken among the scenes of my native country.

We passed a fortnight in these perambulations: my health and spirits had long been restored, and they gained additional strength from the salubrious air I breathed, the natural incidents of our progress, and the conversation of my friend. Study had before secluded me from the intercourse of my fellow-creatures, and rendered me unsocial; but Clerval called forth the better feelings of my heart; he again taught me to love the aspect of nature, and the cheerful faces of children. Excellent friend! how sincerely did you love me, and endeavour to elevate my mind, until it was on a level with your own. A selfish pursuit had cramped and narrowed me, until your gentleness and affection warmed and opened my senses; I became the same happy creature who, a few years ago, loving and beloved by all, had no sorrow or care. When happy, inanimate nature had the power of bestowing on me the most delightful sensations. A serene sky and verdant fields filled me with ecstacy. The present season was indeed divine; the flowers of spring bloomed in the hedges, while those of summer were already in bud: I was undisturbed by thoughts which during the preceding year had pressed upon me, notwithstanding my endeavours to throw them off, with an invincible burden.

Henry rejoiced in my gaiety, and sincerely sympathized in my feelings: he exerted himself to amuse me, while he expressed the sensations that filled his soul. The resources of his mind on this occasion were truly astonishing: his conversation was full of imagination; and very often, in imitation of the Persian and Arabic writers, he invented tales of wonderful fancy and passion. At other times he repeated my favourite poems, or drew me out into arguments, which he supported with great ingenuity.

We returned to our college on a Sunday afternoon: the peasants were dancing, and every one we met appeared gay and happy. My own spirits were high, and I bounded along with feelings of unbridled joy and hilarity.

CHAPTER VI.

On my return, I found the following letter from my father: —

"*To* V. FRANKENSTEIN.

"MY DEAR VICTOR,

"You have probably waited impatiently for a letter to fix the date of your return to us; and I was at first tempted to write only a few lines, merely mentioning the day on which I should expect you. But that would be a cruel kindness, and I dare not do it. What would be your surprise, my son, when you expected a happy and gay welcome, to behold, on the contrary, tears and wretchedness? And how, Victor, can I relate our misfortune? Absence cannot have rendered you callous to our joys and griefs; and how shall I inflict pain on an absent child? I wish to prepare you for the woeful news, but I know it is impossible; even now your eye skims over the page, to seek the words which are to convey to you the horrible tidings.

"William is dead!—that sweet child, whose smiles delighted and warmed my heart, who was so gentle, yet so gay! Victor, he is murdered!

"I will not attempt to console you; but will simply relate the circumstances of the transaction.

"Last Thursday (May 7th) I, my niece, and your two brothers, went to walk in Plainpalais. The evening was warm and serene, and we prolonged our walk farther than usual. It was already dusk before we thought of returning; and then we discovered that William and Ernest, who had gone on before, were not to be found. We accordingly rested on a seat until they should return. Presently Ernest came, and inquired if we had seen his brother: he said, that they had been playing together, that William had run away to hide himself, and that he vainly sought for him, and afterwards waited for him a long time, but that he did not return.

"This account rather alarmed us, and we continued to search for him until night fell, when Elizabeth conjectured that he might have returned to the house. He was not there. We returned again, with torches; for I could not rest, when I thought that my sweet boy had lost himself, and was exposed to all the damps and dews of night: Elizabeth also suffered extreme anguish. About five in the morning I discovered my lovely boy, whom the night before I had seen blooming and active in health, stretched on the grass livid and motionless: the print of the murderer's finger was on his neck.

"He was conveyed home, and the anguish that was visible in my countenance betrayed the secret to Elizabeth. She was very earnest to see the corpse. At first I attempted to prevent her; but she persisted, and entering the room where it lay, hastily examined the neck of the victim, and clasping her hands exclaimed, 'O God! I have murdered my darling infant!'

"She fainted, and was restored with extreme difficulty. When she again lived, it was only to weep and sigh. She told me, that that same evening William had teazed her to let him wear a very valuable miniature that she possessed of your mother. This picture is gone, and was doubtless the temptation which urged the murderer to the deed. We have no trace of him at present, although our exertions to discover him are unremitted; but they will not restore my beloved William.

"Come, dearest Victor; you alone can console Elizabeth. She weeps continually, and accuses herself unjustly as the cause of his death; her words pierce my heart. We are all unhappy; but will not that be an additional motive for you, my son, to return and be our comforter? Your dear mother! Alas, Victor! I now say, Thank God she did not live to witness the cruel, miserable death of her youngest darling!

"Come, Victor; not brooding thoughts of vengeance against the assassin, but with feelings of peace and gentleness, that will heal, instead of festering the wounds of our minds. Enter the house of mourning, my friend, but with kindness and affection for those who love you, and not with hatred for your enemies.

"Your affectionate and afflicted father,
ALPHONSE FRANKENSTEIN.
"Geneva, May 12th, 17—."

Clerval, who had watched my countenance as I read this letter, was surprised to observe the despair that succeeded to the joy I at first expressed on receiving news from my friends. I threw the letter on the table, and covered my face with my hands.

"My dear Frankenstein," exclaimed Henry, when he perceived me weep with bitterness, "are you always to be unhappy? My dear friend, what has happened?"

I motioned to him to take up the letter, while I walked up and down the room in the extremest agitation. Tears also gushed from the eyes of Clerval, as he read the account of my misfortune.

"I can offer you no consolation, my friend," said he; "your disaster is irreparable. What do you intend to do."

"To go instantly to Geneva: come with me, Henry, to order the horses."

During our walk, Clerval endeavoured to raise my spirits. He did not do this by common topics of consolation, but by exhibiting the truest sympathy. "Poor William!" said he, "that dear child; he now sleeps with his angel mother. His friends mourn and weep, but he is at rest: he does not now feel the murderer's grasp; a sod covers his gentle form, and he knows no pain. He can no longer be a fit subject for pity; the survivors are the greatest sufferers, and for them time is the only consolation. Those maxims of the Stoics, that death was no evil, and that the mind of man ought to be superior to despair on the eternal absence of a beloved object, ought not to be urged. Even Cato wept over the dead body of his brother."

Clerval spoke thus as we hurried through the streets; the words impressed themselves on my mind, and I remembered them afterwards in solitude. But now, as soon as the horses arrived, I hurried into a cabriole, and bade farewell to my friend.

My journey was very melancholy. At first I wished to hurry on, for I longed to console and sympathize with my loved and sorrowing friends; but when I drew near my native town, I slackened my progress. I could hardly sustain the multitude of feelings that crowded into my mind. I passed through scenes familiar to my youth, but which I had not seen for nearly six years. How altered every thing might be during that time? One sudden and desolating change had taken place; but a thousand little circumstances might have by degrees worked other alterations which, although they were done more tranquilly, might not be the less decisive. Fear overcame me; I dared not advance, dreading a thousand nameless evils that made me tremble, although I was unable to define them.

I remained two days at Lausanne, in this painful state of mind. I contemplated the lake: the waters were placid; all around was calm, and the snowy mountains, "the palaces of nature," were not changed. By degrees the calm and heavenly scene restored me, and I continued my journey towards Geneva.

The road ran by the side of the lake, which became narrower as I approached my native town. I discovered more distinctly the black sides of Jura, and the bright summit of Mont Blanc; I wept like a child: "Dear mountains! my own beautiful lake! how do you welcome your wanderer? Your summits are clear; the sky and lake are blue and placid. Is this to prognosticate peace, or to mock at my unhappiness?"

I fear, my friend, that I shall render myself tedious by dwelling on these preliminary circumstances; but they were days of comparative happiness, and I think of them with pleasure. My country, my beloved country! who but a native can tell the delight I took in again beholding thy streams, thy mountains, and, more than all, thy lovely lake.

Yet, as I drew nearer home, grief and fear again overcame me. Night also closed around; and when I could hardly see the dark mountains, I felt still more gloomily. The picture appeared a vast and dim scene of evil, and I foresaw obscurely that I was destined to become the most wretched of human beings. Alas! I prophesied truly, and failed only in one single circumstance, that in all the misery I imagined and dreaded, I did not conceive the hundredth part of the anguish I was destined to endure.[58]

It was completely dark when I arrived in the environs of Geneva; the gates of the town were already shut; and I was obliged to pass the night at Secheron, a village half a league to the east of the city. The sky was serene; and, as I was unable to rest, I resolved to visit the spot where my poor William had been murdered. As I could not pass through the town, I was obliged to cross the lake in a boat to arrive at Plainpalais. During this short voyage I saw the lightnings playing on the summit of Mont Blanc in the most beautiful figures. The storm appeared to approach rapidly; and, on landing, I ascended a low hill, that I might observe its progress. It advanced; the heavens were clouded, and I soon felt the rain coming slowly in large drops, but its violence quickly increased.

I quitted my seat, and walked on, although the darkness and storm increased every minute, and the thunder burst with a terrific crash over my head. It was echoed from Salêve, the Juras, and the Alps of Savoy; vivid flashes of lightning dazzled my eyes, illuminating the lake, making it

---

58. Victor links his feelings of foreboding to the romantic notion of the sublime, combining that era's captivation with the immense beauty of the natural world with a perception of its dangers and a willingness to entertain the possibility of personal annihilation. Just before this passage, Victor speaks with tremendous affection and pride about the impressive mountains surrounding his home, using the salutation "Dear" and the possessive pronoun phrase "my own." However, in his encounter with the sublime, he fails to achieve what philosopher Edmund Burke (1729–1797) called "sublime transcendence," which means to experience a sudden relief from horror. Because Victor views the sublime from a position of great personal risk, he can see in this natural vista only his personal suffering and ultimate destruction. This passage also highlights an essential contradiction in Victor's personality: he is both tremendously confident and self-effacing, both a director of his own fate and a passive object at the mercy of uncontrollable forces. As with his renegade approach to scientific discovery, here he simultaneously lauds his powers of prophesy and admits to their deficiencies. Egoism, a flaw that greatly facilitates Victor's hubris, also surfaces here with the repeated use of the first-person pronoun *I*, used to emphasize both his vulnerability and his power.

April Miller.

appear like a vast sheet of fire; then for an instant every thing seemed of a pitchy darkness, until the eye recovered itself from the preceding flash. The storm, as is often the case in Switzerland, appeared at once in various parts of the heavens. The most violent storm hung exactly north of the town, over that part of the lake which lies between the promontory of Belrive and the village of Copêt. Another storm enlightened Jura with faint flashes; and another darkened and sometimes disclosed the Môle, a peaked mountain to the east of the lake.

While I watched the storm, so beautiful yet terrific, I wandered on with a hasty step. This noble war in the sky elevated my spirits; I clasped my hands, and exclaimed aloud, "William, dear angel! this is thy funeral, this thy dirge!" As I said these words, I perceived in the gloom a figure which stole from behind a clump of trees near me; I stood fixed, gazing intently: I could not be mistaken. A flash of lightning illuminated the object, and discovered its shape plainly to me; its gigantic stature, and the deformity of its aspect, more hideous than belongs to humanity, instantly informed me that it was the wretch, the filthy dæmon to whom I had given life. What did he there? Could he be (I shuddered at the conception) the murderer of my brother? No sooner did that idea cross my imagination, than I became convinced of its truth; my teeth chattered, and I was forced to lean against a tree for support.[59] The figure passed me quickly, and I lost it in the gloom. Nothing in human shape could have destroyed that fair child. *He* was the murderer! I could not doubt it. The mere presence of the idea was an irresistible proof of the fact. I thought of pursuing the devil; but it would have been in vain, for another flash discovered him to me hanging among the rocks of the nearly perpendicular ascent of Mont Salêve, a hill that bounds Plainpalais on the South. He soon reached the summit, and disappeared.

I remained motionless. The thunder ceased; but the rain still continued, and the scene was enveloped in an impenetrable darkness. I revolved in my mind the events which I had until now sought to forget: the whole train

59. In Greek myth, Prometheus fashions the clay into which Athena, goddess of wisdom, breathes life, creating the human race. Over the objections of Zeus, Prometheus then provides humans with fire, an element essential for human life. Similarly, Victor uses electricity, a form of fire, to animate his creation. Flashes of light recur throughout the novel, often leading to perceptions by Victor. He continues to characterize the creature as physically "hideous," which he equates with the demonic. The latter is by nature found amid darkness and filth. Victor labors at times to balance what he sees in dreams and what he sees in actual physical existence. Both, however, are for the romantic age sources of knowledge. But having realized he is not simply observing a phantom in the glimpses he catches of the creature, Victor immediately reacts to the "hideous" being as a demon. His realization results in his bodily response of fear as his teeth chatter. (Contrast this interpretation with Charles E. Robinson's; see pp. xxii-xxxiii.)
Joel Gereboff.

of my progress towards the creation; the appearance of the work of my own hands alive at my bed side; its departure. Two years had now nearly elapsed since the night on which he first received life; and was this his first crime? Alas! I had turned loose into the world a depraved wretch, whose delight was in carnage and misery; had he not murdered my brother?

No one can conceive the anguish I suffered during the remainder of the night, which I spent, cold and wet, in the open air. But I did not feel the inconvenience of the weather; my imagination was busy in scenes of evil and despair. I considered the being whom I had cast among mankind, and endowed with the will and power to effect purposes of horror, such as the deed which he had now done, nearly in the light of my own vampire, my own spirit let loose from the grave, and forced to destroy all that was dear to me.

Day dawned; and I directed my steps toward the town. The gates were open; and I hastened to my father's house. My first thought was to discover what I knew of the murderer, and cause instant pursuit to be made. But I paused when I reflected on the story that I had to tell. A being whom I myself had formed, and endued with life, had met me at midnight among the precipices of an inaccessible mountain. I remembered also the nervous fever with which I had been seized just at the time that I dated my creation, and which would give an air of delirium to a tale otherwise so utterly improbable. I well knew that if any other had communicated such a relation to me, I should have looked upon it as the ravings of insanity. Besides, the strange nature of the animal would elude all pursuit, even if I were so far credited as to persuade my relatives to commence it. Besides, of what use would be pursuit? Who could arrest a creature capable of scaling the overhanging sides of Mont Salêve? These reflections determined me, and I resolved to remain silent.

It was about five in the morning when I entered my father's house. I told the servants not to disturb the family, and went into the library to attend their usual hour of rising.

Six years had elapsed, passed as a dream but for one indelible trace, and I stood in the same place where I had last embraced my father before my departure for Ingolstadt. Beloved and respectable parent! He still remained to me. I gazed on the picture of my mother, which stood over the mantle-piece. It was an historical subject, painted at my father's desire, and represented Caroline Beaufort in an agony of despair, kneeling by the coffin of her dead father. Her garb was rustic, and her cheek pale; but there was an air of dignity and beauty, that hardly permitted the sentiment of pity. Below this picture was a miniature of William; and my tears flowed when I looked upon it. While I was thus engaged, Ernest entered: he had heard me arrive, and hastened to welcome me. He expressed a sorrowful delight to see me: "Welcome, my dearest Victor," said he. "Ah! I wish you had come three months ago, and then you would have found us all joyous and delighted. But we are now unhappy; and, I am afraid, tears instead of smiles will be your welcome. Our father looks so sorrowful: this dreadful event seems to have revived in his mind his grief on the death of Mamma. Poor Elizabeth also is quite inconsolable." Ernest began to weep as he said these words.

"Do not," said I, "welcome me thus; try to be more calm, that I may not be absolutely miserable the moment I enter my father's house after so long an absence. But, tell me, how does my father support his misfortunes? and how is my poor Elizabeth?"

"She indeed requires consolation; she accused herself of having caused the death of my brother, and that made her very wretched. But since the murderer has been discovered——"

"The murderer discovered! Good God! how can that be? who could attempt to pursue him? It is impossible; one might as well try to overtake the winds, or confine a mountain-stream with a straw."

"I do not know what you mean; but we were all very unhappy when she was discovered. No one would believe it at first; and even now Elizabeth will not be convinced; notwithstanding all the evidence. Indeed, who would credit that Justine Moritz, who was so amiable, and fond of all the family, could all at once become so extremely wicked?"

"Justine Moritz! Poor, poor girl, is she the accused? But it is wrongfully; every one knows that; no one believes it, surely, Ernest?"

"No one did at first; but several circumstances came out, that have almost forced conviction upon us: and her own behaviour has been so confused, as to add to the evidence of facts a weight that, I fear, leaves no hope for doubt. But she will be tried to-day, and you will then hear all."

He related that, the morning on which the murder of poor William had been discovered, Justine had been taken ill, and confined to her bed; and, after several days, one of the servants, happening to examine the apparel she had worn on the night of the murder, had discovered in her pocket the picture of my mother, which had been judged to be the temptation of the murderer. The servant instantly shewed it to one of the others, who, without saying a word to any of the family, went to a magistrate; and, upon their deposition, Justine was apprehended. On being charged with the fact, the poor girl confirmed the suspicion in a great measure by her extreme confusion of manner.

This was a strange tale, but it did not shake my faith; and I replied earnestly, "You are all mistaken; I know the murderer. Justine, poor, good Justine, is innocent."

At that instant my father entered. I saw unhappiness deeply impressed on his countenance, but he endeavoured to welcome me cheerfully; and, after we had exchanged our mournful greeting, would have introduced some other topic than that of our disaster, had not Ernest exclaimed, "Good God, Papa! Victor says that he knows who was the murderer of poor William."

"We do also, unfortunately," replied my father; "for indeed I had rather have been for ever ignorant than have discovered so much depravity and ingratitude in one I valued so highly."

"My dear father, you are mistaken; Justine is innocent."

"If she is, God forbid that she should suffer as guilty. She is to be tried to-day, and I hope, I sincerely hope, that she will be acquitted."

This speech calmed me. I was firmly convinced in my own mind that Justine, and indeed every human being, was guiltless of this murder. I had no fear, therefore, that any circumstantial evidence could be brought forward strong enough to convict her; and, in this assurance, I calmed myself, expecting the trial with eagerness, but without prognosticating an evil result.

We were soon joined by Elizabeth. Time had made great alterations in her form since I had last beheld her. Six years before she had been a pretty, good-humoured girl, whom every one loved and caressed. She was now a woman in stature and expression of countenance, which was uncommonly lovely. An open and capacious forehead gave indications of a good under-standing, joined to great frankness of disposition. Her eyes were hazel, and expressive of mildness, now through recent affliction allied to sadness. Her hair was of a rich dark auburn, her complexion fair, and her figure slight and graceful. She welcomed me with the greatest affection. "Your arrival, my dear cousin," said she, "fills me with hope. You perhaps will find some means to justify my poor guiltless Justine. Alas! who is safe, if she be con-victed of crime? I rely on her innocence as certainly as I do upon my own. Our misfortune is doubly hard to us; we have not only lost that lovely dar-ling boy, but this poor girl, whom I sincerely love, is to be torn away by even a worse fate. If she is condemned, I never shall know joy more. But she will not, I am sure she will not; and then I shall be happy again, even after the sad death of my little William."

"She is innocent, my Elizabeth," said I, "and that shall be proved; fear nothing, but let your spirits be cheered by the assurance of her acquittal."

"How kind you are! every one else believes in her guilt, and that made me wretched; for I knew that it was impossible: and to see every one else prejudiced in so deadly a manner, rendered me hopeless and despairing." She wept.

"Sweet niece," said my father, "dry your tears. If she is, as you believe, innocent, rely on the justice of our judges, and the activity with which I shall prevent the slightest shadow of partiality."

CHAPTER VII.

We passed a few sad hours, until eleven o'clock, when the trial was to commence. My father and the rest of the family being obliged to attend as witnesses, I accompanied them to the court. During the whole of this wretched mockery of justice, I suffered living torture. It was to be decided, whether the result of my curiosity and lawless devices would cause the death of two of my fellow-beings: one a smiling babe, full of innocence and joy; the other far more dreadfully murdered, with every aggravation of infamy that could make the murder memorable in horror. Justine also was a girl of merit, and possessed qualities which promised to render her life happy: now all was to be obliterated in an ignominious grave; and I the cause! A thousand times rather would I have confessed myself guilty of the crime ascribed to Justine; but I was absent when it was committed, and such a declaration would have been considered as the ravings of a madman, and would not have exculpated her who suffered through me.

The appearance of Justine was calm. She was dressed in mourning; and her countenance, always engaging, was rendered, by the solemnity of her feelings, exquisitely beautiful. Yet she appeared confident in innocence, and did not tremble, although gazed on and execrated by thousands; for all the kindness which her beauty might otherwise have excited, was obliterated in the minds of the spectators by the imagination of the enormity she was supposed to have committed. She was tranquil, yet her tranquillity was evidently constrained; and as her confusion had before been adduced as a proof of her guilt, she worked up her mind to an appearance of courage. When she entered the court, she threw her eyes round it, and quickly discovered where we were seated. A tear seemed to dim her eye when she saw us; but she quickly recovered herself, and a look of sorrowful affection seemed to attest her utter guiltlessness.

The trial began; and after the advocate against her had stated the charge, several witnesses were called. Several strange facts combined against her, which might have staggered any one who had not such proof of her innocence as I had. She had been out the whole of the night on which the murder had been committed, and towards morning had been perceived by a market-woman not far from the spot where the body of the murdered child had been afterwards found. The woman asked her what she did there; but she looked very strangely, and only returned a confused and unintelligible answer. She returned to the house about eight o'clock; and when one inquired where she had passed the night, she replied, that she had been looking for the child, and demanded earnestly, if any thing had been heard concerning him. When shewn the body, she fell into violent hysterics, and kept her bed for several days. The picture was then produced, which the servant had found in her pocket; and when Elizabeth, in a faltering voice, proved that it was the same which, an hour before the child had been missed, she had placed round his neck, a murmur of horror and indignation filled the court.

Justine was called on for her defence. As the trial had proceeded, her countenance had altered. Surprise, horror, and misery, were strongly expressed. Sometimes she struggled with her tears; but when she was desired to plead, she collected her powers, and spoke in an audible although variable voice:—

"God knows," she said, "how entirely I am innocent. But I do not pretend that my protestations should acquit me: I rest my innocence on a plain and simple explanation of the facts which have been adduced against me; and I hope the character I have always borne will incline my judges to a favourable interpretation, where any circumstance appears doubtful or suspicious."

She then related that, by the permission of Elizabeth, she had passed the evening of the night on which the murder had been committed, at the house of an aunt at Chêne, a village situated at about a league from Geneva. On her return, at about nine o'clock, she met a man, who asked her if she had seen any thing of the child who was lost. She was alarmed by this account, and passed several hours in looking for him, when the gates of Geneva were shut, and she was forced to remain several hours of the night in a barn belonging to a cottage, being unwilling to call up the inhabitants, to whom she was well known. Unable to rest or sleep, she quitted her asylum early, that she might again endeavour to find my brother. If she had gone near the spot where his body lay, it was without her knowledge. That she had been bewildered when questioned by the market-woman, was not surprising, since she had passed a sleepless night, and the fate of poor William was yet uncertain. Concerning the picture she could give no account.

"I know," continued the unhappy victim, "how heavily and fatally this one circumstance weighs against me, but I have no power of explaining it; and when I have expressed my utter ignorance, I am only left to conjecture concerning the probabilities by which it might have been placed in my pocket. But here also I am checked. I believe that I have no enemy on earth, and none surely would have been so wicked as to destroy me wantonly. Did the murderer place it there? I know of no opportunity afforded him for so doing; or if I had, why should he have stolen the jewel, to part with it again so soon?

"I commit my cause to the justice of my judges, yet I see no room for hope. I beg permission to have a few witnesses examined concerning my character; and if their testimony shall not overweigh my supposed guilt, I must be condemned, although I would pledge my salvation on my innocence."

Several witnesses were called, who had known her for many years, and they spoke well of her; but fear, and hatred of the crime of which they supposed her guilty, rendered them timorous, and unwilling to come forward. Elizabeth saw even this last resource, her excellent dispositions and irreproachable conduct, about to fail the accused, when, although violently agitated, she desired permission to address the court.

"I am," said she, "the cousin of the unhappy child who was murdered, or rather his sister, for I was educated by and have lived with his parents ever since and even long before his birth. It may therefore be judged indecent in me to come forward on this occasion; but when I see a fellow-creature about to perish through the cowardice of her pretended friends, I wish to be allowed to speak, that I may say what I know of her character. I am well acquainted with the accused. I have lived in the same house with her, at one time for five, and at another for nearly two years. During all that period she appeared to me the most amiable and benevolent of human creatures. She nursed Madame Frankenstein, my aunt, in her last illness with the greatest affection and care; and afterwards attended her own mother during a tedious illness, in a manner that excited the admiration of all who knew her. After which she again lived in my uncle's house, where she was beloved by all the family. She was warmly attached to the child who is now dead, and acted towards him like a most affectionate mother. For my own part, I do not hesitate to say, that, notwithstanding all the evidence produced against her, I believe and rely on her perfect innocence. She had no temptation for such an action: as to the bauble on which the chief proof rests, if she had earnestly desired it, I should have willingly given it to her; so much do I esteem and value her."

Excellent Elizabeth! A murmur of approbation was heard; but it was excited by her generous interference, and not in favour of poor Justine, on whom the public indignation was turned with renewed violence, charging her with the blackest ingratitude. She herself wept as Elizabeth spoke, but she did not answer. My own agitation and anguish was extreme during the whole trial. I believed in her innocence; I knew it. Could the dæmon, who had (I did not for a minute doubt) murdered my brother, also in his hellish sport have betrayed the innocent to death and ignominy. I could not sustain the horror of my situation; and when I perceived that the popular voice, and the countenances of the judges, had already condemned my unhappy victim, I rushed out of the court in agony. The tortures of the accused did not equal mine; she was sustained by innocence, but the fangs of remorse tore my bosom, and would not forego their hold.[60]

I passed a night of unmingled wretchedness. In the morning I went to the court; my lips and throat were parched. I dared not ask the fatal question; but I was known, and the officer guessed the cause of my visit. The ballots had been thrown; they were all black, and Justine was condemned.

I cannot pretend to describe what I then felt. I had before experienced sensations of horror; and I have endeavoured to bestow upon them adequate expressions, but words cannot convey an idea of the heart-sickening despair that I then endured. The person to whom I addressed myself added, that Justine had already confessed her guilt. "That evidence," he observed, "was hardly required in so glaring a case, but I am glad of it; and, indeed, none of our judges like to condemn a criminal upon circumstantial evidence, be it ever so decisive."

When I returned home, Elizabeth eagerly demanded the result.

"My cousin," replied I, "it is decided as you may have expected; all judges had rather that ten innocent should suffer, than that one guilty should escape. But she has confessed."

This was a dire blow to poor Elizabeth, who had relied with firmness upon Justine's innocence. "Alas!" said she, "how shall I ever again believe in human benevolence? Justine, whom I loved and esteemed as my sister,

60. The encounter between Justine and Elizabeth is filled with passion. Justine comes to accept her execution, even if unjust, because she sees it as necessary for her ultimate salvation, and Elizabeth, convinced now of Justine's innocence, is relieved because her trust in Justine has not been betrayed. Such feelings trump concerns for justice. By contrast, Victor's anguish at the injustice and his realization that it is his creation that committed the murder fill him with remorse, an intense correlate of guilt. In current moral thinking, feeling and expressing remorse are essential for seeking forgiveness. But Victor can only hold these feelings within himself because he cannot disclose the truth about his efforts and their impact.

Joel Gereboff.

how could she put on those smiles of innocence only to betray; her mild eyes seemed incapable of any severity or ill-humour, and yet she has committed a murder."

Soon after we heard that the poor victim had expressed a wish to see my cousin. My father wished her not to go; but said, that he left it to her own judgment and feelings to decide. "Yes," said Elizabeth, "I will go, although she is guilty; and you, Victor, shall accompany me: I cannot go alone." The idea of this visit was torture to me, yet I could not refuse.

We entered the gloomy prison-chamber, and beheld Justine sitting on some straw at the further end; her hands were manacled, and her head rested on her knees. She rose on seeing us enter; and when we were left alone with her, she threw herself at the feet of Elizabeth, weeping bitterly. My cousin wept also.

"Oh, Justine!" said she, "why did you rob me of my last consolation. I relied on your innocence; and although I was then very wretched, I was not so miserable as I am now."

"And do you also believe that I am so very, very wicked? Do you also join with my enemies to crush me?" Her voice was suffocated with sobs.

"Rise, my poor girl," said Elizabeth, "why do you kneel, if you are innocent? I am not one of your enemies; I believed you guiltless, notwithstanding every evidence, until I heard that you had yourself declared your guilt. That report, you say, is false; and be assured, dear Justine, that nothing can shake my confidence in you for a moment, but your own confession."

"I did confess; but I confessed a lie. I confessed, that I might obtain absolution; but now that falsehood lies heavier at my heart than all my other sins. The God of heaven forgive me! Ever since I was condemned, my confessor has besieged me; he threatened and menaced, until I almost began to think that I was the monster that he said I was. He threatened excommunication and hell fire in my last moments, if I continued obdurate. Dear lady, I had none to support me; all looked on me as a wretch doomed to ignominy and perdition. What could I do? In an evil hour I subscribed to a lie; and now only am I truly miserable."

She paused, weeping, and then continued—"I thought with horror, my sweet lady, that you should believe your Justine, whom your blessed aunt had so highly honoured, and whom you loved, was a creature capable of a crime which none but the devil himself could have perpetrated. Dear William! dearest blessed child! I soon shall see you again in heaven, where we shall all be happy; and that consoles me, going as I am to suffer ignominy and death."

"Oh, Justine! forgive me for having for one moment distrusted you. Why did you confess? But do not mourn, my dear girl; I will every where proclaim your innocence, and force belief. Yet you must die; you, my playfellow, my companion, my more than sister. I never can survive so horrible a misfortune."

"Dear, sweet Elizabeth, do not weep. You ought to raise me with thoughts of a better life, and elevate me from the petty cares of this world of injustice and strife. Do not you, excellent friend, drive me to despair."

"I will try to comfort you; but this, I fear, is an evil too deep and poignant to admit of consolation, for there is no hope. Yet heaven bless thee, my dearest Justine, with resignation, and a confidence elevated beyond this world. Oh! how I hate its shews and mockeries! when one creature is murdered, another is immediately deprived of life in a slow torturing manner; then the executioners, their hands yet reeking with the blood of innocence, believe that they have done a great deed. They call this *retribution*. Hateful name![61] When that word is pronounced, I know greater and more horrid punishments are going to be inflicted than the gloomiest tyrant has ever invented to satiate his utmost revenge. Yet this is not consolation for you, my Justine, unless indeed that you may glory in escaping from so miserable a den. Alas! I would I were in peace with my aunt and my lovely William, escaped from a world which is hateful to me, and the visages of men which I abhor."

---

61. This passage reflects the type of justice known as retributive, which relies on punishment to balance the wrong done to the victim and his or her family and to act as a deterrent to others from future acts of wrong-doing. In this worldview, justice is served when someone pays for the suffering caused to another. Mary is warning the reader that a rush to judgment, especially if revenge is the driving motive, might hurt innocent people, creating a new form of injustice. This is what happens when the innocent Justine is wrongly executed for the death of William. Science and technology are also implicated in the apparatus of crime and punishment in a number of ways, including the creation of various tools of execution, such as the guillotine—which was a terrible new invention at the time of the French Revolution—the electric chair, lethal injections, and so on. In modern capital punishment in the United States, medical personnel are present to verify the prisoner's death, and psychiatrists play a role in determining whether someone is mentally healthy enough to stand trial or if there are mitigating circumstances due to mental defect. Fingerprinting, handwriting analysis, DNA testing, and other forensic sciences have had disputatious histories, both in terms of how they have been received as evidence in the courtroom and how they have called on courts to understand scientific evidence. Scientific studies have also cast light on the fallibility of eyewitness testimony, and many convictions have been overturned by exculpatory DNA evidence. The power of forensic evidence is such in the public imagination, however, that a "*CSI* effect"—named after the popular television show about crime scene investigators using high-tech forensic analysis—has been identified in jurors who want to see scientific evidence of guilt even if those scientific standards are derived from fiction.

Mary Margaret Fonow.

Justine smiled languidly. "This, dear lady, is despair, and not resignation. I must not learn the lesson that you would teach me. Talk of something else, something that will bring peace, and not increase of misery."

During this conversation I had retired to a corner of the prison-room, where I could conceal the horrid anguish that possessed me. Despair! Who dared talk of that? The poor victim, who on the morrow was to pass the dreary boundary between life and death, felt not as I did, such deep and bitter agony. I gnashed my teeth, and ground them together, uttering a groan that came from my inmost soul. Justine started. When she saw who it was, she approached me, and said, "Dear Sir, you are very kind to visit me; you, I hope, do not believe that I am guilty."

I could not answer. "No, Justine," said Elizabeth; "he is more convinced of your innocence than I was; for even when he heard that you had confessed, he did not credit it."

"I truly thank him. In these last moments I feel the sincerest gratitude towards those who think of me with kindness. How sweet is the affection of others to such a wretch as I am! It removes more than half my misfortune; and I feel as if I could die in peace, now that my innocence is acknowledged by you, dear lady, and your cousin."

Thus the poor sufferer tried to comfort others and herself. She indeed gained the resignation she desired. But I, the true murderer, felt the never-dying worm alive in my bosom, which allowed of no hope or consolation. Elizabeth also wept, and was unhappy; but her's also was the misery of innocence, which, like a cloud that passes over the fair moon, for a while hides, but cannot tarnish its brightness. Anguish and despair had penetrated into the core of my heart; I bore a hell within me, which nothing could extinguish. We staid several hours with Justine; and it was with great difficulty that Elizabeth could tear herself away. "I wish," cried she, "that I were to die with you; I cannot live in this world of misery."

Justine assumed an air of cheerfulness, while she with difficulty repressed her bitter tears. She embraced Elizabeth, and said, in a voice of half-suppressed emotion, "Farewell, sweet lady, dearest Elizabeth, my beloved and only friend; may heaven in its bounty bless and preserve you; may this be the last misfortune that you will ever suffer. Live, and be happy, and make others so."

As we returned, Elizabeth said, "You know not, my dear Victor, how much I am relieved, now that I trust in the innocence of this unfortunate girl. I never could again have known peace, if I had been deceived in my reliance on her. For the moment that I did believe her guilty, I felt an anguish that I could not have long sustained. Now my heart is lightened.

The innocent suffers; but she whom I thought amiable and good has not betrayed the trust I reposed in her, and I am consoled."

Amiable cousin! such were your thoughts, mild and gentle as your own dear eyes and voice. But I—I was a wretch, and none ever conceived of the misery that I then endured.

END OF VOL. I.

VOL. II

CHAPTER I.

Nothing is more painful to the human mind, than, after the feelings have been worked up by a quick succession of events, the dead calmness of inaction and certainty which follows, and deprives the soul both of hope and fear. Justine died; she rested; and I was alive. The blood flowed freely in my veins, but a weight of despair and remorse pressed on my heart, which nothing could remove. Sleep fled from my eyes; I wandered like an evil spirit, for I had committed deeds of mischief beyond description horrible, and more, much more, (I persuaded myself) was yet behind.[1] Yet my heart overflowed with kindness, and the love of virtue. I had begun life with benevolent intentions, and thirsted for the moment when I should put them in practice, and make myself useful to my fellow-beings. Now all was blasted: instead of that serenity of conscience, which allowed me to look back upon the past with self-satisfaction, and from thence to gather promise of new hopes, I was seized by remorse and the sense of guilt, which hurried me away to a hell of intense tortures, such as no language can describe.[2]

This state of mind preyed upon my health, which had entirely recovered from the first shock it had sustained. I shunned the face of man; all sound of joy or complacency was torture to me; solitude was my only consolation—deep, dark, death-like solitude.

1. The concept of guilt may well be a bit more complicated than it first appears. The two most common understandings of guilt are at work in the text, prompting us to think about the idea of guilt in relation to both Victor and the creature. First, guilt describes the person who is responsible for an act that is unethical or illegal or both. Second, guilt describes the feelings that arise after an act—feelings that can be said to haunt a person and potentially shape his or her future actions.

The second understanding of guilt is clarified by psychoanalytic thought, which theorizes that guilt can be at work even when a person does not consciously attribute his or her actions to its effects. For more on this understanding, see Sigmund Freud, *Civilization and Its Discontents* [1930] 1961. Freud's arguments about the inextricable link between guilt and civilization make for a fascinating parallel to *Frankenstein*.

In the first understanding, guilt is also attributed to a person for failing to do what he or she believes is required in a situation. For example, Victor could be seen as guilty for his failure to make the creature's existence public, especially at the trial of Justine. As Shakespeare has Claudius say in *Hamlet*, "[M]y stronger guilt defeats my strong intent" (III.iii.44).

Later in the novel, Victor makes a universal claim about the consequences of guilt: "Ah! it is well for the unfortunate to be resigned, but for the guilty there is no peace" (p. 158).
Ramsey Eric Ramsey.

2. The interior anguish Victor experiences is given heightened expression here. Language has limitations, and Victor finds he cannot disclose his interior conflicts. He has a tortured conscience. Intense sensations of remorse and guilt disrupt his efforts to achieve and maintain a serene conscience, a sense of being right. No words can express the hell and torture he is feeling.
Joel Gereboff.

My father observed with pain the alteration perceptible in my disposition and habits, and endeavoured to reason with me on the folly of giving way to immoderate grief. "Do you think, Victor," said he, "that I do not suffer also? No one could love a child more than I loved your brother"; (tears came into his eyes as he spoke); "but is it not a duty to the survivors, that we should refrain from augmenting their unhappiness by an appearance of immoderate grief? It is also a duty owed to yourself; for excessive sorrow prevents improvement or enjoyment, or even the discharge of daily usefulness, without which no man is fit for society."

This advice, although good, was totally inapplicable to my case; I should have been the first to hide my grief, and console my friends, if remorse had not mingled its bitterness with my other sensations. Now I could only answer my father with a look of despair, and endeavour to hide myself from his view.

About this time we retired to our house at Belrive. This change was particularly agreeable to me. The shutting of the gates regularly at ten o'clock, and the impossibility of remaining on the lake after that hour, had rendered our residence within the walls of Geneva very irksome to me. I was now free. Often, after the rest of the family had retired for the night, I took the boat, and passed many hours upon the water. Sometimes, with my sails set, I was carried by the wind; and sometimes, after rowing into the middle of the lake, I left the boat to pursue its own course, and gave way to my own miserable reflections. I was often tempted, when all was at peace around me, and I the only unquiet thing that wandered restless in a scene so beautiful and heavenly, if I except some bat, or the frogs, whose harsh and interrupted croaking was heard only when I approached the shore—often, I say, I was tempted to plunge into the silent lake, that the waters might close over me and my calamities for ever. But I was restrained, when I thought of the heroic and suffering Elizabeth, whom I tenderly loved, and whose existence was bound up in mine. I thought also of my father, and surviving brother: should I by my base desertion leave them exposed and unprotected to the malice of the fiend whom I had let loose among them?[3]

3. Victor again feels guilt about not disclosing the existence of the destructive creature that he has created. Yet he continues to fail to recognize and concede that his treatment and desertion of the creature, not the initial creation, have brought about the destruction. In this instance, Victor does sense the potential impact of his desertion on his family and others but remains blind to his earlier desertion of his own creation.

Joel Gereboff.

At these moments I wept bitterly, and wished that peace would revisit my mind only that I might afford them consolation and happiness. But that could not be. Remorse extinguished every hope. I had been the author of unalterable evils; and I lived in daily fear, lest the monster whom I had created should perpetrate some new wickedness.[4] I had an obscure feeling that all was not over, and that he would still commit some signal crime, which by its enormity should almost efface the recollection of the past. There was always scope for fear, so long as any thing I loved remained behind. My abhorrence of this fiend cannot be conceived. When I thought of him, I gnashed my teeth, my eyes became inflamed, and I ardently wished to extinguish that life which I had so thoughtlessly bestowed. When I reflected on his crimes and malice, my hatred and revenge burst all bounds of moderation. I would have made a pilgrimage to the highest peak of the Andes, could I, when there, have precipitated him to their base. I wished to see him again, that I might wreak the utmost extent of anger on his head, and avenge the deaths of William and Justine.

Our house was the house of mourning. My father's health was deeply shaken by the horror of the recent events. Elizabeth was sad and desponding; she no longer took delight in her ordinary occupations; all pleasure seemed to her sacrilege towards the dead; eternal woe and tears she then thought was the just tribute she should pay to innocence so blasted and destroyed.

---

4. The remorse Victor expresses is reminiscent of J. Robert Oppenheimer's sentiments when he witnessed the unspeakable power of the atomic bomb. A passage from the Hindu scripture of the Bhagavad-Gita flashed before Oppenheimer's mind: "I am become death, the destroyer of worlds." In this short phrase, Oppenheimer, as one of the architects of the A-bomb, acknowledged that he had unleashed a force that could lead to the annihilation of civilization. He also proclaimed, "The physicists have known sin, and this is a knowledge they cannot lose" (qtd. in Bird and Sherwin 2005, 388).

Victor's responsibility for his horrific scientific experiment has already passed. It appears that the creature is beyond control. All that is left is remorse. Oppenheimer, who witnessed a test of the atomic bomb at Los Alamos in 1945, still had an opportunity to prevent the use of the bomb against humans. Also see Heather E. Douglas's essay "The Bitter Aftertaste of Technical Sweetness" in this volume.

Scientists' responsibility must be engaged before their creations are unleashed; otherwise, the consequences cannot be retracted. Those scientists with high moral conscience view their responsibility to warn about the malevolent uses of scientific results to their students, to their colleagues, and to the public. They would cease and desist from scientific research that has no redeeming value but destruction or baneful dehumanization. Victor's anguish is a warning to those scientists who bracket away the moral quality of their work under a banner of pure inquiry, whatever its outcome. Whether it is cloning a human being, creating a new biological weapon, releasing transgenic species, or designing human genomes, these ends call out for acts and acknowledgments of social responsibility.

Sheldon Krimsky.

She was no longer that happy creature, who in earlier youth wandered with me on the banks of the lake, and talked with ecstacy of our future prospects. She had become grave, and often conversed of the inconstancy of fortune, and the instability of human life.[5]

"When I reflect, my dear cousin," said she, "on the miserable death of Justine Moritz, I no longer see the world and its works as they before appeared to me. Before, I looked upon the accounts of vice and injustice, that I read in books or heard from others, as tales of ancient days, or imaginary evils; at least they were remote, and more familiar to reason than to the imagination; but now misery has come home, and men appear to me as monsters thirsting for each other's blood. Yet I am certainly unjust. Every body believed that poor girl to be guilty; and if she could have committed the crime for which she suffered, assuredly she would have been the most depraved of human creatures. For the sake of a few jewels, to have murdered the son of her benefactor and friend, a child whom she had nursed from its birth, and appeared to love as if it had been her own! I could not consent to the death of any human being; but certainly I should have thought such a creature unfit to remain in the society of men. Yet she was innocent.[6] I know, I feel she was innocent; you are of the same opinion, and that confirms me. Alas! Victor, when falsehood can look so like the truth, who can assure themselves of certain happiness?[7] I feel as if I were

5. After the death of Justine Moritz, Elizabeth is confronted with the unpredictability and temporality of life—that is, the awareness that life is forever changing and moving forward even when its trajectory is one we would never choose for ourselves. In contrast to Victor, who at least initially was preoccupied with notions of fate and destiny, Elizabeth cannot help but see the world as unjust and capricious (see note 11 on existentialism, p. 80 in this volume).
Nicole Piemonte.

6. The nature of truth has been debated by philosophers throughout human history. Difficult decisions about truth or deceit are often made by finding a set of facts to support a preexisting belief. In the legal system, the accused can be convicted based on circumstantial evidence that later turns out to be either patently false or unreliable or full of gaping holes (the Innocence Project is a nonprofit organization that focuses on overturning convictions in such cases). Justine's fate is decided by just that type of evidence. In scientific endeavors, determining what is true from research results likewise requires ensuring that any analysis is independent of personal biases.
Mary Drago.

7. Mary presupposes a direct relationship between knowing the truth and experiencing happiness, though many other works of science fiction suggest otherwise. The Matrix (Lana Wachowski and Lilly Wachowski, 1999) presented a generation of movie-goers with a choice between uncomfortable truths and blissful ignorance: "You take the blue pill, the story ends. You wake up in your bed and believe whatever you want to believe. You take the red pill, you stay in Wonderland, and I show you how deep the rabbit hole goes." One reading of Victor's behavior is his desperate attempt to cling to something like happiness in the face of an increasingly dangerous truth.
Ed Finn.

walking on the edge of a precipice, towards which thousands are crowding, and endeavouring to plunge me into the abyss. William and Justine were assassinated, and the murderer escapes; he walks about the world free, and perhaps respected. But even if I were condemned to suffer on the scaffold for the same crimes, I would not change places with such a wretch."[8]

I listened to this discourse with the extremest agony. I, not in deed, but in effect, was the true murderer. Elizabeth read my anguish in my countenance, and kindly taking my hand said, "My dearest cousin, you must calm yourself. These events have affected me, God knows how deeply; but I am not so wretched as you are. There is an expression of despair, and sometimes of revenge, in your countenance, that makes me tremble. Be calm, my dear Victor; I would sacrifice my life to your peace. We surely shall be happy: quiet in our native country, and not mingling in the world, what can disturb our tranquillity?"

She shed tears as she said this, distrusting the very solace that she gave; but at the same time she smiled, that she might chase away the fiend that lurked in my heart. My father, who saw in the unhappiness that was painted in my face only an exaggeration of that sorrow which I might naturally feel, thought that an amusement suited to my taste would be the best means of restoring to me my wonted serenity. It was from this cause that he had removed to the country; and, induced by the same motive, he now proposed that we should all make an excursion to the valley of Chamounix. I had been there before, but Elizabeth and Ernest never had; and both had often expressed an earnest desire to see the scenery of this place, which had been described to them as so wonderful and sublime. Accordingly we departed from Geneva on this tour about the middle of the month of August, nearly two months after the death of Justine.

The weather was uncommonly fine; and if mine had been a sorrow to be chased away by any fleeting circumstance, this excursion would certainly have had the effect intended by my father. As it was, I was somewhat interested in the scene; it sometimes lulled, although it could not extinguish my grief. During the first day we travelled in a carriage. In the morning we had seen the mountains at a distance, towards which we gradually advanced. We perceived that the valley through which we wound, and which was formed

---

8. This ironic passage speaks of the reality that what appears to be true or what people take to be true is often false. Elizabeth recognizes and expresses to Victor Justine's innocence and the injustice that has been done. But it is in fact Victor's inability to profess the truth about the creature, the murderer, that is the greatest lie. Society can maintain its emotional and moral equilibrium so long as someone has "paid for a crime," even when that person is innocent.
Joel Gereboff.

by the river Arve, whose course we followed, closed in upon us by degrees; and when the sun had set, we beheld immense mountains and precipices overhanging us on every side, and heard the sound of the river raging among rocks, and the dashing of waterfalls around.

The next day we pursued our journey upon mules; and as we ascended still higher, the valley assumed a more magnificent and astonishing character. Ruined castles hanging on the precipices of piny mountains; the impetuous Arve, and cottages every here and there peeping forth from among the trees, formed a scene of singular beauty. But it was augmented and rendered sublime by the mighty Alps, whose white and shining pyramids and domes towered above all, as belonging to another earth, the habitations of another race of beings.

We passed the bridge of Pelissier, where the ravine, which the river forms, opened before us, and we began to ascend the mountain that overhangs it. Soon after we entered the valley of Chamounix. This valley is more wonderful and sublime, but not so beautiful and picturesque as that of Servox, through which we had just passed. The high and snowy mountains were its immediate boundaries; but we saw no more ruined castles and fertile fields. Immense glaciers approached the road; we heard the rumbling thunder of the falling avalanche, and marked the smoke of its passage. Mont Blanc, the supreme and magnificent Mont Blanc, raised itself from the surrounding *aiguilles*, and its tremendous *dome* overlooked the valley.

During this journey, I sometimes joined Elizabeth, and exerted myself to point out to her the various beauties of the scene. I often suffered my mule to lag behind, and indulged in the misery of reflection. At other times I spurred on the animal before my companions, that I might forget them, the world, and, more than all, myself. When at a distance, I alighted, and threw myself on the grass, weighed down by horror and despair. At eight in the evening I arrived at Chamounix. My father and Elizabeth were very much fatigued; Ernest, who accompanied us, was delighted, and in high spirits: the only circumstance that detracted from his pleasure was the south wind, and the rain it seemed to promise for the next day.

We retired early to our apartments, but not to sleep; at least I did not. I remained many hours at the window, watching the pallid lightning that played above Mont Blanc, and listening to the rushing of the Arve, which ran below my window.

CHAPTER II.

The next day, contrary to the prognostications of our guides, was fine, although clouded. We visited the source of the Arveiron, and rode about the valley until evening. These sublime and magnificent scenes afforded me the greatest consolation that I was capable of receiving. They elevated me from all littleness of feeling; and although they did not remove my grief, they subdued and tranquillized it.[9] In some degree, also, they diverted my mind from the thoughts over which it had brooded for the last month. I returned in the evening, fatigued, but less unhappy, and conversed with my family with more cheerfulness than had been my custom for some time. My father was pleased, and Elizabeth overjoyed. "My dear cousin," said she, "you see what happiness you diffuse when you are happy; do not relapse again!"

The following morning the rain poured down in torrents, and thick mists hid the summits of the mountains. I rose early, but felt unusually melancholy. The rain depressed me; my old feelings recurred, and I was miserable. I knew how disappointed my father would be at this sudden change, and I wished to avoid him until I had recovered myself so far as to be enabled to conceal those feelings that overpowered me. I knew that they would remain that day at the inn; and as I had ever inured myself to rain, moisture, and cold, I resolved to go alone to the summit of Montanvert. I remembered the effect that the view of the tremendous and ever-moving glacier had produced upon my mind when I first saw it. It had then filled me with a sublime ecstacy that gave wings to the soul, and allowed it to soar from the obscure world to light and joy. The sight of the awful and majestic in nature had indeed always the effect of solemnizing my mind, and causing me to forget the passing cares of life. I determined to go alone,

9. The idea that exposure to nature (or "scenery") produces unique psychological and spiritual benefits was a common sentiment in romantic literary and artistic circles in the nineteenth century. Ralph Waldo Emerson (1803–1882) and Henry David Thoreau (1817–1862), both part of the tradition of American romanticism known as transcendentalism, celebrated in their writings the value of a life lived close to nature, especially its salutary effect on the poetic and moral imagination. This romantic notion of nature as "balm" would also influence the rise of the urban parks movement, most notably via the work of landscape architect Frederick Law Olmsted (1822–1903) in the mid–nineteenth century. Olmsted's plan for Manhattan's Central Park, for example, was premised on the idea that contemplation of natural scenery had a therapeutic effect on city dwellers. (This view endures today in the concept of "biophilia," the idea that humans are genetically predisposed to love nature and need regular contact with it to thrive.) The romantic understanding of the value of natural scenery was bound up with a pair of distinct aesthetic categories: the "sublime," which referred to feelings of awe and even fear in the face of nature's power and wildness, and the "picturesque," which described the contemplative reaction to a more orderly and human-scaled natural landscape (e.g., the garden motif shaping Olmsted's Central Park design). The notion of the sublime would play a major role in American wilderness appreciation (and eventually protection) throughout the nineteenth and twentieth centuries, animating the work of a diverse community of artists, writers, and advocates, including Albert Bierstadt (1830–1902), John Muir (1838–1914), Ansel Adams (1902–1984), and David Brower (1912–2000).

Ben Minteer.

for I was well acquainted with the path, and the presence of another would destroy the solitary grandeur of the scene.

The ascent is precipitous, but the path is cut into continual and short windings, which enable you to surmount the perpendicularity of the mountain. It is a scene terrifically desolate. In a thousand spots the traces of the winter avalanche may be perceived, where trees lie broken and strewed on the ground; some entirely destroyed, others bent, leaning upon the jutting rocks of the mountain, or transversely upon other trees. The path, as you ascend higher, is intersected by ravines of snow, down which stones continually roll from above; one of them is particularly dangerous, as the slightest sound, such as even speaking in a loud voice, produces a concussion of air sufficient to draw destruction upon the head of the speaker. The pines are not tall or luxuriant, but they are sombre, and add an air of severity to the scene. I looked on the valley beneath; vast mists were rising from the rivers which ran through it, and curling in thick wreaths around the opposite mountains, whose summits were hid in the uniform clouds while rain poured from the dark sky, and added to the melancholy impression I received from the objects around me. Alas! why does man boast of sensibilities superior to those apparent in the brute; it only renders them more necessary beings. If our impulses were confined to hunger, thirst, and desire, we might be nearly free; but now we are moved by every wind that blows, and a chance word or scene that that wind may convey to us.

We rest; a dream has power to poison sleep.
    We rise; one wand'ring thought pollutes the day.
We feel, conceive, or reason; laugh, or weep,
    Embrace fond woe, or cast our cares away;
It is the same: for, be it joy or sorrow,
    The path of its departure still is free.
Man's yesterday may ne'er be like his morrow;
    Nought may endure but mutability![10]

10. Elizabeth attempts to console Victor with the thought of returning to live together in Geneva, unchanging and undisturbed in their peace and bliss. Mary borrows a verse from her husband, Percy, to remind us that this is a fool's errand. Nostalgia for a past both perfect and peaceful is a product of willful forgetting. First, we must forget all those elements of the past that were not peaceful and perfect. Our memory of the past is edited to make it seem preferable to the uncertainties of the present and future. Second, we must make ourselves forget that we are part of a system governed by change in net linear direction. The long arc of history bends toward change, and it is not possible to remove from the world the science and technology we have already introduced and thus return the world to a peaceful but primeval state. It is, therefore, incumbent upon scientists and engineers to think about how their work is embodied in the world and how the world is changed as a result.
Sean A. Hays.

It was nearly noon when I arrived at the top of the ascent. For some time I sat upon the rock that overlooks the sea of ice. A mist covered both that and the surrounding mountains. Presently a breeze dissipated the cloud, and I descended upon the glacier. The surface is very uneven, rising like the waves of a troubled sea, descending low, and interspersed by rifts that sink deep. The field of ice is almost a league in width, but I spent nearly two hours in crossing it. The opposite mountain is a bare perpendicular rock. From the side where I now stood Montanvert was exactly opposite, at the distance of a league; and above it rose Mont Blanc, in awful majesty. I remained in a recess of the rock, gazing on this wonderful and stupendous scene. The sea, or rather the vast river of ice, wound among its dependent mountains, whose aerial summits hung over its recesses. Their icy and glittering peaks shone in the sunlight over the clouds. My heart, which was before sorrowful, now swelled with something like joy; I exclaimed—"Wandering spirits, if indeed ye wander, and do not rest in your narrow beds, allow me this faint happiness, or take me, as your companion, away from the joys of life."

As I said this, I suddenly beheld the figure of a man, at some distance, advancing towards me with superhuman speed. He bounded over the crevices in the ice, among which I had walked with caution; his stature also, as he approached, seemed to exceed that of man. I was troubled: a mist came over my eyes, and I felt a faintness seize me; but I was quickly restored by the cold gale of the mountains. I perceived, as the shape came nearer, (sight tremendous and abhorred!) that it was the wretch whom I had created. I trembled with rage and horror, resolving to wait his approach, and then close with him in mortal combat. He approached; his countenance bespoke bitter anguish, combined with disdain and malignity, while its unearthly ugliness rendered it almost too horrible for human eyes. But I scarcely observed this; anger and hatred had at first deprived me of utterance, and I recovered only to overwhelm him with words expressive of furious detestation and contempt.

"Devil!" I exclaimed, "do you dare approach me? and do not you fear the fierce vengeance of my arm wreaked on your miserable head? Begone, vile insect! or rather stay, that I may trample you to dust! and, oh, that I could, with the extinction of your miserable existence, restore those victims whom you have so diabolically murdered!"

"I expected this reception," said the dæmon. "All men hate the wretched; how then must I be hated, who am miserable beyond all living things! Yet you, my creator, detest and spurn me, thy creature, to whom thou art bound by ties only dissoluble by the annihilation of one of us. You purpose to kill me. How dare you sport thus with life? Do your duty towards me, and I will do mine towards you and the rest of mankind. If you will comply with my conditions, I will leave them and you at peace; but if you refuse, I will glut the maw of death, until it be satiated with the blood of your remaining friends."

"Abhorred monster! fiend that thou art! the tortures of hell are too mild a vengeance for thy crimes. Wretched devil! you reproach me with your creation; come on then, that I may extinguish the spark which I so negligently bestowed."

My rage was without bounds; I sprang on him, impelled by all the feelings which can arm one being against the existence of another.

He easily eluded me, and said,

"Be calm! I entreat you to hear me, before you give vent to your hatred on my devoted head. Have I not suffered enough, that you seek to increase my misery? Life, although it may only be an accumulation of anguish, is dear to me, and I will defend it.[11] Remember, thou hast made me more powerful than thyself; my height is superior to thine; my joints more supple. But I will not be tempted to set myself in opposition to thee. I am thy creature, and I will be even mild and docile to my natural lord and king, if thou wilt also perform thy part, the which thou owest me. Oh, Frankenstein, be not equitable to every other, and trample upon me alone, to whom thy justice, and even thy clemency and affection, is most due. Remember, that I am thy creature: I ought to be thy Adam; but I am rather the fallen angel, whom thou drivest from joy for no misdeed. Every where I see bliss, from which I alone am irrevocably excluded. I was benevolent and good; misery made me a fiend. Make me happy, and I shall again be virtuous."

"Begone! I will not hear you. There can be no community between you and me; we are enemies. Begone, or let us try our strength in a fight, in which one must fall."

11. Though this work well predates such existential writers as Albert Camus (1913–1960) and John Paul Sartre (1905–1980), Mary's narrative grapples with many of the same issues, including feelings of anguish and meaninglessness, especially in the face of suffering and human finitude. Much like the existentialists, who acknowledged the absurdity of making sense of life in a godless world, Victor's creation lives a life full of anguish and isolation, and he has no creator to whom he can turn for answers or consolation. And yet the creation still sees life as "dear" and chooses to "defend it" in spite of this endless misery, a point echoed by the existentialists nearly a century later, who emphasized both the absurdity and the beauty in choosing to continue to live in the face of suffering. Mere existence, in this sense, becomes a form of resistance or rebellion against meaninglessness and our unyielding trajectory toward death. For more on existentialism, see Aho 2014. Nicole Piemonte.

"How can I move thee? Will no entreaties cause thee to turn a favourable eye upon thy creature, who implores thy goodness and compassion? Believe me, Frankenstein: I was benevolent; my soul glowed with love and humanity: but am I not alone, miserably alone? You, my creator, abhor me; what hope can I gather from your fellow-creatures, who owe me nothing? they spurn and hate me. The desert mountains and dreary glaciers are my refuge. I have wandered here many days; the caves of ice, which I only do not fear, are a dwelling to me, and the only one which man does not grudge. These bleak skies I hail, for they are kinder to me than your fellow-beings. If the multitude of mankind knew of my existence, they would do as you do, and arm themselves for my destruction. Shall I not then hate them who abhor me? I will keep no terms with my enemies. I am miserable, and they shall share my wretchedness.[12] Yet it is in your power to recompense me, and deliver them from an evil which it only remains for you to make so great, that not only you and your family, but thousands of others, shall be swallowed up in the whirlwinds of its rage. Let your compassion be moved, and do not disdain me. Listen to my tale: when you have heard that, abandon or commiserate me, as you shall judge that I deserve. But hear me. The guilty are allowed, by human laws, bloody as they may be, to speak in their own defence before they are condemned. Listen to me, Frankenstein. You accuse me of murder; and yet you would, with a satisfied conscience, destroy your own creature. Oh, praise the eternal justice of man![13] Yet I ask you not to spare me: listen to me; and then, if you can, and if you will, destroy the work of your hands."

12. Here we see a classic way the "other" is constructed. The creature, an outcast from human society, begs Victor to hear his story and see things from his, the other's, perspective. He asks, in essence, to be recognized as human. And yet, anticipating rejection, the creature also proclaims his hatred for the humans who can grant him this recognition. This profound ambivalence is in a sense at the core of otherness. The other, as critics from Franz Fanon to Gayatri Spivak have argued, has a split within himself, a wound at the heart of his selfhood. He knows who he is, and yet in the eyes of his fellow humans he sees only the monster they imagine him to be. In this scene, it is also important to consider that the creature's perspective is presented by Victor himself. As readers, we cannot truly know the creature, nor will we ever know what he actually says. We have only Walton's version of Victor's version of the creature's story. It's possible that Victor simply wants us to believe that the creature hates humanity and so has chosen to include only the most terrifying and vengeful statements that the creature makes. Again, this is what it means to construct an other. The truth of the other's experience is barred from us because we have access to it only through representations created by a society that has rejected that other.
Annalee Newitz.

13. The concept of murder functions like a central litmus test here and throughout the novel. On the one hand, if you see Victor's creation as a person, then Victor is countenancing murder as he seeks to destroy his creation. Indeed, it would become very difficult to make a moral distinction between Victor and the creature if this were the case. On the other hand, if the creature is a beast,

"Why do you call to my remembrance circumstances of which I shudder to reflect, that I have been the miserable origin and author? Cursed be the day, abhorred devil, in which you first saw light! Cursed (although I curse myself) be the hands that formed you! You have made me wretched beyond expression. You have left me no power to consider whether I am just to you, or not. Begone! relieve me from the sight of your detested form."

"Thus I relieve thee, my creator," he said, and placed his hated hands before my eyes, which I flung from me with violence; "thus I take from thee a sight which you abhor. Still thou canst listen to me, and grant me thy compassion. By the virtues that I once possessed, I demand this from you. Hear my tale; it is long and strange, and the temperature of this place is not fitting to your fine sensations; come to the hut upon the mountain. The sun is yet high in the heavens; before it descends to hide itself behind yon snowy precipices, and illuminate another world, you will have heard my story, and can decide. On you it rests, whether I quit for ever the neighbourhood of man, and lead a harmless life, or become the scourge of your fellow-creatures, and the author of your own speedy ruin."

As he said this, he led the way across the ice: I followed. My heart was full, and I did not answer him; but, as I proceeded, I weighed the various arguments that he had used, and determined at least to listen to his tale. I was partly urged by curiosity, and compassion confirmed my resolution. I had hitherto supposed him to be the murderer of my brother, and I eagerly sought a confirmation or denial of this opinion. For the first time, also, I felt what the duties of a creator towards his creature were, and that I ought to render him happy before I complained of his wickedness. These motives urged me to comply with his demand. We crossed the ice, therefore, and ascended the opposite rock. The air was cold, and the rain again began to descend: we entered the hut, the fiend with an air of exultation, I with a heavy heart, and depressed spirits. But I consented to listen; and, seating myself by the fire which my odious companion had lighted, he thus began his tale.

---

a piece of property, or a daemon (as Victor often calls him), then it is not possible to murder him because he is not a person. During slavery, this question arose on a number of occasions. Could an owner be prosecuted for murdering a piece of property? The question was highly politicized because to charge an owner with murdering a slave would be to acknowledge the slave's humanity and thus to call into question the entire institution of slavery. Even if the creature in Mary's tale is not human, however, his destruction may still have moral implications for other reasons, but Victor would not be guilty of murder, and the creature would have committed a crime Victor was himself not guilty of. Mary appears to have anticipated by two centuries one of the central ethical concerns of robotics and artificial intelligence. How sophisticated would an artificial intelligence have to be before it could be murdered? If it can be murdered, do we then have to face the issue of its enslavement?

Sean A. Hays.

CHAPTER III.

"It is with considerable difficulty that I remember the original æra of my being: all the events of that period appear confused and indistinct. A strange multiplicity of sensations seized me, and I saw, felt, heard, and smelt, at the same time; and it was, indeed, a long time before I learned to distinguish between the operations of my various senses.[14] By degrees, I remember, a stronger light pressed upon my nerves, so that I was obliged to shut my eyes. Darkness then came over me, and troubled me; but hardly had I felt this, when, by opening my eyes, as I now suppose, the light poured in upon me again. I walked, and, I believe, descended; but I presently found a great alteration in my sensations. Before, dark and opaque bodies had surrounded me, impervious to my touch or sight; but I now found that I could wander on at liberty, with no obstacles which I could not either surmount or avoid. The light became more and more oppressive to me; and, the heat wearying me as I walked, I sought a place where I could receive shade. This was the forest near Ingolstadt; and here I lay by the side of a brook resting from my fatigue, until I felt tormented by hunger and thirst. This roused me from my nearly dormant state, and I ate some berries which I found hanging on the trees, or lying on the ground. I slaked my thirst at the brook; and then lying down, was overcome by sleep.

"It was dark when I awoke; I felt cold also, and half-frightened as it were instinctively, finding myself so desolate. Before I had quitted your apartment, on a sensation of cold, I had covered myself with some clothes; but these were insufficient to secure me from the dews of night. I was a poor, helpless, miserable wretch; I knew, and could distinguish, nothing; but, feeling pain invade me on all sides, I sat down and wept.

"Soon a gentle light stole over the heavens, and gave me a sensation of pleasure. I started up, and beheld a radiant form rise from among the trees. I gazed with a kind of wonder. It moved slowly, but it enlightened my path; and I again went out in search of berries. I was still cold, when under one of the trees I found a huge cloak, with which I covered myself,

14. Although there are separate processing centers in the brain for the various senses, the pattern of how each of these centers processes information is similar. For example, the somatosensory cortex is the area of the brain where touch is processed. Here, different groups of neurons correspond to touch on different parts of the body. Likewise, in the auditory cortex, there are separate regions that process different frequencies of sound. All of these systems work to give us a comprehensive understanding of all our sensory experiences. Upon his creation, the creature is accosted with sensory overload. He initially struggles to distinguish between all of these new sensations, but his brain eventually learns how to process everything in tandem to give him a coherent view of the surrounding world.
Stephanie Naufel.

and sat down upon the ground. No distinct ideas occupied my mind; all was confused. I felt light, and hunger, and thirst, and darkness; innumerable sounds rung in my ears, and on all sides various scents saluted me: the only object that I could distinguish was the bright moon, and I fixed my eyes on that with pleasure.

"Several changes of day and night passed, and the orb of night had greatly lessened when I began to distinguish my sensations from each other. I gradually saw plainly the clear stream that supplied me with drink, and the trees that shaded me with their foliage. I was delighted when I first discovered that a pleasant sound, which often saluted my ears, proceeded from the throats of the little winged animals who had often intercepted the light from my eyes. I began also to observe, with greater accuracy, the forms that surrounded me, and to perceive the boundaries of the radiant roof of light which canopied me. Sometimes I tried to imitate the pleasant songs of the birds, but was unable. Sometimes I wished to express my sensations in my own mode, but the uncouth and inarticulate sounds which broke from me frightened me into silence again.

"The moon had disappeared from the night, and again, with a lessened form, shewed itself, while I still remained in the forest. My sensations had, by this time, become distinct, and my mind received every day additional ideas. My eyes became accustomed to the light, and to perceive objects in their right forms; I distinguished the insect from the herb, and, by degrees, one herb from another. I found that the sparrow uttered none but harsh notes, whilst those of the blackbird and thrush were sweet and enticing.

"One day, when I was oppressed by cold, I found a fire which had been left by some wandering beggars, and was overcome with delight at the warmth I experienced from it. In my joy I thrust my hand into the live embers, but quickly drew it out again with a cry of pain. How strange, I thought, that the same cause should produce such opposite effects![15] I examined the materials of the fire, and to my joy found it to be composed of wood. I quickly collected some branches; but they were wet, and would not burn.

---

15. The emotions of shock and surprise reflect violations of expectations. When you experience a shock or surprise, your physiology causes you to prepare to understand the situation in greater detail. You draw in your breath, widen your eyes, and expand your focus of attention to see what might have caused the violation of expectation. You also get a release of adrenaline in case the surprise reflects a need to fight or flee. A very large violation of expectations, which leads to full-blown shock, can leave someone unable to move or speak for several seconds. This near paralysis provides time to observe what could have caused the surprise and prevents someone from taking an action that might be dangerous for her until she understands the situation more fully.
Arthur B. Markman.

I was pained at this, and sat still watching the operation of the fire. The wet wood which I had placed near the heat dried, and itself became inflamed. I reflected on this; and, by touching the various branches, I discovered the cause, and busied myself in collecting a great quantity of wood, that I might dry it, and have a plentiful supply of fire. When night came on, and brought sleep with it, I was in the greatest fear lest my fire should be extinguished. I covered it carefully with dry wood and leaves, and placed wet branches upon it; and then, spreading my cloak, I lay on the ground, and sunk into sleep.

"It was morning when I awoke, and my first care was to visit the fire. I uncovered it, and a gentle breeze quickly fanned it into a flame. I observed this also, and contrived a fan of branches, which roused the embers when they were nearly extinguished. When night came again, I found, with pleasure, that the fire gave light as well as heat; and that the discovery of this element was useful to me in my food; for I found some of the offals that the travellers had left had been roasted, and tasted much more savoury than the berries I gathered from the trees. I tried, therefore, to dress my food in the same manner, placing it on the live embers. I found that the berries were spoiled by this operation, and the nuts and roots much improved.

"Food, however, became scarce; and I often spent the whole day searching in vain for a few acorns to assuage the pangs of hunger. When I found this, I resolved to quit the place that I had hitherto inhabited, to seek for one where the few wants I experienced would be more easily satisfied. In this emigration, I exceedingly lamented the loss of the fire which I had obtained through accident, and knew not how to re-produce it. I gave several hours to the serious consideration of this deficiency; but I was obliged to relinquish all attempts to supply it; and, wrapping myself up in my cloak, I struck across the wood towards the setting sun. I passed three days in these rambles, and at length discovered the open country. A great fall of snow had taken place the night before, and the fields were of one uniform white; the appearance was disconsolate, and I found my feet chilled by the cold damp substance that covered the ground.

"It was about seven in the morning, and I longed to obtain food and shelter; at length I perceived a small hut, on a rising ground, which had doubtless been built for the convenience of some shepherd. This was a new sight to me; and I examined the structure with great curiosity. Finding the door open, I entered. An old man sat in it, near a fire, over which he was preparing his breakfast. He turned on hearing a noise; and, perceiving me, shrieked loudly, and, quitting the hut, ran across the fields with a speed of which his debilitated form hardly appeared capable. His appearance, different from any I had ever before seen, and his flight, somewhat surprised me. But I was enchanted by the appearance of the hut: here the snow and rain could not penetrate; the ground was dry; and it presented to me then as exquisite and divine a retreat as Pandæmonium appeared to the dæmons of hell after their sufferings in the lake of fire. I greedily devoured the remnants of the shepherd's breakfast, which consisted of bread, cheese, milk, and wine; the latter, however, I did not like. Then, overcome by fatigue, I lay down among some straw, and fell asleep.

"It was noon when I awoke; and, allured by the warmth of the sun, which shone brightly on the white ground, I determined to recommence my travels; and, depositing the remains of the peasant's breakfast in a wallet I found, I proceeded across the fields for several hours, until at sunset I arrived at a village. How miraculous did this appear! the huts, the neater cottages, and stately houses, engaged my admiration by turns. The vegetables in the gardens, the milk and cheese that I saw placed at the windows of some of the cottages, allured my appetite. One of the best of these I entered; but I had hardly placed my foot within the door, before the children shrieked, and one of the women fainted. The whole village was roused; some fled, some attacked me, until, grievously bruised by stones and many other kinds of missile weapons, I escaped to the open country, and fearfully took refuge in a low hovel, quite bare, and making a wretched appearance after the palaces I had beheld in the village. This hovel, however, joined a cottage of a neat and pleasant appearance; but, after my late dearly-bought experience, I dared not enter it. My place of refuge was constructed of wood, but so low, that I could with difficulty sit upright in it. No wood, however, was placed on the earth, which formed the floor, but it was dry; and although the wind entered it by innumerable chinks, I found it an agreeable asylum from the snow and rain.

"Here then I retreated, and lay down, happy to have found a shelter, however miserable, from the inclemency of the season, and still more from the barbarity of man.

"As soon as morning dawned, I crept from my kennel, that I might view the adjacent cottage, and discover if I could remain in the habitation I had found. It was situated against the back of the cottage, and surrounded on the sides which were exposed by a pig-stye and a clear pool of water. One part was open, and by that I had crept in; but now I covered every crevice by which I might be perceived with stones and wood, yet in such a manner that I might move them on occasion to pass out: all the light I enjoyed came through the stye, and that was sufficient for me.

"Having thus arranged my dwelling, and carpeted it with clean straw, I retired; for I saw the figure of a man at a distance, and I remembered too well my treatment the night before, to trust myself in his power. I had first, however, provided for my sustenance for that day, by a loaf of coarse bread, which I purloined, and a cup with which I could drink, more conveniently than from my hand, of the pure water which flowed by my retreat. The floor was a little raised, so that it was kept perfectly dry, and by its vicinity to the chimney of the cottage it was tolerably warm.

"Being thus provided, I resolved to reside in this hovel, until something should occur which might alter my determination. It was indeed a paradise, compared to the bleak forest, my former residence, the rain-dropping branches, and dank earth. I ate my breakfast with pleasure, and was about to remove a plank to procure myself a little water, when I heard a step, and, looking through a small chink, I beheld a young creature, with a pail on her head, passing before my hovel. The girl was young and of gentle demeanour, unlike what I have since found cottagers and farm-house servants to be. Yet she was meanly dressed, a coarse blue petticoat and a linen jacket being her only garb; her fair hair was plaited, but not adorned; she looked patient, yet sad. I lost sight of her; and in about a quarter of an hour she returned, bearing the pail, which was now partly filled with milk. As she walked along, seemingly incommoded by the burden, a young man met her, whose countenance expressed a deeper despondence. Uttering a few sounds with an air of melancholy, he took the pail from her head, and bore it to the cottage himself. She followed, and they disappeared. Presently I saw the young man again, with some tools in his hand, cross the field behind the cottage; and the girl was also busied, sometimes in the house, and sometimes in the yard.

"On examining my dwelling, I found that one of the windows of the cottage had formerly occupied a part of it, but the panes had been filled up with wood. In one of these was a small and almost imperceptible chink, through which the eye could just penetrate. Through this crevice, a small room was visible, white-washed and clean, but very bare of furniture. In one corner, near a small fire, sat an old man, leaning his head on his hands in a disconsolate attitude. The young girl was occupied in arranging the cottage; but presently she took something out of a drawer, which employed her hands, and she sat down beside the old man, who, taking up an instrument, began to play, and to produce sounds, sweeter than the voice of the thrush or the nightingale. It was a lovely sight, even to me, poor wretch! who had never beheld aught beautiful before. The silver hair and benevolent countenance of the aged cottager, won my reverence; while the gentle manners of the girl enticed my love. He played a sweet mournful air, which I perceived drew tears from the eyes of his amiable companion, of which the old man took no notice, until she sobbed audibly; he then pronounced a few sounds, and the fair creature, leaving her work, knelt at his feet. He raised her, and smiled with such kindness and affection, that I felt sensations of a peculiar and overpowering nature: they were a mixture of pain and pleasure, such as I had never before experienced, either from hunger or cold, warmth or food; and I withdrew from the window, unable to bear these emotions.

"Soon after this the young man returned, bearing on his shoulders a load of wood. The girl met him at the door, helped to relieve him of his burden, and, taking some of the fuel into the cottage, placed it on the fire; then she and the youth went apart into a nook of the cottage, and he shewed her a large loaf and a piece of cheese. She seemed pleased; and went into the garden for some roots and plants, which she placed in water, and then upon the fire. She afterwards continued her work, whilst the young man went into the garden, and appeared busily employed in digging and pulling up roots. After he had been employed thus about an hour, the young woman joined him, and they entered the cottage together.

"The old man had, in the mean time, been pensive; but, on the appearance of his companions, he assumed a more cheerful air, and they sat down to eat. The meal was quickly dispatched. The young woman was again occupied in arranging the cottage; the old man walked before the cottage in the sun for a few minutes, leaning on the arm of the youth. Nothing could exceed in beauty the contrast between these two excellent creatures. One was old, with silver hairs and a countenance beaming with benevolence and love; the younger was slight and graceful in his figure, and his features were moulded with the finest symmetry; yet his eyes and attitude expressed the utmost sadness and despondency. The old man returned to the cottage; and the youth, with tools different from those he had used in the morning, directed his steps across the fields.

"Night quickly shut in; but, to my extreme wonder, I found that the cottagers had a means of prolonging light, by the use of tapers, and was delighted to find, that the setting of the sun did not put an end to the pleasure I experienced in watching my human neighbours. In the evening, the young girl and her companion were employed in various occupations which I did not understand; and the old man again took up the instrument, which produced the divine sounds that had enchanted me in the morning. So soon as he had finished, the youth began, not to play, but to utter sounds that were monotonous, and neither resembling the harmony of the old man's instrument or the songs of the birds; I since found that he read aloud, but at that time I knew nothing of the science of words or letters.

"The family, after having been thus occupied for a short time, extinguished their lights, and retired, as I conjectured, to rest.

CHAPTER IV.

"I lay on my straw, but I could not sleep. I thought of the occurrences of the day. What chiefly struck me was the gentle manners of these people; and I longed to join them, but dared not. I remembered too well the treatment I had suffered the night before from the barbarous villagers, and resolved, whatever course of conduct I might hereafter think it right to pursue, that for the present I would remain quietly in my hovel, watching, and endeavouring to discover the motives which influenced their actions.

"The cottagers arose the next morning before the sun. The young woman arranged the cottage, and prepared the food; and the youth departed after the first meal.

"This day was passed in the same routine as that which preceded it. The young man was constantly employed out of doors, and the girl in various laborious occupations within. The old man, whom I soon perceived to be blind, employed his leisure hours on his instrument, or in contemplation. Nothing could exceed the love and respect which the younger cottagers exhibited towards their venerable companion. They performed towards him every little office of affection and duty with gentleness; and he rewarded them by his benevolent smiles.

"They were not entirely happy. The young man and his companion often went apart, and appeared to weep. I saw no cause for their unhappiness; but I was deeply affected by it. If such lovely creatures were miserable, it was less strange that I, an imperfect and solitary being, should be wretched. Yet why were these gentle beings unhappy? They possessed a delightful house (for such it was in my eyes), and every luxury; they had a fire to warm them when chill, and delicious viands when hungry; they were dressed in excellent clothes; and, still more, they enjoyed one another's company and speech, interchanging each day looks of affection and kindness. What did their tears imply? Did they really express pain? I was at first unable to solve these questions; but perpetual attention, and time, explained to me many appearances which were at first enigmatic.

"A considerable period elapsed before I discovered one of the causes of the uneasiness of this amiable family; it was poverty: and they suffered that evil in a very distressing degree. Their nourishment consisted entirely of the vegetables of their garden, and the milk of one cow, which gave very little during the winter, when its masters could scarcely procure food to support it. They often, I believe, suffered the pangs of hunger very poignantly, especially the two younger cottagers; for several times they placed food before the old man, when they reserved none for themselves.

"This trait of kindness moved me sensibly.[16] I had been accustomed, during the night, to steal a part of their store for my own consumption; but when I found that in doing this I inflicted pain on the cottagers, I abstained, and satisfied myself with berries, nuts, and roots, which I gathered from a neighbouring wood.[17]

16. We can think of kindness from two different perspectives: terminating and ongoing. A terminating perspective focuses on an individual act of kindness as not being valuable in itself but mainly valuable in the aim it will achieve. Conversely, an ongoing perspective privileges both the individual act itself and the accumulation of acts over time, which might lead to some particular aim. Both perspectives are rooted in a need to do for others, but the former rejects kindness as a process. The creature seems to understand kindness as a process. Through his many encounters with the family, he develops an ever-deepening recognition and awareness of them as individuals doing for one another. This recognition is significant because spending the time to build awareness of others is part of the mechanism of kindness: thus, when the creature spends this time, he has already begun the process of kindness himself. He progresses from simply recognizing and becoming aware of others to not only refraining from stealing their food but caring for them by chopping wood and leaving it for them at their doorstep. As we can see, he feels tremendous gratification from his actions. Ongoing kindness involves all of the features the creature experiences: recognition, awareness, and care. Scientific endeavors outside of Victor's might be equally rewarded by using ongoing kindness as an ethical approach to research. By recognizing the possible implications of our scientific endeavors, being aware of not only the benefits but potential detriments, and acting with care, we might experience the "true pleasure" in being in service for others.

Jameien Taylor.

17. Although compassion—empathy or sympathy with the plight of others—and other positive sentiments and virtues may seem inherent personal characteristics, Frankenstein makes clear that circumstances can inspire virtues, such as compassion, and changed circumstances can eradicate or obscure them. The creature's observation of the cottagers' poverty as well as of their compassionate behavior toward their elderly relative instructs him in compassion. He stops stealing their food for himself, as he had previously done, and secretly provides them with firewood. But as the novel progresses, the creature suffers increasingly from feelings of abandonment, which inspire acts of revenge against Victor. He can remember that he was once compassionate, but he knows he is no longer so. "I am malicious because I am miserable," he explains. "[I]f I cannot inspire love, I will cause fear" (p. 121). Victor likewise demonstrates compassion when he is happy with himself and the world but intense selfishness and unconcern for others (especially Elizabeth) when he isn't.

If virtue is even partly circumstantial, then all who act in the world, including scientists, must recognize that judgments about their own worth and the value of their work require close scrutiny. Victor acted alone, without consulting anyone about the value of his invention or its potential unintended consequences. If he had conferred with a community of thinkers and innovators with cooler heads, perhaps he could have rekindled his own compassion and avoided the cascading tragedy that emanates from his solitary creation.

Sally Kitch.

"I discovered also another means through which I was enabled to assist their labours. I found that the youth spent a great part of each day in collecting wood for the family fire; and, during the night, I often took his tools, the use of which I quickly discovered, and brought home firing sufficient for the consumption of several days.

"I remember, the first time that I did this, the young woman, when she opened the door in the morning, appeared greatly astonished on seeing a great pile of wood on the outside. She uttered some words in a loud voice, and the youth joined her, who also expressed surprise. I observed, with pleasure, that he did not go to the forest that day, but spent it in repairing the cottage, and cultivating the garden.

"By degrees I made a discovery of still greater moment. I found that these people possessed a method of communicating their experience and feelings to one another by articulate sounds. I perceived that the words they spoke sometimes produced pleasure or pain, smiles or sadness, in the minds and countenances of the hearers. This was indeed a godlike science, and I ardently desired to become acquainted with it. But I was baffled in every attempt I made for this purpose. Their pronunciation was quick; and the words they uttered, not having any apparent connexion with visible objects, I was unable to discover any clue by which I could unravel the mystery of their reference. By great application, however, and after having remained during the space of several revolutions of the moon in my hovel, I discovered the names that were given to some of the most familiar objects of discourse: I learned and applied the words *fire, milk, bread,* and *wood.* I learned also the names of the cottagers themselves. The youth and his companion had each of them several names, but the old man had only one, which was *father.* The girl was called *sister,* or *Agatha*; and the youth *Felix, brother,* or *son.* I cannot describe the delight I felt when I learned the ideas appropriated to each of these sounds, and was able to pronounce them. I distinguished several other words, without being able as yet to understand or apply them; such as *good, dearest, unhappy.*[18]

"I spent the winter in this manner. The gentle manners and beauty of the cottagers greatly endeared them to me: when they were unhappy, I felt depressed; when they rejoiced, I sympathized in their joys. I saw few human beings beside them; and if any other happened to enter the cottage,

---

18. The creature is a good if simple empiricist, understanding words for concrete objects but having more difficulty with words that represent abstract concepts. Perhaps at this stage in his development, he—much like Victor—can master objects but not feelings, causes but not concepts.

David H. Guston.

their harsh manners and rude gait only enhanced to me the superior accomplishments of my friends. The old man, I could perceive, often endeavoured to encourage his children, as sometimes I found that he called them, to cast off their melancholy. He would talk in a cheerful accent, with an expression of goodness that bestowed pleasure even upon me. Agatha listened with respect, her eyes sometimes filled with tears, which she endeavoured to wipe away unperceived; but I generally found that her countenance and tone were more cheerful after having listened to the exhortations of her father. It was not thus with Felix. He was always the saddest of the groupe; and, even to my unpractised senses, he appeared to have suffered more deeply than his friends. But if his countenance was more sorrowful, his voice was more cheerful than that of his sister, especially when he addressed the old man.

"I could mention innumerable instances, which, although slight, marked the dispositions of these amiable cottagers. In the midst of poverty and want, Felix carried with pleasure to his sister the first little white flower that peeped out from beneath the snowy ground. Early in the morning before she had risen, he cleared away the snow that obstructed her path to the milk-house, drew water from the well, and brought the wood from the outhouse, where, to his perpetual astonishment, he found his store always replenished by an invisible hand. In the day, I believe, he worked sometimes for a neighbouring farmer, because he often went forth, and did not return until dinner, yet brought no wood with him. At other times he worked in the garden; but, as there was little to do in the frosty season, he read to the old man and Agatha.

"This reading had puzzled me extremely at first; but, by degrees, I discovered that he uttered many of the same sounds when he read as when he talked. I conjectured, therefore, that he found on the paper signs for speech which he understood, and I ardently longed to comprehend these also; but how was that possible, when I did not even understand the sounds for which they stood as signs? I improved, however, sensibly in this science, but not sufficiently to follow up any kind of conversation, although I applied my whole mind to the endeavour: for I easily perceived that, although I eagerly longed to discover myself to the cottagers, I ought not to make the attempt until I had first become master of their language; which knowledge might enable me to make them overlook the deformity of my figure; for with this also the contrast perpetually presented to my eyes had made me acquainted.[19]

19. The creature here perceives the human tendency to distinguish between members of the in-group and members of the out-group and to fear and despise the latter: "othering," as it is sometimes known. He also suggests, plausibly, that othering occurs where the target is not

"I had admired the perfect forms of my cottagers—their grace, beauty, and delicate complexions: but how was I terrified, when I viewed myself in a transparent pool![20] At first I started back, unable to believe that it was indeed I who was reflected in the mirror; and when I became fully convinced that I was in reality the monster that I am, I was filled with the bitterest sensations of despondence and mortification. Alas! I did not yet entirely know the fatal effects of this miserable deformity.

"As the sun became warmer, and the light of day longer, the snow vanished, and I beheld the bare trees and the black earth. From this time Felix was more employed; and the heart-moving indications of impending famine disappeared. Their food, as I afterwards found, was coarse, but it was wholesome; and they procured a sufficiency of it. Several new kinds of plants sprung up in the garden, which they dressed; and these signs of comfort increased daily as the season advanced.

"The old man, leaning on his son, walked each day at noon, when it did not rain, as I found it was called when the heavens poured forth its waters. This frequently took place; but a high wind quickly dried the earth, and the season became far more pleasant than it had been.

---

simply different from the audience but also not understood, and he hopes to overcome this gap in understanding through communication with the cottagers. As his monologue continues, parallels are drawn between his situation and that of various outsiders and outcasts in history who have also been othered: immigrants (Safie and her father), the poor, the lowborn, and the orphaned. Mary Shelley herself is not immune from this tendency: see, for instance, her rather broad generalizations about women in Islam and her apparent approval of European colonization.

We must recognize that other people, especially those different from us, are not just sources of exclusion and anguish. The creature's monologue is also a story of human development—from securing the most basic means of survival to engaging with language and literature—and it emphasizes, too, the essential role of communing with others unlike us in achieving self-consciousness and fulfillment. Thus, it reveals the creature's deep desire to interact with humans, a different species, and then with a created romantic partner of a different sex.

For another view on how being perceived by others is both essential to achieving self-consciousness and a potential source of deep despair, given our dependency on them for our sense of worth, one might compare Sartre's theory in *Being and Nothingness* ([1943] 2012).
Adam Hosein.

20. The creature experiences fear and terror because his reflection reveals that he looks much different from others whom he has encountered. In this way, his self-knowledge is informed by others—that is, he sees, knows, and understands himself as society sees, knows, and understands him. This scene suggests that individual or personal identity is developed in part via cultural constructions of what it is beautiful, normal, acceptable, moral, and so forth. We come to know ourselves—and even to fear ourselves—through our encounters with others, and what society deems as "normal" often influences our self-perceptions.
Nicole Piemonte.

"My mode of life in my hovel was uniform. During the morning I attended the motions of the cottagers; and when they were dispersed in various occupations, I slept: the remainder of the day was spent in observing my friends. When they had retired to rest, if there was any moon, or the night was star-light, I went into the woods, and collected my own food and fuel for the cottage. When I returned, as often as it was necessary, I cleared their path from the snow, and performed those offices that I had seen done by Felix. I afterwards found that these labours, performed by an invisible hand, greatly astonished them; and once or twice I heard them, on these occasions, utter the words *good spirit, wonderful*; but I did not then understand the signification of these terms.

"My thoughts now became more active, and I longed to discover the motives and feelings of these lovely creatures; I was inquisitive to know why Felix appeared so miserable, and Agatha so sad. I thought (foolish wretch!) that it might be in my power to restore happiness to these deserving people. When I slept, or was absent, the forms of the venerable blind father, the gentle Agatha, and the excellent Felix, flitted before me. I looked upon them as superior beings, who would be the arbiters of my future destiny. I formed in my imagination a thousand pictures of presenting myself to them, and their reception of me. I imagined that they would be disgusted, until, by my gentle demeanour and conciliating words, I should first win their favour, and afterwards their love.

"These thoughts exhilarated me, and led me to apply with fresh ardour to the acquiring the art of language. My organs were indeed harsh, but supple; and although my voice was very unlike the soft music of their tones, yet I pronounced such words as I understood with tolerable ease. It was as the ass and the lap-dog; yet surely the gentle ass, whose intentions were affectionate, although his manners were rude, deserved better treatment than blows and execration.[21]

21. Here the creature refers to one of the fables by Aesop (620–560 BCE). A farmer's donkey becomes jealous of the famer's affection for his pet lap dog. The hard-working donkey tries to get the farmer's attention by imitating the lap dog's playful behavior. When the donkey jumps up on the farmer, expecting to be petted, bystanders become fearful and attack the donkey for acting uncharacteristically. One popular interpretation of the moral of the story is not to try to be someone you are not. Mary turns the meaning of the fable on its head by focusing on the injustice that happens when a creature's efforts to obtain affection are rebuffed and punished. There are many instances throughout the novel where the creature witnesses others expressing love and kindness toward one another, and so he desires to be treated the same. When his bid to be admitted into humanity is rejected, he lashes out. Mary suggests outrage is one possible reaction to rejection and exclusion.

Mary Margaret Fonow.

"The pleasant showers and genial warmth of spring greatly altered the aspect of the earth. Men, who before this change seemed to have been hid in caves, dispersed themselves, and were employed in various arts of cultivation. The birds sang in more cheerful notes, and the leaves began to bud forth on the trees. Happy, happy earth! fit habitation for gods, which, so short a time before, was bleak, damp, and unwholesome. My spirits were elevated by the enchanting appearance of nature; the past was blotted from my memory, the present was tranquil, and the future gilded by bright rays of hope, and anticipations of joy.

CHAPTER V.

"I now hasten to the more moving part of my story. I shall relate events that impressed me with feelings which, from what I was, have made me what I am.

"Spring advanced rapidly; the weather became fine, and the skies cloudless. It surprised me, that what before was desert and gloomy should now bloom with the most beautiful flowers and verdure. My senses were gratified and refreshed by a thousand scents of delight, and a thousand sights of beauty.

"It was on one of these days, when my cottagers periodically rested from labour—the old man played on his guitar, and the children listened to him—I observed that the countenance of Felix was melancholy beyond expression: he sighed frequently; and once his father paused in his music, and I conjectured by his manner that he inquired the cause of his son's sorrow. Felix replied in a cheerful accent, and the old man was recommencing his music, when some one tapped at the door.

"It was a lady on horseback, accompanied by a countryman as a guide. The lady was dressed in a dark suit, and covered with a thick black veil. Agatha asked a question; to which the stranger only replied by pronouncing, in a sweet accent, the name of Felix. Her voice was musical, but unlike that of either of my friends. On hearing this word, Felix came up hastily to the lady; who, when she saw him, threw up her veil, and I beheld a countenance of angelic beauty and expression. Her hair of a shining raven black, and curiously braided; her eyes were dark, but gentle, although animated; her features of a regular proportion, and her complexion wondrously fair, each cheek tinged with a lovely pink.

"Felix seemed ravished with delight when he saw her, every trait of sorrow vanished from his face, and it instantly expressed a degree of ecstatic joy, of which I could hardly have believed it capable; his eyes sparkled, as his cheek flushed with pleasure; and at that moment I thought him as beautiful as the stranger. She appeared affected by different feelings; wiping a few tears from her lovely eyes, she held out her hand to Felix, who kissed it rapturously, and called her, as well as I could distinguish, his sweet Arabian. She did not appear to understand him, but smiled. He assisted her to dismount, and, dismissing her guide, conducted her into the cottage. Some conversation took place between him and his father; and the young stranger knelt at the old man's feet, and would have kissed his hand, but he raised her, and embraced her affectionately.

"I soon perceived, that although the stranger uttered articulate sounds, and appeared to have a language of her own, she was neither understood by, or herself understood, the cottagers. They made many signs which I did not comprehend; but I saw that her presence diffused gladness through the cottage, dispelling their sorrow as the sun dissipates the morning mists. Felix seemed peculiarly happy, and with smiles of delight welcomed his Arabian. Agatha, the ever-gentle Agatha, kissed the hands of the lovely stranger; and, pointing to her brother, made signs which appeared to me to mean that he had been sorrowful until she came. Some hours passed thus, while they, by their countenances, expressed joy, the cause of which I did not comprehend. Presently I found, by the frequent recurrence of one sound which the stranger repeated after them, that she was endeavouring to learn their language; and the idea instantly occurred to me, that I should make use of the same instructions to the same end. The stranger learned about twenty words at the first lesson, most of them indeed were those which I had before understood, but I profited by the others.

"As night came on, Agatha and the Arabian retired early. When they separated, Felix kissed the hand of the stranger, and said, 'Good night, sweet Safie.' He sat up much longer, conversing with his father; and, by the frequent repetition of her name, I conjectured that their lovely guest was the subject of their conversation. I ardently desired to understand them, and bent every faculty towards that purpose, but found it utterly impossible.

"The next morning Felix went out to his work; and, after the usual occupations of Agatha were finished, the Arabian sat at the feet of the old man, and, taking his guitar, played some airs so entrancingly beautiful, that they at once drew tears of sorrow and delight from my eyes. She sang, and her voice flowed in a rich cadence, swelling or dying away, like a nightingale of the woods.

"When she had finished, she gave the guitar to Agatha, who at first declined it. She played a simple air, and her voice accompanied it in sweet accents, but unlike the wondrous strain of the stranger. The old man appeared enraptured, and said some words, which Agatha endeavoured to explain to Safie, and by which he appeared to wish to express that she bestowed on him the greatest delight by her music.

"The days now passed as peaceably as before, with the sole alteration, that joy had taken place of sadness in the countenances of my friends. Safie was always gay and happy; she and I improved rapidly in the knowledge of language, so that in two months I began to comprehend most of the words uttered by my protectors.

"In the meanwhile also the black ground was covered with herbage, and the green banks interspersed with innumerable flowers, sweet to the scent and the eyes, stars of pale radiance among the moonlight woods; the sun became warmer, the nights clear and balmy; and my nocturnal rambles were an extreme pleasure to me, although they were considerably short-ened by the late setting and early rising of the sun; for I never ventured abroad during day-light, fearful of meeting with the same treatment as I had formerly endured in the first village which I entered.

"My days were spent in close attention, that I might more speedily master the language; and I may boast that I improved more rapidly than the Ara-bian, who understood very little, and conversed in broken accents, whilst I comprehended and could imitate almost every word that was spoken.

"While I improved in speech, I also learned the science of letters, as it was taught to the stranger; and this opened before me a wide field for wonder and delight.

"The book from which Felix instructed Safie was Volney's *Ruins of Empires*. I should not have understood the purport of this book, had not Felix, in reading it, given very minute explanations. He had chosen this work, he said, because the declamatory style was framed in imitation of the eastern authors. Through this work I obtained a cursory knowledge of history, and a view of the several empires at present existing in the world; it gave me an insight into the manners, governments, and religions of the different nations of the earth. I heard of the slothful Asiatics; of the stupen-dous genius and mental activity of the Grecians; of the wars and wonder-ful virtue of the early Romans—of their subsequent degeneration—of the decline of that mighty empire; of chivalry, Christianity, and kings. I heard of the discovery of the American hemisphere, and wept with Safie over the hapless fate of its original inhabitants.

"These wonderful narrations inspired me with strange feelings. Was man, indeed, at once so powerful, so virtuous, and magnificent, yet so vicious and base? He appeared at one time a mere scion of the evil principle, and at another as all that can be conceived of noble and godlike. To be a great and virtuous man appeared the highest honour that can befall a sensitive being; to be base and vicious, as many on record have been, appeared the lowest degradation, a condition more abject than that of the blind mole or harmless worm. For a long time I could not conceive how one man could go forth to murder his fellow, or even why there were laws and governments; but when I heard details of vice and bloodshed, my wonder ceased, and I turned away with disgust and loathing.

"Every conversation of the cottagers now opened new wonders to me. While I listened to the instructions which Felix bestowed upon the Arabian, the strange system of human society was explained to me. I heard of the division of property, of immense wealth and squalid poverty; of rank, descent, and noble blood.[22]

"The words induced me to turn towards myself. I learned that the possessions most esteemed by your fellow-creatures were, high and unsullied descent united with riches. A man might be respected with only one of these acquisitions; but without either he was considered, except in very rare instances, as a vagabond and a slave, doomed to waste his powers for the profit of the chosen few. And what was I? Of my creation and creator I was absolutely ignorant; but I knew that I possessed no money, no friends, no kind of property. I was, besides, endowed with a figure hideously deformed and loathsome; I was not even of the same nature as man. I was more agile than they, and could subsist upon coarser diet; I bore the extremes of heat and cold with less injury to my frame; my stature far exceeded their's.[23] When I looked around, I saw and heard of none

22. Much of the novel is inspired by the writings of philosopher Jean-Jacques Rousseau (1712–1778), who believed that humans in their natural state are good and that society corrupts them. Like Rousseau's character Emile (Rousseau [1762] 1979), the creature learns from his environment and only slowly is introduced to society. Whether governments and laws can maintain order or are part of the social ill remains an unanswered question. The two trial scenes in the novel, Justine's and later Victor's, serve as examples of the problems of mobs and the difficulties of attaining justice. It was common during this period to see humans as a link in the "great chain of being": we can climb as high as angels or slip lower than animals on this chain through our moral choices.
Ron Broglio.

23. Scientists have long aspired to improve the human body, or create new bodies, to exceed our natural biological limits. The United States military pursues a range of research areas to enhance the performance of soldiers, from powered exoskeletons granting their users superhuman strength to direct brain interfaces that would allow pilots to fly aircraft by thought alone. More broadly, almost all biomedical technologies can be seen as serving the same purpose, from contact lenses and pacemakers that regulate and improve the function of our organs to antibiotics that make us far more resistant to disease. Many people feel that our bodies' greatest flaw is aging and death.

like me.[24] Was I then a monster, a blot upon the earth, from which all men fled, and whom all men disowned?[25]

"I cannot describe to you the agony that these reflections inflicted upon me; I tried to dispel them, but sorrow only increased with knowledge. Oh, that I had for ever remained in my native wood, nor known or felt beyond the sensations of hunger, thirst, and heat!

"Of what a strange nature is knowledge! It clings to the mind, when it has once seized on it, like a lichen on the rock. I wished sometimes to shake off all thought and feeling; but I learned that there was but one means to overcome the sensation of pain, and that was death—a state which I feared yet did not understand. I admired virtue and good feelings, and loved the gentle manners and amiable qualities of my cottagers; but I was shut out from intercourse with them, except through means which I obtained by stealth, when I was unseen and unknown, and which rather increased

---

Philanthropists like Bill and Melinda Gates and Mark Zuckerberg and Priscilla Chan have invested billions of dollars to eliminate disease and extend human life. Ongoing scientific debates about life extension sometimes echo the quest for the philosopher's stone as researchers contemplate how the human body might be sustained or rejuvenated through genetic modification, personalized drug cocktails, or other means.

Humanity's technological obsession with overcoming our biological limits has a natural parallel in science fiction. Mary's vision of a superhuman creature inspired many others, from comic book superheroes to the robots and replicants populating movies like *The Terminator* (James Cameron, 1984), *Blade Runner* (Ridley Scott, 1982), and *Ex Machina* (Alex Garland, 2015). These stories ask many of the same questions posed in *Frankenstein*: what would a perfected human form really be like? What kind of life would such a creature lead? What consequences would result from a world in which humans and superhumans coexist?

Ed Finn.

24. The creature recounts how his life differs from normal human life. In future narratives, writers directly confront what Mary here only touches upon lightly with allusions to slavery, ownership, and property: that the creature might be "owned" by his creator or that he might be the subject of a patent or that Victor might seek to monetize his investment of time and effort or that his secrecy and obsession are in part motivated by greed as well as a desire for fame and glory.

Robert Cook-Deegan.

25. These musings from Victor's creation invite us to consider what or who determines our self-identity. Do we determine our own ideas of identity? Or do others—family, friends, general society, or a creator—determine them? The creature's social interactions leave him without sympathy from the members of any of these categories, and thus he struggles to understand who or what he is and what his role in life is. Developmental psychologist Erik Eriksen (1902–1994) theorized that identity or our consciousness of self forms in eight stages by evolving through our social interactions. The creature's questions model Eriksen's adolescent stage of asking questions such as "Who am I?" and "What can I be?" by comparing self to others. It is especially poignant that Mary leaves the creature without a name for the duration of the book. His namelessness further highlights the fact that he has no clear identity and no good way to define one.

Stephanie Naufel.

than satisfied the desire I had of becoming one among my fellows. The gentle words of Agatha, and the animated smiles of the charming Arabian, were not for me. The mild exhortations of the old man, and the lively conversation of the loved Felix, were not for me. Miserable, unhappy wretch!

"Other lessons were impressed upon me even more deeply. I heard of the difference of sexes; of the birth and growth of children; how the father doated on the smiles of the infant, and the lively sallies of the older child; how all the life and cares of the mother were wrapt up in the precious charge; how the mind of youth expanded and gained knowledge; of brother, sister, and all the various relationships which bind one human being to another in mutual bonds.[26]

"But where were my friends and relations? No father had watched my infant days, no mother had blessed me with smiles and caresses; or if they had, all my past life was now a blot, a blind vacancy in which I distinguished nothing. From my earliest remembrance I had been as I then was in height and proportion. I had never yet seen a being resembling me, or who claimed any intercourse with me. What was I? The question again recurred, to be answered only with groans.

"I will soon explain to what these feelings tended; but allow me now to return to the cottagers, whose story excited in me such various feelings of indignation, delight, and wonder, but which all terminated in additional love and reverence for my protectors (for so I loved, in an innocent, half painful self-deceit, to call them).

CHAPTER VI.

"Some time elapsed before I learned the history of my friends. It was one which could not fail to impress itself deeply on my mind, unfolding as it did a number of circumstances each interesting and wonderful to one so utterly inexperienced as I was.

---

26. Mary cautions against Victor's myopic perspective that creation—bringing into existence—is all that matters. The creature is made but un-parented, forced into solitary life, and exiled from mainstream society. In his treatment of the creature, Victor shows no concern for social development, the human need for acceptance, and the importance of memory and shared experiences to the creature's initial and eventual selfhood and well-being. Although Victor later recognizes his younger self in Henry Clerval's desire for knowledge, a sign of Victor's own concrete identity, he fails to use any understanding of this self-recognition in his creation. This episode helps us reflect on the idea that scientific discovery and creation are fully value laden, and bound up in the assumptions and guiding philosophies of the scientists who discover and create.
Kerri Slatus.

"The name of the old man was De Lacey. He was descended from a good family in France, where he had lived for many years in affluence, respected by his superiors, and beloved by his equals. His son was bred in the service of his country; and Agatha had ranked with ladies of the highest distinction. A few months before my arrival, they had lived in a large and luxurious city, called Paris, surrounded by friends, and possessed of every enjoyment which virtue, refinement of intellect, or taste, accompanied by a moderate fortune, could afford.

"The father of Safie had been the cause of their ruin. He was a Turkish merchant, and had inhabited Paris for many years, when, for some reason which I could not learn, he became obnoxious to the government. He was seized and cast into prison the very day that Safie arrived from Constantinople to join him. He was tried, and condemned to death. The injustice of his sentence was very flagrant; all Paris was indignant; and it was judged that his religion and wealth, rather than the crime alleged against him, had been the cause of his condemnation.

"Felix had been present at the trial; his horror and indignation were uncontrollable, when he heard the decision of the court. He made, at that moment, a solemn vow to deliver him, and then looked around for the means. After many fruitless attempts to gain admittance to the prison, he found a strongly grated window in an unguarded part of the building, which lighted the dungeon of the unfortunate Mahometan; who, loaded with chains, waited in despair the execution of the barbarous sentence. Felix visited the grate at night, and made known to the prisoner his intentions in his favour. The Turk, amazed and delighted, endeavoured to kindle the zeal of his deliverer by promises of reward and wealth. Felix rejected his offers with contempt; yet when he saw the lovely Safie, who was allowed to visit her father, and who, by her gestures, expressed her lively gratitude, the youth could not help owning to his own mind, that the captive possessed a treasure which would fully reward his toil and hazard.

"The Turk quickly perceived the impression that his daughter had made on the heart of Felix, and endeavoured to secure him more entirely in his interests by the promise of her hand in marriage, so soon as he should be conveyed to a place of safety. Felix was too delicate to accept this offer; yet he looked forward to the probability of that event as to the consummation of his happiness.

"During the ensuing days, while the preparations were going forward for the escape of the merchant, the zeal of Felix was warmed by several letters that he received from this lovely girl, who found means to express her thoughts in the language of her lover by the aid of an old man, a servant of her father's, who understood French. She thanked him in the most ardent terms for his intended services towards her father; and at the same time she gently deplored her own fate.

"I have copies of these letters; for I found means, during my residence in the hovel, to procure the implements of writing; and the letters were often in the hands of Felix or Agatha. Before I depart, I will give them to you, they will prove the truth of my tale; but at present, as the sun is already far declined, I shall only have time to repeat the substance of them to you.

"Safie related, that her mother was a Christian Arab, seized and made a slave by the Turks; recommended by her beauty, she had won the heart of the father of Safie, who married her.[27] The young girl spoke in high and enthusiastic terms of her mother, who, born in freedom spurned the bondage to which she was now reduced. She instructed her daughter in the tenets of her religion, and taught her to aspire to higher powers of intellect, and an independence of spirit, forbidden to the female followers of Mahomet. This lady died; but her lessons were indelibly impressed on the mind of Safie, who sickened at the prospect of again returning to Asia, and the being immured within the walls of a haram, allowed only to occupy herself with puerile amusements, ill suited to the temper of her soul, now accustomed to grand ideas and a noble emulation for virtue. The prospect of marrying a Christian, and remaining in a country where women were allowed to take a rank in society, was enchanting to her.

"The day for the execution of the Turk was fixed; but, on the night previous to it, he had quitted prison, and before morning was distant many leagues from Paris. Felix had procured passports in the name of his father, sister, and himself. He had previously communicated his plan to the former, who aided the deceit by quitting his house, under the pretence of a journey, and concealed himself, with his daughter, in an obscure part of Paris.

27. Mary wrote *Frankenstein* at a time when slavery was still prevalent in Europe and the Americas. Revolutionary France had abolished slavery, but Napoleon reintroduced it after he came to power. In England, the law ending the British slave trade in 1807 culminated a remarkable two decades of abolitionist activism, although slavery itself would persist until the Slavery Abolition Act ended the practice in 1834. William Godwin himself had written about slavery in his most famous work, *An Enquiry Concerning Political Justice*, asking rhetorically, "Have we slaves? We assiduously retain them in ignorance" ([1793] 2013, 461). The Congress of Vienna, through which European nations attempted to settle the consequences of the French Revolution and the Napoleonic Wars, declared its opposition to slavery in 1815. In the United States, many northern states were beginning a slow process of abolition and freeing currently held slaves around the time Mary was writing *Frankenstein*, but the nation as a whole would not abolish slavery until after the Civil War (1861–1865) with the passage of the Fourteenth Amendment to the Constitution.
David H. Guston and Robert Cook-Deegan.

"Felix conducted the fugitives through France to Lyons, and across Mont Cenis to Leghorn, where the merchant had decided to wait a favourable opportunity of passing into some part of the Turkish dominions.

"Safie resolved to remain with her father until the moment of his departure, before which time the Turk renewed his promise that she should be united to his deliverer; and Felix remained with them in expectation of that event; and in the mean time he enjoyed the society of the Arabian, who exhibited towards him the simplest and tenderest affection. They conversed with one another through the means of an interpreter, and sometimes with the interpretation of looks; and Safie sang to him the divine airs of her native country.

"The Turk allowed this intimacy to take place, and encouraged the hopes of the youthful lovers, while in his heart he had formed far other plans. He loathed the idea that his daughter should be united to a Christian; but he feared the resentment of Felix if he should appear lukewarm; for he knew that he was still in the power of his deliverer, if he should choose to betray him to the Italian state which they inhabited. He revolved a thousand plans by which he should be enabled to prolong the deceit until it might be no longer necessary, and secretly to take his daughter with him when he departed. His plans were greatly facilitated by the news which arrived from Paris.

"The government of France were greatly enraged at the escape of their victim, and spared no pains to detect and punish his deliverer. The plot of Felix was quickly discovered, and De Lacey and Agatha were thrown into prison. The news reached Felix, and roused him from his dream of pleasure. His blind and aged father, and his gentle sister, lay in a noisome dungeon, while he enjoyed the free air, and the society of her whom he loved. This idea was torture to him. He quickly arranged with the Turk, that if the latter should find a favourable opportunity for escape before Felix could return to Italy, Safie should remain as a boarder at a convent at Leghorn; and then, quitting the lovely Arabian, he hastened to Paris, and delivered himself up to the vengeance of the law, hoping to free De Lacey and Agatha by this proceeding.

"He did not succeed. They remained confined for five months before the trial took place; the result of which deprived them of their fortune, and condemned them to a perpetual exile from their native country.

"They found a miserable asylum in the cottage in Germany, where I discovered them. Felix soon learned that the treacherous Turk, for whom he and his family endured such unheard-of oppression, on discovering that his deliverer was thus reduced to poverty and impotence, became a traitor to good feeling and honour, and had quitted Italy with his daughter, insultingly sending Felix a pittance of money to aid him, as he said, in some plan of future maintenance.

"Such were the events that preyed on the heart of Felix, and rendered him, when I first saw him, the most miserable of his family. He could have endured poverty, and when this distress had been the meed of his virtue, he would have gloried in it: but the ingratitude of the Turk, and the loss of his beloved Safie, were misfortunes more bitter and irreparable. The arrival of the Arabian now infused new life into his soul.

"When the news reached Leghorn, that Felix was deprived of his wealth and rank, the merchant commanded his daughter to think no more of her lover, but to prepare to return with him to her native country. The generous nature of Safie was outraged by this command; she attempted to expostulate with her father, but he left her angrily, reiterating his tyrannical mandate.

"A few days after, the Turk entered his daughter's apartment, and told her hastily, that he had reason to believe that his residence at Leghorn had been divulged, and that he should speedily be delivered up to the French government; he had, consequently, hired a vessel to convey him to Constantinople, for which city he should sail in a few hours. He intended to leave his daughter under the care of a confidential servant, to follow at her leisure with the greater part of his property, which had not yet arrived at Leghorn.

"When alone, Safie resolved in her own mind the plan of conduct that it would become her to pursue in this emergency. A residence in Turkey was abhorrent to her; her religion and feelings were alike adverse to it. By some papers of her father's, which fell into her hands, she heard of the exile of her lover, and learnt the name of the spot where he then resided. She hesitated some time, but at length she formed her determination. Taking with her some jewels that belonged to her, and a small sum of money, she quitted Italy, with an attendant, a native of Leghorn, but who understood the common language of Turkey, and departed for Germany.

"She arrived in safety at a town about twenty leagues from the cottage of De Lacey, when her attendant fell dangerously ill. Safie nursed her with the most devoted affection; but the poor girl died, and the Arabian was left alone, unacquainted with the language of the country, and utterly ignorant of the customs of the world. She fell, however, into good hands. The Italian had mentioned the name of the spot for which they were bound; and, after her death, the woman of the house in which they had lived took care that Safie should arrive in safety at the cottage of her lover.

CHAPTER VII.

"Such was the history of my beloved cottagers. It impressed me deeply. I learned, from the views of social life which it developed, to admire their virtues, and to deprecate the vices of mankind.[28]

"As yet I looked upon crime as a distant evil; benevolence and generosity were ever present before me, inciting within me a desire to become an actor in the busy scene where so many admirable qualities were called forth and displayed. But, in giving an account of the progress of my intellect, I must not omit a circumstance which occurred in the beginning of the month of August of the same year.

"One night, during my accustomed visit to the neighbouring wood, where I collected my own food, and brought home firing for my protectors, I found on the ground a leathern portmanteau, containing several articles of dress and some books. I eagerly seized the prize, and returned with it to my hovel. Fortunately the books were written in the language the elements of which I had acquired at the cottage; they consisted of *Paradise Lost*, a volume of *Plutarch's Lives*, and the *Sorrows of Werter*.[29] The possession of these treasures gave me extreme delight; I now continually studied and exercised my mind upon these histories, whilst my friends were employed in their ordinary occupations.

"I can hardly describe to you the effect of these books. They produced in me an infinity of new images and feelings, that sometimes raised me to ecstacy, but more frequently sunk me into the lowest dejection. In the *Sorrows of Werter*, besides the interest of its simple and affecting story,

28. A significant part of who we are as individuals is created in response to what we observe in others. The creature, abandoned by his creator, has the good fortune to find a loving and admirable family to watch and attempt to mimic. It is unclear how many of the De Laceys' admirable qualities are genuine and how many are a product of the creature's desire to find in others the qualities he wishes he had found in his creator. What is clear, however, is that the act of creation is only one small component of the creature's tale, and the same is true for any scientific or technological endeavor. The wider social context in which the act of creation takes place will have an impact on the final place and shape of the knowledge or technologies created by the scientist or engineer.

Sean A. Hays.

29. These three texts were on Mary's reading list the summer before she began writing *Frankenstein*. They represent a kind of literary education for the creature. From Plutarch, he would learn about the great leaders of the Greco-Roman world and the nature of politics and public affairs. In Johann Wolfgang von Goethe's *Sorrows of Young Werther* (1774), he would read about domestic life and social relationships, particularly as they apply to the difficult business of adolescence and growing up. Finally, from John Milton's *Paradise Lost* (1667) the creature would learn about faith and the complexities of good and evil. In Milton's story, Satan, the fallen angel, is a charismatic antihero who challenges his creator.

Ed Finn.

so many opinions are canvassed, and so many lights thrown upon what had hitherto been to me obscure subjects, that I found in it a never-ending source of speculation and astonishment. The gentle and domestic manners it described, combined with lofty sentiments and feelings, which had for their object something out of self, accorded well with my experience among my protectors, and with the wants which were for ever alive in my own bosom. But I thought Werter himself a more divine being than I had ever beheld or imagined; his character contained no pretension, but it sunk deep. The disquisitions upon death and suicide were calculated to fill me with wonder. I did not pretend to enter into the merits of the case, yet I inclined towards the opinions of the hero, whose extinction I wept, without precisely understanding it.

"As I read, however, I applied much personally to my own feelings and condition. I found myself similar, yet at the same time strangely unlike the beings concerning whom I read, and to whose conversation I was a listener. I sympathized with, and partly understood them, but I was unformed in mind; I was dependent on none, and related to none. 'The path of my departure was free'; and there was none to lament my annihilation. My person was hideous, and my stature gigantic: what did this mean? Who was I? What was I? Whence did I come? What was my destination? These questions continually recurred, but I was unable to solve them.[30]

30. Who are we really? What are we made of? What is the self? What makes the creation a monster? Of course, answers to the latter question depend on how we define the term *monster*. Victor makes his creation by sewing together the body parts of many individuals, leaving the creation unaware of his own identity. The creature's composite nature, his lack of a singular physical and mental identity, is an important aspect of his monstrosity.

Our current scientific understanding of what we are made of can help us in understanding this idea of monstrosity. Humans and most other forms of life have a genetic conflict within them. This conflict arises from being composed of genetically distinct entities. For example, in "microchimerism," there are genetically distinct cells in a human body that come from a mother or an elder sibling (from the child's perspective) or from a child (from the mother's perspective). There are also genetically distinct gut microbiota, which can influence behavior, as can viral infections such as rabies. In these cases, our physiology and behavior can be influenced by genetically distinct entities that have fitness interests different from our own.

Taking Mary's idea of a monster and joining it with current knowledge about our genetically heterogeneous nature, we arrive at a potentially useful conception of a monster as an individual whose physiology and behavior are (fully or partially) under the control of a genetically distinct individual or population of individuals. Understanding ourselves as biologically heterogeneous, we can more easily and perhaps more sympathetically explore the idea of the monster's composite nature and Victor's struggle with his creation. Unlike Victor, we must face the fact that we are all monsters.

C. Athena Aktipis.

"The volume of *Plutarch's Lives* which I possessed, contained the histories of the first founders of the ancient republics. This book had a far different effect upon me from the *Sorrows of Werter.* I learned from Werter's imaginations despondency and gloom: but Plutarch taught me high thoughts; he elevated me above the wretched sphere of my own reflections, to admire and love the heroes of past ages. Many things I read surpassed my understanding and experience. I had a very confused knowledge of kingdoms, wide extents of country, mighty rivers, and boundless seas. But I was perfectly unacquainted with towns, and large assemblages of men. The cottage of my protectors had been the only school in which I had studied human nature; but this book developed new and mightier scenes of action. I read of men concerned in public affairs governing or massacring their species. I felt the greatest ardour for virtue rise within me, and abhorrence for vice, as far as I understood the signification of those terms, relative as they were, as I applied them, to pleasure and pain alone. Induced by these feelings, I was of course led to admire peaceable law-givers, Numa, Solon, and Lycurgus, in preference to Romulus and Theseus. The patriarchal lives of my protectors caused these impressions to take a firm hold on my mind; perhaps, if my first introduction to humanity had been made by a young soldier, burning for glory and slaughter, I should have been imbued with different sensations.

"But *Paradise Lost* excited different and far deeper emotions. I read it, as I had read the other volumes which had fallen into my hands, as a true history. It moved every feeling of wonder and awe, that the picture of an omnipotent God warring with his creatures was capable of exciting. I often referred the several situations, as their similarity struck me, to my own. Like Adam, I was created apparently united by no link to any other being in existence; but his state was far different from mine in every other respect. He had come forth from the hands of God a perfect creature, happy and prosperous, guarded by the especial care of his Creator; he was allowed to converse with, and acquire knowledge from beings of a superior nature: but I was wretched, helpless, and alone. Many times I considered Satan as the fitter emblem of my condition; for often, like him, when I viewed the bliss of my protectors, the bitter gall of envy rose within me.

"Another circumstance strengthened and confirmed these feelings. Soon after my arrival in the hovel, I discovered some papers in the pocket of the dress which I had taken from your laboratory. At first I had neglected them; but now that I was able to decypher the characters in which they were written, I began to study them with diligence. It was your journal of the four months that preceded my creation. You minutely described in these papers every step you took in the progress of your work; this history was mingled with accounts of domestic occurrences. You, doubtless, recollect these papers. Here they are. Every thing is related in them which bears reference to my accursed origin; the whole detail of that series of disgusting circumstances which produced it is set in view; the minutest description of my odious and loathsome person is given, in language which painted your own horrors, and rendered mine ineffaceable. I sickened as I read. 'Hateful day when I received life!' I exclaimed in agony. 'Cursed creator! Why did you form a monster so hideous that even you turned from me in disgust? God in pity made man beautiful and alluring, after his own image; but my form is a filthy type of your's, more horrid from its very resemblance.[31] Satan had his companions, fellow-devils, to admire and encourage him; but I am solitary and detested.'

"These were the reflections of my hours of despondency and solitude; but when I contemplated the virtues of the cottagers, their amiable and benevolent dispositions, I persuaded myself that when they should become acquainted with my admiration of their virtues, they would compassionate me, and overlook my personal deformity. Could they turn from their door one, however monstrous, who solicited their compassion and friendship? I resolved, at least, not to despair, but in every way to fit myself for an interview with them which would decide my fate. I postponed this attempt for some months longer; for the importance attached to its success inspired me with a dread lest I should fail. Besides, I found that my understanding improved so much with every day's experience, that I was unwilling to commence this undertaking until a few more months should have added to my wisdom.

"Several changes, in the mean time, took place in the cottage. The presence of Safie diffused happiness among its inhabitants; and I also found that a greater degree of plenty reigned there. Felix and Agatha spent more time in amusement and conversation, and were assisted in their labours

31. Here Victor anticipates a problem confronting researchers in the fields of robotics and visual animation as well as related fields. Anyone trying to create lifelike representations of natural organisms will encounter what Japanese roboticist Masahiro Mori ([1970] 2012) calls the "uncanny valley." Humans can feel a strong empathetic connection to creatures that do not closely resemble us or other familiar living things. In film, for example, characters such as the robot Wall-E or the extraterrestrial E.T. gain our sympathy even though they look unfamiliar. But as representations get closer to the human form, they can enter the "uncanny valley," where slight aberrations from our expectations can generate feelings of aversion or disgust.

Mary suggests here that the creature's ugliness derives not from his difference so much as from his uncanny similarity to humans. See also Alfred Nordmann's essay "Undisturbed by Reality" in this volume, which discusses the origins of the notion of the uncanny.

Ed Finn.

by servants. They did not appear rich, but they were contented and happy; their feelings were serene and peaceful, while mine became every day more tumultuous. Increase of knowledge only discovered to me more clearly what a wretched outcast I was. I cherished hope, it is true; but it vanished, when I beheld my person reflected in water, or my shadow in the moonshine, even as that frail image and that inconstant shade.

"I endeavoured to crush these fears, and to fortify myself for the trial which in a few months I resolved to undergo; and sometimes I allowed my thoughts, unchecked by reason, to ramble in the fields of Paradise, and dared to fancy amiable and lovely creatures sympathizing with my feelings and cheering my gloom; their angelic countenances breathed smiles of consolation. But it was all a dream: no Eve soothed my sorrows, or shared my thoughts; I was alone. I remembered Adam's supplication to his Creator; but where was mine? he had abandoned me, and, in the bitterness of my heart, I cursed him.

"Autumn passed thus. I saw, with surprise and grief, the leaves decay and fall, and nature again assume the barren and bleak appearance it had worn when I first beheld the woods and the lovely moon. Yet I did not heed the bleakness of the weather; I was better fitted by my conformation for the endurance of cold than heat. But my chief delights were the sight of the flowers, the birds, and all the gay apparel of summer; when those deserted me, I turned with more attention towards the cottagers. Their happiness was not decreased by the absence of summer. They loved, and sympathized with one another; and their joys, depending on each other, were not interrupted by the casualties that took place around them. The more I saw of them, the greater became my desire to claim their protection and kindness; my heart yearned to be known and loved by these amiable creatures: to see their sweet looks turned towards me with affection, was the utmost limit of my ambition.[32] I dared not think that they would turn them from me with disdain and horror. The poor that stopped at their door were never

32. Communion represents connection, a sharing or holding of things in common that is central to achieving our full humanity. Social scientists today refer to communion in terms of intimacy or perhaps love or even social support. Research has recently discovered what Mary intuited two centuries ago—positive relationships are what keep us healthy and happy. We experience the irony of watching Victor pursue his goal of creating life while isolating himself from what he later learns is most life-giving—communion with family, friends, and lovers. And though he gives biological life to his creation, he fails to give him what is most meaningful—communion. Many of us seem driven to try alternative means of happiness (creation of our own monsters, perhaps) before we realize that relationships are not superfluous but are instead essential in our lives. Victor's disdain for and rejection of his own creation (his dehumanization of the creation) become not only his own undoing but also the causal agent for the transfiguration of his creation's natural state of benevolence to one of violence (the creation's ill-guided attempts at discharging existential loneliness and pain).

driven away. I asked, it is true, for greater treasures than a little food or rest; I required kindness and sympathy; but I did not believe myself utterly unworthy of it.[33]

"The winter advanced, and an entire revolution of the seasons had taken place since I awoke into life. My attention, at this time, was solely directed towards my plan of introducing myself into the cottage of my protectors. I revolved many projects; but that on which I finally fixed was, to enter the dwelling when the blind old man should be alone. I had sagacity enough to discover, that the unnatural hideousness of my person was the chief object of horror with those who had formerly beheld me. My voice, although harsh, had nothing terrible in it; I thought, therefore, that if, in the absence of his children, I could gain the good-will and mediation of the old De Lacey, I might, by his means, be tolerated by my younger protectors.

Had Victor considered communion an essential part of "life," he would have changed the plight of his creation (who notes that communion, with even one person, would change his course) and his own plight. Mary artfully presents the human experience as a process of seeking communion and discharging the pain of disconnection. One is left to wonder if every person must endure loss before understanding the value of communion and whether today's inventors and innovators keep communion more central in their imaginations than Victor does.

Douglas Kelley.

33. Victor's creature has learned about humanity by observing humans and by reading poetry, classical philosophy, and a highly sentimental novel. He believes himself to be worthy of or at least not disqualified from receiving the kindly treatment that he has seen humans accord one another. He has evaluated himself and found himself human.

Self-esteem, the assessment of value that people give themselves and their own behavior, is a relatively recent psychological concept, dating from the late nineteenth century, and this passage can be interpreted as an example of the increased focus on the individual that is associated with the advent of romanticism. However, the process of evaluating one's behavior and ranking it relative to that of other people has been a human concern since the dawn of history. Self-esteem presupposes awareness of self; it may be related to survival-enhancing, neurologically based behaviors common to the many nonhuman social animals in whom self-awareness has been identified. Research has recently been directed at identifying self-esteem-like behavior in primates and other animals.

Victor's creature seems to have, in addition to the desire to evaluate his own behavior, the ability to judge the fairness of that behavior and the behavior of others: that is, he has a sense of justice. There is evidence that an understanding of fairness or equity is a trait shared by many animals, but research remains to be done to understand the mechanism by which various kinds of animals assess whether another's behavior is equitable or not. Even human concepts of justice can be vague and contradictory and may differ from one culture to another, just as individual humans' evaluation of their own behavior is not necessarily accurate and their opinion of themselves is not necessarily shared by others (see Blanchard and Blanchard 2003; Blanchard, Blanchard, and McKittrick 2001; Brosnan 2012; Christen and Glock 2012; and Heatherton and Vohs 2000).

Eileen Gunn.

"One day, when the sun shone on the red leaves that strewed the ground, and diffused cheerfulness, although it denied warmth, Safie, Agatha, and Felix, departed on a long country walk, and the old man, at his own desire, was left alone in the cottage. When his children had departed, he took up his guitar, and played several mournful, but sweet airs, more sweet and mournful than I had ever heard him play before. At first his countenance was illuminated with pleasure, but, as he continued, thoughtfulness and sadness succeeded; at length, laying aside the instrument, he sat absorbed in reflection.

"My heart beat quick; this was the hour and moment of trial, which would decide my hopes, or realize my fears. The servants were gone to a neighbouring fair. All was silent in and around the cottage: it was an excellent opportunity; yet, when I proceeded to execute my plan, my limbs failed me, and I sunk to the ground. Again I rose; and, exerting all the firmness of which I was master, removed the planks which I had placed before my hovel to conceal my retreat. The fresh air revived me, and, with renewed determination, I approached the door of their cottage.

"I knocked. 'Who is there?' said the old man—'Come in.'

"I entered; 'Pardon this intrusion,' said I, 'I am a traveller in want of a little rest; you would greatly oblige me, if you would allow me to remain a few minutes before the fire.'

"'Enter,' said De Lacey; 'and I will try in what manner I can relieve your wants; but, unfortunately, my children are from home, and, as I am blind, I am afraid I shall find it difficult to procure food for you.'

"'Do not trouble yourself, my kind host, I have food; it is warmth and rest only that I need.'

"I sat down, and a silence ensued. I knew that every minute was precious to me, yet I remained irresolute in what manner to commence the interview; when the old man addressed me—

"'By your language, stranger, I suppose you are my countryman;—are you French?'

"'No; but I was educated by a French family, and understand that language only. I am now going to claim the protection of some friends, whom I sincerely love, and of whose favour I have some hopes.'

"'Are these Germans?'

"'No, they are French. But let us change the subject. I am an unfortunate and deserted creature; I look around, and I have no relation or friend upon earth. These amiable people to whom I go have never seen me, and know little of me. I am full of fears; for if I fail there, I am an outcast in the world for ever.'

"Do not despair. To be friendless is indeed to be unfortunate; but the hearts of men, when unprejudiced by any obvious self-interest, are full of brotherly love and charity. Rely, therefore, on your hopes; and if these friends are good and amiable, do not despair.'[34]

"They are kind—they are the most excellent creatures in the world; but, unfortunately, they are prejudiced against me. I have good dispositions; my life has been hitherto harmless, and, in some degree, beneficial; but a fatal prejudice clouds their eyes, and where they ought to see a feeling and kind friend, they behold only a detestable monster.'

"That is indeed unfortunate; but if you are really blameless, cannot you undeceive them?'

"I am about to undertake that task; and it is on that account that I feel so many overwhelming terrors. I tenderly love these friends; I have, unknown to them, been for many months in the habits of daily kindness towards them; but they believe that I wish to injure them, and it is that prejudice which I wish to overcome.'

"Where do these friends reside?'

"Near this spot.'

"The old man paused, and then continued, 'If you will unreservedly confide to me the particulars of your tale, I perhaps may be of use in undeceiving them. I am blind, and cannot judge of your countenance, but there is something in your words which persuades me that you are sincere. I am poor, and an exile; but it will afford me true pleasure to be in any way serviceable to a human creature.'

"Excellent man! I thank you, and accept your generous offer. You raise me from the dust by this kindness; and I trust that, by your aid, I shall not be driven from the society and sympathy of your fellow-creatures.'

---

34. Animal behavior has been shaped by millions of years of evolution. As animals, humans have some behaviors that are conserved and shared with many other species. Fear, for example, is common in the animal kingdom, and it serves a useful purpose by making sure we stay out of dangerous situations. Similarly, selfishness, or the focus on getting the resources we need to survive, is something life has practiced since it began. But what about love? And compassion? What about altruism? Are humans the only creatures to do things that benefit others but don't directly benefit themselves? No. It turns out that altruistic behavior is observed across life— from the prairie dog that will alert its neighbors to a nearby predator (but in doing so puts itself at risk) to slime molds that live most of their lives as single cells but must decide to cooperate if they are to reproduce (and in making that decision become part of the 20 percent that sacrifice themselves). Like many other life forms, humans may be selfish at times but have a tremendous capacity to put the needs of others before themselves. The question is, under what circumstances?

Melissa Wilson Sayres.

"'Heaven forbid! even if you were really criminal; for that can only drive you to desperation, and not instigate you to virtue. I also am unfortunate; I and my family have been condemned, although innocent: judge, therefore, if I do not feel for your misfortunes.'

"'How can I thank you, my best and only benefactor? from your lips first have I heard the voice of kindness directed towards me; I shall be for ever grateful; and your present humanity assures me of success with those friends whom I am on the point of meeting.'

"'May I know the names and residence of those friends?'

"I paused. This, I thought, was the moment of decision, which was to rob me of, or bestow happiness on me for ever. I struggled vainly for firmness sufficient to answer him, but the effort destroyed all my remaining strength; I sank on the chair, and sobbed aloud. At that moment I heard the steps of my younger protectors. I had not a moment to lose; but, seizing the hand of the old man, I cried, 'Now is the time!—save and protect me! You and your family are the friends whom I seek. Do not you desert me in the hour of trial!'

"'Great God!' exclaimed the old man, 'who are you?'

"At that instant the cottage door was opened, and Felix, Safie, and Agatha entered. Who can describe their horror and consternation on beholding me? Agatha fainted; and Safie, unable to attend to her friend, rushed out of the cottage. Felix darted forward, and with supernatural force tore me from his father, to whose knees I clung: in a transport of fury, he dashed me to the ground, and struck me violently with a stick. I could have torn him limb from limb, as the lion rends the antelope. But my heart sunk within me as with bitter sickness, and I refrained. I saw him on the point of repeating his blow, when, overcome by pain and anguish, I quitted the cottage, and in the general tumult escaped unperceived to my hovel.

CHAPTER VIII.

"Cursed, cursed creator! Why did I live? Why, in that instant, did I not extinguish the spark of existence which you had so wantonly bestowed? I know not; despair had not yet taken possession of me; my feelings were those of rage and revenge. I could with pleasure have destroyed the cottage and its inhabitants, and have glutted myself with their shrieks and misery.

"When night came, I quitted my retreat, and wandered in the wood; and now, no longer restrained by the fear of discovery, I gave vent to my anguish in fearful howlings. I was like a wild beast that had broken the toils; destroying the objects that obstructed me, and ranging through the wood with a stag-like swiftness. Oh! what a miserable night I passed! the cold stars shone in mockery, and the bare trees waved their branches above me: now and then the sweet voice of a bird burst forth amidst the universal stillness. All, save I, were at rest or in enjoyment: I, like the arch fiend, bore a hell within me; and, finding myself unsympathized with, wished to tear up the trees, spread havoc and destruction around me, and then to have sat down and enjoyed the ruin.

"But this was a luxury of sensation that could not endure; I became fatigued with excess of bodily exertion, and sank on the damp grass in the sick impotence of despair. There was none among the myriads of men that existed who would pity or assist me; and should I feel kindness towards my enemies? No: from that moment I declared everlasting war against the species, and, more than all, against him who had formed me, and sent me forth to this insupportable misery.[35]

"The sun rose; I heard the voices of men, and knew that it was impossible to return to my retreat during that day. Accordingly I hid myself in some thick underwood, determining to devote the ensuing hours to reflection on my situation.

"The pleasant sunshine, and the pure air of day, restored me to some degree of tranquillity; and when I considered what had passed at the cottage, I could not help believing that I had been too hasty in my conclusions. I had certainly acted imprudently. It was apparent that my conversation had interested the father in my behalf, and I was a fool in having exposed my person to the horror of his children. I ought to have familiarized the old De Lacey to me, and by degrees have discovered myself to the rest of his family, when they should have been prepared for my approach. But I did not believe my errors to be irretrievable; and, after much consideration, I resolved to return to the cottage, seek the old man, and by my representations win him to my party.

35. In this turning point, the creature no longer figures himself as an Adam, the first being of a new creation of humans or humanoids; rather, he opts to be like Milton's Satan, of whom he has read. The epic poem *Paradise Lost* (Milton [1667] 2007) recounts the fall of the angel Satan, who does battle with God, is exiled from heaven, and plots his revenge against his creator with the temptation of Adam and Eve to eat from the forbidden Tree of Knowledge. Sentenced by God to hell, Milton's Satan is determined to make a heaven of his hell and to revel in his punishment, which he sees as unjust. In Mary's story, the creature, having exhausted the limits of reason and compassion when he receives no kindness from humans, cuts himself off from the human race and becomes the antagonist of humankind.

Ron Broglio.

"These thoughts calmed me, and in the afternoon I sank into a profound sleep; but the fever of my blood did not allow me to be visited by peaceful dreams. The horrible scene of the preceding day was for ever acting before my eyes; the females were flying, and the enraged Felix tearing me from his father's feet. I awoke exhausted; and, finding that it was already night, I crept forth from my hiding-place, and went in search of food.

"When my hunger was appeased, I directed my steps towards the well-known path that conducted to the cottage. All there was at peace. I crept into my hovel, and remained in silent expectation of the accustomed hour when the family arose. That hour past, the sun mounted high in the heavens, but the cottagers did not appear. I trembled violently, apprehending some dreadful misfortune. The inside of the cottage was dark, and I heard no motion; I cannot describe the agony of this suspence.

"Presently two countrymen passed by; but, pausing near the cottage, they entered into conversation, using violent gesticulations; but I did not understand what they said, as they spoke the language of the country, which differed from that of my protectors. Soon after, however, Felix approached with another man: I was surprised, as I knew that he had not quitted the cottage that morning, and waited anxiously to discover, from his discourse, the meaning of these unusual appearances.

"'Do you consider,' said his companion to him, 'that you will be obliged to pay three months' rent, and to lose the produce of your garden? I do not wish to take any unfair advantage, and I beg therefore that you will take some days to consider of your determination.'

"'It is utterly useless,' replied Felix, 'we can never again inhabit your cottage. The life of my father is in the greatest danger, owing to the dreadful circumstance that I have related. My wife and my sister will never recover [from] their horror. I entreat you not to reason with me any more. Take possession of your tenement, and let me fly from this place.'

"Felix trembled violently as he said this. He and his companion entered the cottage, in which they remained for a few minutes, and then departed. I never saw any of the family of De Lacey more.

"I continued for the remainder of the day in my hovel in a state of utter and stupid despair. My protectors had departed, and had broken the only link that held me to the world. For the first time the feelings of revenge and hatred filled my bosom, and I did not strive to controul them; but, allowing myself to be borne away by the stream, I bent my mind towards injury and death. When I thought of my friends, of the mild voice of De Lacey, the gentle eyes of Agatha, and the exquisite beauty of the Arabian, these thoughts vanished, and a gush of tears somewhat soothed me. But again, when I reflected that they had spurned and deserted me, anger returned, a rage of anger; and, unable to injure any thing human, I turned my fury towards inanimate objects. As night advanced, I placed a variety of combustibles around the cottage; and, after having destroyed every vestige of cultivation in the garden, I waited with forced impatience until the moon had sunk to commence my operations.

"As the night advanced, a fierce wind arose from the woods, and quickly dispersed the clouds that had loitered in the heavens: the blast tore along like a mighty avalanche, and produced a kind of insanity in my spirits, that burst all bounds of reason and reflection. I lighted the dry branch of a tree, and danced with fury around the devoted cottage, my eyes still fixed on the western horizon, the edge of which the moon nearly touched. A part of its orb was at length hid, and I waved my brand; it sunk, and, with a loud scream, I fired the straw, and heath, and bushes, which I had collected. The wind fanned the fire, and the cottage was quickly enveloped by the flames, which clung to it, and licked it with their forked and destroying tongues.

"As soon as I was convinced that no assistance could save any part of the habitation, I quitted the scene, and sought for refuge in the woods.

"And now, with the world before me, whither should I bend my steps? I resolved to fly far from the scene of my misfortunes; but to me, hated and despised, every country must be equally horrible. At length the thought of you crossed my mind. I learned from your papers that you were my father, my creator; and to whom could I apply with more fitness than to him who had given me life? Among the lessons that Felix had bestowed upon Safie geography had not been omitted: I had learned from these the relative situations of the different countries of the earth. You had mentioned Geneva as the name of your native town; and towards this place I resolved to proceed.

"But how was I to direct myself? I knew that I must travel in a southwesterly direction to reach my destination; but the sun was my only guide. I did not know the names of the towns that I was to pass through, nor could I ask information from a single human being; but I did not despair. From you only could I hope for succour, although towards you I felt no sentiment but that of hatred. Unfeeling, heartless creator! you had endowed me with perceptions and passions, and then cast me abroad an object for the scorn and horror of mankind. But on you only had I any claim for pity and redress, and from you I determined to seek that justice which I vainly attempted to gain from any other being that wore the human form.

"My travels were long, and the sufferings I endured intense. It was late in autumn when I quitted the district where I had so long resided. I travelled only at night, fearful of encountering the visage of a human being. Nature decayed around me, and the sun became heatless; rain and snow poured around me; mighty rivers were frozen; the surface of the earth was hard, and chill, and bare, and I found no shelter. Oh, earth! how often did I imprecate curses on the cause of my being! The mildness of my nature had fled, and all within me was turned to gall and bitterness. The nearer I approached to your habitation, the more deeply did I feel the spirit of revenge enkindled in my heart. Snow fell, and the waters were hardened, but I rested not. A few incidents now and then directed me, and I possessed a map of the country; but I often wandered wide from my path. The agony of my feelings allowed me no respite: no incident occurred from which my rage and misery could not extract its food; but a circumstance that happened when I arrived on the confines of Switzerland, when the sun had recovered its warmth, and the earth again began to look green, confirmed in an especial manner the bitterness and horror of my feelings.

"I generally rested during the day, and travelled only when I was secured by night from the view of man. One morning, however, finding that my path lay through a deep wood, I ventured to continue my journey after the sun had risen; the day, which was one of the first of spring, cheered even me by the loveliness of its sunshine and the balminess of the air. I felt emotions of gentleness and pleasure, that had long appeared dead, revive within me. Half surprised by the novelty of these sensations, I allowed myself to be borne away by them; and, forgetting my solitude and deformity, dared to be happy. Soft tears again bedewed my cheeks, and I even raised my humid eyes with thankfulness towards the blessed sun which bestowed such joy upon me.

"I continued to wind among the paths of the wood, until I came to its boundary, which was skirted by a deep and rapid river, into which many of the trees bent their branches, now budding with the fresh spring. Here I paused, not exactly knowing what path to pursue, when I heard the sound of voices, that induced me to conceal myself under the shade of a cypress. I was scarcely hid, when a young girl came running towards the spot where I was concealed, laughing as if she ran from some one in sport. She continued her course along the precipitous sides of the river, when suddenly her foot slipt, and she fell into the rapid stream. I rushed from my hiding place, and, with extreme labour from the force of the current, saved her, and dragged her to shore. She was senseless; and I endeavoured, by every means in my power, to restore animation, when I was suddenly interrupted by the approach of a rustic, who was probably the person from whom she had playfully fled. On seeing me, he darted towards me, and, tearing the girl from my arms, hastened towards the deeper parts of the wood. I followed speedily, I hardly knew why; but when the man saw me draw near, he aimed a gun, which he carried, at my body, and fired. I sunk to the ground, and my injurer, with increased swiftness, escaped into the wood.

"This was then the reward of my benevolence! I had saved a human being from destruction, and, as a recompence, I now writhed under the miserable pain of a wound, which shattered the flesh and bone. The feelings of kindness and gentleness, which I had entertained but a few moments before, gave place to hellish rage and gnashing of teeth. Inflamed by pain, I vowed eternal hatred and vengeance to all mankind. But the agony of my wound overcame me; my pulses paused, and I fainted.

"For some weeks I led a miserable life in the woods, endeavouring to cure the wound which I had received. The ball had entered my shoulder, and I knew not whether it had remained there or passed through; at any rate I had no means of extracting it. My sufferings were augmented also by the oppressive sense of the injustice and ingratitude of their infliction. My daily vows rose for revenge—a deep and deadly revenge, such as would alone compensate for the outrages and anguish I had endured.

"After some weeks my wound healed, and I continued my journey. The labours I endured were no longer to be alleviated by the bright sun or gentle breezes of spring; all joy was but a mockery, which insulted my desolate state, and made me feel more painfully that I was not made for the enjoyment of pleasure.

"But my toils now drew near a close; and, two months from this time, I reached the environs of Geneva.

"It was evening when I arrived, and I retired to a hiding-place among the fields that surround it, to meditate in what manner I should apply to you. I was oppressed by fatigue and hunger, and far too unhappy to enjoy the gentle breezes of evening, or the prospect of the sun setting behind the stupendous mountains of Jura.

"At this time a slight sleep relieved me from the pain of reflection, which was disturbed by the approach of a beautiful child, who came running into the recess I had chosen with all the sportiveness of infancy. Suddenly, as I gazed on him, an idea seized me, that this little creature was unprejudiced, and had lived too short a time to have imbibed a horror of deformity. If, therefore, I could seize him, and educate him as my companion and friend, I should not be so desolate in this peopled earth.

"Urged by this impulse, I seized on the boy as he passed, and drew him towards me. As soon as he beheld my form, he placed his hands before his eyes, and uttered a shrill scream: I drew his hand forcibly from his face, and said, 'Child, what is the meaning of this? I do not intend to hurt you; listen to me.'

"He struggled violently; 'Let me go,' he cried; 'monster! ugly wretch! you wish to eat me, and tear me to pieces—You are an ogre—Let me go, or I will tell my papa.'

"'Boy, you will never see your father again; you must come with me.'

"'Hideous monster! let me go. My papa is a Syndic—he is M. Frankenstein—he would punish you. You dare not keep me.'

"'Frankenstein! you belong then to my enemy—to him towards whom I have sworn eternal revenge; you shall be my first victim.'

"The child still struggled, and loaded me with epithets which carried despair to my heart: I grasped his throat to silence him, and in a moment he lay dead at my feet.

"I gazed on my victim, and my heart swelled with exultation and hellish triumph: clapping my hands, I exclaimed, 'I, too, can create desolation; my enemy is not impregnable; this death will carry despair to him, and a thousand other miseries shall torment and destroy him.'

"As I fixed my eyes on the child, I saw something glittering on his breast. I took it; it was a portrait of a most lovely woman. In spite of my malignity, it softened and attracted me. For a few moments I gazed with delight on her dark eyes, fringed by deep lashes, and her lovely lips; but presently my rage returned: I remembered that I was for ever deprived of the delights that such beautiful creatures could bestow; and that she whose resemblance I contemplated would, in regarding me, have changed that air of divine benignity to one expressive of disgust and affright.

"Can you wonder that such thoughts transported me with rage? I only wonder that at that moment, instead of venting my sensations in exclamations and agony, I did not rush among mankind, and perish in the attempt to destroy them.

"While I was overcome by these feelings, I left the spot where I had committed the murder, and was seeking a more secluded hiding-place, when I perceived a woman passing near me. She was young, not indeed so beautiful as her whose portrait I held, but of an agreeable aspect, and blooming in the loveliness of youth and health. Here, I thought, is one of those whose smiles are bestowed on all but me; she shall not escape: thanks to the lessons of Felix, and the sanguinary laws of man, I have learned how to work mischief. I approached her unperceived, and placed the portrait securely in one of the folds of her dress.

"For some days I haunted the spot where these scenes had taken place; sometimes wishing to see you, sometimes resolved to quit the world and its miseries for ever. At length I wandered towards these mountains, and have ranged through their immense recesses, consumed by a burning passion which you alone can gratify. We may not part until you have promised to comply with my requisition. I am alone, and miserable; man will not associate with me; but one as deformed and horrible as myself would not deny herself to me.[36] My companion must be of the same species, and have the same defects. This being you must create."

CHAPTER IX.

The being finished speaking, and fixed his looks upon me in expectation of a reply. But I was bewildered, perplexed, and unable to arrange my ideas sufficiently to understand the full extent of his proposition. He continued—

"You must create a female for me, with whom I can live in the interchange of those sympathies necessary for my being. This you alone can do; and I demand it of you as a right which you must not refuse."

The latter part of his tale had kindled anew in me the anger that had died away while he narrated his peaceful life among the cottagers, and, as he said this, I could no longer suppress the rage that burned within me.

"I do refuse it," I replied; "and no torture shall ever extort a consent from me. You may render me the most miserable of men, but you shall never make me base in my own eyes. Shall I create another like yourself, whose joint wickedness might desolate the world. Begone! I have answered you; you may torture me, but I will never consent."

"You are in the wrong," replied the fiend; "and, instead of threatening, I am content to reason with you. I am malicious because I am miserable; am I not shunned and hated by all mankind? You, my creator, would tear me to pieces, and triumph; remember that, and tell me why I should pity man more than he pities me? You would not call it murder, if you could precipitate me into one of those ice-rifts, and destroy my frame, the work of your own hands. Shall I respect man, when he contemns me? Let him live with me in the interchange of kindness, and, instead of injury, I would bestow every benefit upon him with tears of gratitude at his acceptance. But that cannot be; the human senses are insurmountable barriers to our union.

---

36. In furthering the parallel between Victor and the creature and elucidating Mary's feminist themes, the creature wants to instrumentalize the power to create life by having Victor make him a mate who "would not deny herself to me" and would thus satisfy his own selfish feelings of longing. David H. Guston.

Yet mine shall not be the submission of abject slavery. I will revenge my injuries: if I cannot inspire love, I will cause fear; and chiefly towards you my arch-enemy, because my creator, do I swear inextinguishable hatred. Have a care: I will work at your destruction, nor finish until I desolate your heart, so that you curse the hour of your birth."

A fiendish rage animated him as he said this; his face was wrinkled into contortions too horrible for human eyes to behold; but presently he calmed himself, and proceeded—

"I intended to reason. This passion is detrimental to me; for you do not reflect that you are the cause of its excess. If any being felt emotions of benevolence towards me, I should return them an hundred and an hundred fold; for that one creature's sake, I would make peace with the whole kind! But I now indulge in dreams of bliss that cannot be realized. What I ask of you is reasonable and moderate; I demand a creature of another sex, but as hideous as myself: the gratification is small, but it is all that I can receive, and it shall content me. It is true, we shall be monsters, cut off from all the world; but on that account we shall be more attached to one another. Our lives will not be happy, but they will be harmless, and free from the misery I now feel. Oh! my creator, make me happy; let me feel gratitude towards you for one benefit! Let me see that I excite the sympathy of some existing thing; do not deny me my request!"

I was moved. I shuddered when I thought of the possible consequences of my consent; but I felt that there was some justice in his argument. His tale, and the feelings he now expressed, proved him to be a creature of fine sensations; and did I not, as his maker, owe him all the portion of happiness that it was in my power to bestow? He saw my change of feeling, and continued—

"If you consent, neither you nor any other human being shall ever see us again: I will go to the vast wilds of South America. My food is not that of man; I do not destroy the lamb and the kid, to glut my appetite; acorns and berries afford me sufficient nourishment. My companion will be of the same nature as myself, and will be content with the same fare. We shall make our bed of dried leaves; the sun will shine on us as on man, and will ripen our food. The picture I present to you is peaceful and human, and you must feel that you could deny it only in the wantonness of power and cruelty. Pitiless as you have been towards me, I now see compassion in your eyes; let me seize the favourable moment, and persuade you to promise what I so ardently desire."

"You propose," replied I, "to fly from the habitations of man, to dwell in those wilds where the beasts of the field will be your only companions. How can you, who long for the love and sympathy[37] of man, persevere in this exile? You will return, and again seek their kindness, and you will meet with their detestation; your evil passions will be renewed, and you will then have a companion to aid you in the task of destruction. This may not be; cease to argue the point, for I cannot consent."

"How inconstant are your feelings! but a moment ago you were moved by my representations, and why do you again harden yourself to my complaints? I swear to you, by the earth which I inhabit, and by you that made me, that, with the companion you bestow, I will quit the neighbourhood of man, and dwell, as it may chance, in the most savage of places. My evil passions will have fled, for I shall meet with sympathy; my life will flow quietly away, and, in my dying moments, I shall not curse my maker."

His words had a strange effect upon me. I compassionated him, and sometimes felt a wish to console him; but when I looked upon him, when

---

37. The term *sympathy* had multiple meanings in the early nineteenth century, some of which resonate with scientific discourse and some with moral philosophy. The word did mean then what we take it to mean today—a kind of entering into the feelings of another. But it also had embodied, somatic connotations. In *On Sympathy* (2008), Sophie Radcliffe puts it this way: "The uncertainty as to whether 'sympathy' exists as a somatic feeling in itself or as a state of mind resulting from an act of cognition persists through the nineteenth and twentieth centuries, with terms and ideas from scientific discourses drifting into literary works and vice versa" (10).

We can see this view in a definition of the word that is now out of use but was current at the time Mary was writing: "a relation between two bodily organs or parts (or between two persons) such that disorder, or any condition, of the one induces a corresponding condition in the other" (*Oxford English Dictionary*). There was also a question then of whether sympathy is gendered—whether women's minds or bodies are more readily able to engage in admirable moments of communion of feeling as a result of their supposedly shared characteristics of body, mind, or experience. Mothers, in particular, were imagined as having superior abilities for sympathy due to their roles in creating, giving birth to, and raising children. Other questions were posed: Are scientists (largely conceived of as men, as in this novel) capable of engaging in (stereotypically feminine, maternal) sympathy? What do their scientific judgments or achievements lack if they do not have access to the right kind or levels of sympathy, whether from lack of experience or from supposedly biological shortcomings?

Throughout *Frankenstein*, invocations of "sympathy," then, ask readers to investigate what causes a community of feeling among people or creatures and what that feeling means in the act of creating and nurturing new life. Does sympathy arise from the mind? Is it learned through education and the exercise of judgment? In that case, can anyone be taught it? Or does sympathy arise from the body, whether imagined as universally "human" (in which case the creature is a liminal kind) or as differentiated by sex or gender? Mary enters into these debates in her day and, as in this passage, seems to suggest that sympathy fails when there is a lack of identification with the other. This failure, as it relates to the creature, may be read as arising either from the mind or from the body or as arising either from a somatic lack in men or from a somatic lack in humans. Mary does not offer easy answers and leaves many questions for the reader to engage and trouble over in considering where necessary sympathy properly comes from, how it can be exercised, and how it has an impact on scientific discovery.

Devoney Looser.

I saw the filthy mass that moved and talked, my heart sickened, and my feelings were altered to those of horror and hatred. I tried to stifle these sensations; I thought, that as I could not sympathize with him, I had no right to withhold from him the small portion of happiness which was yet in my power to bestow.

"You swear," I said, "to be harmless; but have you not already shewn a degree of malice that should reasonably make me distrust you? May not even this be a feint that will increase your triumph by affording a wider scope for your revenge?"[38]

"How is this? I thought I had moved your compassion, and yet you still refuse to bestow on me the only benefit that can soften my heart, and render me harmless. If I have no ties and no affections, hatred and vice must be my portion; the love of another will destroy the cause of my crimes, and I shall become a thing, of whose existence every one will be ignorant. My vices are the children of a forced solitude that I abhor; and my virtues will necessarily arise when I live in communion with an equal. I shall feel the affections of a sensitive being, and become linked to the chain of existence and events, from which I am now excluded."

I paused some time to reflect on all he had related, and the various arguments which he had employed. I thought of the promise of virtues which he had displayed on the opening of his existence, and the subsequent blight of all kindly feeling by the loathing and scorn which his protectors had manifested towards him. His power and threats were not omitted in my calculations: a creature who could exist in the ice caves of the glaciers, and hide himself from pursuit among the ridges of inaccessible precipices, was a being possessing faculties it would be vain to cope with. After a long pause of reflection, I concluded, that the justice due both to him and my fellow-creatures demanded of me that I should comply with his request. Turning to him, therefore, I said—

"I consent to your demand, on your solemn oath to quit Europe for ever, and every other place in the neighbourhood of man, as soon as I shall deliver into your hands a female who will accompany you in your exile."

38. Victor has reason to distrust the creature. As in Aesop's fable of the boy who cries wolf, once trust is lost, it is difficult to rebuild. Here Victor is moved to compassion by the creature's request, but he remembers the evil acts the creature has performed and now wonders if he can believe anything the creature says. Consider the research claims of scientists who have been caught in a lie—every claim after the lie is suddenly suspect, regardless of its authenticity. For example, Hwang Woo-suk, a Korean scientist, fraudulently claimed he had created human embryonic stem cells through cloning, so his return to the scientific world of cloning has been reduced to the cloning of animals.

Mary Drago.

"I swear," he cried, "by the sun, and by the blue sky of heaven, that if you grant my prayer, while they exist you shall never behold me again. Depart to your home, and commence your labours: I shall watch their progress with unutterable anxiety; and fear not but that when you are ready I shall appear."

Saying this, he suddenly quitted me, fearful, perhaps, of any change in my sentiments. I saw him descend the mountain with greater speed than the flight of an eagle, and quickly lost him among the undulations of the sea of ice.

His tale had occupied the whole day; and the sun was upon the verge of the horizon when he departed. I knew that I ought to hasten my descent towards the valley, as I should soon be encompassed in darkness; but my heart was heavy, and my steps slow. The labour of winding among the little paths of the mountains, and fixing my feet firmly as I advanced, perplexed me, occupied as I was by the emotions which the occurrences of the day had produced. Night was far advanced, when I came to the half-way resting-place, and seated myself beside the fountain. The stars shone at intervals, as the clouds passed from over them; the dark pines rose before me, and every here and there a broken tree lay on the ground: it was a scene of wonderful solemnity, and stirred strange thoughts within me. I wept bitterly; and, clasping my hands in agony, I exclaimed, "Oh! stars, and clouds, and winds, ye are all about to mock me: if ye really pity me, crush sensation and memory; let me become as nought; but if not, depart, depart and leave me in darkness."

These were wild and miserable thoughts; but I cannot describe to you how the eternal twinkling of the stars weighed upon me, and how I listened to every blast of wind, as if it were a dull ugly siroc on its way to consume me.

Morning dawned before I arrived at the village of Chamounix; but my presence, so haggard and strange, hardly calmed the fears of my family, who had waited the whole night in anxious expectation of my return.

The following day we returned to Geneva. The intention of my father in coming had been to divert my mind, and to restore me to my lost tranquillity; but the medicine had been fatal. And, unable to account for the excess of misery I appeared to suffer, he hastened to return home, hoping the quiet and monotony of a domestic life would by degrees alleviate my sufferings from whatsoever cause they might spring.

For myself, I was passive in all their arrangements; and the gentle affection of my beloved Elizabeth was inadequate to draw me from the depth of my despair. The promise I had made to the dæmon weighed upon my mind, like Dante's iron cowl on the heads of the hellish hypocrites. All pleasures of earth and sky passed before me like a dream, and that thought only had to me the reality of life. Can you wonder, that sometimes a kind of insanity possessed me, or that I saw continually about me a multitude of filthy animals inflicting on me incessant torture, that often extorted screams and bitter groans?

By degrees, however, these feelings became calmed. I entered again into the every-day scene of life, if not with interest, at least with some degree of tranquillity.

END OF VOL. II.

CHAPTER I.

Day after day, week after week, passed away on my return to Geneva; and I could not collect the courage to recommence my work. I feared the vengeance of the disappointed fiend, yet I was unable to overcome my repugnance to the task which was enjoined me.[1] I found that I could not compose a female without again devoting several months to profound study and laborious disquisition. I had heard of some discoveries having been made by an English philosopher, the knowledge of which was material to my success, and I sometimes thought of obtaining my father's consent to visit England for this purpose; but I clung to every pretence of delay, and could not resolve to interrupt my returning tranquillity. My health, which had hitherto declined, was now much restored; and my spirits, when unchecked by the memory of my unhappy promise, rose proportionably. My father saw this change with pleasure, and he turned his thoughts towards the best method of eradicating the remains of my melancholy, which every now and then would return by fits, and with a devouring blackness overcast the approaching sunshine. At these moments I took refuge in the most perfect solitude. I passed whole days on the lake alone in a little boat, watching the clouds, and listening to the rippling of the waves, silent and listless. But the fresh air and bright sun seldom failed to restore me to some degree of composure; and, on my return, I met the salutations of my friends with a readier smile and a more cheerful heart.

It was after my return from one of these rambles that my father, calling me aside, thus addressed me:—

"I am happy to remark, my dear son, that you have resumed your former pleasures, and seem to be returning to yourself. And yet you are still unhappy, and still avoid our society. For some time I was lost in conjecture as to the cause of this; but yesterday an idea struck me, and if it is well founded, I conjure you to avow it. Reserve on such a point would be not only useless, but draw down treble misery on us all."

---

1. Victor and his interlocutor, Walton, appear to consider courage to be one of the more mechanical human attributes, one that is shared by some of the lower animals. To be courageous is a means to an end rather than something to be admired in and of itself, or Victor would doubtless have had greater admiration for the creature he creates, and Walton would have found a friend among the sailors of dauntless courage he hired in St. Petersburg. It is Victor's lack of courage that drives the plot for most of the novel. He finds himself motivated to action or inaction by fear, revulsion, and rage but never by courage. If he had the courage to deal directly with the consequences of his experiment, how much pain and grief could have been avoided?

Sean A. Hays.

I trembled violently at this exordium, and my father continued—

"I confess, my son, that I have always looked forward to your marriage with your cousin as the tie of our domestic comfort, and the stay of my declining years. You were attached to each other from your earliest infancy; you studied together, and appeared, in dispositions and tastes, entirely suited to one another. But so blind is the experience of man, that what I conceived to be the best assistants to my plan may have entirely destroyed it. You, perhaps, regard her as your sister, without any wish that she might become your wife. Nay, you may have met with another whom you may love; and, considering yourself as bound in honour to your cousin, this struggle may occasion the poignant misery which you appear to feel."

"My dear father, re-assure yourself. I love my cousin tenderly and sincerely. I never saw any woman who excited, as Elizabeth does, my warmest admiration and affection. My future hopes and prospects are entirely bound up in the expectation of our union."

"The expression of your sentiments on this subject, my dear Victor, gives me more pleasure than I have for some time experienced. If you feel thus, we shall assuredly be happy, however present events may cast a gloom over us. But it is this gloom, which appears to have taken so strong a hold of your mind, that I wish to dissipate. Tell me, therefore, whether you object to an immediate solemnization of the marriage. We have been unfortunate, and recent events have drawn us from that every-day tranquillity befitting my years and infirmities. You are younger; yet I do not suppose, possessed as you are of a competent fortune, that an early marriage would at all interfere with any future plans of honour and utility that you may have formed. Do not suppose, however, that I wish to dictate happiness to you, or that a delay on your part would cause me any serious uneasiness. Interpret my words with candour, and answer me, I conjure you, with confidence and sincerity."

I listened to my father in silence, and remained for some time incapable of offering any reply. I revolved rapidly in my mind a multitude of thoughts, and endeavoured to arrive at some conclusion. Alas! to me the idea of an immediate union with my cousin was one of horror and dismay. I was bound by a solemn promise, which I had not yet fulfilled, and dared not break; or, if I did, what manifold miseries might not impend over me and my devoted family! Could I enter into a festival with this deadly weight yet hanging round my neck, and bowing me to the ground. I must perform my engagement, and let the monster depart with his mate, before I allowed myself to enjoy the delight of an union from which I expected peace.

I remembered also the necessity imposed upon me of either journeying to England, or entering into a long correspondence with those philosophers of that country, whose knowledge and discoveries were of indispensable use to me in my present undertaking. The latter method of obtaining the desired intelligence was dilatory and unsatisfactory: besides, any variation was agreeable to me, and I was delighted with the idea of spending a year or two in change of scene and variety of occupation, in absence from my family; during which period some event might happen which would restore me to them in peace and happiness: my promise might be fulfilled, and the monster have departed; or some accident might occur to destroy him, and put an end to my slavery for ever.

These feelings dictated my answer to my father. I expressed a wish to visit England; but, concealing the true reasons of this request, I clothed my desires under the guise of wishing to travel and see the world before I sat down for life within the walls of my native town.

I urged my entreaty with earnestness, and my father was easily induced to comply; for a more indulgent and less dictatorial parent did not exist upon earth. Our plan was soon arranged. I should travel to Strasburgh, where Clerval would join me. Some short time would be spent in the towns of Holland, and our principal stay would be in England. We should return by France; and it was agreed that the tour should occupy the space of two years.

My father pleased himself with the reflection, that my union with Elizabeth should take place immediately on my return to Geneva. "These two years," said he, "will pass swiftly, and it will be the last delay that will oppose itself to your happiness. And, indeed, I earnestly desire that period to arrive, when we shall all be united, and neither hopes or fears arise to disturb our domestic calm."

"I am content," I replied, "with your arrangement. By that time we shall both have become wiser, and I hope happier, than we at present are." I sighed; but my father kindly forbore to question me further concerning the cause of my dejection, He hoped that new scenes, and the amusement of travelling, would restore my tranquillity.

I now made arrangements for my journey; but one feeling haunted me, which filled me with fear and agitation. During my absence I should leave my friends unconscious of the existence of their enemy, and unprotected from his attacks, exasperated as he might be by my departure. But he had promised to follow me wherever I might go; and would he not accompany me to England? This imagination was dreadful in itself, but soothing, inasmuch as it supposed the safety of my friends. I was agonized with the idea of the possibility that the reverse of this might happen. But through the whole period during which I was the slave of my creature, I allowed myself to be governed by the impulses of the moment;[2] and my present sensations strongly intimated that the fiend would follow me, and exempt my family from the danger of his machinations.

It was in the latter end of August that I departed, to pass two years of exile. Elizabeth approved of the reasons of my departure, and only regretted that she had not the same opportunities of enlarging her experience, and cultivating her understanding.[3] She wept, however, as she bade me farewell, and entreated me to return happy and tranquil. "We all," said she, "depend upon you; and if you are miserable, what must be our feelings?"

I threw myself into the carriage that was to convey me away, hardly knowing whither I was going, and careless of what was passing around. I remembered only, and it was with a bitter anguish that I reflected on it, to order that my chemical instruments should be packed to go with me: for I resolved to fulfil my promise while abroad, and return, if possible, a free man. Filled with dreary imaginations, I passed through many beautiful and majestic scenes; but my eyes were fixed and unobserving. I could only think of the bourne of my travels, and the work which was to occupy me whilst they endured.

After some days spent in listless indolence, during which I traversed many leagues, I arrived at Strasburgh, where I waited two days for Clerval. He came. Alas, how great was the contrast between us! He was alive to every new scene; joyful when he saw the beauties of the setting sun, and more happy when he beheld it rise, and recommence a new day. He pointed out to me the shifting colours of the landscape, and the appearances of the sky. "This is what it is to live"; he cried, "now I enjoy existence! But you, my dear Frankenstein, wherefore are you desponding and sorrowful?"

---

2. As a slave, Victor has lost the capacity to reason through problems and is instead "governed by the impulses of the moment." He recognizes the phenomenon in himself—that one's capacities are shaped by one's social position and relations—but he does not reflect fully on that recognition and allow for it to influence his assessment of the creature.
David H. Guston.

3. In this passage, Mary could be reflecting on her own situation and the social pressures that might have hemmed her in. In theory, Elizabeth could choose, like Mary with Percy, to accompany her paramour in his travels, but in reality her obligations as the woman of Alphonse's house and her bourgeois upbringing make that choice impossible. Other logical possibilities—for example, Elizabeth proposing to Victor that they marry and take the trip together as a honeymoon—are also social impossibilities.
David H. Guston.

In truth, I was occupied by gloomy thoughts, and neither saw the descent of the evening star, nor the golden sun-rise reflected in the Rhine.—And you, my friend, would be far more amused with the journal of Clerval, who observed the scenery with an eye of feeling and delight, than to listen to my reflections. I, a miserable wretch, haunted by a curse that shut up every avenue to enjoyment.

We had agreed to descend the Rhine in a boat from Strasburgh to Rotterdam, whence we might take shipping for London. During this voyage, we passed by many willowy islands, and saw several beautiful towns. We staid a day at Manheim, and, on the fifth from our departure from Strasburgh, arrived at Mayence. The course of the Rhine below Mayence becomes much more picturesque. The river descends rapidly, and winds between hills, not high, but steep, and of beautiful forms. We saw many ruined castles standing on the edges of precipices, surrounded by black woods, high and inaccessible. This part of the Rhine, indeed, presents a singularly variegated landscape. In one spot you view rugged hills, ruined castles overlooking tremendous precipices, with the dark Rhine rushing beneath; and, on the sudden turn of a promontory, flourishing vineyards, with green sloping banks, and a meandering river, and populous towns, occupy the scene.

We travelled at the time of the vintage, and heard the song of the labourers, as we glided down the stream. Even I, depressed in mind, and my spirits continually agitated by gloomy feelings, even I was pleased. I lay at the bottom of the boat, and, as I gazed on the cloudless blue sky, I seemed to drink in a tranquillity to which I had long been a stranger. And if these were my sensations, who can describe those of Henry? He felt as if he had been transported to Fairy-land, and enjoyed a happiness seldom tasted by man. "I have seen," he said, "the most beautiful scenes of my own country; I have visited the lakes of Lucerne and Uri, where the snowy mountains descend almost perpendicularly to the water, casting black and impenetrable shades, which would cause a gloomy and mournful appearance, were it not for the most verdant islands that relieve the eye by their gay appearance; I have seen this lake agitated by a tempest, when the wind tore up whirlwinds of water, and gave you an idea of what the water-spout must be on the great ocean, and the waves dash with fury the base of the mountain, where the priest and his mistress were overwhelmed by an avalanche, and where their dying voices are still said to be heard amid the pauses of the nightly wind; I have seen the mountains of La Valais, and the Pays de Vaud: but this country, Victor, pleases me more than all those wonders. The mountains of Switzerland are more majestic and strange; but there is a charm in the banks of this divine river, that I never before saw equalled.

Look at that castle which overhangs yon precipice; and that also on the island, almost concealed amongst the foliage of those lovely trees; and now that group of labourers coming from among their vines; and that village half-hid in the recess of the mountain. Oh, surely, the spirit that inhabits and guards this place has a soul more in harmony with man, than those who pile the glacier, or retire to the inaccessible peaks of the mountains of our own country."

Clerval! beloved friend! even now it delights me to record your words, and to dwell on the praise of which you are so eminently deserving. He was a being formed in the "very poetry of nature."[4] His wild and enthusiastic imagination was chastened by the sensibility of his heart. His soul over-flowed with ardent affections, and his friendship was of that devoted and wondrous nature that the worldly-minded teach us to look for only in the imagination. But even human sympathies were not sufficient to satisfy his eager mind. The scenery of external nature, which others regard only with admiration, he loved with ardour:

—————"The sounding cataract
Haunted *him* like a passion: the tall rock,
The mountain, and the deep and gloomy wood,
Their colours and their forms, were then to him
An appetite; a feeling, and a love,
That had no need of a remoter charm,
By thought supplied, or any interest
Unborrowed from the eye."[5]

And where does he now exist? Is this gentle and lovely being lost for ever? Has this mind so replete with ideas, imaginations fanciful and mag-nificent, which formed a world, whose existence depended on the life of its creator; has this mind perished? Does it now only exist in my memory? No, it is not thus; your form so divinely wrought, and beaming with beauty, has decayed, but your spirit still visits and consoles your unhappy friend.

Pardon this gush of sorrow; these ineffectual words are but a slight tribute to the unexampled worth of Henry, but they soothe my heart, over-flowing with the anguish which his remembrance creates. I will proceed with my tale.

4. Leigh Hunt's "Rimini." [Mary's note]
5. Wordsworth's "Tintern Abbey." [Mary's note]

Beyond Cologne we descended to the plains of Holland; and we resolved to post the remainder of our way; for the wind was contrary, and the stream of the river was too gentle to aid us.

Our journey here lost the interest arising from beautiful scenery; but we arrived in a few days at Rotterdam, whence we proceeded by sea to England. It was on a clear morning, in the latter days of September, that I first saw the white cliffs of Britain. The banks of the Thames presented a new scene; they were flat, but fertile, and almost every town was marked by the remembrance of some story. We saw Tilbury Fort, and remembered the Spanish armada; Gravesend, Woolwich, and Greenwich, places which I had heard of even in my country.

At length we saw the numerous steeples of London, St. Paul's towering above all, and the Tower famed in English history.

CHAPTER II.

London was our present point of rest; we determined to remain several months in this wonderful and celebrated city. Clerval desired the intercourse of the men of genius and talent who flourished at this time; but this was with me a secondary object; I was principally occupied with the means of obtaining the information necessary for the completion of my promise, and quickly availed myself of the letters of introduction that I had brought with me, addressed to the most distinguished natural philosophers.[6]

If this journey had taken place during my days of study and happiness, it would have afforded me inexpressible pleasure. But a blight had come over my existence, and I only visited these people for the sake of the information they might give me on the subject in which my interest was so terribly profound. Company was irksome to me; when alone, I could fill my mind with the sights of heaven and earth; the voice of Henry soothed me, and I could thus cheat myself into a transitory peace. But busy uninteresting joyous faces brought back despair to my heart. I saw an insurmountable barrier placed between me and my fellow-men; this barrier was sealed with the blood of William and Justine; and to reflect on the events connected with those names filled my soul with anguish.

6. Among these leading natural philosophers of the period were William Nicholson (1753–1815), whom Mary's father, William Godwin, often turned to for scientific advice, and Humphry Davy (1778–1829), a young chemist who would dazzle London and the scientific world from the era in which *Frankenstein* is set to Mary's own. Davy was a frequent guest at the Godwin house during Mary's childhood and was part of an important ongoing conversation with Godwin and the poet Samuel Taylor Coleridge about the relationship between science, creativity, and poetry. Ed Finn.

But in Clerval I saw the image of my former self; he was inquisitive, and anxious to gain experience and instruction. The difference of manners which he observed was to him an inexhaustible source of instruction and amusement. He was for ever busy; and the only check to his enjoyments was my sorrowful and dejected mien. I tried to conceal this as much as possible, that I might not debar him from the pleasures natural to one who was entering on a new scene of life, undisturbed by any care or bitter recollection. I often refused to accompany him, alleging another engagement, that I might remain alone. I now also began to collect the materials necessary for my new creation, and this was to me like the torture of single drops of water continually falling on the head. Every thought that was devoted to it was an extreme anguish, and every word that I spoke in allusion to it caused my lips to quiver, and my heart to palpitate.

After passing some months in London, we received a letter from a person in Scotland, who had formerly been our visitor at Geneva. He mentioned the beauties of his native country, and asked us if those were not sufficient allurements to induce us to prolong our journey as far north as Perth, where he resided. Clerval eagerly desired to accept this invitation; and I, although I abhorred society, wished to view again mountains and streams, and all the wondrous works with which Nature adorns her chosen dwelling-places.

We had arrived in England at the beginning of October, and it was now February. We accordingly determined to commence our journey towards the north at the expiration of another month. In this expedition we did not intend to follow the great road to Edinburgh, but to visit Windsor, Oxford, Matlock, and the Cumberland lakes, resolving to arrive at the completion of this tour about the end of July. I packed my chemical instruments, and the materials I had collected, resolving to finish my labours in some obscure nook in the northern highlands of Scotland.

We quitted London on the 27th of March, and remained a few days at Windsor, rambling in its beautiful forest. This was a new scene to us mountaineers; the majestic oaks, the quantity of game, and the herds of stately deer, were all novelties to us.

From thence we proceeded to Oxford. As we entered this city, our minds were filled with the remembrance of the events that had been transacted there more than a century and a half before. It was here that Charles I. had collected his forces. This city had remained faithful to him, after the whole nation had forsaken his cause to join the standard of parliament and liberty. The memory of that unfortunate king, and his companions, the amiable Falkland, the insolent Goring, his queen, and son, gave a peculiar interest to every part of the city, which they might be supposed to have inhabited. The spirit of elder days found a dwelling here, and we delighted to trace its footsteps. If these feelings had not found an imaginary gratification, the appearance of the city had yet in itself sufficient beauty to obtain our admiration. The colleges are ancient and picturesque; the streets are almost magnificent; and the lovely Isis, which flows beside it through meadows of exquisite verdure, is spread forth into a placid expanse of waters, which reflects its majestic assemblage of towers, and spires, and domes, embosomed among aged trees.

I enjoyed this scene; and yet my enjoyment was embittered both by the memory of the past, and the anticipation of the future. I was formed for peaceful happiness. During my youthful days discontent never visited my mind; and if I was ever overcome by *ennui*, the sight of what is beautiful in nature, or the study of what is excellent and sublime in the productions of man, could always interest my heart, and communicate elasticity to my spirits. But I am a blasted tree; the bolt has entered my soul; and I felt then that I should survive to exhibit, what I shall soon cease to be—a miserable spectacle of wrecked humanity, pitiable to others, and abhorrent to myself.

We passed a considerable period at Oxford, rambling among its environs, and endeavouring to identify every spot which might relate to the most animating epoch of English history. Our little voyages of discovery were often prolonged by the successive objects that presented themselves. We visited the tomb of the illustrious Hampden, and the field on which that patriot fell. For a moment my soul was elevated from its debasing and miserable fears to contemplate the divine ideas of liberty and self-sacrifice, of which these sights were the monuments and the remembrancers. For an instant I dared to shake off my chains, and look around me with a free and lofty spirit; but the iron had eaten into my flesh, and I sank again, trembling and hopeless, into my miserable self.

We left Oxford with regret, and proceeded to Matlock, which was our next place of rest. The country in the neighbourhood of this village resembled, to a greater degree, the scenery of Switzerland; but every thing is on a lower scale, and the green hills want the crown of distant white Alps, which always attend on the piny mountains of my native country. We visited the wondrous cave, and the little cabinets of natural history, where the curiosities are disposed in the same manner as in the collections at Servox and Chamounix. The latter name made me tremble, when pronounced by Henry; and I hastened to quit Matlock, with which that terrible scene was thus associated.

From Derby still journeying northward, we passed two months in Cumberland and Westmoreland. I could now almost fancy myself among the Swiss mountains. The little patches of snow which yet lingered on the northern sides of the mountains, the lakes, and the dashing of the rocky streams, were all familiar and dear sights to me. Here also we made some acquaintances, who almost contrived to cheat me into happiness. The delight of Clerval was proportionably greater than mine; his mind expanded in the company of men of talent, and he found in his own nature greater capacities and resources than he could have imagined himself to have possessed while he associated with his inferiors. "I could pass my life here," said he to me; "and among these mountains I should scarcely regret Switzerland and the Rhine."

But he found that a traveller's life is one that includes much pain amid its enjoyments. His feelings are for ever on the stretch; and when he begins to sink into repose, he finds himself obliged to quit that on which he rests in pleasure for something new, which again engages his attention, and which also he forsakes for other novelties.

We had scarcely visited the various lakes of Cumberland and Westmoreland, and conceived an affection for some of the inhabitants, when the period of our appointment with our Scotch friend approached, and we left them to travel on. For my own part I was not sorry. I had now neglected my promise for some time, and I feared the effects of the dæmon's disappointment. He might remain in Switzerland, and wreak his vengeance on my relatives. This idea pursued me, and tormented me at every moment from which I might otherwise have snatched repose and peace. I waited for my letters with feverish impatience: if they were delayed, I was miserable, and overcome by a thousand fears; and when they arrived, and I saw the superscription of Elizabeth or my father, I hardly dared to read and ascertain my fate. Sometimes I thought that the fiend followed me, and might expedite my remissness by murdering my companion. When these thoughts possessed me, I would not quit Henry for a moment, but followed him as his shadow, to protect him from the fancied rage of his destroyer. I felt as if I had committed some great crime, the consciousness of which haunted me. I was guiltless, but I had indeed drawn down a horrible curse upon my head, as mortal as that of crime.[7]

7. Victor gives expression to his conflicting feelings. His conscience haunts him for the crime he feels he has committed. But he confesses his innocence—an ironic juxtaposition with Justine's untruthful confession of guilt. In part, this passage expresses the difficulty of conscience serving as a reliable guide. Do feelings serve as a better source of moral discernment?
Joel Gereboff.

I visited Edinburgh with languid eyes and mind; and yet that city might have interested the most unfortunate being. Clerval did not like it so well as Oxford; for the antiquity of the latter city was more pleasing to him. But the beauty and regularity of the new town of Edinburgh, its romantic castle, and its environs, the most delightful in the world, Arthur's Seat, St. Bernard's Well, and the Pentland Hills, compensated him for the change, and filled him with cheerfulness and admiration. But I was impatient to arrive at the termination of my journey.

We left Edinburgh in a week, passing through Coupar, St. Andrews, and along the banks of the Tay, to Perth, where our friend expected us. But I was in no mood to laugh and talk with strangers, or enter into their feelings or plans with the good humour expected from a guest; and accordingly I told Clerval that I wished to make the tour of Scotland alone. "Do you," said I, "enjoy yourself, and let this be our rendezvous. I may be absent a month or two; but do not interfere with my motions, I entreat you: leave me to peace and solitude for a short time; and when I return, I hope it will be with a lighter heart, more congenial to your own temper."

Henry wished to dissuade me; but, seeing me bent on this plan, ceased to remonstrate. He entreated me to write often. "I had rather be with you," he said, "in your solitary rambles, than with these Scotch people, whom I do not know: hasten then, my dear friend, to return, that I may again feel myself somewhat at home, which I cannot do in your absence."

Having parted from my friend, I determined to visit some remote spot of Scotland, and finish my work in solitude. I did not doubt but that the monster followed me, and would discover himself to me when I should have finished, that he might receive his companion.

With this resolution I traversed the northern highlands, and fixed on one of the remotest of the Orkneys as the scene of my labours. It was a place fitted for such a work, being hardly more than a rock, whose high sides were continually beaten upon by the waves. The soil was barren, scarcely affording pasture for a few miserable cows, and oatmeal for its inhabitants, which consisted of five persons, whose gaunt and scraggy limbs gave tokens of their miserable fare. Vegetables and bread, when they indulged in such luxuries, and even fresh water, was to be procured from the main land, which was about five miles distant.

On the whole island there were but three miserable huts, and one of these was vacant when I arrived. This I hired. It contained but two rooms, and these exhibited all the squalidness of the most miserable penury. The thatch had fallen in, the walls were unplastered, and the door was off its hinges. I ordered it to be repaired, bought some furniture, and took possession; an incident which would, doubtless, have occasioned some surprise, had not all the senses of the cottagers been benumbed by want and squalid poverty. As it was, I lived ungazed at and unmolested, hardly thanked for the pittance of food and clothes which I gave; so much does suffering blunt even the coarsest sensations of men.

In this retreat I devoted the morning to labour; but in the evening, when the weather permitted, I walked on the stony beach of the sea, to listen to the waves as they roared, and dashed at my feet. It was a monotonous, yet ever-changing scene. I thought of Switzerland; it was far different from this desolate and appalling landscape. Its hills are covered with vines, and its cottages are scattered thickly in the plains. Its fair lakes reflect a blue and gentle sky; and, when troubled by the winds, their tumult is but as the play of a lively infant, when compared to the roarings of the giant ocean.

In this manner I distributed my occupations when I first arrived; but, as I proceeded in my labour, it became every day more horrible and irksome to me. Sometimes I could not prevail on myself to enter my laboratory for several days; and at other times I toiled day and night in order to complete my work. It was indeed a filthy process in which I was engaged. During my first experiment, a kind of enthusiastic frenzy had blinded me to the horror of my employment; my mind was intently fixed on the sequel of my labour, and my eyes were shut to the horror of my proceedings. But now I went to it in cold blood, and my heart often sickened at the work of my hands.

Thus situated, employed in the most detestable occupation, immersed in a solitude where nothing could for an instant call my attention from the actual scene in which I was engaged, my spirits became unequal; I grew restless and nervous. Every moment I feared to meet my persecutor. Sometimes I sat with my eyes fixed on the ground, fearing to raise them lest they should encounter the object which I so much dreaded to behold. I feared to wander from the sight of my fellow-creatures, lest when alone he should come to claim his companion.

In the mean time I worked on, and my labour was already considerably advanced. I looked towards its completion with a tremulous and eager hope, which I dared not trust myself to question, but which was intermixed with obscure forebodings of evil, that made my heart sicken in my bosom.

CHAPTER III.

I sat one evening in my laboratory; the sun had set, and the moon was just rising from the sea; I had not sufficient light for my employment, and

I remained idle, in a pause of consideration of whether I should leave my labour for the night, or hasten its conclusion by an unremitting attention to it. As I sat, a train of reflection occurred to me, which led me to consider the effects of what I was now doing. Three years before I was engaged in the same manner, and had created a fiend whose unparalleled barbarity had desolated my heart, and filled it for ever with the bitterest remorse. I was now about to form another being, of whose dispositions I was alike ignorant; she might become ten thousand times more malignant than her mate, and delight, for its own sake, in murder and wretchedness. He had sworn to quit the neighbourhood of man, and hide himself in deserts; but she had not; and she, who in all probability was to become a thinking and reasoning animal, might refuse to comply with a compact made before her creation. They might even hate each other; the creature who already lived loathed his own deformity, and might he not conceive a greater abhorrence for it when it came before his eyes in the female form? She also might turn with disgust from him to the superior beauty of man; she might quit him, and he be again alone, exasperated by the fresh provocation of being deserted by one of his own species.[8]

Even if they were to leave Europe, and inhabit the deserts of the new world, yet one of the first results of those sympathies for which the dæmon thirsted would be children, and a race of devils would be propagated upon the earth, who might make the very existence of the species of man a condition precarious and full of terror. Had I a right, for my own benefit, to inflict this curse upon everlasting generations? I had before been moved by the sophisms of the being I had created; I had been struck senseless by his fiendish threats: but now, for the first time, the wickedness of my promise burst upon me; I shuddered to think that future ages might curse

8. For Mary, the daughter of early feminist philosopher Mary Wollstonecraft, women's status as "the other" was painfully and personally obvious. Men ruled the world, and therefore almost every philosophical, scientific, and political tract about the meaning of selfhood assumed that the "self" is male. Women's experiences were considered at best irrelevant and at worst monstrous. It is therefore delightfully sneaky that Mary has figured out a way to turn the female perspective into something more relatable than the male, as Victor imagines his new creation—"a thinking and reasoning animal"—asserting her own will in the face of the first creature's desire. Victor is also forced to imagine the creature's perspective as he looks for the first time into the eyes of "his own species." When Victor imagines the two creatures looking upon each other for the first time, he calls to mind Jean-Paul Sartre's classic notion that humans learn selfhood when we are first seen by the "other." In *Being and Nothingness* ([1943] 2012), Sartre argues that we cannot have a self until we are recognized by an other, which allows us to see both the other in ourselves and the selfhood in others. Victor typically cannot imagine the two creatures having selves at all. So he suggests they will be "repulsed" rather than find sympathy in one another's eyes.

Annalee Newitz.

me as their pest, whose selfishness had not hesitated to buy its own peace at the price perhaps of the existence of the whole human race.[9]

I trembled, and my heart failed within me; when, on looking up, I saw, by the light of the moon, the dæmon at the casement. A ghastly grin wrinkled his lips as he gazed on me, where I sat fulfilling the task which he had allotted to me. Yes, he had followed me in my travels; he had loitered in forests, hid himself in caves, or taken refuge in wide and desert heaths; and he now came to mark my progress, and claim the fulfilment of my promise.

As I looked on him, his countenance expressed the utmost extent of malice and treachery. I thought with a sensation of madness on my promise of creating another like to him, and, trembling with passion, tore to pieces the thing on which I was engaged. The wretch saw me destroy the creature on whose future existence he depended for happiness, and, with a howl of devilish despair and revenge, withdrew.

I left the room, and, locking the door, made a solemn vow in my own heart never to resume my labours; and then, with trembling steps, I sought my own apartment. I was alone; none were near me to dissipate the gloom, and relieve me from the sickening oppression of the most terrible reveries.

Several hours past, and I remained near my window gazing on the sea; it was almost motionless, for the winds were hushed, and all nature reposed under the eye of the quiet moon. A few fishing vessels alone specked the water, and now and then the gentle breeze wafted the sound of voices, as the fishermen called to one another. I felt the silence, although I was hardly conscious of its extreme profundity, until my ear was suddenly arrested by the paddling of oars near the shore, and a person landed close to my house.

In a few minutes after, I heard the creaking of my door, as if some one endeavoured to open it softly. I trembled from head to foot; I felt a presentiment of who it was, and wished to rouse one of the peasants who dwelt in a cottage not far from mine; but I was overcome by the sensation of helplessness, so often felt in frightful dreams, when you in vain endeavour to fly from an impending danger, and was rooted to the spot.

---

9. Pondering the unknowns and potential horrors the future mate for the creature might perpetrate, Victor thinks through these possibilities and resolves not to continue his efforts. Perhaps overestimating his creative prowess, he now recognizes that his own selfishness might result in the destruction of the whole human race. Although some emotions may prove reliable guides for behavior, selfishness is never appropriate because it leads only to destruction, be it of the self or of others.

Joel Gereboff.

Presently I heard the sound of footsteps along the passage; the door opened, and the wretch whom I dreaded appeared. Shutting the door, he approached me, and said, in a smothered voice—

"You have destroyed the work which you began; what is it that you intend? Do you dare to break your promise? I have endured toil and misery: I left Switzerland with you; I crept along the shores of the Rhine, among its willow islands, and over the summits of its hills. I have dwelt many months in the heaths of England, and among the deserts of Scotland. I have endured incalculable fatigue, and cold, and hunger; do you dare destroy my hopes?"

"Begone! I do break my promise; never will I create another like yourself, equal in deformity and wickedness."

"Slave, I before reasoned with you, but you have proved yourself unworthy of my condescension. Remember that I have power; you believe yourself miserable, but I can make you so wretched that the light of day will be hateful to you. You are my creator, but I am your master;—obey!"[10]

"The hour of my weakness is past, and the period of your power is arrived. Your threats cannot move me to do an act of wickedness; but they confirm me in a resolution of not creating you a companion in vice. Shall I, in cool blood, set loose upon the earth a dæmon, whose delight is in death and wretchedness. Begone! I am firm, and your words will only exasperate my rage."

The monster saw my determination in my face, and gnashed his teeth in the impotence of anger. "Shall each man," cried he, "find a wife for his bosom, and each beast have his mate, and I be alone? I had feelings of affection, and they were requited by detestation and scorn. Man, you may hate; but beware! Your hours will pass in dread and misery, and soon the bolt will fall which must ravish from you your happiness for ever.

10. A great deal is going on in this paragraph. First, the creature continues to speak as though he has adopted the mantle of Milton's Satan: "I before reasoned with you" evokes Isaiah's "Come, let us reason together" (1.18), a biblical voice that echoes in a great deal of Satan's language in *Paradise Lost* (Milton [1667] 2007). Second, the creature has a sophisticated understanding of Victor's psychology and social context, perhaps more so than Victor does, in his claim that he can render Victor even more miserable than he is. Third, even as Victor manages to achieve some measure of foresight and the ability to view a situation from a perspective other than his own (importantly, from the female creature's perspective; see note 6), the creature has understood that his physical prowess has utterly transformed the dynamic between them. This inversion of the master–slave relationship is every slave master's fear and perhaps the reason why, for example, the novel was banned in apartheid South Africa and why it has become such a fertile source for narratives on robotics and artificial intelligence. Victor must have some measure of physical courage to stand up to the creature here, but does he have moral courage as well?

David H. Guston.

Are you to be happy, while I grovel in the intensity of my wretchedness? You can blast my other passions; but revenge remains—revenge, henceforth dearer than light or food! I may die; but first you, my tyrant and tormentor, shall curse the sun that gazes on your misery. Beware; for I am fearless, and therefore powerful. I will watch with the wiliness of a snake, that I may sting with its venom. Man, you shall repent of the injuries you inflict."

"Devil, cease; and do not poison the air with these sounds of malice. I have declared my resolution to you, and I am no coward to bend beneath words. Leave me; I am inexorable."

"It is well. I go; but remember, I shall be with you on your wedding-night."

I started forward, and exclaimed, "Villain! before you sign my death-warrant, be sure that you are yourself safe."

I would have seized him; but he eluded me, and quitted the house with precipitation: in a few moments I saw him in his boat, which shot across the waters with an arrowy swiftness, and was soon lost amid the waves.

All was again silent; but his words rung in my ears. I burned with rage to pursue the murderer of my peace, and precipitate him into the ocean. I walked up and down my room hastily and perturbed, while my imagination conjured up a thousand images to torment and sting me. Why had I not followed him, and closed with him in mortal strife? But I had suffered him to depart, and he had directed his course towards the main land. I shuddered to think who might be the next victim sacrificed to his insatiate revenge. And then I thought again of his words—"*I will be with you on your wedding-night.*" That then was the period fixed for the fulfilment of my destiny. In that hour I should die, and at once satisfy and extinguish his malice. The prospect did not move me to fear; yet when I thought of my beloved Elizabeth,—of her tears and endless sorrow, when she should find her lover so barbarously snatched from her,—tears, the first I had shed for many months, streamed from my eyes, and I resolved not to fall before my enemy without a bitter struggle.

The night passed away, and the sun rose from the ocean; my feelings became calmer, if it may be called calmness, when the violence of rage sinks into the depths of despair. I left the house, the horrid scene of the last night's contention, and walked on the beach of the sea, which I almost regarded as an insuperable barrier between me and my fellow-creatures; nay, a wish that such should prove the fact stole across me. I desired that I might pass my life on that barren rock, wearily it is true, but uninterrupted by any sudden shock of misery. If I returned, it was to be sacrificed, or to see those whom I most loved die under the grasp of a dæmon whom I had myself created.

I walked about the isle like a restless spectre, separated from all it loved, and miserable in the separation. When it became noon, and the sun rose higher, I lay down on the grass, and was overpowered by a deep sleep. I had been awake the whole of the preceding night, my nerves were agitated, and my eyes inflamed by watching and misery. The sleep into which I now sunk refreshed me; and when I awoke, I again felt as if I belonged to a race of human beings like myself, and I began to reflect upon what had passed with greater composure; yet still the words of the fiend rung in my ears like a death-knell, they appeared like a dream, yet distinct and oppressive as a reality.

The sun had far descended, and I still sat on the shore, satisfying my appetite, which had become ravenous, with an oaten cake, when I saw a fishing-boat land close to me, and one of the men brought me a packet; it contained letters from Geneva, and one from Clerval, entreating me to join him. He said that nearly a year had elapsed since we had quitted Switzerland, and France was yet unvisited. He entreated me, therefore, to leave my solitary isle, and meet him at Perth, in a week from that time, when we might arrange the plan of our future proceedings. This letter in a degree recalled me to life, and I determined to quit my island at the expiration of two days.

Yet, before I departed, there was a task to perform, on which I shuddered to reflect: I must pack my chemical instruments; and for that purpose I must enter the room which had been the scene of my odious work, and I must handle those utensils, the sight of which was sickening to me. The next morning, at day-break, I summoned sufficient courage, and unlocked the door of my laboratory. The remains of the half-finished creature, whom I had destroyed, lay scattered on the floor, and I almost felt as if I had mangled the living flesh of a human being. I paused to collect myself, and then entered the chamber. With trembling hands I conveyed the instruments out of the room; but I reflected that I ought not to leave the relics of my work to excite the horror and suspicion of the peasants, and I accordingly put them into a basket, with a great quantity of stones, and laying them up, determined to throw them into the sea that very night; and in the mean time I sat upon the beach, employed in cleaning and arranging my chemical apparatus.

Nothing could be more complete than the alteration that had taken place in my feelings since the night of the appearance of the dæmon. I had before regarded my promise with a gloomy despair, as a thing that, with whatever consequences, must be fulfilled; but I now felt as if a film had been taken from before my eyes, and that I, for the first time, saw clearly.

The idea of renewing my labours did not for one instant occur to me; the threat I had heard weighed on my thoughts, but I did not reflect that a voluntary act of mine could avert it. I had resolved in my own mind, that to create another like the fiend I had first made would be an act of the basest and most atrocious selfishness; and I banished from my mind every thought that could lead to a different conclusion.

Between two and three in the morning the moon rose; and I then, putting my basket aboard a little skiff, sailed out about four miles from the shore. The scene was perfectly solitary: a few boats were returning towards land, but I sailed away from them. I felt as if I was about the commission of a dreadful crime, and avoided with shuddering anxiety any encounter with my fellow-creatures. At one time the moon, which had before been clear, was suddenly overspread by a thick cloud, and I took advantage of the moment of darkness, and cast my basket into the sea; I listened to the gurgling sound as it sunk, and then sailed away from the spot. The sky became clouded; but the air was pure, although chilled by the north-east breeze that was then rising. But it refreshed me, and filled me with such agreeable sensations, that I resolved to prolong my stay on the water, and fixing the rudder in a direct position, stretched myself at the bottom of the boat. Clouds hid the moon, every thing was obscure, and I heard only the sound of the boat, as its keel cut through the waves; the murmur lulled me, and in a short time I slept soundly.

I do not know how long I remained in this situation, but when I awoke I found that the sun had already mounted considerably. The wind was high, and the waves continually threatened the safety of my little skiff. I found that the wind was north-east, and must have driven me far from the coast from which I had embarked. I endeavoured to change my course, but quickly found that if I again made the attempt the boat would be instantly filled with water. Thus situated, my only resource was to drive before the wind. I confess that I felt a few sensations of terror. I had no compass with me, and was so little acquainted with the geography of this part of the world that the sun was of little benefit to me. I might be driven into the wide Atlantic, and feel all the tortures of starvation, or be swallowed up in the immeasurable waters that roared and buffeted around me. I had already been out many hours, and felt the torment of a burning thirst, a prelude to my other sufferings. I looked on the heavens, which were covered by clouds that flew before the wind only to be replaced by others: I looked upon the sea, it was to be my grave. "Fiend," I exclaimed, "your task is already fulfilled!" I thought of Elizabeth, of my father, and of Clerval; and sunk into a reverie, so despairing and frightful, that even now, when the scene is on the point of closing before me for ever, I shudder to reflect on it.

Some hours passed thus; but by degrees, as the sun declined towards the horizon, the wind died away into a gentle breeze, and the sea became free from breakers. But these gave place to a heavy swell; I felt sick, and hardly able to hold the rudder, when suddenly I saw a line of high land towards the south.

Almost spent, as I was, by fatigue, and the dreadful suspense I endured for several hours, this sudden certainty of life rushed like a flood of warm joy to my heart, and tears gushed from my eyes.

How mutable are our feelings, and how strange is that clinging love we have of life even in the excess of misery! I constructed another sail with a part of my dress, and eagerly steered my course towards the land. It had a wild and rocky appearance; but as I approached nearer, I easily perceived the traces of cultivation. I saw vessels near the shore, and found myself suddenly transported back to the neighbourhood of civilized man. I eagerly traced the windings of the land, and hailed a steeple which I at length saw issuing from behind a small promontory. As I was in a state of extreme debility, I resolved to sail directly towards the town as a place where I could most easily procure nourishment. Fortunately I had money with me. As I turned the promontory, I perceived a small neat town and a good harbour, which I entered, my heart bounding with joy at my unexpected escape.

As I was occupied in fixing the boat and arranging the sails, several people crowded towards the spot. They seemed very much surprised at my appearance; but, instead of offering me any assistance, whispered together with gestures that at any other time might have produced in me a slight sensation of alarm. As it was, I merely remarked that they spoke English; and I therefore addressed them in that language: "My good friends," said I, "will you be so kind as to tell me the name of this town, and inform me where I am?"

"You will know that soon enough," replied a man with a gruff voice. "May be you are come to a place that will not prove much to your taste; but you will not be consulted as to your quarters, I promise you."

I was exceedingly surprised on receiving so rude an answer from a stranger; and I was also disconcerted on perceiving the frowning and angry countenances of his companions. "Why do you answer me so roughly?" I replied: "surely it is not the custom of Englishmen to receive strangers so inhospitably."

"I do not know," said the man, "what the custom of the English may be; but it is the custom of the Irish to hate villains."

While this strange dialogue continued, I perceived the crowd rapidly increase. Their faces expressed a mixture of curiosity and anger, which annoyed, and in some degree alarmed me. I inquired the way to the inn; but no one replied. I then moved forward, and a murmuring sound arose from the crowd as they followed and surrounded me; when an ill-looking man approaching, tapped me on the shoulder, and said, "Come, Sir, you must follow me to Mr. Kirwin's, to give an account of yourself."

"Who is Mr. Kirwin? Why am I to give an account of myself? Is not this a free country?"

"Aye, Sir, free enough for honest folks. Mr. Kirwin is a magistrate; and you are to give an account of the death of a gentleman who was found murdered here last night."

This answer startled me; but I presently recovered myself. I was innocent; that could easily be proved: accordingly I followed my conductor in silence, and was led to one of the best houses in the town. I was ready to sink from fatigue and hunger; but, being surrounded by a crowd, I thought it politic to rouse all my strength, that no physical debility might be construed into apprehension or conscious guilt. Little did I then expect the calamity that was in a few moments to overwhelm me, and extinguish in horror and despair all fear of ignominy or death.

I must pause here; for it requires all my fortitude to recall the memory of the frightful events which I am about to relate, in proper detail, to my recollection.

CHAPTER IV.

I was soon introduced into the presence of the magistrate, an old benevolent man, with calm and mild manners. He looked upon me, however, with some degree of severity; and then, turning towards my conductors, he asked who appeared as witnesses on this occasion.

About half a dozen men came forward; and one being selected by the magistrate, he deposed, that he had been out fishing the night before with his son and brother-in-law, Daniel Nugent, when, about ten o'clock, they observed a strong northerly blast rising, and they accordingly put in for port. It was a very dark night, as the moon had not yet risen; they did not land at the harbour, but, as they had been accustomed, at a creek about two miles below. He walked on first, carrying a part of the fishing tackle, and his companions followed him at some distance. As he was proceeding along the sands, he struck his foot against something, and fell all his length on the ground. His companions came up to assist him; and, by the light of their lantern, they found that he had fallen on the body of a man, who was to all appearance dead. Their first supposition was, that it was the corpse of some person who had been drowned, and was thrown on shore by the waves; but, upon examination, they found that the clothes were not wet, and even that the body was not then cold. They instantly carried it to the cottage of an old woman near the spot, and endeavoured, but in vain, to restore it to life. He appeared to be a handsome young man, about five and twenty years of age. He had apparently been strangled; for there was no sign of any violence, except the black mark of fingers on his neck.

The first part of this deposition did not in the least interest me; but when the mark of the fingers was mentioned, I remembered the murder of my brother, and felt myself extremely agitated; my limbs trembled, and a mist came over my eyes, which obliged me to lean on a chair for support. The magistrate observed me with a keen eye, and of course drew an unfavourable augury from my manner,

The son confirmed his father's account: but when Daniel Nugent was called, he swore positively that, just before the fall of his companion, he saw a boat, with a single man in it, at a short distance from the shore; and, as far as he could judge by the light of a few stars, it was the same boat in which I had just landed.

A woman deposed, that she lived near the beach, and was standing at the door of her cottage, waiting for the return of the fishermen, about an hour before she heard of the discovery of the body, when she saw a boat, with only one man in it, push off from that part of the shore where the corpse was afterwards found.

Another woman confirmed the account of the fishermen having brought the body into her house; it was not cold. They put it into a bed, and rubbed it; and Daniel went to the town for an apothecary, but life was quite gone.

Several other men were examined concerning my landing; and they agreed, that, with the strong north wind that had arisen during the night, it was very probable that I had beaten about for many hours, and had been obliged to return nearly to the same spot from which I had departed. Besides, they observed that it appeared that I had brought the body from another place, and it was likely, that as I did not appear to know the shore, I might have put into the harbour ignorant of the distance of the town of —————— from the place where I had deposited the corpse.

Mr. Kirwin, on hearing this evidence, desired that I should be taken into the room where the body lay for interment that it might be observed what effect the sight of it would produce upon me. This idea was probably suggested by the extreme agitation I had exhibited when the mode of the murder had been described. I was accordingly conducted, by the magistrate and several other persons, to the inn. I could not help being struck by the strange coincidences that had taken place during this eventful night; but, knowing that I had been conversing with several persons in the island I had inhabited about the time that the body had been found, I was perfectly tranquil as to the consequences of the affair.

I entered the room where the corpse lay, and was led up to the coffin. How can I describe my sensations on beholding it? I feel yet parched with horror, nor can I reflect on that terrible moment without shuddering and agony, that faintly reminds me of the anguish of the recognition. The trial, the presence of the magistrate and witnesses, passed like a dream from my memory, when I saw the lifeless form of Henry Clerval stretched before me. I gasped for breath; and, throwing myself on the body, I exclaimed, "Have my murderous machinations deprived you also, my dearest Henry, of life? Two I have already destroyed; other victims await their destiny: but you, Clerval, my friend, my benefactor"——

The human frame could no longer support the agonizing suffering that I endured, and I was carried out of the room in strong convulsions.

A fever succeeded to this. I lay for two months on the point of death: my ravings, as I afterwards heard, were frightful; I called myself the murderer of William, of Justine, and of Clerval. Sometimes I entreated my attendants to assist me in the destruction of the fiend by whom I was tormented; and, at others, I felt the fingers of the monster already grasping my neck, and screamed aloud with agony and terror. Fortunately, as I spoke my native language, Mr. Kirwin alone understood me; but my gestures and bitter cries were sufficient to affright the other witnesses.

Why did I not die? More miserable than man ever was before, why did I not sink into forgetfulness and rest? Death snatches away many blooming children, the only hopes of their doating parents: how many brides and youthful lovers have been one day in the bloom of health and hope, and the next a prey for worms and the decay of the tomb! Of what materials was I made, that I could thus resist so many shocks, which, like the turning of the wheel, continually renewed the torture.

But I was doomed to live; and, in two months, found myself as awaking from a dream, in a prison, stretched on a wretched bed, surrounded by gaolers, turnkeys, bolts, and all the miserable apparatus of a dungeon. It was morning, I remember, when I thus awoke to understanding: I had forgotten the particulars of what had happened, and only felt as if some great misfortune had suddenly overwhelmed me; but when I looked around, and saw the barred windows, and the squalidness of the room in which I was, all flashed across my memory, and I groaned bitterly.

This sound disturbed an old woman who was sleeping in a chair beside me. She was a hired nurse, the wife of one of the turnkeys, and her countenance expressed all those bad qualities which often characterize that class. The lines of her face were hard and rude, like that of persons accustomed to see without sympathizing in sights of misery. Her tone expressed her entire indifference; she addressed me in English, and the voice struck me as one that I had heard during my sufferings:

"Are you better now, Sir?" said she.

I replied in the same language, with a feeble voice, "I believe I am; but if it be all true, if indeed I did not dream, I am sorry that I am still alive to feel this misery and horror."

"For that matter," replied the old woman, "if you mean about the gentleman you murdered, I believe that it were better for you if you were dead, for I fancy it will go hard with you; but you will be hung when the next sessions come on. However, that's none of my business, I am sent to nurse you, and get you well; I do my duty with a safe conscience, it were well if every body did the same."

I turned with loathing from the woman who could utter so unfeeling a speech to a person just saved, on the very edge of death; but I felt languid, and unable to reflect on all that had passed. The whole series of my life appeared to me as a dream; I sometimes doubted if indeed it were all true, for it never presented itself to my mind with the force of reality.

As the images that floated before me became more distinct, I grew feverish; a darkness pressed around me; no one was near me who soothed me with the gentle voice of love; no dear hand supported me. The physician came and prescribed medicines, and the old woman prepared them for me; but utter carelessness was visible in the first, and the expression of brutality was strongly marked in the visage of the second. Who could be interested in the fate of a murderer, but the hangman who would gain his fee?

These were my first reflections; but I soon learned that Mr. Kirwin had shewn me extreme kindness. He had caused the best room in the prison to be prepared for me (wretched indeed was the best); and it was he who had provided a physician and a nurse. It is true, he seldom came to see me; for, although he ardently desired to relieve the sufferings of every human creature, he did not wish to be present at the agonies and miserable ravings of a murderer. He came, therefore, sometimes to see that I was not neglected; but his visits were short, and at long intervals.

One day, when I was gradually recovering, I was seated in a chair, my eyes half open, and my checks livid like those in death, I was overcome by gloom and misery, and often reflected I had better seek death than remain miserably pent up only to be let loose in a world replete with wretchedness. At one time I considered whether I should not declare myself guilty, and suffer the penalty of the law, less innocent than poor Justine had been. Such were my thoughts, when the door of my apartment was opened, and Mr. Kirwin entered. His countenance expressed sympathy and compassion; he drew a chair close to mine, and addressed me in French—

"I fear that this place is very shocking to you; can I do any thing to make you more comfortable?"

"I thank you; but all that you mention is nothing to me: on the whole earth there is no comfort which I am capable of receiving."

"I know that the sympathy of a stranger can be but of little relief to one borne down as you are by so strange a misfortune. But you will, I hope, soon quit this melancholy abode; for, doubtless, evidence can easily be brought to free you from the criminal charge."

"That is my least concern: I am, by a course of strange events, become the most miserable of mortals. Persecuted and tortured as I am and have been, can death be any evil to me?"

"Nothing indeed could be more unfortunate and agonizing than the strange chances that have lately occurred. You were thrown, by some surprising accident, on this shore, renowned for its hospitality, seized immediately, and charged with murder. The first sight that was presented to your eyes was the body of your friend, murdered in so unaccountable a manner, and placed, as it were, by some fiend across your path."

As Mr. Kirwin said this, notwithstanding the agitation I endured on this retrospect of my sufferings, I also felt considerable surprise at the knowledge he seemed to possess concerning me. I suppose some astonishment was exhibited in my countenance; for Mr. Kirwin hastened to say—

"It was not until a day or two after your illness that I thought of examining your dress, that I might discover some trace by which I could send to your relations an account of your misfortune and illness. I found several letters, and, among others, one which I discovered from its commencement to be from your father. I instantly wrote to Geneva: nearly two months have elapsed since the departure of my letter.—But you are ill; even now you tremble: you are unfit for agitation of any kind."

"This suspense is a thousand times worse than the most horrible event: tell me what new scene of death has been acted, and whose murder I am now to lament."

"Your family is perfectly well," said Mr. Kirwin, with gentleness; "and some one, a friend, is come to visit you."

I know not by what chain of thought the idea presented itself, but it instantly darted into my mind that the murderer had come to mock at my misery, and taunt me with the death of Clerval, as a new incitement for me to comply with his hellish desires. I put by hand before my eyes, and cried out in agony—

"Oh! take him away! I cannot see him; for God's sake, do not let him enter!"

Mr. Kirwin regarded me with a troubled countenance. He could not help regarding my exclamation as a presumption of my guilt, and said, in rather a severe tone—

"I should have thought, young man, that the presence of your father would have been welcome, instead of inspiring such violent repugnance."

"My father!" cried I, while every feature and every muscle was relaxed from anguish to pleasure. "Is my father, indeed, come? How kind, how very kind. But where is he, why does he not hasten to me?"

My change of manner surprised and pleased the magistrate; perhaps he thought that my former exclamation was a momentary return of delirium, and now he instantly resumed his former benevolence. He rose, and quitted the room with my nurse, and in a moment my father entered it.

Nothing, at this moment, could have given me greater pleasure than the arrival of my father. I stretched out my hand to him, and cried—

"Are you then safe—and Elizabeth—and Ernest?"

My father calmed me with assurances of their welfare, and endeavoured, by dwelling on these subjects so interesting to my heart, to raise my desponding spirits; but he soon felt that a prison cannot be the abode of cheerfulness. "What a place is this that you inhabit, my son!" said he, looking mournfully at the barred windows, and wretched appearance of the room. "You travelled to seek happiness, but a fatality seems to pursue you. And poor Clerval—"

The name of my unfortunate and murdered friend was an agitation too great to be endured in my weak state; I shed tears.

"Alas! yes, my father," replied I; "some destiny of the most horrible kind hangs over me, and I must live to fulfil it, or surely I should have died on the coffin of Henry."

We were not allowed to converse for any length of time, for the precarious state of my health rendered every precaution necessary that could insure tranquillity. Mr. Kirwin came in, and insisted that my strength should not be exhausted by too much exertion. But the appearance of my father was to me like that of my good angel, and I gradually recovered my health.

As my sickness quitted me, I was absorbed by a gloomy and black melancholy, that nothing could dissipate. The image of Clerval was for ever before me, ghastly and murdered. More than once the agitation into which these reflections threw me made my friends dread a dangerous relapse. Alas! why did they preserve so miserable and detested a life? It was surely that I might fulfil my destiny, which is now drawing to a close. Soon, oh, very soon, will death extinguish these throbbings, and relieve me from the mighty weight of anguish that bears me to the dust; and, in executing the award of justice, I shall also sink to rest. Then the appearance of death was distant, although the wish was ever present to my thoughts; and I often sat for hours motionless and speechless, wishing for some mighty revolution that might bury me and my destroyer in its ruins.

The season of the assizes approached. I had already been three months in prison; and although I was still weak, and in continual danger of a relapse, I was obliged to travel nearly a hundred miles to the county-town, where the court was held. Mr. Kirwin charged himself with every care of collecting witnesses, and arranging my defence. I was spared the disgrace of appearing publicly as a criminal, as the case was not brought before the court that decides on life and death. The grand jury rejected the bill, on its being proved that I was on the Orkney Islands at the hour the body of my friend was found, and a fortnight after my removal I was liberated from prison.

My father was enraptured on finding me freed from the vexations of a criminal charge, that I was again allowed to breathe the fresh atmosphere, and allowed to return to my native country. I did not participate in these feelings; for to me the walls of a dungeon or a palace were alike hateful. The cup of life was poisoned for ever;[11] and although the sun shone upon me, as upon the happy and gay of heart, I saw around me nothing but a dense and frightful darkness, penetrated by no light but the glimmer of two eyes that glared upon me. Sometimes they were the expressive eyes of Henry, languishing in death, the dark orbs nearly covered by the lids, and the long black lashes that fringed them; sometimes it was the watery clouded eyes of the monster, as I first saw them in my chamber at Ingolstadt.

11. Victor's misery is all consuming, and it colors the way he sees his whole world, regardless of his circumstances. As he states in this passage, to him "the walls of a dungeon or a palace were alike hateful." Such a perspective challenges the notion that there is an objective reality "out there," considering that Victor's reality—his "cup of life"—is so significantly shaped by his personal misery and grief.

Nicole Piemonte.

My father tried to awaken in me the feelings of affection. He talked of Geneva, which I should soon visit—of Elizabeth, and Ernest; but these words only drew deep groans from me. Sometimes, indeed, I felt a wish for happiness; and thought, with melancholy delight, of my beloved cousin; or longed, with a devouring *maladie du pays*, to see once more the blue lake and rapid Rhone, that had been so dear to me in early childhood: but my general state of feeling was a torpor, in which a prison was as welcome a residence as the divinest scene in nature; and these fits were seldom interrupted, but by paroxysms of anguish and despair. At these moments I often endeavoured to put an end to the existence I loathed; and it required unceasing attendance and vigilance to restrain me from committing some dreadful act of violence.

I remember, as I quitted the prison, I heard one of the men say, "He may be innocent of the murder, but he has certainly a bad conscience." These words struck me. A bad conscience! yes, surely I had one. William, Justine, and Clerval, had died through my infernal machinations; "And whose death," cried I, "is to finish the tragedy? Ah! my father, do not remain in this wretched country; take me where I may forget myself, my existence, and all the world."

My father easily acceded to my desire; and, after having taken leave of Mr. Kirwin, we hastened to Dublin. I felt as if I was relieved from a heavy weight, when the packet sailed with a fair wind from Ireland, and I had quitted for ever the country which had been to me the scene of so much misery.

It was midnight. My father slept in the cabin; and I lay on the deck, looking at the stars, and listening to the dashing of the waves. I hailed the darkness that shut Ireland from my sight, and my pulse beat with a feverish joy, when I reflected that I should soon see Geneva. The past appeared to me in the light of a frightful dream; yet the vessel in which I was, the wind that blew me from the detested shore of Ireland, and the sea which surrounded me, told me too forcibly that I was deceived by no vision, and that Clerval, my friend and dearest companion, had fallen a victim to me and the monster of my creation. I repassed, in my memory, my whole life; my quiet happiness while residing with my family in Geneva, the death of my mother, and my departure for Ingolstadt. I remembered shuddering at the mad enthusiasm that hurried me on to the creation of my hideous enemy, and I called to mind the night during which he first lived. I was unable to pursue the train of thought; a thousand feelings pressed upon me, and I wept bitterly.

Ever since my recovery from the fever I had been in the custom of taking every night a small quantity of laudanum; for it was by means of this drug only that I was enabled to gain the rest necessary for the preservation of life. Oppressed by the recollection of my various misfortunes, I now took a double dose, and soon slept profoundly. But sleep did not afford me respite from thought and misery; my dreams presented a thousand objects that scared me. Towards morning I was possessed by a kind of night-mare; I felt the fiend's grasp in my neck, and could not free myself from it; groans and cries rung in my ears. My father, who was watching over me, perceiving my restlessness, awoke me, and pointed to the port of Holyhead, which we were now entering.

CHAPTER V.

We had resolved not to go to London, but to cross the country to Portsmouth, and thence to embark for Havre. I preferred this plan principally because I dreaded to see again those places in which I had enjoyed a few moments of tranquillity with my beloved Clerval. I thought with horror of seeing again those persons whom we had been accustomed to visit together, and who might make inquiries concerning an event, the very remembrance of which made me again feel the pang I endured when I gazed on his lifeless form in the inn at ———.

As for my father, his desires and exertions were bounded to the again seeing me restored to health and peace of mind. His tenderness and attentions were unremitting; my grief and gloom was obstinate, but he would not despair. Sometimes he thought that I felt deeply the degradation of being obliged to answer a charge of murder, and he endeavoured to prove to me the futility of pride.

"Alas! my father," said I, "how little do you know me. Human beings, their feelings and passions, would indeed be degraded, if such a wretch as I felt pride. Justine, poor unhappy Justine, was as innocent as I, and she suffered the same charge; she died for it; and I am the cause of this—I murdered her. William, Justine, and Henry—they all died by my hands."

My father had often, during my imprisonment, heard me make the same assertion; when I thus accused myself, he sometimes seemed to desire an explanation, and at others he appeared to consider it as caused by delirium, and that, during my illness, some idea of this kind had presented itself to my imagination, the remembrance of which I preserved in my convalescence. I avoided explanation, and maintained a continual silence concerning the wretch I had created. I had a feeling that I should be supposed mad, and this for ever chained my tongue, when I would have given the whole world to have confided the fatal secret.

Upon this occasion my father said, with an expression of unbounded wonder, "What do you mean, Victor? are you mad? My dear son, I entreat you never to make such an assertion again."

"I am not mad," I cried energetically; "the sun and the heavens, who have viewed my operations, can bear witness of my truth. I am the assassin of those most innocent victims; they died by my machinations. A thousand times would I have shed my own blood, drop by drop, to have saved their lives; but I could not, my father, indeed I could not sacrifice the whole human race."

The conclusion of this speech convinced my father that my ideas were deranged, and he instantly changed the subject of our conversation, and endeavoured to alter the course of my thoughts. He wished as much as possible to obliterate the memory of the scenes that had taken place in Ireland, and never alluded to them, or suffered me to speak of my misfortunes.

As time passed away I became more calm: misery had her dwelling in my heart, but I no longer talked in the same incoherent manner of my own crimes; sufficient for me was the consciousness of them. By the utmost self-violence, I curbed the imperious voice of wretchedness, which sometimes desired to declare itself to the whole world; and my manners were calmer and more composed than they had ever been since my journey to the sea of ice.

We arrived at Havre on the 8th of May, and instantly proceeded to Paris, where my father had some business which detained us a few weeks. In this city, I received the following letter from Elizabeth:—

"*To* VICTOR FRANKENSTEIN.
"MY DEAREST FRIEND,

"It gave me the greatest pleasure to receive a letter from my uncle dated at Paris; you are no longer at a formidable distance, and I may hope to see you in less than a fortnight. My poor cousin, how much you must have suffered! I expect to see you looking even more ill than when you quitted Geneva. This winter has been passed most miserably, tortured as I have been by anxious suspense; yet I hope to see peace in your countenance, and to find that your heart is not totally devoid of comfort and tranquillity.

"Yet I fear that the same feelings now exist that made you so miserable a year ago, even perhaps augmented by time. I would not disturb you at this period, when so many misfortunes weigh upon you; but a conversation that I had with my uncle previous to his departure renders some explanation necessary before we meet.

"Explanation! you may possibly say; what can Elizabeth have to explain? If you really say this, my questions are answered, and I have no more to do than to sign myself your affectionate cousin. But you are distant from me, and it is possible that you may dread, and yet be pleased with this explanation; and, in a probability of this being the case, I dare not any longer postpone writing what, during your absence, I have often wished to express to you, but have never had the courage to begin.

"You well know, Victor, that our union had been the favourite plan of your parents ever since our infancy. We were told this when young, and taught to look forward to it as an event that would certainly take place. We were affectionate playfellows during childhood, and, I believe, dear and valued friends to one another as we grew older. But as brother and sister often entertain a lively affection towards each other, without desiring a more intimate union, may not such also be our case? Tell me, dearest Victor. Answer me, I conjure you, by our mutual happiness, with simple truth—Do you not love another?

"You have travelled; you have spent several years of your life at Ingolstadt; and I confess to you, my friend, that when I saw you last autumn so unhappy, flying to solitude, from the society of every creature, I could not help supposing that you might regret our connexion, and believe yourself bound in honour to fulfil the wishes of your parents, although they opposed themselves to your inclinations. But this is false reasoning. I confess to you, my cousin, that I love you, and that in my airy dreams of futurity you have been my constant friend and companion. But it is your happiness I desire as well as my own, when I declare to you, that our marriage would render me eternally miserable, unless it were the dictate of your own free choice. Even now I weep to think, that, borne down as you are by the cruelest misfortunes, you may stifle, by the word *honour*, all hope of that love and happiness which would alone restore you to yourself. I, who have so interested an affection for you, may increase your miseries ten-fold, by being an obstacle to your wishes. Ah, Victor, be assured that your cousin and playmate has too sincere a love for you not to be made miserable by this supposition. Be happy, my friend; and if you obey me in this one request, remain satisfied that nothing on earth will have the power to interrupt my tranquillity.

"Do not let this letter disturb you; do not answer it to-morrow, or the next day, or even until you come, if it will give you pain. My uncle will send me news of your health; and if I see but one smile on your lips when we meet, occasioned by this or any other exertion of mine, I shall need no other happiness.

"ELIZABETH LAVENZA.
"Geneva, May 18th, 17—."

This letter revived in my memory what I had before forgotten, the threat of the fiend—"*I will be with you on your wedding-night!*" Such was my sentence, and on that night would the dæmon employ every art to destroy me, and tear me from the glimpse of happiness which promised partly to console my sufferings. On that night he had determined to consummate his crimes by my death. Well, be it so; a deadly struggle would then assuredly take place, in which if he was victorious, I should be at peace, and his power over me be at an end. If he were vanquished, I should be a free man. Alas! what freedom? such as the peasant enjoys when his family have been massacred before his eyes, his cottage burnt, his lands laid waste, and he is turned adrift, homeless, pennyless, and alone, but free. Such would be my liberty, except that in my Elizabeth I possessed a treasure; alas! balanced by those horrors of remorse and guilt, which would pursue me until death.

Sweet and beloved Elizabeth! I read and re-read her letter, and some softened feelings stole into my heart, and dared to whisper paradisaical dreams of love and joy; but the apple was already eaten, and the angel's arm bared to drive me from all hope. Yet I would die to make her happy. If the monster executed his threat, death was inevitable; yet, again, I considered whether my marriage would hasten my fate. My destruction might indeed arrive a few months sooner; but if my torturer should suspect that I postponed it, influenced by his menaces, he would surely find other, and perhaps more dreadful means of revenge. He had vowed *to be with me on my wedding-night*, yet he did not consider that threat as binding him to peace in the mean time; for, as if to shew me that he was not yet satiated with blood, he had murdered Clerval immediately after the enunciation of his threats. I resolved, therefore, that if my immediate union with my cousin would conduce either to her's or my father's happiness, my adversary's designs against my life should not retard it a single hour.[12]

---

12. Altruism, typically conceived of as selfless concern for the best interest of others, is usually seen as a positive quality. Though Victor does appear altruistic here, he never shows selfless concern for his creation and instead shirks responsibility for the creature and his well-being. Moreover, in the context of scientific research, it is important to consider the tireless or "altruistic" behavior of the researcher that leads to the complete abnegation of the self, resulting in unreflective decisions and actions. Perhaps if Victor had taken the time to reflect on himself—his motives, decisions, desires, and actions—during his scientific pursuits, he would have refrained from bringing his creature to life in the first place.

Nicole Piemonte.

In this state of mind I wrote to Elizabeth. My letter was calm and affectionate. "I fear, my beloved girl," I said, "little happiness remains for us on earth; yet all that I may one day enjoy is concentered in you. Chase away your idle fears; to you alone do I consecrate my life, and my endeavours for contentment. I have one secret, Elizabeth, a dreadful one; when revealed to you, it will chill your frame with horror, and then, far from being surprised at my misery, you will only wonder that I survive what I have endured. I will confide this tale of misery and terror to you the day after our marriage shall take place; for, my sweet cousin, there must be perfect confidence between us. But until then, I conjure you, do not mention or allude to it. This I most earnestly entreat, and I know you will comply."

In about a week after the arrival of Elizabeth's letter, we returned to Geneva. My cousin welcomed me with warm affection; yet tears were in her eyes, as she beheld my emaciated frame and feverish cheeks. I saw a change in her also. She was thinner, and had lost much of that heavenly vivacity that had before charmed me; but her gentleness, and soft looks of compassion, made her a more fit companion for one blasted and miserable as I was.

The tranquillity which I now enjoyed did not endure. Memory brought madness with it; and when I thought on what had passed, a real insanity possessed me; sometimes I was furious, and burnt with rage, sometimes low and despondent. I neither spoke nor looked, but sat motionless, bewildered by the multitude of miseries that overcame me.

Elizabeth alone had the power to draw me from these fits; her gentle voice would soothe me when transported by passion, and inspire me with human feelings when sunk in torpor. She wept with me, and for me. When reason returned, she would remonstrate, and endeavour to inspire me with resignation. Ah! it is well for the unfortunate to be resigned, but for the guilty there is no peace. The agonies of remorse poison the luxury there is otherwise sometimes found in indulging the excess of grief.

Soon after my arrival my father spoke of my immediate marriage with my cousin. I remained silent.

"Have you, then, some other attachment?"

"None on earth. I love Elizabeth, and look forward to our union with delight. Let the day therefore be fixed; and on it I will consecrate myself, in life or death, to the happiness of my cousin."

"My dear Victor, do not speak thus. Heavy misfortunes have befallen us; but let us only cling closer to what remains, and transfer our love for those whom we have lost to those who yet live. Our circle will be small, but bound close by the ties of affection and mutual misfortune. And when time shall have softened your despair, new and dear objects of care will be born to replace those of whom we have been so cruelly deprived."

Such were the lessons of my father. But to me the remembrance of the threat returned: nor can you wonder, that, omnipotent as the fiend had yet been in his deeds of blood, I should almost regard him as invincible; and that when he had pronounced the words, "*I shall be with you on your wedding-night*," I should regard the threatened fate as unavoidable. But death was no evil to me, if the loss of Elizabeth were balanced with it; and I therefore, with a contented and even cheerful countenance, agreed with my father, that if my cousin would consent, the ceremony should take place in ten days, and thus put, as I imagined, the seal to my fate.

Great God! if for one instant I had thought what might be the hellish intention of my fiendish adversary, I would rather have banished myself for ever from my native country, and wandered a friendless outcast over the earth, than have consented to this miserable marriage. But, as if possessed of magic powers, the monster had blinded me to his real intentions; and when I thought that I prepared only my own death, I hastened that of a far dearer victim.

As the period fixed for our marriage drew nearer, whether from cowardice or a prophetic feeling, I felt my heart sink within me. But I concealed my feelings by an appearance of hilarity, that brought smiles and joy to the countenance of my father, but hardly deceived the ever-watchful and nicer eye of Elizabeth. She looked forward to our union with placid contentment, not unmingled with a little fear, which past misfortunes had impressed, that what now appeared certain and tangible happiness, might soon dissipate into an airy dream, and leave no trace but deep and everlasting regret.

Preparations were made for the event; congratulatory visits were received; and all wore a smiling appearance. I shut up, as well as I could, in my own heart the anxiety that preyed there, and entered with seeming earnestness into the plans of my father, although they might only serve as the decorations of my tragedy. A house was purchased for us near Cologny, by which we should enjoy the pleasures of the country, and yet be so near Geneva as to see my father every day; who would still reside within the walls, for the benefit of Ernest, that he might follow his studies at the schools.

In the mean time I took every precaution to defend my person, in case the fiend should openly attack me. I carried pistols and a dagger constantly about me, and was ever on the watch to prevent artifice; and by these means gained a greater degree of tranquillity. Indeed, as the period approached, the threat appeared more as a delusion, not to be regarded as worthy to disturb my peace, while the happiness I hoped for in my marriage wore a greater appearance of certainty, as the day fixed for its solemnization drew nearer, and I heard it continually spoken of as an occurrence which no accident could possibly prevent.

Elizabeth seemed happy; my tranquil demeanour contributed greatly to calm her mind. But on the day that was to fulfil my wishes and my destiny, she was melancholy, and a presentiment of evil pervaded her; and perhaps also she thought of the dreadful secret, which I had promised to reveal to her the following day. My father was in the mean time overjoyed, and, in the bustle of preparation, only observed in the melancholy of his niece the diffidence of a bride.

After the ceremony was performed, a large party assembled at my father's; but it was agreed that Elizabeth and I should pass the afternoon and night at Evian, and return to Cologny the next morning. As the day was fair, and the wind favourable, we resolved to go by water.

Those were the last moments of my life during which I enjoyed the feeling of happiness. We passed rapidly along: the sun was hot, but we were sheltered from its rays by a kind of canopy, while we enjoyed the beauty of the scene, sometimes on one side of the lake, where we saw Mont Salêve, the pleasant banks of Montalêgre, and at a distance, surmounting all, the beautiful Mont Blanc, and the assemblage of snowy mountains that in vain endeavour to emulate her; sometimes coasting the opposite banks, we saw the mighty Jura opposing its dark side to the ambition that would quit its native country, and an almost insurmountable barrier to the invader who should wish to enslave it.

I took the hand of Elizabeth: "You are sorrowful, my love. Ah! if you knew what I have suffered, and what I may yet endure, you would endeavour to let me taste the quiet, and freedom from despair, that this one day at least permits me to enjoy."

"Be happy, my dear Victor," replied Elizabeth; "there is, I hope, nothing to distress you; and be assured that if a lively joy is not painted in my face, my heart is contented. Something whispers to me not to depend too much on the prospect that is opened before us; but I will not listen to such a sinister voice. Observe how fast we move along, and how the clouds which sometimes obscure, and sometimes rise above the dome of Mont Blanc, render this scene of beauty still more interesting. Look also at the innumerable fish that are swimming in the clear waters, where we can distinguish every pebble that lies at the bottom. What a divine day! how happy and serene all nature appears!"

Thus Elizabeth endeavoured to divert her thoughts and mine from all reflection upon melancholy subjects. But her temper was fluctuating; joy for a few instants shone in her eyes, but it continually gave place to distraction and reverie.

The sun sunk lower in the heavens; we passed the river Drance, and observed its path through the chasms of the higher, and the glens of the lower hills. The Alps here come closer to the lake, and we approached the amphitheatre of mountains which forms its eastern boundary. The spire of Evian shone under the woods that surrounded it, and the range of mountain above mountain by which it was overhung.

The wind, which had hitherto carried us along with amazing rapidity, sunk at sunset to a light breeze; the soft air just ruffled the water, and caused a pleasant motion among the trees as we approached the shore, from which it wafted the most delightful scent of flowers and hay. The sun sunk beneath the horizon as we landed; and as I touched the shore, I felt those cares and fears revive, which soon were to clasp me, and cling to me for ever.

CHAPTER VI.

It was eight o'clock when we landed; we walked for a short time on the shore, enjoying the transitory light, and then retired to the inn, and contemplated the lovely scene of waters, woods, and mountains, obscured in darkness, yet still displaying their black outlines.

The wind, which had fallen in the south, now rose with great violence in the west. The moon had reached her summit in the heavens, and was beginning to descend; the clouds swept across it swifter than the flight of the vulture, and dimmed her rays, while the lake reflected the scene of the busy heavens, rendered still busier by the restless waves that were beginning to rise. Suddenly a heavy storm of rain descended.

I had been calm during the day; but so soon as night obscured the shapes of objects, a thousand fears arose in my mind. I was anxious and watchful, while my right hand grasped a pistol which was hidden in my bosom; every sound terrified me; but I resolved that I would sell my life dearly, and not relax the impending conflict until my own life, or that of my adversary, were extinguished.

Elizabeth observed my agitation for some time in timid and fearful silence; at length she said, "What is it that agitates you, my dear Victor? What is it you fear?"

"Oh! peace, peace, my love," replied I, "this night, and all will be safe: but this night is dreadful, very dreadful."

I passed an hour in this state of mind, when suddenly I reflected how dreadful the combat which I momentarily expected would be to my wife, and I earnestly entreated her to retire, resolving not to join her until I had obtained some knowledge as to the situation of my enemy.

She left me, and I continued some time walking up and down the passages of the house, and inspecting every corner that might afford a retreat to my adversary. But I discovered no trace of him, and was beginning to conjecture that some fortunate chance had intervened to prevent the execution of his menaces; when suddenly I heard a shrill and dreadful scream. It came from the room into which Elizabeth had retired. As I heard it, the whole truth rushed into my mind, my arms dropped, the motion of every muscle and fibre was suspended; I could feel the blood trickling in my veins, and tingling in the extremities of my limbs. This state lasted but for an instant; the scream was repeated, and I rushed into the room.

Great God! why did I not then expire! Why am I here to relate the destruction of the best hope, and the purest creature of earth? She was there, lifeless and inanimate, thrown across the bed, her head hanging down, and her pale and distorted features half covered by her hair. Every where I turn I see the same figure—her bloodless arms and relaxed form flung by the murderer on its bridal bier. Could I behold this, and live? Alas! life is obstinate, and clings closest where it is most hated. For a moment only did I lose recollection; I fainted.

When I recovered, I found myself surrounded by the people of the inn; their countenances expressed a breathless terror: but the horror of others appeared only as a mockery, a shadow of the feelings that oppressed me. I escaped from them to the room where lay the body of Elizabeth, my love, my wife, so lately living, so dear, so worthy. She had been moved from the posture in which I had first beheld her; and now, as she lay, her head upon her arm, and a handkerchief thrown across her face and neck, I might have supposed her asleep. I rushed towards her, and embraced her with ardour; but the deathly languor and coldness of the limbs told me, that what I now held in my arms had ceased to be the Elizabeth whom I had loved and cherished. The murderous mark of the fiend's grasp was on her neck, and the breath had ceased to issue from her lips.

While I still hung over her in the agony of despair, I happened to look up. The windows of the room had before been darkened; and I felt a kind of panic on seeing the pale yellow light of the moon illuminate the chamber. The shutters had been thrown back; and, with a sensation of horror not to be described, I saw at the open window a figure the most hideous and abhorred. A grin was on the face of the monster; he seemed to jeer, as with his fiendish finger he pointed towards the corpse of my wife. I rushed towards the window, and drawing a pistol from my bosom, shot; but he eluded me, leaped from his station, and, running with the swiftness of lightning, plunged into the lake.

The report of the pistol brought a crowd into the room. I pointed to the spot where he had disappeared, and we followed the track with boats; nets were cast, but in vain. After passing several hours, we returned hopeless, most of my companions believing it to have been a form conjured by my fancy. After having landed, they proceeded to search the country, parties going in different directions among the woods and vines.

I did not accompany them; I was exhausted: a film covered my eyes, and my skin was parched with the heat of fever. In this state I lay on a bed, hardly conscious of what had happened; my eyes wandered round the room, as if to seek something that I had lost.

At length I remembered that my father would anxiously expect the return of Elizabeth and myself, and that I must return alone. This reflection brought tears into my eyes, and I wept for a long time; but my thoughts rambled to various subjects, reflecting on my misfortunes, and their cause. I was bewildered in a cloud of wonder and horror. The death of William, the execution of Justine, the murder of Clerval, and lastly of my wife; even at that moment I knew not that my only remaining friends were safe from the malignity of the fiend; my father even now might be writhing under his grasp, and Ernest might be dead at his feet. This idea made me shudder, and recalled me to action. I started up, and resolved to return to Geneva with all possible speed.

There were no horses to be procured, and I must return by the lake; but the wind was unfavourable, and the rain fell in torrents. However, it was hardly morning, and I might reasonably hope to arrive by night. I hired men to row, and took an oar myself, for I had always experienced relief from mental torment in bodily exercise.[13] But the overflowing misery I now felt, and the excess of agitation that I endured, rendered me incapable of any exertion. I threw down the oar; and, leaning my head upon my hands, gave way to every gloomy idea that arose. If I looked up, I saw the scenes which were familiar to me in my happier time, and which I had

---

13. After the deaths of his brother, his friend, and his bride, Victor seeks refuge from his grief in strenuous exercise, just as he walked the streets of Ingolstadt after creating the creature. Influential thinkers of the Enlightenment vigorously pursued theories about the relationship between the mind and the body and about the place that exercise holds in physical and mental health. René Descartes, the seventeenth-century French scientific philosopher, promulgated the idea that humans have a dual nature—a material body and a nonmaterial mind—and that although they are separate, each can influence the other via the pineal gland. Joseph Addison (1672–1718), an influential thinker and essayist of the early eighteenth century, held a broad view about the means by

contemplated but the day before in the company of her who was now but a shadow and a recollection. Tears streamed from my eyes. The rain had ceased for a moment, and I saw the fish play in the waters as they had done a few hours before; they had then been observed by Elizabeth. Nothing is so painful to the human mind as a great and sudden change. The sun might shine, or the clouds might lour; but nothing could appear to me as it had done the day before. A fiend had snatched from me every hope of future happiness: no creature had ever been so miserable as I was; so frightful an event is single in the history of man.

But why should I dwell upon the incidents that followed this last overwhelming event. Mine has been a tale of horrors; I have reached their *acme*, and what I must now relate can but be tedious to you. Know that, one by one, my friends were snatched away; I was left desolate. My own strength is exhausted; and I must tell, in a few words, what remains of my hideous narration.

I arrived at Geneva. My father and Ernest yet lived; but the former sunk under the tidings that I bore. I see him now, excellent and venerable old man! his eyes wandered in vacancy, for they had lost their charm and their delight—his niece, his more than daughter, whom he doated on with all that affection which a man feels, who, in the decline of life, having few affections, clings more earnestly to those that remain. Cursed, cursed be the fiend that brought misery on his grey hairs, and doomed him to waste in wretchedness! He could not live under the horrors that were accumulated around him; an apoplectic fit was brought on, and in a few days he died in my arms.

What then became of me? I know not; I lost sensation, and chains and darkness were the only objects that pressed upon me. Sometimes, indeed, I dreamt that I wandered in flowery meadows and pleasant vales with the friends of my youth; but awoke, and found myself in a dungeon.

---

which the body could influence the mind and wrote extensively on the usefulness of exercise in avoiding "melancholic spleen" in men and "the vapours" in women. "Whatever we do," Addison wrote, "we should keep up the cheerfulness of our spirits and never let them sink below an inclination at least to be well-pleased. The way of this is to keep our bodies in exercise, our minds at ease" (1711). Victor Frankenstein, in exercising to alleviate his mental anguish, has taken to heart Addison's advice from a century earlier. Present-day neuroscientists likewise theorize that vigorous exercise stimulates the pituitary gland to release endorphins, substances that can alleviate pain and induce euphoria, the well-known "runner's high," and have found evidence that regular physical activity reduces anxiety and depression (see Anderson and Shivakumar 2013; Batchelder 2012; Leuenberger 2006).

Eileen Gunn.

Melancholy followed, but by degrees I gained a clear conception of my miseries and situation, and was then released from my prison. For they had called me mad; and during many months, as I understood, a solitary cell had been my habitation.

But liberty had been a useless gift to me had I not, as I awakened to reason, at the same time awakened to revenge. As the memory of past misfortunes pressed upon me, I began to reflect on their cause—the monster whom I had created, the miserable dæmon whom I had sent abroad into the world for my destruction. I was possessed by a maddening rage when I thought of him, and desired and ardently prayed that I might have him within my grasp to wreak a great and signal revenge on his cursed head.

Nor did my hate long confine itself to useless wishes; I began to reflect on the best means of securing him; and for this purpose, about a month after my release, I repaired to a criminal judge in the town, and told him that I had an accusation to make; that I knew the destroyer of my family; and that I required him to exert his whole authority for the apprehension of the murderer.

The magistrate listened to me with attention and kindness: "Be assured, sir," said he, "no pains or exertions on my part shall be spared to discover the villain."

"I thank you," replied I; "listen, therefore, to the deposition that I have to make. It is indeed a tale so strange, that I should fear you would not credit it, were there not something in truth which, however wonderful, forces conviction. The story is too connected to be mistaken for a dream, and I have no motive for falsehood." My manner, as I thus addressed him, was impressive, but calm; I had formed in my own heart a resolution to pursue my destroyer to death; and this purpose quieted my agony, and provisionally reconciled me to life. I now related my history briefly, but with firmness and precision, marking the dates with accuracy, and never deviating into invective or exclamation.

The magistrate appeared at first perfectly incredulous, but as I continued he became more attentive and interested; I saw him sometimes shudder with horror, at others a lively surprise, unmingled with disbelief, was painted on his countenance.

When I had concluded my narration, I said, "This is the being whom I accuse, and for whose detection and punishment I call upon you to exert your whole power. It is your duty as a magistrate, and I believe and hope that your feelings as a man will not revolt from the execution of those functions on this occasion."

This address caused a considerable change in the physiognomy of my auditor. He had heard my story with that half kind of belief that is given to a tale of spirits and supernatural events; but when he was called upon to act officially in consequence, the whole tide of his incredulity returned. He, however, answered mildly, "I would willingly afford you every aid in your pursuit; but the creature of whom you speak appears to have powers which would put all my exertions to defiance. Who can follow an animal which can traverse the sea of ice, and inhabit caves and dens, where no man would venture to intrude? Besides, some months have elapsed since the commission of his crimes, and no one can conjecture to what place he has wandered, or what region he may now inhabit."

"I do not doubt that he hovers near the spot which I inhabit; and if he has indeed taken refuge in the Alps, he may be hunted like the chamois, and destroyed as a beast of prey. But I perceive your thoughts: you do not credit my narrative, and do not intend to pursue my enemy with the punishment which is his desert."

As I spoke, rage sparkled in my eyes; the magistrate was intimidated; "You are mistaken," said he, "I will exert myself; and if it is in my power to seize the monster, be assured that he shall suffer punishment proportionate to his crimes. But I fear, from what you have yourself described to be his properties, that this will prove impracticable, and that, while every proper measure is pursued, you should endeavour to make up your mind to disappointment."

"That cannot be; but all that I can say will be of little avail. My revenge is of no moment to you; yet, while I allow it to be a vice, I confess that it is the devouring and only passion of my soul. My rage is unspeakable, when I reflect that the murderer, whom I have turned loose upon society, still exists. You refuse my just demand: I have but one resource; and I devote myself, either in my life or death, to his destruction." [14]

14. Retribution is punishment for an injury, wrongdoing, or crime. In organized societies, the law imposes retribution in the form of penalties such as imprisonment. In the absence or failure of law, individuals may seek to impose retribution in the wild, unrestrained form of revenge—one of this novel's major themes. The creature, abandoned by his creator and rejected by the family he hoped to befriend, furiously vows "eternal hatred and vengeance to all mankind" (p. 118). His desire for vengeance ultimately zeroes in on Victor's loved ones, and so he destroys William, Justine, Clerval, and Elizabeth in turn. After Elizabeth's death, Victor significantly first seeks retribution through law, urging a judge to bring the creature to justice. When the judge explains his powerlessness to help in the pursuit—that is, when society fails Victor—he becomes a mirror of the creature in his obsession with vengeance. As a consequence, Victor loses both the rationality of the scientist and the normal connections and affections of a civilized person. His search for the creature eventually leads him to the icy region of the North Pole—a journey symbolizing the freezing out of human

I trembled with excess of agitation as I said this; there was a phrenzy in my manner, and something, I doubt not, of that haughty fierceness, which the martyrs of old are said to have possessed. But to a Genevan magistrate, whose mind was occupied by far other ideas than those of devotion and heroism, this elevation of mind had much the appearance of madness. He endeavoured to soothe me as a nurse does a child, and reverted to my tale as the effects of delirium.

"Man," I cried, "how ignorant art thou in thy pride of wisdom! Cease; you know not what it is you say."[15]

I broke from the house angry and disturbed, and retired to meditate on some other mode of action.

CHAPTER VII.

My present situation was one in which all voluntary thought was swallowed up and lost. I was hurried away by fury; revenge alone endowed me with strength and composure; it modelled my feelings, and allowed me to be calculating and calm, at periods when otherwise delirium or death would have been my portion.

My first resolution was to quit Geneva for ever; my country, which, when I was happy and beloved, was dear to me, now, in my adversity, became hateful. I provided myself with a sum of money, together with a few jewels which had belonged to my mother, and departed.

And now my wanderings began, which are to cease but with life. I have traversed a vast portion of the earth, and have endured all the hardships which travellers, in deserts and barbarous countries, are wont to meet. How I have lived I hardly know; many times have I stretched my failing limbs upon the sandy plain, and prayed for death. But revenge kept me alive; I dared not die, and leave my adversary in being.

---

feeling that comes with the blind pursuit of vengeance. The destructive nature of such a pursuit has been a theme of literature since the time of the ancient Greeks. Here Mary adds the troubling notion that science itself—however based in rationality and a drive for human progress—may inadvertently create disruptions that unleash the most irrational and violent of human feelings, which override the ability of society's institutions to contain them.
Mike Stanford.

15. Victor's objection here is that the Genevan magistrate is being arrogant in assuming a position of understanding that he (the magistrate) feels is necessary to dispense absolution. The moment foreshadows the anxiety of contemporary citizens who feel that they simply don't know enough to engage in discussions of scientific morality.
Chris Hanlon.

When I quitted Geneva, my first labour was to gain some clue by which I might trace the steps of my fiendish enemy. But my plan was unsettled; and I wandered many hours around the confines of the town, uncertain what path I should pursue. As night approached, I found myself at the entrance of the cemetery where William, Elizabeth, and my father, reposed. I entered it, and approached the tomb which marked their graves. Every thing was silent, except the leaves of the trees, which were gently agitated by the wind; the night was nearly dark; and the scene would have been solemn and affecting even to an uninterested observer. The spirits of the departed seemed to flit around, and to cast a shadow, which was felt but seen not, around the head of the mourner.

The deep grief which this scene had at first excited quickly gave way to rage and despair. They were dead, and I lived; their murderer also lived, and to destroy him I must drag out my weary existence. I knelt on the grass, and kissed the earth, and with quivering lips exclaimed, "By the sacred earth on which I kneel, by the shades that wander near me, by the deep and eternal grief that I feel, I swear; and by thee, O Night, and by the spirits that preside over thee, I swear to pursue the dæmon, who caused this misery, until he or I shall perish in mortal conflict. For this purpose I will preserve my life: to execute this dear revenge, will I again behold the sun, and tread the green herbage of earth, which otherwise should vanish from my eyes for ever. And I call on you, spirits of the dead; and on you, wandering ministers of vengeance, to aid and conduct me in my work. Let the cursed and hellish monster drink deep of agony; let him feel the despair that now torments me."

I had begun my adjuration with solemnity, and an awe which almost assured me that the shades of my murdered friends heard and approved my devotion; but the furies possessed me as I concluded, and rage choaked my utterance.

I was answered through the stillness of night by a loud and fiendish laugh. It rung on my ears long and heavily; the mountains re-echoed it, and I felt as if all hell surrounded me with mockery and laughter. Surely in that moment I should have been possessed by phrenzy, and have destroyed my miserable existence, but that my vow was heard, and that I was reserved for vengeance. The laughter died away; when a well-known and abhorred voice, apparently close to my ear, addressed me in an audible whisper— "I am satisfied: miserable wretch! you have determined to live, and I am satisfied."

I darted towards the spot from which the sound proceeded; but the devil eluded my grasp. Suddenly the broad disk of the moon arose, and shone full upon his ghastly and distorted shape, as he fled with more than mortal speed.

I pursued him; and for many months this has been my task. Guided by a slight clue, I followed the windings of the Rhone, but vainly. The blue Mediterranean appeared; and, by a strange chance, I saw the fiend enter by night, and hide himself in a vessel bound for the Black Sea. I took my passage in the same ship; but he escaped, I know not how.

Amid the wilds of Tartary and Russia, although he still evaded me, I have ever followed in his track. Sometimes the peasants, scared by this horrid apparition, informed me of his path; sometimes he himself, who feared that if I lost all trace I should despair and die, often left some mark to guide me. The snows descended on my head, and I saw the print of his huge step on the white plain. To you first entering on life, to whom care is new, and agony unknown, how can you understand what I have felt, and still feel? Cold, want, and fatigue, were the least pains which I was destined to endure; I was cursed by some devil, and carried about with me my eternal hell; yet still a spirit of good followed and directed my steps, and, when I most murmured, would suddenly extricate me from seemingly insurmountable difficulties. Sometimes, when nature, overcome by hunger, sunk under the exhaustion, a repast was prepared for me in the desert, that restored and inspirited me. The fare was indeed coarse, such as the peasants of the country ate; but I may not doubt that it was set there by the spirits that I had invoked to aid me. Often, when all was dry, the heavens cloudless, and I was parched by thirst, a slight cloud would bedim the sky, shed the few drops that revived me, and vanish.[16]

I followed, when I could, the courses of the rivers; but the dæmon generally avoided these, as it was here that the population of the country chiefly collected. In other places human beings were seldom seen; and I generally subsisted on the wild animals that crossed my path. I had money with me, and gained the friendship of the villagers by distributing it, or bringing with me some food that I had killed, which, after taking a small part, I always presented to those who had provided me with fire and utensils for cooking.

---

16. Most people attribute their successes to their own efforts. People pride themselves on great preparation and stellar execution. Most, however, do not recognize how often their success is a result of the world lining up in exactly the right way so that this effort and preparation can pay off. When you look back on your life, though, you may recognize that luck and happenstance led to your successes. In this passage, Victor reflects on the role that chance and serendipity have played in his successes. Just when things look darkest, circumstances align to allow him to continue his pursuit of the creature.

Arthur B. Markman.

My life, as it passed thus, was indeed hateful to me, and it was during sleep alone that I could taste joy. O blessed sleep! often, when most miserable, I sank to repose, and my dreams lulled me even to rapture. The spirits that guarded me had provided these moments, or rather hours, of happiness, that I might retain strength to fulfil my pilgrimage. Deprived of this respite, I should have sunk under my hardships. During the day I was sustained and inspirited by the hope of night: for in sleep I saw my friends, my wife, and my beloved country; again I saw the benevolent countenance of my father, heard the silver tones of my Elizabeth's voice, and beheld Clerval enjoying health and youth. Often, when wearied by a toilsome march, I persuaded myself that I was dreaming until night should come, and that I should then enjoy reality in the arms of my dearest friends. What agonizing fondness did I feel for them! how did I cling to their dear forms, as sometimes they haunted even my waking hours, and persuade myself that they still lived! At such moments vengeance, that burned within me, died in my heart, and I pursued my path towards the destruction of the dæmon, more as a task enjoined by heaven, as the mechanical impulse of some power of which I was unconscious, than as the ardent desire of my soul.

What his feelings were whom I pursued, I cannot know. Sometimes, indeed, he left marks in writing on the barks of the trees, or cut in stone, that guided me, and instigated my fury. "My reign is not yet over," (these words were legible in one of these inscriptions); "you live, and my power is complete. Follow me; I seek the everlasting ices of the north, where you will feel the misery of cold and frost, to which I am impassive. You will find near this place, if you follow not too tardily, a dead hare; eat, and be refreshed. Come on, my enemy; we have yet to wrestle for our lives; but many hard and miserable hours must you endure, until that period shall arrive."

Scoffing devil! Again do I vow vengeance; again do I devote thee, miserable fiend, to torture and death. Never will I omit my search, until he or I perish; and then with what ecstacy shall I join my Elizabeth, and those who even now prepare for me the reward of my tedious toil and horrible pilgrimage.

As I still pursued my journey to the northward, the snows thickened, and the cold increased in a degree almost too severe to support. The peasants were shut up in their hovels, and only a few of the most hardy ventured forth to seize the animals whom starvation had forced from their hiding-places to seek for prey. The rivers were covered with ice, and no fish could be procured; and thus I was cut off from my chief article of maintenance.

The triumph of my enemy increased with the difficulty of my labours. One inscription that he left was in these words: "Prepare! your toils only begin: wrap yourself in furs, and provide food, for we shall soon enter upon a journey where your sufferings will satisfy my everlasting hatred."

My courage and perseverance were invigorated by these scoffing words; I resolved not to fail in my purpose; and, calling on heaven to support me, I continued with unabated fervour to traverse immense deserts, until the ocean appeared at a distance, and formed the utmost boundary of the horizon. Oh! how unlike it was to the blue seas of the south! Covered with ice, it was only to be distinguished from land by its superior wildness and ruggedness. The Greeks wept for joy when they beheld the Mediterranean from the hills of Asia, and hailed with rapture the boundary of their toils. I did not weep; but I knelt down, and, with a full heart, thanked my guiding spirit for conducting me in safety to the place where I hoped, notwithstanding my adversary's gibe, to meet and grapple with him.

Some weeks before this period I had procured a sledge and dogs, and thus traversed the snows with inconceivable speed. I know not whether the fiend possessed the same advantages; but I found that, as before I had daily lost ground in the pursuit, I now gained on him; so much so, that when I first saw the ocean, he was but one day's journey in advance, and I hoped to intercept him before he should reach the beach. With new courage, therefore, I pressed on, and in two days arrived at a wretched hamlet on the sea-shore. I inquired of the inhabitants concerning the fiend, and gained accurate information. A gigantic monster, they said, had arrived the night before, armed with a gun and many pistols; putting to flight the inhabitants of a solitary cottage, through fear of his terrific appearance. He had carried off their store of winter food, and, placing it in a sledge, to draw which he had seized on a numerous drove of trained dogs, he had harnessed them, and the same night, to the joy of the horror-struck villagers, had pursued his journey across the sea in a direction that led to no land; and they conjectured that he must speedily be destroyed by the breaking of the ice, or frozen by the eternal frosts.

On hearing this information, I suffered a temporary access of despair. He had escaped me; and I must commence a destructive and almost endless journey across the mountainous ices of the ocean,—amidst cold that few of the inhabitants could long endure, and which I, the native of a genial and sunny climate, could not hope to survive. Yet at the idea that the fiend should live and be triumphant, my rage and vengeance returned, and, like a mighty tide, overwhelmed every other feeling. After a slight repose, during which the spirits of the dead hovered round, and instigated me to toil and revenge, I prepared for my journey.

I exchanged my land sledge for one fashioned for the inequalities of the frozen ocean; and, purchasing a plentiful stock of provisions, I departed from land.

I cannot guess how many days have passed since then; but I have endured misery, which nothing but the eternal sentiment of a just retribution burning within my heart could have enabled me to support. Immense and rugged mountains of ice often barred up my passage, and I often heard the thunder of the ground sea, which threatened my destruction. But again the frost came, and made the paths of the sea secure.

By the quantity of provision which I had consumed I should guess that I had passed three weeks in this journey; and the continual protraction of hope, returning back upon the heart, often wrung bitter drops of despondency and grief from my eyes. Despair had indeed almost secured her prey, and I should soon have sunk beneath this misery; when once, after the poor animals that carried me had with incredible toil gained the summit of a sloping ice mountain, and one sinking under his fatigue died, I viewed the expanse before me with anguish, when suddenly my eye caught a dark speck upon the dusky plain. I strained my sight to discover what it could be, and uttered a wild cry of ecstacy when I distinguished a sledge, and the distorted proportions of a well-known form within. Oh! with what a burning gush did hope revisit my heart! warm tears filled my eyes, which I hastily wiped away, that they might not intercept the view I had of the dæmon; but still my sight was dimmed by the burning drops, until, giving way to the emotions that oppressed me, I wept aloud.

But this was not the time for delay; I disencumbered the dogs of their dead companion, gave them a plentiful portion of food; and, after an hour's rest, which was absolutely necessary, and yet which was bitterly irksome to me, I continued my route. The sledge was still visible; nor did I again lose sight of it, except at the moments when for a short time some ice rock concealed it with its intervening crags. I indeed perceptibly gained on it; and when, after nearly two days' journey, I beheld my enemy at no more than a mile distant, my heart bounded within me.

But now, when I appeared almost within grasp of my enemy, my hopes were suddenly extinguished, and I lost all trace of him more utterly than I had ever done before. A ground sea was heard; the thunder of its progress, as the waters rolled and swelled beneath me, became every moment more ominous and terrific. I pressed on, but in vain. The wind arose; the sea roared; and, as with the mighty shock of an earthquake, it split, and cracked with a tremendous and overwhelming sound. The work was soon finished: in a few minutes a tumultuous sea rolled between me and my enemy, and I was left drifting on a scattered piece of ice, that was continually lessening, and thus preparing for me a hideous death.

In this manner many appalling hours passed; several of my dogs died; and I myself was about to sink under the accumulation of distress, when I saw your vessel riding at anchor, and holding forth to me hopes of succour and life. I had no conception that vessels ever came so far north, and was astounded at the sight. I quickly destroyed part of my sledge to construct oars, and by these means was enabled, with infinite fatigue, to move my ice-raft in the direction of your ship. I had determined, if you were going southward, still to trust myself to the mercy of the seas, rather than abandon my purpose. I hoped to induce you to grant me a boat with which I could still pursue my enemy. But your direction was northward. You took me on board when my vigour was exhausted, and I should soon have sunk under my multiplied hardships into a death, which I still dread,—for my task is unfulfilled.

Oh! when will my guiding spirit, in conducting me to the dæmon, allow me the rest I so much desire; or must I die, and he yet live? If I do, swear to me, Walton, that he shall not escape; that you will seek him, and satisfy my vengeance in his death. Yet, do I dare ask you to undertake my pilgrimage, to endure the hardships that I have undergone? No; I am not so selfish. Yet, when I am dead, if he should appear; if the ministers of vengeance should conduct him to you, swear that he shall not live—swear that he shall not triumph over my accumulated woes, and live to make another such a wretch as I am. He is eloquent and persuasive; and once his words had even power over my heart: but trust him not. His soul is as hellish as his form, full of treachery and fiend-like malice. Hear him not; call on the manes[17] of William, Justine, Clerval, Elizabeth, my father, and of the wretched Victor, and thrust your sword into his heart. I will hover near, and direct the steel aright.

---

17. Mary's use of "manes" here is a reference to the Latin meaning: ghosts or spirits of the deceased.

Joey Eschrich.

WALTON, *IN CONTINUATION.*

August 26th, 17—.

You have read this strange and terrific story, Margaret; and do you not feel your blood congealed with horror, like that which even now curdles mine? Sometimes, seized with sudden agony, he could not continue his tale; at others, his voice broken, yet piercing, uttered with difficulty the words so replete with agony. His fine and lovely eyes were now lighted up with indignation, now subdued to downcast sorrow, and quenched in infinite wretchedness. Sometimes he commanded his countenance and tones, and related the most horrible incidents with a tranquil voice, suppressing every mark of agitation; then, like a volcano bursting forth, his face would suddenly change to an expression of the wildest rage, as he shrieked out imprecations on his persecutor.

His tale is connected, and told with an appearance of the simplest truth; yet I own to you that the letters of Felix and Safie, which he shewed me, and the apparition of the monster, seen from our ship, brought to me a greater conviction of the truth of his narrative than his asseverations, however earnest and connected. Such a monster has then really existence; I cannot doubt it; yet I am lost in surprise and admiration. Sometimes I endeavoured to gain from Frankenstein the particulars of his creature's formation; but on this point he was impenetrable.

"Are you mad, my friend?" said he, "or whither does your senseless curiosity lead you? Would you also create for yourself and the world a demoniacal enemy? Or to what do your questions tend? Peace, peace! learn my miseries, and do not seek to increase your own."

Frankenstein discovered that I made notes concerning his history: he asked to see them, and then himself corrected and augmented them in many places; but principally in giving the life and spirit to the conversations he held with his enemy. "Since you have preserved my narration," said he, "I would not that a mutilated one should go down to posterity."

Thus has a week passed away, while I have listened to the strangest tale that ever imagination formed. My thoughts, and every feeling of my soul, have been drunk up by the interest for my guest, which this tale, and his own elevated and gentle manners have created. I wish to soothe him; yet can I counsel one so infinitely miserable, so destitute of every hope of consolation, to live? Oh, no! the only joy that he can now know will be when he composes his shattered feelings to peace and death. Yet he enjoys one comfort, the offspring of solitude and delirium: he believes, that, when in dreams he holds converse with his friends, and derives from that communion consolation for his miseries, or excitements to his vengeance, that they are not the creations of his fancy, but the real beings who visit him from the regions of a remote world. This faith gives a solemnity to his reveries that render them to me almost as imposing and interesting as truth.

Our conversations are not always confined to his own history and misfortunes. On every point of general literature he displays unbounded knowledge, and a quick and piercing apprehension. His eloquence is forcible and touching; nor can I hear him, when he relates a pathetic incident, or endeavours to move the passions of pity or love, without tears. What a glorious creature must he have been in the days of his prosperity, when he is thus noble and godlike in ruin. He seems to feel his own worth, and the greatness of his fall.

"When younger," said he, "I felt as if I were destined for some great enterprise. My feelings are profound; but I possessed a coolness of judgment that fitted me for illustrious achievements. This sentiment of the worth of my nature supported me, when others would have been oppressed; for I deemed it criminal to throw away in useless grief those talents that might be useful to my fellow-creatures. When I reflected on the work I had completed, no less a one than the creation of a sensitive and rational animal, I could not rank myself with the herd of common projectors. But this feeling, which supported me in the commencement of my career, now serves only to plunge me lower in the dust. All my speculations and hopes are as nothing; and, like the archangel who aspired to omnipotence, I am chained in an eternal hell. My imagination was vivid, yet my powers of analysis and application were intense; by the union of these qualities I conceived the idea, and executed the creation of a man.[18] Even now I cannot recollect, without passion, my reveries while the work was incomplete. I trod heaven in my thoughts, now exulting in my powers, now burning with the idea of their effects. From my infancy I was imbued with high hopes and a lofty ambition; but how am I sunk! Oh! my friend, if you had known me as I once was, you would not recognize me in this state of degradation.

18. At his entrance to the wider world, Victor felt he had talents that he could use to benefit society. He expected to put forth greatness in the world and chose the lofty goal of creating life, but without thinking of the consequences. His high expectations for himself did not temper his ability to create, and although his accomplishment is amazing, it only serves to torture him until the bitter end—when he has come to some recognition of the monstrosity of his own behavior, likening himself to Satan, just as the creature has done. At the start of his efforts to create life, Victor might have benefited from thinking about the greater repercussions of those efforts. If it is criminal to throw away those talents, is it not also criminal to use those talents to invent without caution?

Stephanie Naufel.

Despondency rarely visited my heart; a high destiny seemed to bear me on, until I fell, never, never again to rise."

Must I then lose this admirable being? I have longed for a friend; I have sought one who would sympathize with and love me. Behold, on these desert seas I have found such a one; but, I fear, I have gained him only to know his value, and lose him. I would reconcile him to life, but he repulses the idea.

"I thank you, Walton," he said, "for your kind intentions towards so miserable a wretch; but when you speak of new ties, and fresh affections, think you that any can replace those who are gone? Can any man be to me as Clerval was; or any woman another Elizabeth? Even where the affections are not strongly moved by any superior excellence, the companions of our childhood always possess a certain power over our minds, which hardly any later friend can obtain. They know our infantine dispositions, which, however they may be afterwards modified, are never eradicated; and they can judge of our actions with more certain conclusions as to the integrity of our motives. A sister or a brother can never, unless indeed such symptoms have been shewn early, suspect the other of fraud or false dealing, when another friend, however strongly he may be attached, may, in spite of himself, be invaded with suspicion.[19] But I enjoyed friends, dear not only through habit and association, but from their own merits; and, wherever I am, the soothing voice of my Elizabeth, and the conversation of Clerval, will be ever whispered in my ear. They are dead; and but one feeling in such a solitude can persuade me to preserve my life. If I were engaged in any high undertaking or design, fraught with extensive utility to my fellow-creatures, then could I live to fulfil it.[20] But such is not my destiny; I must pursue and destroy the being to whom I gave existence; then my lot on earth will be fulfilled, and I may die."

19. In this passage, Victor highlights the effect others have on the formation of the self and the development of personal identity. Others can have, as he points out, "a certain power over our minds." Similar to the way others' perceptions and fears of the creature inevitably influence how the creature sees himself (as ugly, frightening, and loathsome), Victor's close companions have shaped the way he sees himself. As the philosopher Mikhail Bakhtin (1895–1975) proposes, "A person has no sovereign internal territory, he is wholly and always on the boundary; looking inside himself, he looks into the eyes of another or with the eyes of another" (1984, 287). Because a person cannot help but see herself with the eyes of another, Bakhtin says that she becomes conscious of herself, in fact "becomes herself," only through her engagement with other people. Indeed, Victor himself says that Elizabeth's "existence was bound up in mine" (p. 72).
Nicole Piemonte.

20. Scientific research today extends Victor's position here in two conflicting ways. On the one hand, science is generally perceived as altruistic, a "high undertaking" that produces discoveries and technologies that can benefit humanity. Over the course of the nineteenth century, the often

September 2d.

MY BELOVED SISTER,

I write to you, encompassed by peril, and ignorant whether I am ever doomed to see again dear England, and the dearer friends that inhabit it. I am surrounded by mountains of ice, which admit of no escape, and threaten every moment to crush my vessel. The brave fellows, whom I have persuaded to be my companions, look towards me for aid; but I have none to bestow. There is something terribly appalling in our situation, yet my courage and hopes do not desert me. We may survive; and if we do not, I will repeat the lessons of my Seneca,[21] and die with a good heart.

Yet what, Margaret, will be the state of your mind? You will not hear of my destruction, and you will anxiously await my return. Years will pass, and you will have visitings of despair, and yet be tortured by hope.

---

ethereal realm of natural philosophy gradually evolved into the practical, empire-building work of scientific progress. Sir Humphry Davy was urged by his British compatriots to shine the light of his intellect not just on abstract questions in chemistry but also on the plight of working people in the midst of the industrial revolution (leading to his invention of a revolutionary new safety lamp for miners). Benjamin Franklin was iconic not just as a scientist but an inventor and entrepreneur.

On the other hand, the twentieth century saw a new rhetoric come into play. During and after World War II, an argument emerged to justify scientific research with the claim that humanity benefits most when scientists *selfishly* pursue knowledge for its own sake, just as Victor did. Many science advocates today fiercely defend the principle of basic research, unconstrained by any attempt to identify pragmatic or utilitarian outcomes.

But it's the melding of inquiry and practicality that makes science a deeply human pursuit, and which Victor sees as his only path to redemption. Franklin's lightening rod, Pasteur's rabies vaccine, Bessemer's steel, Roebling's Brooklyn Bridge, Edison's power station, water and sewer lines, hybrid corn and refrigerators, lasers and fiber optic cables, all are "fraught with extensive utility" (p. 176) and together add up to that most unpoetic word, "infrastructure," without which life would still be fairly nasty, brutish, and short—and science would be nothing but hobbyism.

Daniel Sarewitz and Ed Finn.

21. Seneca: Lucius Annaeus Seneca (ca. 4 BCE–65 CE), "Seneca the Younger," Roman Stoic philosopher, playwright, essayist, and tutor and advisor to emperor Nero. Stoicism valued self-restraint over passion, yet Seneca's immersion in the excesses of empire brought accusations of hypocrisy during his lifetime. When he was entangled, possibly falsely, in a plot to assassinate Nero, Seneca was forced to commit suicide. As recorded by Roman historian Tacitus, his death was intended to be quick and painless, but became a drawn-out ordeal of bleeding and poison. Joined forever with the earlier, ennobling death of criminalized philosopher Socrates, Seneca's demise is depicted and interpreted in later art and literature as one that cleanses and redeems, and even baptizes him, as he died in a basin of water. Mary's Captain Walton, facing his potential mortality surrounded by ice, notes that he will "die with a good heart," as did Seneca. Is it possible that Mary offers him (and, likewise, Victor) "the lessons" of Seneca—and of Socrates—as redemption in the wake of his overly passionate pursuit of knowledge, when he should have practiced greater self-restraint?

Judith Guston.

Oh! my beloved sister, the sickening failings of your heart-felt expectations are, in prospect, more terrible to me than my own death. But you have a husband, and lovely children; you may be happy: heaven bless you, and make you so!

My unfortunate guest regards me with the tenderest compassion. He endeavours to fill me with hope; and talks as if life were a possession which he valued. He reminds me how often the same accidents have happened to other navigators, who have attempted this sea, and, in spite of myself, he fills me with cheerful auguries. Even the sailors feel the power of his eloquence: when he speaks, they no longer despair; he rouses their energies, and, while they hear his voice, they believe these vast mountains of ice are mole-hills, which will vanish before the resolutions of man. These feelings are transitory; each day's expectation delayed fills them with fear, and I almost dread a mutiny caused by this despair.

September 5th.

A scene has just passed of such uncommon interest, that although it is highly probable that these papers may never reach you, yet I cannot forbear recording it.

We are still surrounded by mountains of ice, still in imminent danger of being crushed in their conflict. The cold is excessive, and many of my unfortunate comrades have already found a grave amid this scene of desolation. Frankenstein has daily declined in health: a feverish fire still glimmers in his eyes; but he is exhausted, and, when suddenly roused to any exertion, he speedily sinks again into apparent lifelessness.

I mentioned in my last letter the fears I entertained of a mutiny. This morning, as I sat watching the wan countenance of my friend—his eyes half closed, and his limbs hanging listlessly,—I was roused by half a dozen of the sailors, who desired admission into the cabin. They entered; and their leader addressed me. He told me that he and his companions had been chosen by the other sailors to come in deputation to me, to make me a demand, which, in justice, I could not refuse. We were immured in ice, and should probably never escape; but they feared that if, as was possible, the ice should dissipate, and a free passage be opened, I should be rash enough to continue my voyage, and lead them into fresh dangers, after they might happily have surmounted this. They desired, therefore, that I should engage with a solemn promise, that if the vessel should be freed, I would instantly direct my course southward.

This speech troubled me. I had not despaired; nor had I yet conceived the idea of returning, if set free. Yet could I, in justice, or even in possibility, refuse this demand? I hesitated before I answered; when Frankenstein, who had at first been silent, and, indeed, appeared hardly to have force enough to attend, now roused himself; his eyes sparkled, and his cheeks flushed with momentary vigour. Turning towards the men, he said—

"What do you mean? What do you demand of your captain? Are you then so easily turned from your design? Did you not call this a glorious expedition? and wherefore was it glorious? Not because the way was smooth and placid as a southern sea, but because it was full of dangers and terror; because, at every new incident, your fortitude was to be called forth, and your courage exhibited; because danger and death surrounded, and these dangers you were to brave and overcome. For this was it a glorious, for this was it an honourable undertaking. You were hereafter to be hailed as the benefactors of your species; your names adored, as belonging to brave men who encountered death for honour and the benefit of mankind. And now, behold, with the first imagination of danger, or, if you will, the first mighty and terrific trial of your courage, you shrink away, and are content to be handed down as men who had not strength enough to endure cold and peril; and so, poor souls, they were chilly, and returned to their warm fire-sides. Why, that requires not this preparation; ye need not have come thus far, and dragged your captain to the shame of a defeat, merely to prove yourselves cowards. Oh! be men, or be more than men. Be steady to your purposes, and firm as a rock. This ice is not made of such stuff as your hearts might be; it is mutable, cannot withstand you, if you say that it shall not. Do not return to your families with the stigma of disgrace marked on your brows. Return as heroes who have fought and conquered, and who know not what it is to turn their backs on the foe."[22]

He spoke this with a voice so modulated to the different feelings expressed in his speech, with an eye so full of lofty design and heroism, that can you wonder that these men were moved. They looked at one another,

22. Here, Victor implores the crewmen to continue their expedition, calling them to be brave and altruistic in the face of danger. It is ironic that he is encouraging them to do so because they will be "adored" or "hailed as the benefactors of [their] species," when similar motives drove the construction of his creature and ultimately led to his own misery and demise. This passage illustrates the complexity of Victor's—and perhaps humankind's—motives and desires; altruistic motives can be mingled with hubris and pride. As such, introspection and intentional self-reflection are necessary for uncovering what is driving our decision making, especially in high-stakes situations.

Nicole Piemonte.

and were unable to reply. I spoke; I told them to retire, and consider of what had been said: that I would not lead them further north, if they strenuously desired the contrary; but that I hoped that, with reflection, their courage would return.

They retired, and I turned towards my friend; but he was sunk in languor, and almost deprived of life.

How all this will terminate, I know not; but I had rather die, than return shamefully,—my purpose unfulfilled. Yet I fear such will be my fate; the men, unsupported by ideas of glory and honour, can never willingly continue to endure their present hardships.

September 7th.

The die is cast; I have consented to return, if we are not destroyed. Thus are my hopes blasted by cowardice and indecision; I come back ignorant and disappointed. It requires more philosophy than I possess, to bear this injustice with patience.[23]

September 12th.

It is past; I am returning to England. I have lost my hopes of utility and glory;—I have lost my friend. But I will endeavour to detail these bitter circumstances to you, my dear sister; and, while I am wafted towards England, and towards you, I will not despond.

September 9th, the ice began to move, and roarings like thunder were heard at a distance, as the islands split and cracked in every direction. We were in the most imminent peril; but, as we could only remain passive, my chief attention was occupied by my unfortunate guest, whose illness increased in such a degree, that he was entirely confined to his bed. The ice cracked behind us, and was driven with force towards the north; a breeze sprung from the west, and on the 11th the passage towards the south became perfectly free. When the sailors saw this, and that their return to their native country was apparently assured, a shout of tumultuous joy

23. In many ways, Walton appears to be the embodiment of everything Victor is not. He rescues and befriends a man who at the beginning of his tale is more of a monster than his creation and at the end is on equal terms with the creature in that both have been twisted by grief, rage, and the desire for vengeance. Walton undertakes a quest for knowledge with the awareness that it may cost him his life. He makes and endeavors to fulfill promises to Victor based solely on the bonds of platonic friendship. When the ice threatens to kill him and his mates in his pursuit of knowledge, he does not flinch, and initially from his perspective it is only the cowardice of lesser men that turns him aside.

Sean A. Hays.

broke from them, loud and long-continued. Frankenstein, who was dozing, awoke, and asked the cause of the tumult. "They shout," I said, "because they will soon return to England."

"Do you then really return?"

"Alas! yes; I cannot withstand their demands. I cannot lead them unwillingly to danger, and I must return."

"Do so, if you will; but I will not. You may give up your purpose; but mine is assigned to me by heaven, and I dare not. I am weak; but surely the spirits who assist my vengeance will endow me with sufficient strength." Saying this, he endeavoured to spring from the bed, but the exertion was too great for him; he fell back, and fainted.

It was long before he was restored; and I often thought that life was entirely extinct. At length he opened his eyes, but he breathed with difficulty, and was unable to speak. The surgeon gave him a composing draught, and ordered us to leave him undisturbed. In the mean time he told me, that my friend had certainly not many hours to live.

His sentence was pronounced; and I could only grieve, and be patient. I sat by his bed watching him; his eyes were closed, and I thought he slept; but presently he called to me in a feeble voice, and, bidding me come near, said—"Alas! the strength I relied on is gone; I feel that I shall soon die, and he, my enemy and persecutor, may still be in being. Think not, Walton, that in the last moments of my existence I feel that burning hatred, and ardent desire of revenge, I once expressed, but I feel myself justified in desiring the death of my adversary. During these last days I have been occupied in examining my past conduct; nor do I find it blameable. In a fit of enthusiastic madness I created a rational creature, and was bound towards him, to assure, as far as was in my power, his happiness and well-being. This was my duty; but there was another still paramount to that. My duties towards my fellow-creatures had greater claims to my attention,[24] because

24. Mary's "creature" is vegetarian: "My food is not that of man; I do not destroy the lamb and the kid, to glut my appetite; acorns and berries afford me sufficient nourishment" (p. 121). The creature rationalizes and demonstrates his "humanity" in exhibiting empathy toward other creatures that he likens similar to himself, and therefore Mary more than hints that this creature has a nurturing side. Naming a pet makes it more than animal, and Victor never gives a name to his experimental human. Despite his admission so late in the narrative that his creation is rational and deserves well-being, for Victor the creature never ceases to be his laboratory "rat." Western objectivity proceeds from the European Enlightenment; however, we identify with emotionally engaging things such as embryonic stem cells because they derive from human embryos and are the stems of all human cells. Are all "harvested" embryonic stem cells in a situational and transitory "disposition" of animacy, with innate capacity to transform and mature into a human if placed within a womb rather than in a lab to be used for research? Is Mary's creature, in stating that he does not eat meat (use the flesh) of other animals, indicating that he is more humane in some respects

they included a greater proportion of happiness or misery. Urged by this view, I refused, and I did right in refusing, to create a companion for the first creature. He shewed unparalleled malignity and selfishness, in evil: he destroyed my friends; he devoted to destruction beings who possessed exquisite sensations, happiness, and wisdom; nor do I know where this thirst for vengeance may end. Miserable himself, that he may render no other wretched, he ought to die. The task of his destruction was mine, but I have failed. When actuated by selfish and vicious motives, I asked you to undertake my unfinished work; and I renew this request now, when I am only induced by reason and virtue.

"Yet I cannot ask you to renounce your country and friends, to fulfil this task; and now, that you are returning to England, you will have little chance of meeting with him. But the consideration of these points, and the well-balancing of what you may esteem your duties, I leave to you; my judgment and ideas are already disturbed by the near approach of death. I dare not ask you to do what I think right, for I may still be misled by passion.

"That he should live to be an instrument of mischief disturbs me; in other respects this hour, when I momentarily expect my release, is the only happy one which I have enjoyed for several years. The forms of the beloved dead flit before me, and I hasten to their arms. Farewell, Walton! Seek happiness in tranquillity, and avoid ambition, even if it be only the apparently innocent one of distinguishing yourself in science and discoveries. Yet why do I say this? I have myself been blasted in these hopes, yet another may succeed."[25]

---

than humans? Embryonic stem cells, during and after research, are eventually destroyed, so do they have the same life value as a "the lamb and the kid," or do they have less? More? Or none? How would Mary's "creature," the vegetarian, answer the previous question?

Miguel Astor-Aguilera.

25. Despite praising his friend Walton for his virtuous actions, particularly in the episode of love he recounts, Victor criticizes his lack of imagination. He further suggests that the inability to think further than the ship's ropes and shroud (the nautical term for a cable, typically part of a pattern of lines used to stay a ship's mast) is the result of having spent his life aboard a ship. Mary encapsulates an important romantic idea in this suggestion. Empiricists of the time argued for the metaphor of the tabula rasa to explain the concept that people's minds, like a wax tablet, encounter the world blank and directly collect impressions. They held that human minds could be made blank for observation. In contrast, the romantics developed a view that what can be observed is affected by what is already in the mind. This theory explains the difference in perceptions that two people might have in encountering the same landscape, personage, or natural wonder. To Victor, Walton has a limited imagination because his experience has been limited to life aboard a ship, in contrast to Victor's own childhood and educational experiences, which he believes shaped his mind for scientific work.

Hannah Rogers.

His voice became fainter as he spoke; and at length, exhausted by his effort, he sunk into silence. About half an hour afterwards he attempted again to speak, but was unable; he pressed my hand feebly, and his eyes closed for ever, while the irradiation of a gentle smile passed away from his lips.

Margaret, what comment can I make on the untimely extinction of this glorious spirit? What can I say, that will enable you to understand the depth of my sorrow? All that I should express would be inadequate and feeble. My tears flow; my mind is overshadowed by a cloud of disappointment. But I journey towards England, and I may there find consolation.

I am interrupted. What do these sounds portend? It is midnight; the breeze blows fairly, and the watch on deck scarcely stir. Again; there is a sound as of a human voice, but hoarser; it comes from the cabin where the remains of Frankenstein still lie. I must arise, and examine. Good night, my sister.

Great God! what a scene has just taken place! I am yet dizzy with the remembrance of it. I hardly know whether I shall have the power to detail it; yet the tale which I have recorded would be incomplete without this final and wonderful catastrophe.

I entered the cabin, where lay the remains of my ill-fated and admirable friend. Over him hung a form which I cannot find words to describe; gigantic in stature, yet uncouth and distorted in its proportions. As he hung over the coffin, his face was concealed by long locks of ragged hair; but one vast hand was extended, in colour and apparent texture like that of a mummy. When he heard the sound of my approach, he ceased to utter exclamations of grief and horror, and sprung towards the window. Never did I behold a vision so horrible as his face, of such loathsome, yet appalling hideousness. I shut my eyes involuntarily, and endeavoured to recollect what were my duties with regard to this destroyer. I called on him to stay.

He paused, looking on me with wonder; and, again turning towards the lifeless form of his creator, he seemed to forget my presence, and every feature and gesture seemed instigated by the wildest rage of some uncontrollable passion.

"That is also my victim!" he exclaimed; "in his murder my crimes are consummated; the miserable series of my being is wound to its close! Oh, Frankenstein! generous and self-devoted being! what does it avail that I now ask thee to pardon me? I, who irretrievably destroyed thee by destroying all thou lovedst. Alas! he is cold; he may not answer me."

His voice seemed suffocated; and my first impulses, which had suggested to me the duty of obeying the dying request of my friend, in destroying his enemy, were now suspended by a mixture of curiosity and compassion. I approached this tremendous being; I dared not again raise my looks upon his face, there was something so scaring and unearthly in his ugliness. I attempted to speak, but the words died away on my lips. The monster continued to utter wild and incoherent self-reproaches. At length I gathered resolution to address him, in a pause of the tempest of his passion: "Your repentance," I said, "is now superfluous. If you had listened to the voice of conscience,[26] and heeded the stings of remorse, before you had urged your diabolical vengeance to this extremity, Frankenstein would yet have lived."

"And do you dream?" said the dæmon; "do you think that I was then dead to agony and remorse?—He," he continued, pointing to the corpse, "he suffered not more in the consummation of the deed;—oh! not the tenthousandth portion of the anguish that was mine during the lingering detail of its execution. A frightful selfishness hurried me on, while my heart was poisoned with remorse. Think ye that the groans of Clerval were music to my ears? My heart was fashioned to be susceptible of love and sympathy; and, when wrenched by misery to vice and hatred, it did not endure the violence of the change without torture, such as you cannot even imagine.

"After the murder of Clerval, I returned to Switzerland, heart-broken and overcome. I pitied Frankenstein; my pity amounted to horror: I abhorred myself. But when I discovered that he, the author at once of my existence and of its unspeakable torments, dared to hope for happiness; that while he accumulated wretchedness and despair upon me, he sought his own enjoyment in feelings and passions from the indulgence of which I was for ever barred, then impotent envy and bitter indignation filled me with an insatiable thirst for vengeance. I recollected my threat, and resolved that it should be accomplished. I knew that I was preparing for myself a deadly torture; but I was the slave, not the master of an impulse, which I detested, yet could not disobey. Yet when she died!—nay, then I was not miserable. I had cast off all feeling, subdued all anguish to riot in the excess of my despair. Evil thenceforth became my good. Urged thus far, I had no choice but to adapt my nature to an element which I had willingly chosen. The completion of my demoniacal design became an insatiable passion. And now it is ended; there is my last victim!"

---

26. Having heard the creature's expression of appreciation for Victor's efforts and his remorse for his own inexcusable actions, spoken to the now dead Victor, Walton rejects these statements as vain. The creature could have chosen to listen to his conscience, which was able to discern right from wrong, instead of seeking vengeance. The creature's gratitude should have overcome whatever sense of rejection he experienced.
Joel Gereboff.

I was at first touched by the expressions of his misery; yet when I called to mind what Frankenstein had said of his powers of eloquence and persuasion, and when I again cast my eyes on the lifeless form of my friend, indignation was re-kindled within me. "Wretch!" I said, "it is well that you come here to whine over the desolation that you have made. You throw a torch into a pile of buildings, and when they are consumed you sit among the ruins, and lament the fall. Hypocritical fiend! if he whom you mourn still lived, still would he be the object, again would he become the prey of your accursed vengeance. It is not pity that you feel; you lament only because the victim of your malignity is withdrawn from your power."

"Oh, it is not thus—not thus," interrupted the being; "yet such must be the impression conveyed to you by what appears to be the purport of my actions. Yet I seek not a fellow-feeling in my misery. No sympathy may I ever find. When I first sought it, it was the love of virtue, the feelings of happiness and affection with which my whole being overflowed, that I wished to be participated. But now, that virtue has become to me a shadow, and that happiness and affection are turned into bitter and loathing despair, in what should I seek for sympathy? I am content to suffer alone, while my sufferings shall endure: when I die, I am well satisfied that abhorrence and opprobrium should load my memory. Once my fancy was soothed with dreams of virtue, of fame, and of enjoyment. Once I falsely hoped to meet with beings, who, pardoning my outward form, would love me for the excellent qualities which I was capable of bringing forth. I was nourished with high thoughts of honour and devotion. But now vice has degraded me beneath the meanest animal. No crime, no mischief, no malignity, no misery, can be found comparable to mine. When I call over the frightful catalogue of my deeds, I cannot believe that I am he whose thoughts were once filled with sublime and transcendant visions of the beauty and the majesty of goodness. But it is even so; the fallen angel becomes a malignant devil. Yet even that enemy of God and man had friends and associates in his desolation; I am quite alone.

"You, who call Frankenstein your friend, seem to have a knowledge of my crimes and his misfortunes. But, in the detail which he gave you of them, he could not sum up the hours and months of misery which I endured, wasting in impotent passions. For whilst I destroyed his hopes, I did not satisfy my own desires. They were for ever ardent and craving; still I desired love and fellowship, and I was still spurned. Was there no injustice in this? Am I to be thought the only criminal, when all human kind sinned against me? Why do you not hate Felix, who drove his friend from his door with contumely? Why do you not execrate the rustic who sought to destroy the saviour of his child? Nay, these are virtuous and immaculate beings! I, the miserable and the abandoned, am an abortion, to be spurned at, and kicked, and trampled on. Even now my blood boils at the recollection of this injustice.

"But it is true that I am a wretch. I have murdered the lovely and the helpless; I have strangled the innocent as they slept, and grasped to death his throat who never injured me or any other living thing. I have devoted my creator, the select specimen of all that is worthy of love and admiration among men, to misery; I have pursued him even to that irremediable ruin. There he lies, white and cold in death. You hate me; but your abhorrence cannot equal that with which I regard myself. I look on the hands which executed the deed; I think on the heart in which the imagination of it was conceived, and long for the moment when they will meet my eyes, when it will haunt my thoughts, no more.

"Fear not that I shall be the instrument of future mischief. My work is nearly complete. Neither your's nor any man's death is needed to consummate the series of my being, and accomplish that which must be done; but it requires my own.[27] Do not think that I shall be slow to perform this sacrifice. I shall quit your vessel on the ice-raft which brought me hither, and shall seek the most northern extremity of the globe; I shall collect my funeral pile, and consume to ashes this miserable frame, that its remains may afford no light to any curious and unhallowed wretch, who would create such another as I have been. I shall die. I shall no longer feel the agonies which now consume me, or be the prey of feelings unsatisfied, yet unquenched. He is dead who called me into being; and when I shall be no more, the very remembrance of us both will speedily vanish. I shall no longer see the sun or stars, or feel the winds play on my cheeks. Light, feeling, and sense, will pass away; and in this condition must I find my happiness.

27. Here Mary anticipates one of the most serious debates about unintended consequences confronting contemporary scientists and technologists. How can we be sure that new creations we bring into the world will remain constrained, controlled, and limited in the ways that we expect them to be? One popular example of this discussion is the "grey goo" argument. Imagine a modern-day Victor creating a kind of self-replicating nanotechnology that can harness certain resources in the environment to copy itself. Without the proper controls, such an entity could destroy everything on the planet within a matter of days, turning the world into a grey goo of seething nanobots.

The creature's description of his plan for self-destruction is one of the most poignant explorations of a correlated problem—if the new technology in question is not only autonomous but in some way self-aware, the imposition of safety limits may mean asking our creations to enact a kind of suicide.

Ed Finn.

Some years ago, when the images which this world affords first opened upon me, when I felt the cheering warmth of summer, and heard the rustling of the leaves and the chirping of the birds, and these were all to me, I should have wept to die; now it is my only consolation. Polluted by crimes, and torn by the bitterest remorse, where can I find rest but in death?

"Farewell! I leave you, and in you the last of human kind whom these eyes will ever behold. Farewell, Frankenstein! If thou wert yet alive, and yet cherished a desire of revenge against me, it would be better satiated in my life than in my destruction. But it was not so; thou didst seek my extinction, that I might not cause greater wretchedness; and if yet, in some mode unknown to me, thou hast not yet ceased to think and feel, thou desirest not my life for my own misery. Blasted as thou wert, my agony was still superior to thine; for the bitter sting of remorse may not cease to rankle in my wounds until death shall close them for ever.

"But soon," he cried, with sad and solemn enthusiasm, "I shall die, and what I now feel be no longer felt. Soon these burning miseries will be extinct. I shall ascend my funeral pile triumphantly, and exult in the agony of the torturing flames.[28] The light of that conflagration will fade away; my ashes will be swept into the sea by the winds. My spirit will sleep in peace; or if it thinks, it will not surely think thus. Farewell."

He sprung from the cabin-window, as he said this, upon the ice-raft which lay close to the vessel. He was soon borne away by the waves, and lost in darkness and distance.

THE END.

28. The creature's final words describe his plans for a noble suicide (see note 21 on the death of Seneca, and note 27 on self-sacrificing technologies). The creature's decision to "repeat the lessons of my Seneca, and die with a good heart" (p. 177) has many echoes in contemporary representations of some autonomous technology sacrificing itself for the good of humanity. In *Terminator 2: Judgment Day*, the superhuman robot played by Arnold Schwarzenegger makes a similar sacrifice, lowering itself into a pool of molten metal in order to protect John and Sarah Connor.

As autonomous systems become more prevalent—think of self-driving cars—the question of how to encode ethical judgment in them has become far more pressing. Perhaps it seems obvious that a self-driving car should sacrifice itself before allowing a human pedestrian to be harmed. But how should such a system react when it must choose between injuring its driver or hitting a pedestrian? As Victor and the creature have discovered, most of our moral decisions involve some risk of harming others and force us to grapple with ethical ambiguity.

Ed Finn.

The Publishers of the Standard Novels, in selecting "Frankenstein" for one of their series, expressed a wish that I should furnish them with some account of the origin of the story. I am the more willing to comply, because I shall thus give a general answer to the question, so frequently asked me—"How I, then a young girl, came to think of, and to dilate upon, so very hideous an idea?" It is true that I am very averse to bringing myself forward in print; but as my account will only appear as an appendage to a former production, and as it will be confined to such topics as have connection with my authorship alone, I can scarcely accuse myself of a personal intrusion.

It is not singular that, as the daughter of two persons of distinguished literary celebrity, I should very early in life have thought of writing. As a child I scribbled; and my favourite pastime, during the hours given me for recreation, was to "write stories." Still I had a dearer pleasure than this, which was the formation of castles in the air—the indulging in waking dreams—the following up trains of thought, which had for their subject the formation of a succession of imaginary incidents. My dreams were at once more fantastic and agreeable than my writings. In the latter I was a close imitator—rather doing as others had done, than putting down the suggestions of my own mind. What I wrote was intended at least for one other eye—my childhood's companion and friend; but my dreams were all my own; I accounted for them to nobody; they were my refuge when annoyed—my dearest pleasure when free.

I lived principally in the country as a girl, and passed a considerable time in Scotland. I made occasional visits to the more picturesque parts; but my habitual residence was on the blank and dreary northern shores of the Tay, near Dundee. Blank and dreary on retrospection I call them; they were not so to me then. They were the eyry of freedom, and the pleasant region where unheeded I could commune with the creatures of my fancy. I wrote then—but in a most common-place style. It was beneath the trees of the grounds belonging to our house, or on the bleak sides of the woodless mountains near, that my true compositions, the airy flights of my imagination, were born and fostered. I did not make myself the heroine of my tales.

Life appeared to me too common-place an affair as regarded myself. I could not figure to myself that romantic woes or wonderful events would ever be my lot; but I was not confined to my own identity, and I could people the hours with creations far more interesting to me at that age, than my own sensations.

After this my life became busier, and reality stood in place of fiction. My husband, however, was from the first, very anxious that I should prove myself worthy of my parentage, and enrol myself on the page of fame. He was for ever inciting me to obtain literary reputation, which even on my own part I cared for then, though since I have become infinitely indifferent to it. At this time he desired that I should write, not so much with the idea that I could produce any thing worthy of notice, but that he might himself judge how far I possessed the promise of better things hereafter. Still I did nothing. Travelling, and the cares of a family, occupied my time; and study, in the way of reading, or improving my ideas in communication with his far more cultivated mind, was all of literary employment that engaged my attention.

In the summer of 1816, we visited Switzerland, and became the neighbours of Lord Byron. At first we spent our pleasant hours on the lake, or wandering on its shores; and Lord Byron, who was writing the third canto of Childe Harold, was the only one among us who put his thoughts upon paper. These, as he brought them successively to us, clothed in all the light and harmony of poetry, seemed to stamp as divine the glories of heaven and earth, whose influences we partook with him.

But it proved a wet, ungenial summer, and incessant rain often confined us for days to the house. Some volumes of ghost stories, translated from the German into French, fell into our hands. There was the History of the Inconstant Lover, who, when he thought to clasp the bride to whom he had pledged his vows, found himself in the arms of the pale ghost of her whom he had deserted. There was the tale of the sinful founder of his race, whose miserable doom it was to bestow the kiss of death on all the younger sons of his fated house, just when they reached the age of promise. His gigantic, shadowy form, clothed like the ghost in Hamlet, in complete armour, but with the beaver up, was seen at midnight, by the moon's fitful beams, to advance slowly along the gloomy avenue. The shape was lost beneath the shadow of the castle walls; but soon a gate swung back, a step was heard, the door of the chamber opened, and he advanced to the couch of the blooming youths, cradled in healthy sleep. Eternal sorrow sat upon his face as he bent down and kissed the forehead of the boys, who from that hour withered like flowers snapt upon the stalk. I have not seen these stories since then; but their incidents are as fresh in my mind as if I had read them yesterday.

"We will each write a ghost story," said Lord Byron; and his proposition was acceded to. There were four of us. The noble author began a tale, a fragment of which he printed at the end of his poem of Mazeppa. Shelley, more apt to embody ideas and sentiments in the radiance of brilliant imagery, and in the music of the most melodious verse that adorns our language, than to invent the machinery of a story, commenced one founded on the experiences of his early life. Poor Polidori had some terrible idea about a skull-headed lady, who was so punished for peeping through a key-hole— what to see I forget—something very shocking and wrong of course; but when she was reduced to a worse condition than the renowned Tom of Coventry, he did not know what to do with her, and was obliged to despatch her to the tomb of the Capulets, the only place for which she was fitted. The illustrious poets also, annoyed by the platitude of prose, speedily relinquished the uncongenial task.

I busied myself *to think of a story,*—a story to rival those which had excited us to this task. One which would speak to the mysterious fears of our nature, and awaken thrilling horror—one to make the reader dread to look round, to curdle the blood, and quicken the beatings of the heart. If I did not accomplish these things, my ghost story would be unworthy of its name. I thought and pondered—vainly. I felt that blank incapability of invention which is the greatest misery of authorship, when dull Nothing replies to our anxious invocations. *Have you thought of a story?* I was asked each morning, and each morning I was forced to reply with a mortifying negative.

Every thing must have a beginning, to speak in Sanchean phrase; and that beginning must be linked to something that went before. The Hindoos give the world an elephant to support it, but they make the elephant stand upon a tortoise. Invention, it must be humbly admitted, does not consist in creating out of void, but out of chaos; the materials must, in the first place, be afforded: it can give form to dark, shapeless substances, but cannot bring into being the substance itself. In all matters of discovery and invention, even of those that appertain to the imagination, we are continually reminded of the story of Columbus and his egg. Invention consists in the capacity of seizing on the capabilities of a subject, and in the power of moulding and fashioning ideas suggested to it.

Many and long were the conversations between Lord Byron and Shelley, to which I was a devout but nearly silent listener. During one of these, various philosophical doctrines were discussed, and among others the nature of the principle of life, and whether there was any probability of its ever being discovered and communicated. They talked of the experiments of Dr. Darwin, (I speak not of what the Doctor really did, or said that he did, but, as more to my purpose, of what was then spoken of as having been done by him,) who preserved a piece of vermicelli in a glass case, till by some extraordinary means it began to move with voluntary motion. Not thus, after all, would life be given. Perhaps a corpse would be re-animated; galvanism had given token of such things: perhaps the component parts of a creature might be manufactured, brought together, and endued with vital warmth.

Night waned upon this talk; and even the witching hour had gone by, before we retired to rest. When I placed my head on my pillow, I did not sleep, nor could I be said to think. My imagination, unbidden, possessed and guided me, gifting the successive images that arose in my mind with a vividness far beyond the usual bounds of reverie. I saw—with shut eyes, but acute mental vision—I saw the pale student of unhallowed arts kneeling beside the thing he had put together. I saw the hideous phantasm of a man stretched out, and then, on the working of some powerful engine, show signs of life, and stir with an uneasy, half vital motion. Frightful must it be; for supremely frightful would be the effect of any human endeavour to mock the stupendous mechanism of the Creator of the world. His success would terrify the artist; he would rush away from his odious handywork, horror-stricken. He would hope that, left to itself, the slight spark of life which he had communicated would fade; that this thing, which had received such imperfect animation, would subside into dead matter; and he might sleep in the belief that the silence of the grave would quench for ever the transient existence of the hideous corpse which he had looked upon as the cradle of life. He sleeps; but he is awakened; he opens his eyes; behold the horrid thing stands at his bedside, opening his curtains, and looking on him with yellow, watery, but speculative eyes.

I opened mine in terror. The idea so possessed my mind, that a thrill of fear ran through me, and I wished to exchange the ghastly image of my fancy for the realities around. I see them still; the very room, the dark *parquet*, the closed shutters, with the moonlight struggling through, and the sense I had that the glassy lake and white high Alps were beyond. I could not so easily get rid of my hideous phantom; still it haunted me. I must try to think of something else. I recurred to my ghost story,—my tiresome unlucky ghost story! O! if I could only contrive one which would frighten my reader as I myself had been frightened that night!

Swift as light and as cheering was the idea that broke in upon me. "I have found it! What terrified me will terrify others; and I need only describe the spectre which had haunted my midnight pillow." On the morrow I announced that I had *thought of a story*. I began that day with the words, *It was on a dreary night of November*, making only a transcript of the grim terrors of my waking dream.

At first I thought but of a few pages—of a short tale; but Shelley urged me to develope the idea at greater length. I certainly did not owe the suggestion of one incident, nor scarcely of one train of feeling, to my husband, and yet but for his incitement, it would never have taken the form in which it was presented to the world. From this declaration I must except the preface. As far as I can recollect, it was entirely written by him.

And now, once again, I bid my hideous progeny go forth and prosper. I have an affection for it, for it was the offspring of happy days, when death and grief were but words, which found no true echo in my heart. Its several pages speak of many a walk, many a drive, and many a conversation, when I was not alone; and my companion was one whom, in this world, I shall never see more. But this is for myself; my readers have nothing to do with these associations.

I will add but one word as to the alterations I have made. They are principally those of style. I have changed no portion of the story, nor introduced any new ideas or circumstances. I have mended the language where it was so bald as to interfere with the interest of the narrative; and these changes occur almost exclusively in the beginning of the first volume. Throughout they are entirely confined to such parts as are mere adjuncts to the story, leaving the core and substance of it untouched.

M.W.S.
London, October 15, 1831.

CHRONOLOGY OF SCIENCE AND
MARY WOLLSTONECRAFT SHELLEY

· **1745**	Ewald Jürgen Georg von Kleist develops the first capacitor, the Leyden jar.
· **1750**	Joseph Black describes latent heat.
· **1751**	Benjamin Franklin demonstrates that lightning is electrical.
· **1761**	Mikhail Lomonosov discovers the atmosphere of Venus.
· **1763**	Thomas Bayes publishes the first version of Bayes's theorem, paving the way for Bayesian probability.
· **1771**	Charles Messier publishes catalog of astronomical objects (Messier Objects), now known to include galaxies, star clusters, and nebulae.
· **1778**	Antoine Lavoisier and Joseph Priestley discover oxygen, leading to the end of phlogiston theory.
· **1780**	Luigi Galvani makes the legs of dead frogs twitch by connecting them to an electrical current, discovering what we call bioelectricity.
· **1781**	William Herschel announces discovery of Uranus, expanding the known boundaries of the solar system for the first time in modern history.
· **1785**	William Withering publishes the first definitive account of the use of foxglove (digitalis) for treating dropsy.
· **1787**	Jacques Charles develops the law of ideal gas.
· **1789**	Antoine Lavoisier develops the law of conservation of mass, a beginning of modern chemistry.
· **1796**	Georges Cuvier establishes extinction as a fact.
· **1796**	Edward Jenner provides an historical accounting of smallpox.
· **1797**	Mary Wollstonecraft Godwin is born in London on August 30.
· **1797**	Mary's mother dies at age thirty-eight, ten days after giving birth to Mary.
· **1800**	Alessandro Volta discovers electrochemical series and invents the battery.
· **1800**	William Herschel discovers infrared radiation.

· **1802**	Jean-Baptiste Lamarck defines teleological evolution.
· **1804**	Hanaoka Seishū conducts first operation using general anesthesia.
· **1805**	John Dalton explains atomic theory in chemistry.
· **1812**	Humphry Davy publishes *Elements of Chemical Philosophy*; knighted the same year.
· **1814**	Mary and Percy Bysshe Shelley leave England to live together in France but return a month later when they run out of money.
· **1815**	Mary gives birth to a daughter prematurely, and the infant dies at six weeks of age.
· **1816**	A son, William, is born to Mary and Percy Shelley in January; Mary has visions of her novel, *Frankenstein*; Mary's half-sister commits suicide; Percy's first wife commits suicide by drowning; Mary and Percy wed at the end of the year.
· **1817**	Mary finishes writing *Frankenstein* and gives birth to daughter Clara.
· **1818**	*Frankenstein* is published in three volumes with no author identified, but the name "Shelley" appears on the spine of the book, and people think Percy wrote it; daughter Clara dies.
· **1819**	Son William dies; Mary finishes the novella *Mathilda*; Mary gives birth to son Percy Florence.
· **1820**	Hans Christian Ørsted discovers that a current passed through a wire will deflect the needle of a compass, thus establishing a deep relationship between electricity and magnetism (electromagnetism).
· **1822**	Mary almost dies from miscarriage; Percy drowns one month before he would have been thirty.
· **1823**	The second edition of *Frankenstein* is published.
· **1824**	Nicolas Carnot describes the Carnot cycle, the idealized heat engine.
· **1827**	Georg Ohm develops Ohm's law (electricity).
· **1827**	Amedeo Avogadro develops Avogadro's law (gas law).
· **1828**	Friedrich Wöhler synthesizes urea, destroying the theory of vitalism.
· **1830**	Nikolai Lobachevsky creates non-Euclidean geometry.
· **1831**	Michael Faraday discovers electromagnetic induction; Mary publishes a revised version of *Frankenstein*, with an additional introduction explaining how she conceived and wrote the work.
· **1851**	Mary Shelley dies in London at the age of fifty-three.

CHRONOLOGY OF SCIENCE AND MARY WOLLSTONECRAFT SHELLEY

ESSAYS

TRAUMATIC RESPONSIBILITY
VICTOR FRANKENSTEIN AS CREATOR AND CASUALTY

JOSEPHINE JOHNSTON

A rich theme running through Mary Shelley's *Frankenstein* is responsibility. In a straightforward—even didactic—way, the novel chronicles the devastating consequences for an inventor and those he loves of his utter failure to anticipate the harm that can result from raw, unchecked scientific curiosity. The novel not only explores the responsibility that Victor Frankenstein has *for* the destruction caused by his creation but also examines the responsibility he owes *to* him. The creature is a new being, with emotions and desires and dreams that he quickly learns cannot be satisfied by humans, who are repulsed by his appearance and terrified of his brute strength. So the creature comes to Victor, pleading—and then demanding—that he create a female companion with whom he can experience peace and love. While Victor is grappling intellectually and practically with the implications of being responsible both for and to the creature, he is also *experiencing* responsibility as a devastating physical and emotional state. In this way, Mary Shelley raises a third aspect of responsibility—its impact on the self.

What Is Responsibility?

The word *responsibility* is a noun defined as either a *duty* to take care of something or someone or the *state* of being the cause of an outcome. The word is familiar to everyone. Indeed, we order our daily lives based on our ideas about responsibility, whether we are referring to the duties we have to care for others—for instance, children—or our understandings about who or what has caused there to be food on our plates or a drought in California. The concept is especially important to students of philosophy and law.

In philosophy, special attention is paid to the concept of "moral responsibility," which refers not to a cause-and-effect relationship nor to the duties that come with occupying particular roles in society but to the determination that someone deserves praise or blame for an outcome or state of affairs. Humans' ability to be held morally responsible is closely tied up with the ideas about the nature of persons—specifically that persons have the capacity to be morally responsible agents. In *Frankenstein*, Mary raises questions about who is and is not capable of moral responsibility. At the beginning of the book, she introduces a protagonist who appears capable of being held morally responsible for his actions and an antagonist (the creature) who does not. But as the story develops, she raises questions about which of the two is the truly rational actor—Victor, who is addled by ambition, fever, and guilt, or the creature, who acquires emotion, language, and an intellect.

In law, responsibility is generally attributed in a two-step process. Judges and juries are first asked to determine whether the person *caused* the outcome in question—Did the accused pull the trigger on the gun that fired the bullet that killed the victim? They must then decide whether the person did so with the requisite intent, called *mens rea*. A killer who intended to kill the victim could be guilty of first-degree murder, but the legal responsibility assigned to someone who shot the victim accidentally might be manslaughter or another less-serious offense. A number of factors can interfere with legal responsibility, such as age (children are generally excused), compulsion (if someone has a gun to your head, you might not be held responsible for the actions they instruct you to perform), and mental defect (e.g., insanity). As with the determination of moral responsibility in a court of law, an attempt to attribute legal responsibility in *Frankenstein* quickly becomes complex. Although it might initially seem that Victor should be the one held legally responsible not just for the existence of the creature but for the havoc he wreaks, we also must consider that the creature quickly develops the capacity for rational thought, raising the possibility that he may qualify as an actor capable of both causing harm and forming the intention to do so. Given the sophisticated way the creature develops, by the end of the book he alone might be held legally responsible for the deaths he causes.

Victor experiences the two basic meanings of the word *responsibility*. He creates the creature (he causes it to exist), and therefore he has at least some responsibility for what the creature goes on to do. As the creature's maker, Victor also has both a duty to others to keep them safe from his creation and, Mary seems to be saying, a duty to his creation to ensure that his existence is worthwhile. We will turn to these two ideas now—responsibility for and responsibility to.

Responsibility for Our Creations

In a very straightforward way, Victor *causes* the monster to exist. He builds him, freely and with the hope, indeed the intention, that he will come to life.

This creation is no accident. Although many factors can arguably interfere with attributions of responsibility—including compulsion and delusion—there is no suggestion that Victor does not intend to make the creature, despite the frenzied way he goes about it. Indeed, Victor anticipates his future responsibility for the existence of the creature with pleasure and excitement—even triumph: "A new species would bless me as its creator and source; many happy and excellent natures would owe their being to me. No father could claim the gratitude of his child so completely as I should deserve their's" (p. 37).

Victor's error is failing to think harder about the potential repercussions of his work. Although he says that he hesitated for a long time about how to use the "astonishing" (p. 35) power to "bestow animation upon lifeless matter" (p. 37), this hesitation is due to the many technical hurdles that he needs to overcome rather than to any concern for the questionable results of success. He considers the good that might come from his discovery—it might lead to development of a method for bringing the dead back to life—but he fails to consider the future of his initial experimental creation. Although he is aware that the single-minded pursuit of his scientific goals is throwing his life out of balance, he utterly fails to consider the possibility that the form he has stitched together and will soon animate may go on to cause harm to anyone, including Victor himself. We might compare Victor to some modern scientists who have stopped their work to consider its potential for harm, such as those who gathered at Asilomar in the mid-1970s to consider the implications of research on recombinant DNA or those who recently called for a moratorium on germline gene editing.

Victor's failure to thoroughly anticipate responsibility—to consider that there might be both upsides and downsides to his technical achievement—is his downfall. As soon as the creature opens his "dull yellow eye" (p. 41), Victor is filled with "breathless horror and disgust" (p. 42). He flees, initially so agitated he is unable to stand still, eventually falling into a nightmare-filled sleep in which he sees his fiancée, Elizabeth, first "in the bloom of health" (p. 43) and then as a rotting corpse. Victor is woken by the creature but "escape[s]" again (p. 43). He is unable to face his creation and is unprepared for the creature's independent existence.

As the story progresses, Victor's initial emotional reactions to seeing the creature come to life—disgust and horror—are substantiated by the creature's actions. Victor learns that the creature has killed his young brother William, whose death is then blamed on a family friend, Justine. But Victor knows the truth. He understands that he would be implicated in her execution if she is convicted as well as in the murder of his brother—"the result of my curiosity and lawless devices would cause the death of two of my fellow-beings" (p. 62). He suffers greatly under this guilt—"the tortures of the accused did not equal mine; she was sustained by innocence, but the fangs of remorse tore my bosom, and would not forego their hold" (p. 65). But he does nothing to intervene. The girl is unjustly convicted. "I, not in deed, but in effect, was the true murderer" (p. 75).

Victor continues to hold himself responsible for both the existence of the horrifying creature and the creature's deadly deeds. He spends his remaining days on earth chasing the creature across the Arctic, intending to kill him. But in this understanding of his responsibility, he is alone—no one else in the novel sees Victor as anything but a casualty of unspeakable misfortune. Although he is at one time accused of murdering his friend Henry Clerval—who is killed by the creature—that charge is eventually dropped (ironically, as Victor leaves the prison, an observer remarks, "He may be innocent of the murder, but he has certainly a bad conscience" [p. 153]). Even Robert Walton, the explorer who encounters Victor on the ice and to whom Victor narrates his entire story, judges him to be noble, gentle, and wise. It is left to Victor's own conscience—and to the reader—to assess the extent to which he should be held responsible for the creature's deeds. On this question, Victor is resolved. Although he allows that he did not intend to create a creature capable of such evil, he continues to hold himself responsible for the creature's existence and for the deaths the creature causes, and he dies believing himself duty bound toward his fellow creatures to destroy his creation.

Responsibility to Our Creations

On his deathbed, Victor also acknowledges that he is not just responsible *for* the creature but also responsible *to* him: "I … was bound towards him, to assure, as far as was in my power, his happiness and well-being" (p. 181). The creature himself makes this argument forcefully when he confronts Victor in the mountains overlooking the Chamonix Valley. The creature relates all that has transpired since Victor abandoned him. He has learned to find food and shelter. By closely observing a human family, he has learned about emotion and relationships as well as how to speak and read. By finding a collection of books, he learns the rudiments of human society and history. Yet on each attempt to engage with humans, the creature is disastrously rejected—sometimes even attacked. He learns that humans are repulsed by him. Concluding that humans will never accept him into their moral community, he comes to see humans as the enemy. He now lays his pain and loneliness at Victor's feet: "Unfeeling, heartless creator! you had endowed me with perceptions and passions, and then cast me abroad an object for the scorn and horror of mankind. But on you only had I any claim for pity and redress, and from you I determined to seek that justice which I vainly attempted to gain from any other being that wore the human form" (p. 116).

To assuage his loneliness, rage, and pain, the creature demands that Victor "create a female for me, with whom I can live in the interchange of those sympathies necessary for my being" (p. 120). The creature tries to reason with Victor: "Oh! my creator, make me happy; let me feel gratitude towards you for one benefit! Let me see that I excite the sympathy of some existing thing; do not deny me my request!" (p. 121). Although Victor's sympathies are stirred by the creature's story and his plea for companionship, Victor immediately refuses out of a sense of responsibility to protect the world from "wickedness" (p. 139).

By having her inventor create a sentient being—in particular one whose intellect and emotions rival or surpass those of her supposed protagonist—Mary sharpens the point about the responsibility that we might owe to our creations. Parents understand this point (and in many ways Victor is placed in the role of a parent—albeit one who rejects and abandons his child). And so must scientists working to create new or modified life-forms carry a responsibility to their creations. We can take the point even further: a sense of responsibility can be experienced by anyone who pours time and energy into a project, even if that project does not result in a new life form. We can legitimately speak about feeling an obligation *to* our work—including to our results, our ideas, or our findings—that it deserves to be published or further developed or recognized as valuable not only because it can benefit others or result in glory for ourselves but because of the intrinsic value of new knowledge.

Responsibility as an Experience

One of the most striking aspects of Mary's treatment of responsibility is her depiction of its emotional and physical toll. Before Victor gains any insight into the deadly consequences of his scientific work or the onerous duties he has thereby acquired, he experiences responsibility as an emotional and physical state. At the very moment he animates his creation, "the beauty of the dream vanished, and breathless horror and disgust filled my heart" (p. 42). He runs from the room, paces back and forth, "unable to compose my mind to sleep" (p. 42), falls into a sleep filled with nightmares portending the death of his fiancée, and wakes in a cold sweat with his limbs convulsing. He goes outside and by chance meets his friend Henry Clerval, who notices his agitated mood and then spends several months nursing Victor through a "nervous fever" during which "the form of the monster on whom I had bestowed existence was for ever before my eyes, and I raved incessantly concerning him" (p. 46).

Victor recovers from this first episode, but his recovery is short-lived. As the creature kills his family and friends, Victor grapples with the realization that he is responsible for the existence of the creature and to a certain extent is therefore responsible for the creature's deeds. His grief at the death of little William and then of Henry are compounded and tainted by his guilt at the role he has played in their deaths. He cannot sleep, and his physical health declines. His concerned father implores him to move beyond his grief and reenter the world, "for excessive sorrow prevents improvement or enjoyment, or even the discharge of daily usefulness, without which no man is fit for society." But Victor is unable to respond: "I should have been the first to hide my grief, and console my friends, if remorse had not mingled its bitterness with my other sensations" (p. 72).

As the story progresses, Victor continues to suffer emotionally and physically. His family and friends are alarmed and try to help him, but Victor cannot be reached. He withdraws from their company, floating aimlessly on a boat on the lake, unable to find peace. He hikes in the mountains during a rainstorm. He travels to England, ostensibly to see the world before settling down in marriage but in reality to build another creature. He describes the time as "two years of exile" (p. 130), and he bemoans his inability to enjoy the journey or the people he meets on his way. He describes a visit to Oxford, noting that he "enjoyed this scene; and yet my enjoyment was embittered both by the memory of the past, and the anticipation of the future. ... I am a blasted tree; the bolt has entered my soul; and I felt then that I should survive to exhibit, what I shall soon cease to be—a miserable spectacle of wrecked humanity, pitiable to others, and abhorrent to myself" (p. 135).

As the book concludes, Victor lay dying in Walton's boat. The explorer and the reader are left in no doubt about what has killed him. When the creature boards the boat and sees the newly dead Victor, he claims responsibility for his death—"That is also my victim!" the creature exclaims. "I, who irretrievably destroyed thee by destroying all thou lovedst" (p. 183). Yet it is not only the loss of his family and friends that destroys Victor but also the guilt and remorse that came with being the one who so naively created the creature and gave him life.

Conclusion

In *Frankenstein*, Mary Shelley explores at least three aspects of responsibility: Victor's responsibility *for* the deadly actions committed by his creation and the threat the creature's existence poses to his family, friends, and, Victor fears, the entire world; Victor's responsibility *to* his creation for the creature's welfare and well-being; and the consequences of this weighty responsibility for Victor both physically and emotionally.

The novel is a gothic horror—the plot is fantastical, the scenery dramatic, and the hero doomed. But it is also a cautionary tale, with a serious message about scientists' and engineers' social responsibility. Mary conveys a concern that unchecked scientific enthusiasm can cause unanticipated harm. For Victor, scientific curiosity threatens the integrity of his family and disrupts his ability to engage with nature and enter into relationships. By supplying a protagonist who suffers so greatly as a result of failing to anticipate the consequences of his work, Mary urges upon her readers the virtues of humility and restraint. In her development of a creature who suffers so greatly because he is despised and rejected by an intolerant human society, she asks us to consider our obligations to our creations before we bring them into being.

The reader is left to wonder whether the story could have unfolded differently if Victor were to have behaved more responsibly. Might he have anticipated the brute strength of his creation and decided not to create it, or might he have altered his plan so that the creature would be less powerful and less terrifying? Rather than abandoning the creature, might he have stepped into his parental role and worked to ensure the creature's happy existence? Mary does not tell us what Victor should have done differently—that is the reflective work that we readers must do as we consider our own responsibility to and for our modern-day creations.

I'VE CREATED A MONSTER! (AND SO CAN YOU)

CORY DOCTOROW

When it comes to predicting the future, science fiction writers are Texas marksmen: they fire a shotgun into the side of a barn, draw a target around the place where the pellets hit, and proclaim their deadly accuracy to anyone who'll listen. They have made a *lot* of "predictions," before and after Mary Shelley wrote her "modern Prometheus" story about a maker and his creature. Precious few of those predictions have come true, which is only to be expected: throw enough darts, and you'll get a bull's eye eventually, even if you're wearing a blindfold.

Predicting the future is a mug's game, anyway. If the future can be predicted, then it is inevitable. If it's inevitable, then what we do doesn't matter. If what we do doesn't matter, why bother getting out of bed in the morning? Science fiction does something better than predict the future: it *influences* it.

The science fiction stories that we remember—such as *Frankenstein*—are ones that resonate with the public imagination. Most science fiction is forgotten shortly after it's published, but a few of those tales live on for years, decades—even centuries in the case of *Frankenstein*. The fact that a story captures the public imagination doesn't mean that it will come true in the future, but it tells you something about the *present*. You learn something about the world when a vision of the future becomes a subject of controversy or delight.

If some poor English teacher has demanded that you identify the "themes" of Mary's *Frankenstein*, the obvious correct answer is that she is referring to ambition and hubris. Ambition because Victor Frankenstein has challenged death itself, one of the universe's eternal verities. Everything dies: whales and humans and dogs and cats and stars and galaxies. Hubris—"extreme pride or self-confidence" (thanks, *Wikipedia*!)—because as Victor brings his creature to life, he is so blinded by his own ambition that he fails to consider the moral consequences of his actions. He fails to ask himself how the thinking, living being he is creating will feel about being stitched together, imbued with life force, and ushered into the uncaring universe.

Many critics panned *Frankenstein* when it was first published, but the crowds loved it—made it a best seller and packed the theaters where it was performed on the stage. Mary had awoken something in the public imagination, and it's not hard to understand what that was: a story about technology mastering humans rather than serving them.

When Mary published *Frankenstein* in 1818, England was getting completely upended by runaway technological innovation in the Industrial Revolution. Ways of life that had endured for centuries disappeared in the blink of an eye. William Wordsworth would soon write mournful letters and poems about railroads ruining his beloved countryside. Ancient trades disappeared without fanfare; new careers appeared overnight. Every constant was unmade; the maps were redrawn; and the old, steady rhythm of life stuttered and pulsed erratically. Young Mary, eighteen years old when she started writing *Frankenstein*, felt revolution in the air.

In 1999, Douglas Adams—another prodigious predictor of the present—made a keen observation about the relationship of young people to technology:

I've come up with a set of rules that describe our reactions to technologies:

1. Anything that is in the world when you're born is normal and ordinary and is just a natural part of the way the world works.
2. Anything that's invented between when you're fifteen and thirty-five is new and exciting and revolutionary and you can probably get a career in it.
3. Anything invented after you're thirty-five is against the natural order of things.

Depending on your age, the truth of Adams's law—and the terror of the nineteenth-century readers who relished *Frankenstein*'s cautionary message about technology mastering its creator—may not be immediately apparent to you. But we assuredly live in a world of continuous technological upheaval, an Information Revolution that makes Mary's piddling Industrial Revolution seem mild by comparison, and that is the reason we still care about a two-hundred-year-old novel imagining a scientifically inarticulate project to bring the dead back to life.

"Technological change" isn't a force of nature, though. The way technology changes and the way it changes us are the result of choices that we make as toolsmiths, individual users, and groups.

Where Does Technological Change Come From?

Robert Heinlein, a titan of science fiction (as well as a titanically problematic figure), wrote in *The Door into Summer* (1957), a time-travel novel all about technological revolution, "When railroading time comes you can railroad—but not before" (120). All through history, inventors doodled things that looked like helicopters, including, famously, Leonardo da Vinci. But helicopters didn't come into existence until a lot of other stuff was in place: metallurgy, engine design, aerodynamics, and so on. The idea of helicopters was floating around in our ether, occurring and recurring in the minds of dreamers, but just because you can think up and design a rotor, it doesn't mean you can design a diesel motor, let alone build a Sikorsky that can lift a tank.

This theory of technological progress is called the "adjacent possible." Fanciful inspiration strikes all the time as a consequence of our playful, unpredictable imaginations. Fancy becomes reality when enough of the necessary stuff is in place. When it's railroading time, you get railroads. Writers had long dreamed of animating dead matter—think of the dirt that became Adam or the clay that rabbis turned into golems. Mary, living in the world of Galvinism, industrial and democratic revolution, and the newfound delight in rationalism, was able to give us a golem without resorting to the supernatural.

But railroading time didn't just give us railroads: it gave us robber barons who built huge corporate "trusts" that stole from the masses to enrich the few. It gave us forced laborers, kidnapped or tricked out of China or shipped from slave plantations, to do the back-breaking work of laying the tracks. Railroads may have been inevitable, given steel and tracks and land and engines. Slave labor was not inevitable. It was a choice.

Once the railroads were built, though, choices got harder to make. Railroads changed the way that farmers sold their wares, changed the way that settlements were opened and serviced, changed all those things that freaked out Wordsworth, redrew maps, made industries disappear, and created new ones. Living as though the railroad didn't exist was hard, got harder, and eventually became virtually impossible. Whether it was your distant business correspondents expecting quick responses to their letters or what kinds of jobs your kids could get, you couldn't just opt out of railroads—not without opting out of all the activities your pals and loved ones undertook on the trains.

How the railroads were built was the result of individual and often immoral choices. How the railroads were *used* was the result of a collective choice made by all the people in your social network: family, friends, bosses, and teachers.

That's why there's no such thing as an Amish village of one. To be Amish is to agree with all the people who matter to you to make the same choices about which technologies you'll use and how you'll use them.

Let's Talk about Facebook, the Amish Village with a Billion People in It

Internet social networks were already huge before Facebook: Sixdegrees, Friendster, Myspace, Bebo, and dozens of others had already come and gone. There was an adjacent possible in play: the Internet and the Web existed, and it had grown enough that many of the people you wanted to talk to could be found online, if only someone would design a service to facilitate finding or meeting them.

A service like Facebook was inevitable, but how Facebook works was not. Facebook is designed like a casino game where the jackpots are attention from other people (likes and messages) and the playing surface is a vast board whose parts can't be seen most of the time. You place bets on what kind of personal revelation will ring the cherries, pull the lever—hit "post"—and wait while the wheel spins to see if you'll win big. As in all casino games, in the Facebook game there's one universal rule: the house always wins. Facebook continuously fine-tunes its algorithms to maximize the amount that you disclose to the service because it makes money by selling that personal information to advertisers. The more personal information you give up, the more ways they can sell you—if an advertiser wants to sell sugar water or subprime mortgages to nineteen-year-old engineering freshmen whose parents rent in a large northeastern city, then disclosing all those facts about you converts you from a user to a vendible asset.

Adding the surveillance business model to Facebook was an individual choice. But using Facebook—now that it is dominant—is a group choice.

I'm a Facebook vegan. I won't even use Whatsapp or Instagram because they're owned by Facebook. That means I basically never get invited to parties; I can't keep up with what's going on in my daughter's school; I can't find my old school friends or participate in the online memorials when one of them dies. Unless everyone you know chooses along with you not to use Facebook, being a Facebook vegan is hard. But it also lets you see the casino for what it is and make a more informed choice about what technologies you depend on.

Mary Shelley understood social exile. She walked away from the social network of England—ran away, really, at the age of sixteen with a married man, Percy Bysshe Shelley, and conceived two children with him before they finally married. Shelley's life is a story about the adjacent possible of belonging, and *Frankenstein* is a story about the adjacent possible of deliciously credible catastrophes in an age of technological whiplash and massive dislocation.

In 1989, the Berlin Wall fell, and the end of the ironically named German Democratic Republic was at hand. The GDR—often called "East Germany"—was one of the most spied-upon countries in the history of the world. The Stasi, its secret police force, were synonymous with totalitarian control, and their name struck terror wherever it was whispered.

The Stasi employed one snitch for every sixty people in the GDR: an army to surveil a nation.

Today, the US National Security Agency (NSA) has *the entire world* under surveillance more totally than the Stasi ever dreamed of. It has one employee for every twenty thousand people it spies on—not counting the contractors.

The NSA uses a workforce less than one-tenth the size of the Stasi to surveil *a planet*.

How does the NSA do it? How did we get to the point where the labor costs of surveillance have plummeted so far in a few decades?

By enlisting the spied upon to do the spying. Your mobile device, your social media accounts, your search queries, and your Facebook posts—those juicy, detailed, revelatory Facebook posts—contain everything the NSA can possibly want to know about whole populations, and those populations foot the bill for its gathering of that information.

The adjacent possible made Facebook inevitable, but individual choices by technologists and entrepreneurs made Facebook into a force for mass surveillance. Opting out of Facebook is not a personal choice but a social one, one that you brave on your own at the cost of your social life and your ability to stay in touch with the people you love.

Frankenstein warns of a world where technology controls people instead of the other way around. Victor has choices to make about what he does with technology, and he gets those choices wrong again and again. But technology doesn't control people: people wield technology to control other people.

The world's adjacent possibles will enable you to dream up many technologies throughout your life. But what you do with them can take away other people's possibilities. The decision to use a widely adopted technology is never entirely in your personal hands, but what about the decision to *make* that technology and *how* you make it?

That's up to you.

CHANGING CONCEPTIONS OF HUMAN NATURE
JANE MAIENSCHEIN AND KATE MACCORD

Aristotle

Frankenstein is a bit like the proverbial elephant, with all those blind men seeing different things as they touch the trunk or tail or skin. Viewers read Mary Shelley's novel and see many wildly different things. The nearly fifty million Google hits for the word *Frankenstein* exceed the number of hits for the word *Macbeth*, suggesting the popularity and staying power of this text. Here we ask what the story tells us about conceptions of human nature and how those conceptions have changed over time.

While we are looking back two hundred years, let us look back a couple of millennia more. In the fourth century BCE, the Greek philosopher Aristotle set the stage for thinking in terms of "monsters" as deviations from the normal essence of a species. As a keen observer of nature, Aristotle also recognized that individuals go through a development process that unfolds over time. Both of these themes are important for Mary Shelley.

First, about the idea of an essence for a species, or essentialism: Aristotle was convinced based on what he could observe that the world consists of different types of organisms. Each organism falls into a particular species type, in our case the human type. For Aristotle, each type has four causes that make an individual: the material cause provides the substance; the formal cause provides a plan that determines the shape; the efficient cause involves the construction process that make the material the right shape over time; and the final cause makes an organism come alive as it actualizes the potential for life (Lawrence 2010). These causes require time to interact, meaning that an organism can become recognized as a member of its natural type only at the end of the *process* of generation.

In addition, all living organisms also have what Aristotle called a vegetative soul (which makes it alive); animals have locomotory souls (which allow them to move around); and humans have rational souls (which give us reason and emotions). Aristotle's idea of soul was not religious, but it was part of his attempt to explain how something could look exactly the same one minute when a person was alive and different the next minute when the person is dead. Aristotle explained the difference in terms of the action of the final cause and the soul (see Aristotle 1943).

Second is Aristotle's recognition that making something alive requires time. It involves a developmental process to bring all these causes and factors together. Much later the Catholic Church added the idea of "hominization" to indicate the moment when a person becomes alive as a human being. Aristotle would have insisted that becoming alive does not happen at one moment but rather only as a process over time. Several millennia of thinkers have agreed with Aristotle on this point, which remains, at its heart, the best understanding of development.

Victor Frankenstein and His Creature

Like other intellectuals at the beginning of the nineteenth century, Mary Wollstonecraft Shelley lived in the shadow of Aristotle. The period later named the Scientific Revolution (approximately the sixteenth through the eighteenth centuries) sought to replace parts of Aristotelian natural philosophy with materialism, empiricism, and experimentation. Materialism emphasized the importance of thinking in terms of material and the roles of matter in motion as causing what happens in the world, including life. Materialists rejected, for example, the idea that there is some special life force and maintained that living organisms are made of matter that changes over time. In contrast, vitalists believed that there is some kind of vital or life force that makes things come alive—that it takes a life force to make something a living organism rather than a hunk of clay or other material. Through these new explanatory frameworks, people began to explore the living world and ask what causes life to appear in the first place and then continues to make something alive rather than dead.

Those various attempts to understand life obviously influenced Mary's thinking. Empiricism and experimentation called for people to try things out—that is, not just to rely on past knowledge or what can be learned from books but to look for ourselves. Victor Frankenstein embraces the call for experimentation.

Yet Victor seems not to have had a clear view of what makes life happen or about human nature. For some thinkers, such as Paracelsus, among those who were called the iatrochemists of the seventeenth century, life requires a particular chemical interaction. For others, electricity imparts life. Still others thought that heat is the driving factor. Some believed that life arises through some form of unexplained spontaneous generation. Or perhaps there is some other life force that drives material to become animated or alive. Although Victor seems not to have a clear view about what it is that causes life, he is driven by a conviction that he can make a

JANE MAIENSCHEIN AND KATE MACCORD

creature and cause that creature to acquire whatever it takes and thereby to become alive. He wants to create life, and Mary uses the term *create* quite consciously (Westfall 1977, 82–104).

We are just as fascinated today as Mary's contemporary readers would have been about what it takes to make material come to life and what makes up what we think of as human nature. Today scientists often point to something about the way cells in embryos divide to produce more and more cells out of an initially fertilized egg. Those cells contain nucleic acids, which seem to be essential for life. Strands of deoxyribonucleic acids (DNA) replicate themselves in ways that allow cells to divide and multicellular organisms to grow and develop over time. We continue to think of life as having a material basis. Perhaps unlike Mary's Victor, we know much more about what makes something alive, and we also realize how much more we do not yet know.

What Makes the Unnamed Creature a "Monster"?

In Victor's creature, we are introduced to a conundrum about human nature—What makes a monster? Is it physical appearance? This is a strong possibility; after all, the creature is bigger and stronger than the people it encounters and "endowed with a figure hideously deformed and loathsome" (p. 98). In Aristotle's parlance of causes, we could read within the creature an interrupted set of formal and efficient causes—that is, an interruption in the plan and the construction of the material that makes a shape.

Maybe it behooves us, however, to look a little deeper at the nature of this creature's putative monstrosity. Although physically aberrant, he is constructed from human parts and so is endowed with some level of humanness, at least in the material sense. And although the people whom the creature encounters recoil from his physical appearance, his form is recognizable as that of a man rather than that of some other type. In this sense, he has the essence or "nature" of a human.

What about the creature's rational "soul" or his intellectual faculties, which also include emotion and sensations? Are his deficits here what makes him a monster? This is another strong possibility. He displays behaviors that challenge his contemporaries' moral sensibilities—violence, vengeance, and murder. But these acts are also committed by many people to whom the label *monster* might not apply.

To delve a bit deeper into the monstrous nature of Victor's creation, let's return for a moment to Aristotle. Recall that as generation unfolds, the four causes interact to give rise to a fully realized organism of a particular type. That is, a person is a person and has the nature of a human in particular only because of the *process* of development.

Why Development Matters

Let's take a moment to consider the importance of there being a process of development and why this matters for the creation of a monster and whether he can become a human person without appropriate development. Throughout his monologues to his creator, the creature explains that he had no parents to raise him and that he had to pick up his morals through stolen conversations and observations. Victor carried out his experiment and then ran away from it, leaving the mind and behavior of a newborn bound within an adult body. Victor made the fatal mistake of failing to understand that producing a life, in the sense of a fully and properly functioning living human, requires development. Babies do not know what is right and wrong; they have to learn about morals as well as about how to walk and talk and ride a bicycle and read a book and such things. Aristotle knew this. Yet some of the enthusiastic materialists of the Scientific Revolution thought that material and material forces might be enough. It is not clear whether Victor or Mary learned the lesson that development matters or fell for the illusion that matter is enough.

Mary surely wants us to see that Victor oversteps the bounds of proper science and medicine with his experiments. The morality tale suggests that we humans should not try to overreach and create novel beings. We are, it seems, likely to get it wrong and create a monster.

Yet perhaps this is not the right conclusion. Perhaps instead we should note that Victor himself also lacks a proper education that has developed over time. He does not develop his understanding of the world in a systematic way. He seems to jump from one passion to another. At first, he enthuses about some texts that appeal to him, only to discard them and embrace others. Then he seeks teachers and learns from them but also pursues his own secret agenda. We do not get a clear sense of why but might interpret that, like the creature he produces, Victor also fails to develop appropriate feelings and rationality about the world, including a feeling for proper scientific experimentation and what it can or cannot tell us.

The point here is that the moral of Mary's tale is not simply restrictive—that is, "do not mess with creating life"—but also instructive—that is, be aware that organisms, especially humans, require time and particular stimuli to realize fully the norms of their species.

JANE MAIENSCHEIN AND KATE MACCORD

Normal and Aberrant Development

For Aristotle, the four causes interact throughout the generative process, giving rise to an adult of a particular type. Type (in our case, being human) is thus the outcome of a regular process of generation. What, then, is the outcome of an interrupted generative process? And how have people understood this interrupted generative process through time?

There are two points to consider here: type and deviation from the regular process of development (i.e., the normal way in which something achieves a type). Within the Aristotelian worldview, a type is a natural unit, and its members are endowed with particular features that make them recognizable as belonging to that unit (so long as they go through the regular course of development). In Aristotle's estimation, types are essential—that is, they are constituted by sets of attributes that make their members fundamentally what they are. Essence defines the type but also defines and gives rise to the organisms within a type.

Let's look at the idea of type a little bit more closely. The type concept persisted long beyond Aristotle. Just as Aristotle had done, natural historians of the seventeenth through the nineteenth centuries sought to make sense of and to order the natural world. This ordering often required recognizing distinctions between organisms and grouping them into neat, tidy types.

In Aristotle's estimation, types are unchanging entities, but by the time Mary wrote *Frankenstein*, the concept that species are fixed had begun to be challenged. Part of this challenge came from recognizing that the environment can affect an organism throughout the process of development; the other part involved understanding that these changes can be passed from one generation to the next. These two pieces of the puzzle became the basis for evolutionary theory: Darwin understood them but had no way of knowing how changes during development could be passed on; this understanding would not come until the twentieth century once the process and material nature of inheritance were understood.

In Mary's time, deviation from the regular process of development was understood to create monsters. In the early nineteenth century, for instance, Johann Friedrich Meckel (1781–1833) spent the majority of his career looking for and describing embryological aberrations (O'Connell 2013a). To Meckel, these monstrosities could be explained on the basis of interrupted development. They were recognized by their deviations from the norms of development (i.e., their nonadherence to the norms of the human type). What's more, these monsters, according to Meckel, represented arrests of development in which the embryo or fetus was stuck at a stage representing a lower organism in the animal kingdom (Meckel was a proponent of the idea that development is a readout of evolutionary history long before Ernst Haeckel [1834–1919] offered his famous recapitulation theory) (Barnes 2014b; O'Connell 2013b). In this system, an interrupted generative process creates a transgression of types.

Theories of deviation from the normal type and altered developmental processes were co-opted in the later nineteenth century by some scientists seeking to explain both development and evolution. For instance, Edward Drinker Cope (1840–1897) and Henry Fairfield Osborn (1857–1935) understood there to be tooth types that organisms could move between throughout evolution. This move, according to Cope and Osborn, was brought about by changes in the organism's developmental trajectory (Barnes 2014a). In this later context, types and movement between them became not so much about monsters but about evolution.

And in Conclusion, Was the Creature Human?

A human, according to Aristotle, is a being of the human type. It is a creature that has gained the proper form and has followed the proper course of development (both physically and rationally/emotionally) for the human type. According to Aristotle's estimation, then, Victor Frankenstein's creature cannot be considered a human. We agree.

Victor wants to see the creature as human; after all, he went through the arduous process of gathering human materials and conducting the experiments necessary to (re)create life. But in the end Victor doesn't want to do the proper developmental work—he abandons his creation, leaving him in an incomplete state of development. In Aristotelian language, Victor disturbs the formal, efficient, and final causes, leaving the creature with an ill-formed body and mind of material cause alone.

What if we abandon the Aristotelian framework of the four causes and focus on the ways in which others among Mary Shelley's contemporaries explained life? Let's return for a moment to the materialists. For a strict materialist, the only thing necessary to designate something as human is that it be constructed of the proper matter. Because process isn't an issue here, a pure materialist may well deem the creature to be human. However, very few people have ever been strict materialists in this sense. Material alone is not enough. A much more common view was that of the mechanist materialist, who required both that the proper material be present and that this material be in motion in the correct way. Such a thinker would not see the creature as human. The mechanistic aspect requires process, and the motions of material must be started and continued in the right way.

In closing, let's consider a modern implication of one question *Frankenstein* raises for our views of human nature. Being a human means being of the human type, which requires both the form of the matter and also the process of its development. Only when the matter and process are achieved together in the proper way can an individual's humanity be achieved. The concept of personhood carries additional social interpretations and is ultimately defined through social convention, yet in our view personhood requires at the very least being fully human in the sense of form and development.

We recognize that there are many different opinions about what can and should be counted as a person. Yet development is crucial, and material alone is not enough. Genes and inherited material are not enough. In this light, personhood, or the designation of a being as a person, can be conferred only once the process of development is sufficiently complete. Determining what counts as sufficient to count as a person is a social issue. Biologically, what counts as a human being is the ability to live independently, with "living" defined according to the best scientific and medical standards of the day.

To look more concretely at a topic of current interest, some people claim that embryos have personhood and should be given the legal rights of a human being. In the sense of humanity or personhood explained here, this definition would be an inaccurate assessment of embryos. Embryos are materially of the human type, but they have not yet gone through the process of development and are not yet persons in this sense. Some people like to suggest that embryos are potential persons in that they might, under the right circumstances, become persons. Or to put it biologically, perhaps an embryo or a "monster" that is not a fully formed human might be taken as having the potential to become a human being. But potential is not actual. Most of us have many potentials that we never put into action. It does not make sense to act as if every one of us is already an Olympic star or concert pianist or math genius just because we may each have the potential to become these things. It is the actual that matters. The creature is not an actual human in that he has not developed fully. Even after two centuries, Victor and his not-human creature help inform our understanding of human nature.

UNDISTURBED BY REALITY
VICTOR FRANKENSTEIN'S TECHNOSCIENTIFIC DREAM OF REASON
ALFRED NORDMANN

Animated by an Almost Supernatural Enthusiasm

"Learn from me ... how dangerous is the acquirement of knowledge" (p. 35). Victor Frankenstein's warning is one reason why his story continues to fascinate and why books like the present volume are written. The terrible repercussions of the ambition to become like Prometheus and "animate the lifeless clay" (p. 39) hold a stark lesson for today. This lesson, however, is not quite what it is often made out to be. Early on in the book, Victor— the "modern Prometheus" of Mary Shelley's subtitle—lets on that his inclination is not so modern after all but is indebted to premodern, mystical authors such as the alchemists Cornelius Agrippa (Heinrich Cornelius Agrippa von Nettesheim, 1486–1535) and Albertus Magnus (c. 1200–1280):

> I should certainly have thrown Agrippa aside, and, with my imagination warmed as it was, should probably have applied myself to the more rational theory of chemistry which has resulted from modern discoveries. It is even possible, that the train of my ideas would never have received the fatal impulse that led to my ruin. ...
>
> It may appear very strange, that a disciple of Albertus Magnus should arise in the eighteenth century; but our family was not scientifical, and I had not attended any of the lectures given at the schools of Geneva. My dreams were therefore undisturbed by reality; and I entered with the greatest diligence into the search of the philosopher's stone and the elixir of life. (pp. 21, 22)

For Mary's readers in 1818, Victor's aspirations did not fit "in this enlightened and scientific age" (p. 28); they were out of sync with rational theory and the modern discoveries of chemistry.

So the creature is not a product of modern science, and yet we fancy Victor as a mad scientist in a laboratory filled with fumes and sparks from modern apparatus. How is it that this premodern mystical alchemist appears so contemporary today? The answer is as easy as it is provocative: perhaps today's "Frankenfoods" and "Frankenmaterials" are not the products of modern science, either, but a return to alchemical dreams of reason (Krimsky 1982; Turney 1998).[1] Undisturbed by reality, they are "animated by an almost supernatural enthusiasm" (p. 33).

Indeed, Mary's novel suggests not only that magic and alchemy preceded science but also that science can infuse and revive their prescientific ambitions. Victor's teacher M. Waldman points him in this direction when he portrays modern science as a rite of passage that will allow Victor to reclaim the alchemist's desire to "bestow animation upon lifeless matter" (p. 37). In and of itself, the world of science is a disenchanted world with causal knowledge about the arrangements of facts. But before and beyond the enlightened and scientific age lies a rather more magical world, enchanted and animated by almost unlimited powers:

> "The ancient teachers of this science," said he, "promised impossibilities, and performed nothing. The modern masters promise very little; they know that metals cannot be transmuted, and that the elixir of life is a chimera. But these philosophers, whose hands seem only made to dabble in dirt, and their eyes to pore over the microscope or crucible, have indeed performed miracles. They penetrate into the recesses of nature, and shew how she works in her hiding places. They ascend into the heavens; they have discovered how the blood circulates, and the nature of the air we breathe. They have acquired new and almost unlimited powers; they can command the thunders of heaven, mimic the earthquake, and even mock the invisible world with its own shadows. (p. 30)

This description is an apt one, not only of those attempts that are most readily identified with Victor's ambitions—to genetically engineer plants and animals, to technologically enhance human nature, to create artificial life, and to "banish disease from the human frame, and render man invulnerable to any but a violent death" (p. 23)—but also of the far more mundane achievements of today's synthetic chemistry, nanotechnology, and materials science, with ordinary plastics first in line to mock the world with its own shadows. In 1957, Roland Barthes discussed plastics not as an application of polymer science but as "the magical operation par excellence: the transmutation of matter":

> This is because the quick-change artistry of plastic is absolute: it can become buckets as well as jewels. Hence a perpetual amazement. ... And this amazement is a pleasurable one, since the scope of the transformations gives man the measure of his power. ... [T]he age-old function of nature is modified: it is no longer the Idea, the pure Substance to be regained or imitated: an artificial Matter, more bountiful than all the natural deposits, is about to replace her, and to determine the very invention of forms. ([1957] 1991, 97–98)

Plastic signifies the malleability—indeed, the plasticity—of the material world. With sufficient ingenuity, anything can become anything else; the wealth of natural forms is mocked by the unbounded inventiveness of designers; and, in the words of nanotechnologist Gerd Binnig, we are witnesses and shapers of a second creation: "We have to become familiar with the idea that there is nothing inferior about dead matter. All the wonders of the world are contained, for example, in a stone, as all the laws of nature (and thus all the possibilities that can emerge from them) are reflected in it" (1989, 23). If plastic, according to Barthes, "is in essence the stuff of alchemy" ([1957] 1991, 97), so are ongoing attempts to transform dead matter into smart materials, to declare that dirt-repellant coatings make for self-cleaning surfaces, and to teach refrigerators to report back to us about milk going bad and eggs running low. These attempts to animate things, to give them intelligence, or to make them come to life are undisturbed by reality in that they do not accept things as they are in virtue of their first or original creation. They instead make things subject to a second creation, presumably of our own making.

Realities of Little Worth

Mary's tale is not one of modern science. On the contrary, it tells the limits of science and dreams the dream of technoscience, a dream that gains power in the plastic world of Frankenmaterials.

Science is the theoretical knowledge produced by those who seek to describe or represent the world and are aided in this quest by technology. The person who pursues this science is *Homo depictor*, the Representer; technoscience is technological knowledge produced by those who seek to control how things work together and are aided by theory in this effort; the person who pursues technoscience is *Homo faber*, the Maker.

Science seeks to understand the world to the extent and in the ways that humans can comprehend it. Because the human mind is limited, science is essentially modest—the transmutation of matter and the making of gold from base metals are not on its agenda. Scientists are not interested in creating the philosopher's stone to transform lead into gold or the elixir of life. "It was very different," says a crestfallen Victor, "when the masters of the science sought immortality and power; such views, although futile, were grand: but now the scene was changed. The ambition of the inquirer seemed to limit itself to the annihilation of those visions on which my interest in science was chiefly founded. I was required to exchange chimeras of boundless grandeur for realities of little worth" (p. 29). By definition, perhaps, what the mind can comprehend is well proportioned, measured, and not apt to provoke awe. When we make a model, for example, and liken the inside of an atom to a miniaturized solar system with planets orbiting its core, we effectively create a mental image that cuts things down to size so that we can easily comprehend them. We do so even as we acknowledge that, really, electrons are not like solid bodies at all but something that eludes our commonsense conceptions. If science formerly relied on simplification in order to reduce complexity, to picture and explain things, this reliance did not stifle the ambition to be creative and generate complexity even where it surpasses our intellectual powers. The history of technology testifies to this ambition, and the technology of the computer allows us to exceed the limits of our science. The statements that represent slices of reality—each of little worth—can be built into a complex system of statements simulating a dynamic process that may also be observed in nature or that is entirely artificial. Either way, with statements that reduce complexity and simplify things for the purpose of human understanding, one can now generate a system that quickly becomes too complex for the human mind: too many lines of code, too many parameters to keep track of.

On the basis of science but far beyond its limits, we have "acquired new and almost unlimited powers … can command the thunders of heaven, mimic the earthquake, and even mock the invisible world with its own shadows" (p. 30). We have made a machine that serves to model and predict the behavior of complex systems and, in effect, does the work of thinking for us. Quite independently of whether we have solved the problem of "artificial intelligence" and as unspectacular as the invention of plastic, this achievement is yet another example of bestowing animation upon lifeless matter. It is also another example of being undisturbed by reality—that is, by the limitations of the human mind: "Whence, I often asked myself, did the principle of life proceed? It was a bold question, and one which has ever been considered as a mystery; yet with how many things are we upon the brink of becoming acquainted, if cowardice or carelessness did not restrain our inquiries" (p. 33).

Insensible to the Charms of Nature

Unrestrained by cowardice and carelessness, Victor pursues his inquiries obsessively: "It was a most beautiful season; never did the fields bestow a more plentiful harvest, or the vines yield a more luxuriant vintage: but my eyes were insensible to the charms of nature" (p. 40). In more ways than one, to the obsessive gaze the world takes on a dual aspect: "To examine the causes of life, we must first have recourse to death. I became acquainted with the science of anatomy: but this was not sufficient; I must also observe the natural decay and corruption of the human body" (p. 33). Nothing is what it seems: the lively charms of nature harbor decay and corruption; what is naturally given is a promise or sign of what can be technologically; and lifeless matter is imbued by a mind, whereas our brain for climate change is a mere machine.

When things take on such a dual aspect, when they are not what they appear to be but endowed with secret powers, they become uncanny. This is the starting point for Sigmund Freud's famous analysis of the uncanny. Quoting Erich Rentsch, Freud notes that, "in telling a story, one of the most successful devices for easily creating uncanny effects is to leave the reader in uncertainty whether a particular figure in the story is a human being or an automaton" ([1919] 1955, 227)—or, one might add, whether that figure is lifeless matter from the graveyard or a living being. Today, it is not just the robots and zombies in the movies but also the devices that surround us that, as Freud explains, instill "doubts whether an apparently animate being is really alive; or conversely, whether a lifeless object might not be in fact animate" (227). Consider, for example, the ambition to create ambient intelligence in smart environments. As we move through the world, a network of sensors would collect background information about the quality of air; it would attach *Wikipedia* entries to the streets and houses we pass; it would signal the presence of friends, charging stations, and goods. This world would be a magical one in which all things are endowed with meaning, subject to our wishes, which may be granted if we conjure the powers properly—not by praying but by speaking to them or choosing the right app. With ambient intelligence and ubiquitous computing, the natural environment takes on a dual aspect, and aided by modern science and technology we advance to a premodern animistic world.[2]

Not Befitting the Human Mind

Contemporary technoscience is undisturbed by reality in that it flaunts its inventions that surpass the limited vocabulary of forms and shapes in nature; it is undisturbed by reality in that it draws on scientific understanding to generate a degree of complexity that exceeds the natural intellectual power of human minds; and it is undisturbed by reality in that it creates monsters—lifeless things that appear to be animated by a mind or a soul as well as lively, talkative, and animated things that are merely machines. And as we are learning to live and interact with such monsters, there is nothing particularly terrible or frightening about them, although they are sometimes a bit unsettling, uncanny, leaving us unsure just what and who we are dealing with when we eat genetically modified foods, when we talk to our cell phones, when we watch a computer generate on screen the right path for a hurricane, when we try to imagine that we wade all the time through a sea of information-laden radio waves or are surrounded by electrical wiring in every room of every house.

The dreams of materials science, of information and communication technology, of biomedical research, of synthetic biology seek to overcome or transgress the limits of the given world with an almost supernatural enthusiasm. In the midst of this story, it might be worthwhile to pause and reflect—only to discover, as Victor did, "that I am moralizing in the most interesting part of my tale" (p. 40):

> A human being in perfection ought always to preserve a calm and peaceful mind, and never to allow passion or a transitory desire to disturb his tranquillity. I do not think that the pursuit of knowledge is an exception to this rule. If the study to which you apply yourself has a tendency to weaken your affections, and to destroy your taste for those simple pleasures in which no alloy can possibly mix, then that study is certainly unlawful, that is to say, not befitting the human mind. (p. 40)

In an age of technoscience, it has become quite difficult even to understand this injunction. Are we supposed to achieve perfection merely by taking pleasure in unadulterated things that are unspoiled by excessive ambition? The dispassionate scientist describes things peacefully as they are, no matter what good or ill they signify. But there is no such tranquility when Victor or one of our contemporary technoscientists seeks to perfect his or her powers on "a dreary night of November": "With an anxiety that almost amounted to agony, I collected the instruments of life around me, that I might infuse a spark of being into the lifeless thing that lay at my feet" (p. 41).

NOTES

1. As a term for genetically engineered food, *Frankenfood* was coined around 1992 and found its way into dictionaries. Regarding "Frankenmaterial," see the discussion later in this essay.

2. Compare Freud's essay "The Uncanny" ([1919] 1955, 247–248). Tellingly, Freud offers the "reality principle" as an antidote to the "pleasure principle" of magical wish fulfillment. See also Nordmann 2008.

FRANKENSTEIN REFRAMED; OR, THE TROUBLE WITH PROMETHEUS

ELIZABETH BEAR

Mary Shelley's enduring novel *Frankenstein*, considered by some to be the first science fiction novel in the English language, is often read as a cautionary tale about science and secrets man was not meant to know. I contend that this interpretation is not so much accurate as incomplete and that in fact Victor Frankenstein's choices are fatal not in his desire for knowledge but in his avoidance of it.

Victor's crime is not pursuing science but in failing to consider the well-being of others and the consequences of his actions. I contend also that Mary's great work is a tale not about the dangers of a man's quest for knowledge but about the ethics of his failure to attempt to anticipate and take responsibility for the results of that quest. There is a strong link between Victor's failure of empathy for his creature and the particular kind of hubris that allows for the discarding of other people's lives in service to an ambition. This failure of empathy is closely connected to the moral cowardice of refusing to take responsibility for one's actions or for the outcomes derived from one's research.

Explicitly in the subtitle of the novel, Mary identifies Victor with the Greek immortal and trickster figure Prometheus, who among other adventures steals fire from the gods and gives it to man. The trouble with comparing Victor to Prometheus, however, is that in stealing fire, Prometheus actually accomplishes something of great utility to humanity and is punished by the gods for his temerity. Victor does indeed step into a role previously defined by his society as being appropriate to a god—that of progenitor of life—but Mary makes it evident from the beginning that any scientific utility in his work is of very little interest to him. He undertakes his research in a spirit of self-aggrandizement: it's not knowledge he seeks but power and renown, and this ambition leads him to become far more of a monster than the creature he creates.

This motivation is reflected early in his life when he rejects the painstaking and boring—by his standards—research done by contemporary natural philosophers (who at the turn of the nineteenth century were beginning to make some real progress in developing the foundations of science as we practice it today) in favor of the type of research done by the ancients, whose untested ideas, although widely accepted in the medieval period, had already been discredited by Mary's time. So Victor seeks the philosopher's stone, a mythical substance alchemists believed could grant eternal life, because it is sexy and because he sees "little worth" in modern—to him—science.

His purpose in this quest is quite patently glory and fame, not the betterment of the human condition. He gains interest in his contemporary science only when it seems to offer him a path to this same aggrandizement. This narcissism, this inability to engage with other creatures beyond their utility to him and his desire for glory, is his fatal flaw—his hamartia—that will lead him to isolation, to monstrosity, and—most particularly—to the destruction of himself and others.

Victor also fails as a parallel to Prometheus in that his eventual failure and punishment are delineated not by divine retribution but by the inevitable consequences of his own ill-considered choices and refusal to accept responsibility for the results of his actions. In the course of his self-appointed work, Victor withdraws from the world, his family, and his schooling. He isolates himself in an obsessive quest to create life from death, and as soon as he succeeds, he rejects his creation for the dubious sin of being unattractive, abandons it, and takes to his bed in a fit of emo pique.

As soon as he achieves his obsession, he rejects the accomplishment, and catastrophe results.

It's relevant to this point that Mary's text is marked by a cursory and much-undermined veneer of Christianity. For the time, this irreligion is unusual, though it appears typical of Mary's life experience. And yet Christianity is often portrayed as the religion of compassion: the word *compassion* itself derives from that religion, from *com* (with) and *passion* (suffering), as in "the Passion of the Christ." Compassion is literally, then, to experience suffering in empathy with another.

Victor himself professes to be a Christian, and a great deal of his internal conflict stems from his feelings that he has betrayed his faith and usurped the rights of his creator in imbuing life into dead flesh. But he never considers that he has failed in a far more sacred duty of Christianity: the Golden Rule upon which the religion is founded. He's such an incredible narcissist that instead of offering this *compassion*, this sharing of the suffering of others, he discards people when they are inconvenient, including his supposedly beloved family and fiancée. His treatment of his creation is really no different.

So, in other words, Victor professes Christianity, but he is a terrible example of it—especially to his creation. He's a lousy parent—a lousy creator—because of his selfishness, his self-absorption, and his lack of foresight. He makes no sacrifices of the kind that would be appropriate for the education and upbringing of a sentient creature whose existence he is responsible for. He cannot even accept his creation as a fellow sufferer in need of succor and charity. And when confronted with the terrible murders of those close to him, rather than feeling pity or compassion, he uses his religiosity to justify how much worse his suffering is than theirs because they are dead and in heaven, while he remains on earth, suffering guilt. (But one of the victims dies while her soul is burdened with a false confession, which seems, in a Christian worldview, as if it might result in a little time in purgatory, at the very least.)

Although we can't know, of course, what Mary's religious outlook was in its entirety, we do know that she was raised by free thinkers, married an atheist, and was a social radical for her time, with determined opinions about the equality of women and the role of liberated sexuality in society. Significantly, one of her more noble and courageous characters, the beautiful Arabian Safie, is the product of a Muslim father and a Christian mother. Safie chooses to espouse her mother's religion seemingly not out of any deep conviction but rather entirely because it offers her greater freedom and legal protection.

Safie is also a marginalized person—a woman and a Muslim—but even she can find at least a flawed asylum in a family where women are treated as human beings even if not as equals. Her experience raises the question of where the creature might seek such asylum—then as now.

Victor, in other words, is as tremendous a religious hypocrite as he is a scientific one. His monstrousness and abnormality are manifest in his behavior, even though Robert Walton, the ship's captain and explorer to whom he relates his tale and who serves as the reader's intermediary for understanding Victor's life, sees him as nobly countenanced and well spoken. Victor is a beautiful man and fairly obviously a spoiled and indulged one, though he himself does not realize this, even at the end of his life. Victor and those around him think of him as a noble intellectual. But his intellectual achievements pale in comparison to those of his creation, who teaches himself in the span of a few years to read, to speak several languages, to navigate a ship, and to comprehend the nuances and hypocrisies of human society.

And yet because the creature is ugly, he is spurned first by his creator and then by every other human person he meets, despite the apparently innate goodness of his impulses. Mary makes it plain that though the creature is manufactured as a blank and willing pupil, he is benevolent in spirit and wishes only to help, to be accepted by human society, to find companionship. It is only after repeated abandonments and rejections that he becomes violent and vengeful.

Victor, the hypocrite, has no such excuse for his own monstrosity. He simply is incapable of considering the needs or desires or even the safety of anyone beyond his own immediate gratification. He cannot rise above his own innate selfishness and his ingrained tendency to dismiss, deny, and abandon something he considers ugly and unnatural—even though it is his own creation. Even worse, Walton—who in many ways represents the better aspects of human character—cannot see his way past Victor's beauty and the creature's ugliness to the truth of their relationship and of Victor's abandonment and abuse of his creation. As with all literature, the reader sees his or her own best and worst aspects reflected in the narrative, externalized so they can be examined with new insight.

Victor is such a narcissist, in fact, that it never occurs to him that the creature might take revenge for Victor's refusal to manufacture a companion for him by killing Victor's own intended wife and life companion. He assumes that he himself will be the focus of any such revenge.

Victor is incurious about the results of his actions, which is an enormous failing in a scientist. I admit, personally, to a fair quantity of scientific curiosity about exactly how Victor preserves the "materials" he uses, as he so euphemistically describes them. His world is one without refrigeration beyond ice houses, and he mentions spending months collecting body parts and then assembling his creations before imbuing the first one, at least, with the "spark of life." To the scientifically minded reader of 1818, this phrase would have been a transparent reference to the explorations of such near-contemporaneous scientists as Luigi Galvani (1737–1798), Giovanni Aldini (1762–1834), and Benjamin Franklin (1706–1790) as well as to a long-brewing debate over vitalism and the origins of life. Many early nineteenth-century readers would have been familiar with and perhaps even have witnessed infamous public experiments where human and animal corpses jerked briefly to life through the application of electricity.

The novel is pointedly vague on the details of Victor's work. I have a rather unpleasant image of Victor wandering around England for some time with two hundred pounds of grave-robbed body parts in a steamer trunk, taking them out each night to dry them on racks before the fire.

Walton's description of the creature—the only actual description of him, other than Victor's noting his filmed eye, great stature, and horrible countenance—mentions that his hand is "in colour and apparent texture like that of a mummy" (p. 183).

I also find myself wondering, in the interests of science, if Victor's fears of the monster breeding with the bride Victor begins to make for him could not be simply addressed by, oh, leaving out the ovaries and womb of the female creature? One does rather wonder how effective mummified testes are in producing viable creature germ cells. …

My point here is to reinforce that Victor really doesn't think things through, which is an aspect of his monstrosity: the fatal flaws that result in his destruction are that incuriousness and that narcissism.

But the creature has a fatal flaw as well: it is his desire for vengeance when he is ostracized. Whereas Victor's self-isolation is a symptom of his innate monstrosity, it is his ostracization of the creature—the creature's othering, to use the modern parlance—that turns his creation into a monster.

Thus, failing to consider the impact of his decisions on the creature he creates and then compounding that failure with selfishness and lack of compassion, Victor causes the very carnage that so desolates him. And so he becomes the author of his own ruined life and of the ruined lives of so many more innocent others.

This relationship is pointed out quite brilliantly at the climax of the book, when Walton is confronted by the remainder of his fast-dying crew, who wish to abandon their quest for the Northwest Passage and return to warmer southern waters. Victor berates them as cowards, almost literally with his last breath. And yet, in the end, Walton chooses his men's safety over his own selfish desire for glory and discovery as well as over Victor's demand that he continue the obsessive, vengeful quest to destroy Victor's creation.

Walton stands in contrast to Victor in this choice, which creates a thematic counterpoint to those decisions Victor makes that destroy him and his much-abused family and friends. In fact, Walton treats his own quest for knowledge responsibly. He considers the well-being of others, and he maintains his human connection to his family—personified by a beloved sister to whom he writes at every opportunity—throughout his adventures. That he turns back is not a scientific defeat—he makes no grand declarations about the impossibility of his quest for knowledge and pens no polemics about the uselessness of further ventures.

Rather, Walton demonstrates a simple acceptance that Victor never manages to embrace: other human lives have worth and value. Even those of a group of nameless sailors.

Victor himself states the problem, even as he is unable to comprehend how thoroughly he has failed to compass it: "In a fit of enthusiastic madness I created a rational creature, and was bound towards him, to assure, as far as was in my power, his happiness and well-being. This was my duty; but there was another still paramount to that. My duties towards my fellow-creatures had greater claims to my attention, because they included a greater proportion of happiness or misery" (pp. 181–182). He does not number his own creation among his fellow creatures, although in truth he owes it a greater debt than he does to any other person because he is responsible for its existence and abandonment. As the creature itself says, "Am I to be thought the only criminal, when all human kind sinned against me?" (p. 185).

Because the creature looks like a monster, he is treated as one despite his initial benevolence, and so he becomes one. Because Victor looks like an angel, he is treated as one despite being a monster, and he never grows and changes. The great tragedy of his life is that if he had simply considered the moral implications of his work and chosen a different course or if he had accepted his own debt of care to his creation from the beginning and nurtured it—if he had, in other words, behaved as a responsible scientist—every tragedy for which he bears the guilt would have been averted (and he might have received the accolades he so desired).

FRANKENSTEIN, GENDER, AND MOTHER NATURE
ANNE K. MELLOR

On 16 June 1816, Mary Wollstonecraft Godwin gave birth to one of the enduring myths of modern civilization, the narrative of the scientist who single-handedly creates a new species, a humanoid form that need not die. In her novel *Frankenstein, or The Modern Prometheus* (1818), Victor Frankenstein robs both cemeteries and slaughterhouses in order to suture together a creature composed of dead animal and human body parts, a creature he then animates with the "spark of being" (p. 41). In doing so, he claims he has renewed life where death had apparently devoted the body to corruption. Victor thus realizes the age-old wish of humankind to transcend mortality, to become a god. And like Prometheus, who in ancient myth both shapes the human species out of clay and then steals fire from the Olympian gods to give to man, Victor expects to be revered, even worshipped.

But in his hubristic quest to become God, to create an immortal species, Victor constructs a creature that eventually destroys his wife, his best friend, and his baby brother, so exhausting Victor that he dies at an early age. Mary Shelley's novel has thus become the paradigm for every scientific effort to harness the uncontrollable powers of Nature and the unintended consequences that those efforts have produced, be they nuclear fission, genetic engineering, stem cell cloning, or bioterrorism. The popular conflation of the scientist *with* his creation—such that "Frankenstein" is as often the name of the creature as of his maker—only points to a profound understanding of Mary's novel in which Victor finally becomes as filled with hatred, revenge, and the desire to destroy as the creature he hunts across the Arctic wastes. The novel implicitly suggests an alternative. Had Victor Frankenstein taken responsibility for his creation, had he loved, nurtured, and disciplined his creature, he might have created the superior species of which he dreamed.

How did the eighteen-year-old Mary Wollstonecraft Godwin (later Shelley) come to write a tale so prescient of modern science? Two years earlier, on 28 July 1814, Mary had left her home in London to go to France with the married poet Percy Shelley. Seven months later she gave birth prematurely to a baby girl, called Clara, who lived only two weeks, after which she had a recurrent dream that her little baby came to life again, that it had only been cold, and that she rubbed it before the fire, and it lived. Immediately pregnant again, Mary gave birth to her son William on 24 January 1816. Four months later Mary, Percy, and her stepsister Claire left England to join Claire's new lover, Lord Byron, and his doctor, John William Polidori, in Geneva. Kept indoors by the coldest summer in a century following the eruption of the volcano Tambora in the Indonesian archipelago in April 1815 (which threw so much debris into the stratosphere that the sun was literally blocked out across India, Europe, and North America), reading ghost stories for their amusement, the four friends decided on 16 June 1816 to have a contest to see who could write the most frightening story.

That night Mary had the "waking dream" or reverie that provided the germ of *Frankenstein*. Born from Mary's own deepest pregnancy anxieties (What if I give birth to a monster? Could I ever wish to kill my own child?), her novel brilliantly explores what happens when a man attempts to have a baby without a woman (Victor Frankenstein immediately abandons his creature); why an abandoned and unloved creature becomes a monster; the predictable consequences of her day's cutting-edge research in chemistry, physics, and electricity (most notably the experiments conducted by Erasmus Darwin [1731–1802], Humphry Davy [1778–1829], and Luigi Galvani [1737–1798]); and the violent aftermath of the French Revolution. Mary drew psychologically on her own childhood experiences of isolation and abandonment after her mother's death in childbirth and her father's remarriage to a hostile stepmother to articulate the creature's overwhelming desire for a family, a mate of his own, and the consequences of his violent anger when he is rejected by all whom he approaches, even an innocent young boy, William Frankenstein (modeled on William Shelley), and then his maker. By including an image of the murder of her own son, William, in the novel, Mary articulated her deepest fear that an unloved (and psychologically abused) child, such as she herself had been, could become an unloving, abusive mother, even a murdering monster.

Given Mary's parentage, it is unsurprising that gendered constructions of the universe are everywhere apparent in *Frankenstein*: for example, Victor's identification of Nature as female—"I pursued nature to *her* hiding places" (p. 38, emphasis added). Victor's scientific and technological exploitation of female Nature is only one way in which the novel consistently represents the female as passive and able to be possessed, the willing receptacle of male desire. Victor's usurpation of the natural mode of human reproduction implies a kind of destruction of the female. We see this destruction erupt symbolically in his nightmare following the animation of his creature: while in his embrace, Elizabeth, his bride-to-be, is transformed into the corpse of his dead mother—"a shroud enveloped her form, and I saw the grave-worms crawling in the folds of the flannel" (p. 43). By stealing the female's control over natural reproduction, Victor has eliminated the female's primary biological function and source of cultural power. Indeed, as a male scientist who creates a male creature, Victor eliminates the biological necessity for females at all. One of the deepest horrors of this novel is his implicit goal of creating a society for men only: Victor's creature is male; he refuses to create a female; there is no reason why the race of immortal beings he hopes to propagate should not be exclusively male.

On the cultural and social level, Victor's scientific project—to become the sole creator of a superior human being—supports a patriarchal denial of the value of women and of female sexuality. Victor's nineteenth-century Genevan society is founded on a rigid division of sex roles: men inhabit the public sphere, women are relegated to the private or domestic sphere. The men work outside the home, as public servants (Alphonse Frankenstein), as scientists (Victor), as merchants (Henry Clerval and his father), and as explorers (Walton). The women are confined to the home, kept either as a kind of pet (Victor "loved to tend on" Elizabeth "as ... on a favourite animal" [p. 18]) or as housewives, childcare providers, and nurses (Caroline Beaufort, Elizabeth, Margaret Saville) or as servants (Justine Moritz).

As a consequence of this division, public intellectual activity is segregated from private emotional activity: Victor cannot work and love at the same time. He cannot feel empathy for his creature and chooses to work with large body pieces because doing so is easier and faster, despite the fact that his creature will be a deformed giant. And he remains so self-absorbed that he cannot imagine his creature might threaten someone other than himself on his wedding night. The separation of the sphere of public (masculine) power from the sphere of private (feminine) affection also causes the destruction of most of the women in the novel. Caroline Beaufort dies from scarlet fever caught when she alone volunteers to nurse the contagious Elizabeth. Justine, unable to prove her innocence in the death of William, is condemned to death by Victor's refusal to take responsibility for his creature's actions. And Elizabeth is murdered on her wedding night. The novel offers an alternative to this gendered division of labor in the egalitarian relationships in the De Lacey family, where brother and sister together share the duties of supporting their father, and Safie (an independent woman based on Mary Shelley's feminist mother, Mary Wollstonecraft) is welcomed as Felix's partner. But this ideal family is ripped out of the novel when the creature enters their household, suggesting that Mary herself did not think such an ideal family could prosper in her time.

Why does Victor finally refuse to create a mate for his creature, an Eve for his Adam, after having promised to do so? He rationalizes his decision to destroy the half-formed female creature:

> I was now about to form another being, of whose dispositions I was alike ignorant; she might become ten thousand times more malignant that her mate, and delight, for its own sake, in murder and wretchedness. He had sworn to quit the neighbourhood of man, and hide himself in deserts; but she had not; and she, who in all probability was to become a thinking and reasoning animal, might refuse to comply with a compact made before her creation. They might even hate each other; the creature who already lived loathed his own deformity, and might he not conceive a greater abhorrence for it when it came before his eyes in the female form? She also might turn with disgust from him to the superior beauty of man; she might quit him, and he be again alone, exasperated by the fresh provocation of being deserted by one of his own species.
>
> Even if they were to leave Europe, and inhabit the deserts of the new world, yet one of the first results of those sympathies for which the dæmon thirsted would be children, and a race of devils would be propagated upon the earth, who might make the very existence of the species of man a condition precarious and full of terror. Had I a right, for my own benefit, to inflict this curse upon everlasting generations? (p. 139)

What does Victor truly fear that causes him to rip up his half-finished female creature? First, he is afraid that this female will have desires and opinions that cannot be controlled by his male creature. Like French Genevan philosopher Jean-Jacques Rousseau's (1712–1778) natural man, she might refuse to comply with a social contract made by another person before her birth—namely, between the creature and Victor himself; she might assert the revolutionary right to determine her own existence. A second fear is that her uninhibited female desires might be sadistic: Victor imagines a female creature "ten thousand times" more evil than her mate, who would "delight" in murder for its own sake. Third, he fears that his female creature will be uglier than his male creature, so much so that even the male will turn from her in disgust. Fourth, he fears that she will prefer to mate with ordinary human males; implicit here is Frankenstein's horror that, given this female creature's gigantic strength, she would have the ability to seize and even rape a man she might choose. And, finally, he is

ANNE K. MELLOR

afraid of her reproductive powers, her capacity to generate an entire race of similar creatures.

What Victor truly fears is female sexuality as such. A woman who is sexually liberated, free to choose her own life and her own sexual partner (by force, if necessary), and able to propagate at will can only appear monstrously ugly, even evil, to him because she defies the sexist aesthetic that insists that women should be small, delicate, modest, passive, and sexually pleasing but available only to their lawful husbands. Horrified by this image of uninhibited female sexual desire and power, Victor violently reasserts a male control over the female body, penetrating and mutilating the female creature in an image that suggests a violent rape: "trembling with passion, [I] tore to pieces the thing on which I was engaged" (p. 140). The next morning, when he returns to the scene, "the remains of the half-finished creature, whom I had destroyed, lay scattered on the floor, and I almost felt as if I had mangled the living flesh of a human being" (p. 143).

However, in Mary's feminist novel, Victor's efforts to control and even to eliminate female sexuality altogether is portrayed not only as horrifying and finally unattainable but also as self-destructive. For Nature is not the passive, inert, or "dead" matter that he imagines. Victor assumes that he can violate Nature and pursue her to her hiding places with impunity. But Mother Nature both resists and revenges herself upon his attempts. During his research, Nature denies to Victor Frankenstein both mental and physical health: "Every night I was oppressed by a slow fever, and I became nervous to a most painful degree" (p. 41). When he decides to create a second creature and again defy natural reproduction, his mental illness returns: "[E]very word that I spoke in allusion to it caused my lips to quiver, and my heart to palpitate. ... [M]y spirits became unequal; I grew restless and nervous" (pp. 134, 138). Finally, Victor's obsession with destroying his male creature exposes him to such mental and physical fatigue that he dies of natural causes at the age of twenty-five.

Appropriately, Nature prevents Victor from constructing a normal human being: his unnatural method of reproduction spawns an unnatural being, a freak of gigantic stature, watery eyes, shriveled complexion, and straight black lips. His creature's physiognomy then causes Victor's revulsion from his child–invention and sets in motion the series of events that finally produces the monster that destroys his family, friends, and self.

Moreover, Nature pursues Victor with the very electricity, the "spark of being," that he has stolen: lightning, thunder, and rain rage around him as he works. Rain pours down on the "dreary night of November" on which he completes his experiment (p. 41). When he returns to Geneva, he glimpses his creature on the Alps through a violent storm and flash of lightning. After destroying the female creature, he sets sail to dispose of the remains in the ocean and is caught up by a fierce wind and high waves that portend his own death—"I looked upon the sea, it was to be my grave" (p. 144). Victor ends his life in the arctic regions, surrounded by the ice, the aurora borealis, and the electromagnetic field of the North Pole. The novel's atmospheric effects, which most readers have dismissed as the traditional trappings of gothic fiction, in fact manifest the power of Nature to punish those who transgress her boundaries. The elemental forces that Victor has released pursue him to his hiding places, raging around him like the female spirits of vengeance, the Furies of Greek drama.

Mary's novel not only portrays the penalties of violating Nature but also celebrates an all-creating Nature that is loved and revered by human beings. Those characters capable of feeling the beauties of Nature are rewarded with physical and mental health. Henry Clerval's relationship to Nature, for example, represents one moral touchstone in the novel. Because he "loved with ardour" "the scenery of external nature" (p. 132), he is endowed with a generous sympathy, a vivid imagination, a sensitive intelligence, and an unbounded capacity for devoted friendship. And it is no accident that the only member of the Frankenstein family still alive at the end of the novel is Ernest, who rejects the career of lawyer to become instead a farmer, one who must live in harmony and cooperation with the forces of Nature, one who lives "a very healthy happy life; and ... the most beneficial profession of any" (p. 48).

As *Frankenstein* finally shows, an unmothered child, like a scientific experiment that is performed without consideration of its probable or even its unintended results and that radically changes the natural order, can become a monster, one capable of destroying its maker. The novel implicitly endorses instead a science that seeks to understand rather than to change the workings of Mother Nature. Mary's novel thus resonates powerfully with the ethical problems inherent in the most recent advances in genetics: the introduction of germ-line engineering through CRISPR-Cas9 techniques of DNA alteration and the current scientific possibility of producing what Victor Frankenstein dreamed of, a superhuman "designer baby." At the same time, the novel vividly illustrates the terrifying ramifications and unintended consequences of such attempts to "improve" the human species.

ANNE K. MELLOR

THE BITTER AFTERTASTE OF TECHNICAL SWEETNESS
HEATHER E. DOUGLAS

Technical sweetness. Scientists and engineers use this phrase when a puzzle's solution presents itself, when all the pieces fit beautifully and functionally together, when success at the particular endeavor presents itself in a neat package. Technical sweetness is alluring, consuming, and, as we can see in the story of Victor Frankenstein, potentially blinding to what might follow from the solution being sought. Scientists who are driven by technical sweetness can fail to see what might be obvious to those with a bit more distance—that despite some projects' allure, sometimes completing the project is not desirable.

When Victor first discovers the secret to life, he is so overwhelmed by his success that he fails to share it with his colleagues and instead accelerates toward a full-fledged test of his insight—Can he animate a body devoid of life? In his desperation to complete this test, he pushes himself to the breaking point, fully in the thrall of the technical sweetness of his work. He stops communicating with his friends and family and disengages from the social connections that might give him a better perspective on his pursuits. He senses that all is not right—that his reluctance to share his work might mean something more than a desire to guard the secret until confirmation is achieved; only once his creation awakes does he realize that it might not have been a good idea to create such life. Indeed, he recoils from what he has done, running from his creation for two years. In the end, he spends the rest of his life in a dark dance with the creature, attempting to forestall further horrors from being inflicted upon humanity.

Victor is, of course, a fictional character in a gothic horror story, but the arc of his work—from the capture of his imagination by an idea to the theoretical discovery (which he refuses to share), to the sequestration of his work until a complete empirical manifestation of it, to a revulsion in his ultimate success, and finally to an embrace of his responsibility and pursuit of his creation in an attempt to restrain it—is not something that resides solely in the realm of fiction. Such an arc can be found in one of the most momentous scientific projects of the twentieth century: the creation of the first atomic bombs.

The story of the pursuit of the atom bomb is not a perfect reflection of Victor's story because the former involves the work of many scientists, not just one. It is also the story of an endeavor that was constantly in the shadow of fraught moral decisions and catastrophic world war. But much of the arc of this story mirrors the arc of *Frankenstein*, and the lesson of the need to resist the allure of technical sweetness is made manifest even amid the complexities.

In late 1938, Lise Meitner and Otto Frisch discovered the process of fission in atomic nuclei and spread the word throughout the international physics community. Before this discovery, most physicists thought that using nuclear physics for practical purposes like energy production and weapons was utterly impractical, and indeed some relished this lack of practical application of their work. But with the discovery of fission, all that changed. The nuclear physics community in the United Kingdom and the United States immediately began not only to speculate about but also directly to investigate whether fission opened the door to practical use, whether enough neutrons resulted from the fission of a uranium nucleus to support a chain reaction, and what sorts of materials could be used to increase the likelihood of a chain reaction. By December 1942, Italian physicist Enrico Fermi created the first self-sustained nuclear reaction (with slow neutrons) in a laboratory located in the squash courts beneath Stagg Field at the University of Chicago, and the Manhattan Project to build that bomb (a fast neutron reaction) was well under way. The Manhattan Project comprised research and development at many sites, especially large industrial sites at Oak Ridge, Tennessee, and Hanford, Washington, as well as the building of Los Alamos Laboratory, where scientists were sequestered to research how to design and test the first atomic weapons.

Scientists traveled to the isolated Los Alamos site under secrecy and, once there, were under strict orders not to discuss the project outside of the inner laboratories, called the Technical Area. Scientists were focused on achieving the goal, a workable atomic weapon, and not on whether doing so was a good idea. Given most scientists' impetus—concern that the Nazis might develop such a weapon first—such a focus was understandable.

Situated at the timberline more than seven thousand feet atop a mesa in New Mexico, Los Alamos was a heady atmosphere in which to work: led by the brilliant J. Robert Oppenheimer, filled with past and future Nobel Prize winners, and pressurized by the war. The site grew rapidly from about one hundred people in the spring of 1943 to more than six thousand by the end of the war (Bird and Sherwin 2005, 210). The scientists at Los Alamos confronted a number of technical challenges, particularly regarding how to ensure that maximum energy would be released from the hard-to-collect fissile material being produced at Oak Ridge (enriched uranium) and Hanford (plutonium) (Rhodes 1986, 460–464). But by late 1944, the initial impetus behind the program was undermined. Reports coming back from successful Allied pushes into German territory revealed that the Nazis' atomic efforts were nowhere close to producing weapons. In fact, Germany had failed to produce a functioning nuclear reactor, something achieved in the United States two years earlier.

For one scientist, Polish physicist Joseph Rotblat, the realization that the original motivation to produce an atomic weapon had evaporated provided sufficient reason to leave the project. He resigned from Los Alamos in December 1944. However, before his departure, he was forbidden from discussing his decision with the other scientists at Los Alamos (Brown 2012, 55). A moment for moral reflection among the Los Alamos scientists was lost.

By May 1945, even as the European war came to an end, work on the weapon accelerated. Oppenheimer recalled later that the scientists never worked harder than in the summer of 1945 (Szasz 1984, 25). Producing a weapon before the end of the war, that could be used to end the war, became a paramount driver, in part because many of the scientists at Los Alamos had shifted their justification for pursuing the weapon to the ending of *all* wars. Many thought that only if the weapon were used to end the current war would humanity appreciate how truly destructive such weapons could be and thus be motivated to end war permanently.

Efforts at Los Alamos from February 1945 through the summer were focused on a test of the plutonium bomb. Because of the much more complex mechanism needed to produce a weapon with plutonium, scientists were quite unsure whether it would work. Only a trial with real plutonium could produce an adequate test of the mechanism. This test would be the Trinity test, the first atomic explosion on the planet, held on 16 July 1945.

The work leading up to this test was nothing short of feverish. Getting all the technical details, calibrating measuring equipment, and creating contingency plans took massive effort. Three possible outcomes presented themselves: (1) the test weapon could be a dud, no more powerful than a usual ordnance explosion; (2) it could be massively destructive, killing many on site and causing a national emergency; or (3) it could be the weapon they hoped for, impressive but not out of control (Szasz 1984, 79). Much to the relief of the scientists present, the last possibility proved accurate, which meant that their work was a success and that they had produced a usable weapon. They had not wasted their effort during the war, and they had survived to tell the tale.

The scientists reacted in different ways to their success. The first thing Oppenheimer said when the bomb went off was an exultant "It worked!" The scientists had mostly expected a much smaller explosion, as revealed by the betting pool for the yield at Trinity (Szasz 1984, 65–66). Oppenheimer picked the equivalent of three hundred tons of TNT; most scientists picked yields much less than ten thousand tons. In fact, the weapon produced a yield closer to twenty thousand tons of TNT. Along with relief and excitement at the technical success, the visual and visceral impact of the explosion impressed many of the witnesses. Oppenheimer later recalled that these words from the Bhagavad Gita went through his mind: "I am become death, the destroyer of worlds" (quoted in Szasz 1984, 89). I. I. Rabi was at first thrilled but then overwhelmed by the implications of what he and his fellow scientists had done (Szasz 1984, 90). As Victor Weisskopf wrote, "Our first feeling was one of elation, then we realized we were tired, and then we were worried" (quoted in Szasz 1984, 91). The technical sweetness of the project was over, and now the scientists had to confront what their success meant in the full complexity of the world. Test director Kenneth Bainbridge quipped, "Now we are all sons-of-bitches" (quoted in Bird and Sherwin 2005, 309).

It took time for some of the scientists to fully grasp the moral weight of what they had done. After the use of the weapons at Hiroshima and Nagasaki, which helped bring a sudden end to the war, many of the enlisted men at Los Alamos celebrated, but the scientists were subdued and sometimes physically sick, overwhelmed by what they had helped achieve (Bird and Sherwin 2005, 317). When Phil Morrison and Bob Serber returned from Japan to Los Alamos at the end of October 1945 with firsthand accounts of the impacts of the bombs (Bird and Sherwin 2005, 321), scientists who had worked on the project now faced the grim reality of their success and, seeing it clearly, committed themselves to making their work as beneficial for humanity as possible.

Different scientists sought to shoulder responsibility for their creation in different ways. Some worked to ensure that atomic power was placed under civilian control, and their efforts led to the US Atomic Energy Commission. Some sought to forestall an arms race with the Soviets by advocating for international control of atomic technology. Some spread the word of how destructive the bombs were, hoping to prevent all future wars. Some pursued even more powerful weapons, their sights set on keeping Soviet totalitarianism at bay. And some pursued the peaceful uses of the atom. None escaped a sense of responsibility for their work.

We can see in the arc of the story of scientists at Los Alamos echoes of Victor Frankenstein's story. From the intense pursuit to the dawning realization of the downsides of success and the attempt to ameliorate such success, such parallels were noted at the time. In notes for a meeting of the Interim Committee (a high-level policy committee for nuclear weapons) on 31 May 1945, Secretary of War Henry Stimson wrote that the bomb "May *destroy* or *perfect* International *Civilization*, May [be] *Frankenstein or* means for World Peace" (quoted in Rhodes 1986, 642, emphasis and capitalization in the original). For the scientists engaged in the project, the Frankenstein nature of it remained out of focus until its completion. With technical success and technical sweetness attained, the fraught moral questions that came with success clarified painfully.

Mary Shelley's novel *Frankenstein* is a prescient parable, a gripping nontheistic version of Goethe's *Faust* that spells out the horror that can accompany success as we pursue science and technology. Even as science has grown as an enterprise, even as the collective nature of the scientific endeavor has become clear and big science has taken a more central place in scientific culture, the arc followed by Victor—the solitary scientist—is still relevant. Whether scientists work by themselves or in collaboration, they continue to confront the allure of technical sweetness and its blinding power as they grapple with their responsibilities for their work in the twenty-first century.

Scientists whose work suddenly raises the red flag—for example, those whose work gets labeled "potential dual-use research of concern"—often balk at the imposition of restrictions and the requirement of deeper reflection. The lure of technical sweetness, of continuing to pursue success in their area of expertise, makes it hard for those scientists to see, much less weigh seriously, the downsides of their work. Even with increasing efforts to create structures through which scientists can address the thorny problems that can arise when pursuing new scientific and technical capacities, technical sweetness can still blind them to the need to reflect on the implications of their work and the imperative to act, before completion, to ameliorate the impact of success.

APPENDIXES

REFERENCES

Adams, Douglas. 1999. How to Stop Worrying and Learn to Love the Internet. *Sunday Times* (London), August 29. http://www.douglasadams.com/dna/19990901-00-a.html. Accessed October 19, 2016.

Addison, Joseph. 1711. *Spectator*, No. 143, August 14.

Aho, Kevin. 2014. *Existentialism: An Introduction*. Cambridge, UK: Polity Press.

Anderson, Elizabeth, and Geetha Shivakumar. 2013. Effects of Exercise and Physical Activity on Anxiety. *Frontiers in Psychiatry* 4. doi:10.3389/fpsyt.2013.00027.

Aristotle. 1943. *Generation of Animals*. Translated by A. L. Peck. Cambridge, MA: Harvard University Press. https://archive.org/details/generationofanim00arisuoft.

Astor-Aguilera, Miguel Angel. 2010. *The Maya World of Communicating Objects: Quadripartite Crosses, Trees, and Stones*. Albuquerque: University of New Mexico Press.

Bakhtin, Mikhail. 1984. *Problems of Dostoevsky's Poetics*. Edited and translated by Caryl Emerson. Minneapolis: University of Minnesota Press.

Bandura, Albert. 1994. Regulative Function of Perceived Self-Efficacy. In *Personnel Selection and Classification*, edited by Michael G. Rumsey, Clinton B. Walker, and James H. Harris, 261–272. Hillsdale, NJ: Lawrence Erlbaum Associates.

Barnes, M. Elizabeth. 2014a. Edward Drinker Cope's Law of the Acceleration of Growth. In *Embryo Project Encyclopedia*. http://embryo.asu.edu/handle/10776/8067. Last modified August 6, 2014.

Barnes, M. Elizabeth. 2014b. Ernst Haeckel's Biogenetic Law (1866). In *Embryo Project Encyclopedia*. http://embryo.asu.edu/handle/10776/7825. Last modified May 3, 2014.

Barthes, Roland. [1957] 1991. *Mythologies*. New York: Noonday Press.

Batchelder, Robert. 2012. Thinking about the Gym: Greek Ideals, Newtonian Bodies, and Exercise in Early Eighteenth-Century Britain. *Journal for Eighteenth Century Studies* 35 (2): 185–197. doi: 10.1111/j.1754-0208.2012.00496.

Bieri, James. 2008. *Percy Bysshe Shelley: A Biography*. Baltimore: Johns Hopkins University Press.

Binnig, Gert. 1989. *Aus dem Nichts: Über die Kreativität von Natur und Mensch.* Munich: Piper.

Bird, Kai, and Martin J. Sherwin. 2005. *American Prometheus: The Triumph and Tragedy of J. Robert Oppenheimer.* New York: Vintage Books.

Blanchard, D. Caroline, and Robert J. Blanchard. 2003. Bringing Natural Behaviors into the Laboratory: A Tribute to Paul MacLean. *Physiology & Behavior* 79 (3): 515–524. doi:10.1016/S0031-9384(03)00157-4.

Blanchard, Robert J., D. Caroline Blanchard, and Christina R. McKittrick. 2001. Animal Models of Social Stress: Effects on Behavior and Brain Neurochemical Systems. *Physiology & Behavior* 73 (3): 261–271. doi:10.1016/S0031-9384(01)00449-8.

Bolton, Gillie. 2014. *Reflective Practice: Writing and Professional Development.* 4th ed. Thousand Oaks, CA: SAGE.

Brosnan, Sarah F. 2012. Introduction to "Justice in Animals." *Social Justice Research* 25 (2): 109–121. doi:10.1007/s11211-012-0156-9.

Brown, Andrew. 2012. *Keeper of the Nuclear Conscience: The Life and Work of Joseph Rotblat.* Oxford: Oxford University Press.

Bush, Vannevar. 1945. *Science, the Endless Frontier: A Report to the President.* Washington, DC: U.S. Office of Scientific Research and Development.

Butler, Judith. 2010. *Frames of War: When Is Life Grievable?* New York: Verso.

Butler, Marilyn. 1993a. The First Frankenstein and Radical Science: How the Original Version of Mary Shelley's Novel Drew Inspiration from the Early Evolutionists. *Times Literary Supplement (London)*, April 9.

Butler, Marilyn. 1993b. The Shelleys and Radical Science. In Mary Wollstonecraft Shelley, *Frankenstein; or, the Modern Prometheus: The 1818 Text*, edited by Marilyn Butler, xv–xx. London: Pickering. Reprinted in Mary Wollstonecraft Shelley, with Percy Bysshe Shelley, *The Original Frankenstein; or, the Modern Prometheus: The Original Two-Volume Novel of 1816–1817 from the Bodleian Library Manuscripts,* edited by Charles E. Robinson, xv–xxi. Oxford: Bodleian Library, University of Oxford, 2008.

Čapek, Karel, and Josef Čapek. 1920. *R. U. R. and the Insect Play.* London: Oxford University Press.

Chess, Stella, and Mahin Hassibi. 1978. *Principles and Practice of Child Psychiatry.* New York: Plenum Press.

Christen, Markus, and Hans-Johann Glock. 2012. The (Limited) Space for Justice in Social Animals. *Social Justice Research* 25 (3): 298–326. doi:10.1007/s11211-012-0163-x.

Coleridge, Samuel Taylor. [1817] 1907. *Biographia literaria.* Edited by John Shawcross. Oxford: Clarendon Press.

Crook, Nora. 1996. Introductory Note. In Mary Wollstonecraft Shelley, *Frankenstein; or the Modern Prometheus*, edited by Nora Crook, xciii–xcviii. London: Pickering.

D'Arcy Wood, Gillen. 2014. *Tambora: The Eruption That Changed the World.* Princeton, NJ: Princeton University Press.

Freud, Sigmund. [1919] 1955. The Uncanny. In *The Complete Psychological Works of Sigmund Freud*, vol. 17, edited by James Strachey, 217–252. London: Hogarth Press.

Freud, Sigmund. [1923] 1960. *The Ego and the Id.* Translated by James Strachey. New York: Norton.

Freud, Sigmund. [1930] 1961. *Civilization and Its Discontents.* Translated by James Strachey. New York: Norton.

Garrett, Martin. 2002. *A Mary Shelley Chronology.* Author Chronologies Series. New York: Palgrave.

Glut, Donald F. 1984. *The Frankenstein Catalog: Being a Comprehensive Listing of Novels, Translations, Adaptations, Stories, Critical Works, Popular Articles, Series, Fumetti, Verse, Stage Plays, Films, Cartoons, Puppetry, Radio & Television Programs, Comics, Satire & Humor, Spoken & Musical Recordings, Tapes, and Sheet Music Featuring Frankenstein's Monster and / or Descended from Mary Shelley's Novel.* Jefferson, NC: McFarland.

Godwin, William. 2012. *William Godwin's Diary.* Edited by David O'Shaughnessy, Mark Philp, and Victoria Myers. Bodleian Library, University of Oxford. http:/godwindiary.bodleian.ox.ac.uk/index2.html. Accessed March 23, 2016.

Godwin, William. [1793] 2013. *An Enquiry Concerning Political Justice.* Edited by Mark Philp. Oxford: Oxford University Press.

Golinksi, Jan. 2016. *The Experimental Self: Humphry Davy and the Making of a Man of Science.* Chicago: University of Chicago Press.

Heatherton, Todd F., and Kathleen D. Vohs. 2000. Interpersonal Evaluations Following Threats to Self: Role of Self-Esteem. *Journal of Personality and Social Psychology* 78 (4): 725–736. doi:10.1037/0022-3514.78.4.725.

Heinlein, Robert A. 1957. *The Door into Summer.* Garden City, NY: Doubleday.

Hunt, Leigh. [1816] 1817. *The Story of Rimini: A Poem.* Internet Archive. https://archive.org/details/storyofriminipoe00huntiala. Accessed March 23, 2016.

Krimsky, Sheldon. 1982. *Genetic Alchemy: The Social History of the Recombinant DNA Controversy.* Cambridge, MA: MIT Press.

Lawrence, Cera R. 2010. On the Generation of Animals, by Aristotle. In *Embryo Project Encyclopedia.* http://embryo.asu.edu/handle/10776/2063. Last modified September 25, 2013.

Leuenberger, Andrea. 2006. Endorphins, Exercise, and Addictions: A Review of Exercise Dependence. *Impulse: The Premier Journal for Undergraduate Publications in the Neurosciences* 2006:1–9.

Locke, John. 1821. *Two Treatises of Government.* London: Whitemore and Fenn.

Mellor, Anne K. 1987. *Frankenstein*: A Feminist Critique of Science. In *One Culture: Essays in Science and Literature*, edited by George Levine and Alan Rauch, 287–312. Madison: University of Wisconsin Press. http://knarf.english.upenn.edu/Articles/mellor1.html.

Milton, John. [1667] 2007. *Paradise Lost*. Edited by Barbara Kiefer Lewalski. Malden, MA: Blackwell.

Mori, Masahiro. [1970] 2012. *The Uncanny Valley*. Translated by Karl F. Mac Dorman and Norri Kageki. IEEE Spectrum, June 12. http://spectrum.ieee.org/automaton/robotics/humanoids/the-uncanny-valley.

Newton, John Frank. [1811] 2015. *The Return to Nature, or a Defence of the Vegetable Regimen: With Some Account of an Experiment Made during the Last Three or Four Years in the Author's Family*. London: Forgotten Books.

Noble, David F. 1997. *The Religion of Technology: The Divinity of Man and the Spirit of Invention*. Vol. 1. New York: Knopf.

Nordmann, Alfred. 2008. Technology Naturalized: A Challenge to Design for the Human Scale. In *Philosophy and Design: From Engineering to Architecture*, edited by Pieter E. Vermaas, Peter Kroes, Andrew Light, and Steven A. Moore, 173–184. Dordrecht, Netherlands: Springer.

O'Connell, Lindsey. 2013a. Johann Friedrich Meckel, the Younger (1781–1833). In *Embryo Project Encyclopedia*. http://embryo.asu.edu/handle/10776/6282. Last modified February 9, 2015.

O'Connell, Lindsey. 2013b. The Meckel–Serres Conception of Recapitulation. In *Embryo Project Encyclopedia*. http://embryo.asu.edu/handle/10776/5916. Last modified February 17, 2015.

Plato. 1999. *The Symposium*. Edited by Christopher Gill. New York: Penguin.

Polanyi, Michael. 1962. The Republic of Science: Its Political and Economic Theory. *Minerva* 1:54–74.

Prior, Stuart. 2015. Meet the Real Frankenstein: Pioneering Scientist Who May Have Inspired Mary Shelley. *The Conversation*, December 4. http://theconversation.com/meet-the-real-frankenstein-pioneering-scientist-who-may-have-inspired-mary-shelley-51833.

Prophets of Science Fiction. 2011. Episode 1: Mary Shelley. Aired November 9. Produced by Ridley Scott, Gary Auerbach, Julie Auerbach, Henry Capanna, Mary Lisio, David Cargill, and David W. Zucker. Hosted by Ridley Scott. Science Channel.

Radcliffe, Sophie. 2008. *On Sympathy*. New York: Oxford University Press.

Review of *Frankenstein*. 1818. *British Critic* 9 (April): 432–438.

Rhodes, Richard. 1986. *The Making of the Atomic Bomb*. New York: Simon and Schuster.

Robinson, Charles E. 2013. *Frankenstein* Filmography. In *Frankenstein, or The Modern Prometheus [by] Mary Shelley*, appendices, chronology, filmography, and suggested further reading by Charles E. Robinson, 307–330. New York: Penguin Books.

Robinson, Charles E. 2015. Percy Bysshe Shelley's Text(s) in Mary Wollstonecraft Shelley's *Frankenstein*. In *The Neglected Shelley*, edited by Alan M. Weinberg and Timothy Webb, 117–136. Farnham, UK: Ashgate.

Robinson, Charles E. 2016a. Frankenstein Chronology. In Mary Wollstonecraft Shelley, *The Frankenstein Notebooks: A Facsimile Edition of Mary Shelley's*

Manuscript Novel, 1816–17 as It Survives in Draft and Fair Copy, 2 vols., edited by Charles E. Robinson, 1:lxxvi–cx. New York: Routledge.

Robinson, Charles E. 2016b. Introduction to the Frankenstein Notebooks. In Mary Wollstonecraft Shelley, *The Frankenstein Notebooks: A Facsimile Edition of Mary Shelley's Manuscript Novel, 1816–1817 as It Survives in Draft and Fair Copy*, 2 vols., edited by Charles E. Robinson, 1:xxv–lxxv. New York: Routledge.

Rousseau, Jean-Jacques. [1762] 1979. *Emile: Or, On Education*. New York: Basic Books.

Rushton, Sharon. 2016. The Science of Life and Death in Mary Shelley's *Frankenstein*. In *Discovering Literature: Romantics and Victorians*. British Library. http://www.bl.uk/romantics-and-victorians/articles/the-science-of-life-and-death-in-mary-shelleys-frankenstein. Accessed March 23.

Sartre, Jean-Paul. [1943] 2012. *Being and Nothingness*. New York: Philosophical Library/Open Road.

Shelley, Mary Wollstonecraft. 1980. *The Letters of Mary Wollstonecraft Shelley*. 3 vols. Edited by Betty T. Bennett. Baltimore: Johns Hopkins University Press.

Shelley, Mary Wollstonecraft. 1987. *The Journals of Mary Shelley*. Edited by Paula R. Feldman and Diana Scott-Kilvert. Baltimore: Johns Hopkins University Press.

Shelley, Mary Wollstonecraft. [1831] 2000. *Frankenstein: Complete, Authoritative Text with Biographical, Historical, and Cultural Contexts, Critical History, and Essays from Contemporary Critical Perspectives*. 2nd ed. Edited by Johanna M. Smith. Boston: Bedford/St. Martin's.

Shelley, Mary Wollstonecraft, with Percy Bysshe Shelley. 2008. *The Original Frankenstein; or, the Modern Prometheus: The Original Two-Volume Novel of 1816–1817 from the Bodleian Library Manuscripts*. Edited by Charles E. Robinson. Oxford: Bodleian Library, University of Oxford.

Shelley, Percy Bysshe. 2002. *Shelley's Poetry and Prose: Authoritative Texts, Criticism*. 2nd ed. Edited by Donald H. Reiman and Neil Fraistat. New York: Norton.

Snow, C. P. [1959] 2013. *The Two Cultures and the Scientific Revolution*. Eastford, CT: Martino Fine Books.

St. Clair, William. [1989] 1991. *The Godwins and Shelleys: A Biography of a Literary Family*. Baltimore: Johns Hopkins University Press.

Szasz, Ferenc Morton. 1984. *The Day the Sun Rose Twice: The Story of the Trinity Site Nuclear Explosion, July 16, 1945*. Albuquerque: University of New Mexico Press.

Tennyson, Lord Alfred. 2004. *Selected Poems*. London: Penguin.

Turney, Jon. 1998. *Frankenstein's Footsteps: Science, Genetics, and Popular Culture*. New Haven, CT: Yale University Press.

Vygotsky, L. S. 1978. *Mind in Society: The Development of Higher Psychological Processes*. Edited by Michael Cole, Vera John-Steiner, Sylvia Scribner, and Ellen Souberman. Cambridge, MA: Harvard University Press.

Westfall, Richard S. 1977. *The Construction of Modern Science: Mechanisms and Mechanics*. New York: Cambridge University Press.

FURTHER READING

Anthes, Emily. *Frankenstein's Cat: Cuddling Up to Biotech's Brave New Beasts.* New York: Farrar, Straus and Giroux, 2013.

Ashcroft, Frances. *The Spark of Life: Electricity in the Human Body.* New York: Norton, 2012.

Duchaney, Brian N. *The Spark of Fear: Technology, Society and the Horror Film.* Jefferson, NC: MacFarland, 2015.

Friedman, Lester D., and Allison B. Kavey. *Monstrous Progeny: A History of the Frankenstein Narratives.* New Brunswick, NJ: Rutgers University Press, 2016.

Gordon, Charlotte. *Romantic Outlaws: The Extraordinary Lives of Mary Wollstonecraft and Her Daughter Mary Shelley.* New York: Random House, 2015.

Hitchcock, Susan Tyler. *Frankenstein: A Cultural History.* New York: Norton, 2007.

Holmes, Richard. *The Age of Wonder: The Romantic Generation and the Discovery of the Beauty and Terror of Science.* New York: Vintage Books, 2010.

Kaplan, Matt. *The Science of Monsters: Why Monsters Came to Be and What Made Them so Terrifying.* London: Constable, 2012.

Lederer, Susan E. *Frankenstein: Penetrating the Secrets of Nature.* New Brunswick, NJ: Rutgers University Press, 2002.

Mellor, Anne K. *Mary Shelley: Her Life, Her Fiction, Her Monsters.* New York: Routledge, 1989.

Montillo, Roseanne. *The Lady and Her Monsters: A Tale of Dissections, Real-Life Dr. Frankensteins, and the Creation of Mary Shelley's Masterpiece.* New York: Morrow, 2013.

Shelley, Mary Wollstonecraft. *Frankenstein: The Original 1818 Text.* 2nd ed. Edited by D. L. Macdonald and Kathleen Scherf. Peterborough, Canada: Broadview Press, 1999.

Townshend, Dale, ed. *Terror and Wonder: The Gothic Imagination.* London: The British Library, 2014.

Winner, Langdon. *Autonomous Technology: Technics-out-of-Control as a Theme in Political Thought.* Cambridge, MA: MIT Press, 1977.

Young, Elizabeth. *Black Frankenstein: The Making of an American Metaphor.* New York: New York University Press, 2008.

DISCUSSION QUESTIONS

VOLUME I

PREFACE

Many have identified Frankenstein as a book of science fiction—indeed, as even the first of that genre in the English language. In the preface, Mary Shelley writes, "The event on which the interest of the story depends ... was recommended by the novelty of the situations which it developes; and, however impossible as a physical fact, affords a point of view to the imagination for the delineating of human passions" (p. 1). What is she suggesting about the relationship between science fiction and truth? Do you agree with her? Why or why not?

LETTERS

Why has Mary included the letters Captain Walton writes to his sister, Margaret? Do they help you understand the scientific context in which Victor (and Mary) operate? The social context? In what ways is Captain Walton like Victor? In what ways is he different? Do your views of him change from the beginning to the end of the novel?

In the last of the letters, Victor slips into the language of fate and predetermination. In what ways is his future fated, and in what ways is it of his own making? Why is he here using the language of fate?

CHAPTER I

What do we learn about Victor, his family, and his friends from this opening chapter of Mary's narrative? Would you call Victor's childhood "Edenic"? What are the implications of identifying it as such?

How did the young Victor approach reading, learning, and science? What kind of things impressed him or failed to impress him?

CHAPTER II

When Victor goes off to the University of Ingolstadt, he has become a "mother-less child," believing himself "totally unfitted for the company of strangers" (p. 28). How does this view of himself influence the way he approaches his studies? Have you ever felt this way when you have gone off to school or camp or elsewhere? If so, how did it affect the way you approached your tasks?

Have you ever had a teacher accuse you of reading "nonsense," as M. Krempe does of Victor? If so, how did you react? How is M. Krempe correct or incorrect in his assessment of Albertus Magnus and Paracelsus?

Who might be on the reading lists that M. Krempe and M. Waldman provide Victor (roughly around 1790)? M. Waldman shows Victor the machines in his laboratory. What might those machines have been? What did a laboratory of the late eighteenth century or early nineteenth century look like?

CHAPTER III

How does Victor approach his studies at the University of Ingolstadt? How is this approach different from your approach to your studies? How does Victor choose a mentor? Do you have a mentor? How would your studies be different if your mentoring situation were different?

How does Victor learn about "the principle of life" (p. 33)? In what venues do his inquiries take place? Are his inquiries limited to the laboratory? In what ways does contemporary research span laboratory research and research outside the laboratory?

What biological materials are used in a modern university? What rules govern the their use? How did these rules come about? Are rules different for human biological materials and nonhuman materials? Should they be?

Has discovering something about the natural world ever made you unhappy? Has learning something new in any endeavor ever made you unhappy? In either case, did you decide in the end that it was better to know or not to know? What other stories, fact or fiction, can you think of about knowledge causing unhappiness?

Why does Victor choose not to reveal his discovery to anyone or to consult with anyone about his determination to animate a creature based on his discovery? Is it right to keep discoveries secret? Are there examples of discoveries that have been kept secret, at least for a time? Should they have been kept secret?

Have you ever neglected other duties—your friends or family, your other classes, sports or art or entertainment—because of your commitment to a scientific or creative endeavor? How did it feel while you were doing this? How did it feel afterward?

CHAPTER IV

Why is Mary's description of the laboratory context of the "instruments of life" (p. 41) so vague? Compare this scene to the many film reenactments of it (especially the Edison Studios film in 1910, the Universal Pictures film directed by James Whale in 1931, and the TriStar Pictures film directed by Kenneth Branagh in 1994). How are they different? How are they the same? Do the different media give you different ideas about what the science is like? What the ethics are like?

Does Victor use both human and animal material in making his creature? What is the textual evidence, one way or the other? Does it matter to your understanding of the creature's status if it has animal as well as human parts? Does it matter to your understanding of contemporary human beings if doctors repair their hearts with valves from pigs or transplant baboon hearts into their chests? What about plastic valves, metal joints, or artificial hearts? What about artificial brains?

Some (feminist) critiques of *Frankenstein* point out that Victor succeeds in creating a motherless creature. Would a female creator have behaved differently toward her creature? Could a woman have done what Victor did in his day? Can a female scientist do what a male scientist can do today? Would a female scientist have made the creature? Do women do different science or do science differently than men?

CHAPTER V

Victor "conceived a violent antipathy even to the name of natural philosophy" (p. 51). Is there any extent to which he might be right in blaming the entire field of study or its overall perspective? Are there fields of inquiry to which you have an "antipathy," if not a violent one? What is that hostility based on? Is it moral? Is it metaphysical?

Parenthood can be emotionally challenging, as exemplified by the prevalence of post-partum depression among new mothers. Victor also falls ill in the wake of his animation of the creature, and his friend Henry Clerval nurses him back to health. Why in this period, which goes on for many months, does Victor completely ignore the creature's disappearance? What is his emotional state during this time, and in what ways is he like or unlike a parent?

CHAPTER VI

Upon returning to Geneva following William's death and seeing his creature there, illuminated by a flash of lightning, Victor states that "[t]he mere presence of the idea was an irresistible proof of the fact" (p. 58) that the creature was the murderer. Have you ever had such leaps of intuition that you immediately knew they were true, even without evidence or investigation? Is that the kind of understanding you associate with a scientist?

CHAPTER VII

Justine is convicted in a murder trial largely on the basis of circumstantial evidence. She was found in possession of the locket that had been on the murdered boy William and could not provide an alibi. How is the use of knowledge different in the law and in science? Are the stakes different? Should knowledge in law and science be identical? Should justice always be predicated on truth?

Why do you think Elizabeth's testimony has no influence on the jury?

How does religion influence the creation of knowledge in Justine's trial? How does it influence Victor's and Elizabeth's response to the execution of Justine? Why does Justine confess to a crime she did not commit and does not even understand, whereas Victor refuses to provide evidence about which he is certain?

VOLUME II

CHAPTER I

Victor does not seek forgiveness from those he loves, choosing instead to withdraw further from human society. Are his choices so far forgivable? Why or why not?

CHAPTER II

Why would Mary choose such an awe-filled and sublime environment as the Alpine glacier for the confrontation between Victor and the creature? Is it just dumb luck that both Victor and the creature end up there?

Why does the creature not accept Victor's offer to fight, a fight that the creature would most surely win?

In this chapter, Victor finally expresses some ambivalence and even self-doubt—about the circumstances of William's murder and about his treatment of the creature. Why?

CHAPTER III

How credible do you find the creature's account (or, rather, Walton's account of Frankenstein's account of the creature's account) of his early days and weeks? Do you find it surprising that the creature is such an exacting observer? Why or why not?

Why do the people the creature meets react to him with fear or hostility or both? Is it the same fear with which Frankenstein reacts?

How are the creature's "childhood days" like or unlike Victor's described at the outset of the novel?

CHAPTER IV

What do we learn about the creature from his interaction with the old man and the two young people who live in the cottage? What does the creature learn about himself?

What is the creature's view of spoken language? Of what importance is it for him to say that he "learned *and* applied" (p. 91, emphasis added) specific words? What is the difference between the words he learns and applies quickly and those that are still difficult for him?

How does the creature hope to overcome the "deformity" to which he attributes the inspiration of fear and hostility in the humans he meets? Is this hope reasonable?

CHAPTER V

What is the significance for the creature of Safie's arrival at the cottage? What does her presence mean for his understanding of language? Of emotion?

Again like Victor earlier in the novel, the creature experiences the ambivalence of the acquisition of knowledge—sometimes it is greatly for his benefit, but sometimes it causes pain. How does the creature experience this ambivalence? How does he propose to manage it?

Whereas the earlier chapters—for example, those about Victor's gathering of research materials—remind us more of contemporary biomedical research, the narrative of the later chapters, when the creature starts to find his own voice, is more reminiscent of issues with artificial intelligence. How do you imagine the creature's experience compares with that of a machine that has a dawning consciousness?

DISCUSSION QUESTIONS

CHAPTER VI

Why does the creature think that he has to produce copies of the letters between Safie and Felix in order for Victor to believe him?

What is the purpose of the creature's long digression into the affairs of the De Lacey family and of Safie and her family? What can we learn about Victor and the creature through comparison with these two families' experiences?

CHAPTER VII

Mary has the creature stumble upon *Paradise Lost* (Milton), *Plutarch's Lives*, and *The Sorrows of Young Werther* (Goethe). What three poems, histories, or novels (or even songs or other creative works) would you choose to educate a creature created today?

Each of us imagines that we are a singular "I" with a unitary body and mind and genetic makeup. At various times, this imagination comes under assault: Freud opened up the world of the subconscious, fracturing the unitary mind. More contemporary discoveries of the importance of microbiota pose the problem of a fragmented body, even after a long history of replacement of lost limbs with prostheses. Contemporary discoveries of chimerism can fragment our genetic unity. In so many ways, the "I" is really a complex collective. What are the implications of such fragmentation, and what are its consequences for understanding who we are as well for the pursuit of science and technology? Does it provide us with new motivations? Does it result in different kinds of knowledge or different kinds of technologies?

The creature says he read *Paradise Lost* as a "true history." What mistakes do we make when we read fiction as fact? How do we know?

It turns out that Victor did make notes or keep a journal of his experiments, and the creature finds them and reads them, although the reader is never given any details from them. How would these notes differ from the letters exchanged elsewhere in the novel?

If you were designing a creature that you intended to be sentient and sapient, what form or type would you give it? Why? Would it depend on its function? Would you take into account its feelings, if any, regarding how it looks, or would you take into account the feelings of the people among whom it would live and work?

The creature refers to his designed encounter with the elder De Lacey as a "trial." How is this trial like or not like the other trials in the novel—for instance, those of Justine and Victor?

CHAPTER VIII

When the creature arrives in Geneva and meets William, the child's identity is unknown to him, and he does not have murder on his mind. He imagines that William is too young to have formed a prejudice against his deformity, but he is wrong and in his anger and discovery of William's identity strangles the boy. Where does William's prejudice (or fear) come from? Why is the creature wrong about William's innocence of such knowledge?

At the end of the chapter, the creature announces his plan to Victor: that Victor create for him "one as deformed and horrible as myself [who] would not deny herself to me" (p. 120). The creature recognizes himself as intelligent, and he has all of Victor's notes about how he was made. So why doesn't the creature himself make his mate or propose to Victor that he teach him or that they collaborate in the making of his mate? Why does he demand, "This being you must create" (p. 120)?

CHAPTER IX

Victor concludes about the creature's proposition that "justice due both to him and my fellow-creatures demanded of me that I should comply with his request" (p. 123). What competing forms or definitions of justice are at play here?

If you were Victor, would you agree to make the creature a mate? Why or why not? Are there perhaps other, unexplored possibilities?

VOLUME III

CHAPTER I

Why does Victor delay fulfilling his promise to the creature? What reason do you think is most important?

Mary is very self-conscious of the social impossibilities in her world—for example, that women, people from lower social classes, immigrants, non-Christians, and slaves cannot partake in the full range of social and political possibilities that are reserved for people (usually men) of privilege. This problem is represented in this chapter by Elizabeth's inability to accompany Victor on his two-year jaunt across Europe. *Frankenstein* is also a novel about technical possibilities and impossibilities. How do social (im)possibilities and technical (im)possibilities play into each other in the novel? Does the relative lack of technical impossibility help us understand or feel differently toward the presence of social impossibility?

CHAPTER II

Why is there no account of what Frankenstein learns from his contacts in London, "the information necessary for the completion of my promise" (p. 133)? What might Victor need to learn to assemble a female creature that he did not already know?

Victor refers to himself as "a blasted tree; the bolt has entered my soul" (p. 135). To what does this refer? How might you compare Victor's metaphor of being struck by lightning to the creature's experience of the "spark of life"?

There are differences between how Victor approaches his first experiment and how he approaches his second experiment, despite his solitude in the latter. What are they? Is there a relationship between his different attitudes and their respective outcomes? Does Victor have a clearer sense of the second experiment's potential outcomes? Why? Can we fully think things out in advance?

CHAPTER III

Why does Victor decide to destroy the new creature? Is it simply because of the first creature's appearance and a "countenance [that] expressed the utmost extent of malice and treachery" (p. 140), observed in the dimmest of light? If the creature had not appeared, would Victor have finished his work?

The confrontation between the creature—"You are my creator, but I am your master; —obey!" (p. 141)—and Victor in this chapter is perhaps the most dramatic scene in the novel. Is the creature's wrath justified? Have the tables turned as thoroughly as the creature imagines? Does Victor fully understand the scope of his decision not to cooperate with the creature's demands?

What else must Victor believe if he believes that creating a new creature would be an act of "the basest and most atrocious selfishness" (p. 144)? Can he reasonably hold this belief in his head while at the same time feeling that he "was about the commission of a dreadful crime" (p. 144) when he is disposing of the torn-apart remains of the second creature?

CHAPTER IV

Victor refers to destiny often in this chapter. Is choice now extinguished for him, and is fulfilling his destiny all that he has left to do? In what does Victor see his destiny? Are there points when he could have changed it? Is destiny the same thing as path dependency?

Compare the respective legal cases against Justine and Victor and how they play out. What are the crucial pieces of evidence? How do the accused and the judicial authorities behave? How do the physical evidence, the circumstances, and other factors come together for a verdict?

CHAPTER V

Why does Victor continue to insist to his father that he is a murderer?

CHAPTER VI

Why does Victor not tell Elizabeth about the creature, especially before or at least on their wedding night? Are his potential reasons the same as or different from his reasons for not telling his father or Clerval?

Why does Victor skip quickly over his period of madness after Elizabeth's murder and his father's consequent death? Might he have been subject to another trial, this time for the murder of his bride?

Victor finally tells the whole story to someone in this chapter—a magistrate of Geneva—who listens politely and then interestedly but uses elements of Victor's own story about the timeline and the creature's superior power in his refusal to assist Victor. Is this denial ironic? A condemnation of bureaucracy? A convenient plot device?

CHAPTER VII

Victor expresses an extensive oath (or small prayer?) in this chapter, seemingly the first time he has invoked some religious or quasi-religious power. Where does this oath come from? Does his turn to spirituality here have anything to do with his experience with science? With law?

Why does Victor makes a distinction between the "ardent desire of [his] soul" and "the mechanical impulse of some [external] power" (p. 170)? Is this distinction easy to make for him? For us? Can Victor's creature make such a distinction? If we were to make such a creature today, would it be able to do so?

WALTON'S LETTERS (CONTINUED)

Why, in his letter to Margaret, does Captain Walton tell her that he really believes Victor's story? Is Victor's account sufficient?

Even if science fiction, Mary's novel is set in the past. Given that the novel is told through letters and stories passed from one person to another, do you think the readers of its day might have taken it as a real-life, nonfiction account? As an alternate history? As something like the radio broadcast of H. G. Wells's *The War of the Worlds* in 1938?

Walton quotes Victor as calling the creature a "sensitive and rational animal" (p. 175) and then shortly afterward "a man" (p. 175). Is the former a good and full definition of the latter? How do we define personhood today? Can personhood include nonrational animals? Rational nonanimals? Is personhood unitary, or can there be different varieties of it?

Victor recognizes that he has a duty to support "his [creature's] happiness and well-being" and a duty to humanity "paramount to that" (p. 181). What is the logic of Victor's assigning the duty to humanity the paramount value? Is this view utilitarian—emphasizing the good of the many over the good of the one? Is it communitarian—that the creature really doesn't belong to a broader community, whose values and safety are more important than the outsider's? Is Victor's logic here instead simply an excuse for his earlier mistakes? Are there times when the logic of privileging the larger number over the smaller number is incorrect and we should risk the well-being of the community for the individual?

Across the novel, there is something of a comparative ethics of suffering: Victor asserts that his suffering is greater than Justine's, and Walton overhears the creature claiming that his suffering is greater than Victor's. Is there any sense to be made of these comparisons? Can one being suffer more than another? Can suffering be objectively determined? Or is it entirely subjective? Is my suffering always more than yours simply because it is mine?

Do you agree with Walton that the creature does not feel true remorse but instead feels only frustrated that Victor is now free of him?

Do you believe the creature will extinguish himself? If you believe that promise, then do you believe the rest of his representations of his feelings and intentions? Why or why not?

ESSAYS

JOSEPHINE JOHNSTON, "TRAUMATIC RESPONSIBILITY"

The novel portrays an extreme case of scientific responsibility, but all of us are implicated in situations where we are responsible to moral standards, to particular ideas, and to other people. What kinds of responsibility do you have as a scientist, a citizen, a creator, a human being? How do you define these responsibilities? And what does it mean to "feel" them?

Johnston argues that Victor experiences two forms of responsibility: responsibility *for* and responsibility *to*. Are there other kinds of responsibility, in particular forms of shared or collective responsibility?

CORY DOCTOROW, "I'VE CREATED A MONSTER! (AND SO CAN YOU)"

Doctorow's essay argues that science fiction is not really about predicting the future but rather about understanding the present. What does Mary's novel, which was presumably written for a present two hundred years old, have to tell us about scientific practices today? Is it still relevant, or do we need new stories to confront the present?

According to the theory of the "adjacent possible," technological change comes "when enough of the necessary stuff is in place" (p. 201). According to this logic, discovery can proceed only through so many pathways, and what's coming always depends on what has come. Do you agree with this view, or do you think that true surprise and serendipity are possible? Is the direction of scientific progress somehow predetermined?

Doctorow argues that although technological changes are often the result of individual choices, how they are used becomes a collective choice. Using the example of Facebook, he talks about how disavowing a surveillance society is a difficult social choice—but still one that you can make as an individual. What collective choices concerning contemporary technologies do you disagree with, and what would it take for you to opt out?

JANE MAIENSCHEIN AND KATE MACCORD, "CHANGING CONCEPTIONS OF HUMAN NATURE"

Maienschein and MacCord believe that Mary's story is both "restrictive" and "instructive." What do you think they mean by this? Do you agree with their assertion? Does *Frankenstein* go beyond these parameters?

What is your answer to the authors' question "Is the creature human?"? If the creature is not human by the end of the novel, is there any way for it to become so?

What do you think the relationship is between what the authors call the biological concept of "human" and the social concept of "person"? Can one easily or neatly demarcate the social from the biological in this way?

ALFRED NORDMANN, "UNDISTURBED BY REALITY"

Nordmann's essay suggests that modern incarnations of the creature, such as "Frankenfoods" and "Frankenmaterials," are not scientific outcomes but a throwback to alchemy and the supernatural. What is the relationship between science and belief today? When we entrust ourselves to an airplane or an algorithmic credit-scoring system, are we engaging in an act of reason or a leap of faith?

The publication of Mary's novel predated the modern term *scientist* by almost twenty years, and Nordmann argues that her novel is "not one of modern science" (p. 223). Is Victor a scientist? Would we recognize him as one today? If not, how would you describe him in contemporary terms?

Nordmann argues that contemporary technoscience is "undisturbed by reality"; in other words, we are creating materials, ideas, and life-forms that have no corollary in nature. At its most fundamental level, is science about understanding the natural world or about creating a structure of knowledge that may or may not resemble the reality we perceive?

ELIZABETH BEAR, *"FRANKENSTEIN* REFRAMED; OR, THE TROUBLE WITH PROMETHEUS"

Bear suggests that Victor's central character flaw is his lack of empathy. Do you agree? Is empathy an important faculty for the conducting of scientific research?

The other great character flaw that Bear highlights is Victor's narcissism. The great critique of scientific reason at the dawn of the Enlightenment was precisely this: that it was pure hubris for humanity to imagine itself at the center of the universe, to displace the external existence of God for a structure of knowledge built within our minds. Do you think the pursuit of scientific discovery is a fundamentally narcissistic enterprise or a humbling one? Can one be a successful *and* humble scientist, engineer, or creator?

Bear talks about the fact that Victor's beauty, his handsomeness, leads people to treat him better than they treat his creature. What role do you think beauty plays or should play in scientific discovery? Is the search for truth also a search for beauty, to paraphrase the poet Jonathan Keats, Mary's contemporary?

ANNE K. MELLOR, *"FRANKENSTEIN,* GENDER, AND MOTHER NATURE"

Frankenstein was initially published anonymously, and some critics or reviewers speculated that Percy Shelley wrote it. Do you think a man could have written *Frankenstein* as Mary Shelley wrote it?

Given Mellor's interpretation of the novel, what do you make of contemporary accounts that change Victor's gender—for example, the PBS digital series *Frankenstein, MD,* featuring a Victoria Frankenstein, or the children's book series *Franny K. Stein* by Jim Benton? If the creator at the center of the story was raised and socialized as a woman, in Shelley's time or today, would her relationship with her creation change? If so, how?

Are today's scientists and engineers who are involved in synthetic biology and other similar endeavors engaged in motherless creation?

HEATHER E. DOUGLAS, "THE BITTER AFTERTASTE OF TECHNICAL SWEETNESS"

How close is the analogy between Victor's work and the work of the atomic scientists in the 1930s and 1940s?

Do you believe that the pursuit of "technical sweetness" is one reason why Victor completes his experiment?

If creating life is so technically sweet and technical sweetness is important in making the creature, why doesn't Victor make the creature a mate?

CONTRIBUTORS

VOLUME EDITORS

DAVID H. GUSTON is professor and founding director of the School for the Future of Innovation in Society at Arizona State University. His *Between Politics and Science* (Cambridge, 2000) was awarded the 2002 Don K. Price Prize by the American Political Science Association for best book in science and technology policy. He is the founding editor of the *Journal of Responsible Innovation* (Taylor & Francis). A fellow of the American Association for the Advancement of Science, he cochaired the 2008 Gordon Research Conference on Science and Technology Policy, "Governing Emerging Technologies." He holds a B.A. from Yale University and a Ph.D. from the Massachusetts Institute of Technology.

ED FINN is the founding director of the Center for Science and the Imagination at Arizona State University, where he is an assistant professor with a joint appointment in the School of Arts, Media and Engineering and the Department of English. Ed's research and teaching explore digital narratives, contemporary culture, and the intersection of the humanities, arts, and sciences. He is the author of *What Algorithms Want: Imagination in the Age of Computing* (MIT Press, 2017) and coeditor of *Hieroglyph: Stories and Visions for a Better Future* (William Morrow, 2014). He holds a B.A. from Princeton University and an M.A. and Ph.D. from Stanford University.

JASON SCOTT ROBERT holds the Lincoln Chair in Ethics and serves as senior ethics advisor to the provost at Arizona State University. He is also director of ASU's Lincoln Center for Applied Ethics, and dean's distinguished professor in the School of Life Sciences. His teaching and research are at the intersection of bioethics and the philosophy of biology. He is the author of the book *Embryology, Epigenesis and Evolution: Taking Development Seriously* (Cambridge, 2004). He holds a B.A. from Queen's University at Kingston and an M.A. and Ph.D. from McMaster University.

ESSAYISTS

Elizabeth Bear, science fiction and fantasy author

Cory Doctorow, science fiction author, activist, journalist, blogger, coeditor of *Boing Boing*

Heather E. Douglas, associate professor and Waterloo Chair in Science and Society, University of Waterloo

Josephine Johnston, director of research and research scholar, The Hastings Center

Kate MacCord, PhD candidate, School of Life Sciences, Arizona State University

Jane Maienschein, Regent's Professor, School of Life Sciences, and director of the Center for Biology and Society, Arizona State University

Anne K. Mellor, Distinguished Professor of English Literature and Women's Studies, University of California, Los Angeles

Alfred Nordmann, professor of philosophy, Technische Universität Darmstadt

Charles E. Robinson, professor emeritus, Department of English, University of Delaware

ANNOTATORS

C. Athena Aktipis, assistant professor, Department of Psychology, Arizona State University

Braden Allenby, professor, School of Sustainable Engineering and the Built Environment, Arizona State University

Ariel Anbar, professor, School of Earth and Space Exploration, Arizona State University

Miguel Astor-Aguilera, associate professor, School of Historical, Philosophical, and Religious Studies, Arizona State University

Dominic Berry, research fellow, Science, Technology, and Innovation Studies, University of Edinburgh

Ron Broglio, associate professor, Department of English, Arizona State University

Sara Brownell, assistant professor, School of Life Sciences, Arizona State University

Carlos Castillo-Chavez, professor, Mathematical, Computational, and Modeling Sciences Center, Arizona State University

Robert Cook-Deegan, professor, School for the Future of Innovation in Society, Arizona State University

Mary Drago, independent scholar

Joey Eschrich, editor and program manager, Center for Science and the Imagination, Arizona State University

Ed Finn, assistant professor, School of Arts, Media and Engineering and Department of English, and founding director, Center for Science and the Imagination, Arizona State University

Mary Margaret Fonow, professor, School of Social Transformation, Arizona State University

Joel Gereboff, associate professor, School of Historical, Philosophical, and Religious Studies, Arizona State University

Eileen Gunn, science fiction author and editor

David H. Guston, professor and founding director, School for the Future of Innovation in Society, Arizona State University

Judith Guston, curator and director of collections, Rosenbach Museum and Library

Chris Hanlon, associate professor, School of Humanities, Arts, and Cultural Studies, Arizona State University

Dehlia Hannah, visiting assistant professor, School for the Future of Innovation in Society, Arizona State University

Sean A. Hays, independent scholar

Nicole Herbots, professor emerita, Department of Physics, Arizona State University

Adam Hosein, assistant professor, Department of Philosophy, University of Colorado at Boulder

Allison Kavey, associate professor, John Jay School of Criminal Justice, City University of New York

Jonathon Keats, writer, artist, and experimental philosopher

Douglas Kelley, professor, School of Social and Behavioral Sciences, Arizona State University

Sally Kitch, Regents' Professor, School of Social Transformation, Arizona State University

Joel A. Klein, lecturer, Department of History, and postdoctoral research fellow, Center for Science and Society, Columbia University

Sheldon Krimsky, professor, Department of Urban and Environmental Policy and Planning, Tufts University

JJ LaTourelle, PhD candidate, School of Life Sciences, Arizona State University

Devoney Looser, professor, Department of English, Arizona State University

Arthur B. Markman, professor, Department of Psychology, University of Texas at Austin

April Miller, honors faculty fellow, Barrett Honors College, Arizona State University

Ben Minteer, professor, School of Life Sciences, Arizona State University

Stephanie Naufel, PhD candidate, Department of Biomedical Engineering, Northwestern University

Annalee Newitz, fiction and nonfiction journalist, editor, and author

Nicole Piemonte, postdoctoral associate, Lincoln Center for Applied Ethics, Arizona State University

Ramsey Eric Ramsey, associate dean, Barrett Honors College, Arizona State University

Jason Scott Robert, Lincoln Chair in Ethics, Lincoln Center for Applied Ethics, and associate professor, School of Life Sciences, Arizona State University

Hannah Rogers, instructor, University Writing Program, Columbia University

Daniel Sarewitz, professor, School for the Future of Innovation in Society, and codirector, Consortium for Science, Policy and Outcomes, Arizona State University

Pablo Schyfter, lecturer, Science, Technology, and Innovation Studies, University of Edinburgh

Kerri Slatus, Visiting Affiliate Assistant Professor, Loyola University Maryland

Mike Stanford, principal lecturer, Barrett Honors College, Arizona State University

Jameien Taylor, PhD student, Hugh Downs School of Human Communication, Arizona State University

Melissa Wilson Sayres, assistant professor, School of Life Sciences, Arizona State University

Stephani Etheridge Woodson, associate professor, School of Film, Dance, and Theater, Arizona State University

"This new, remarkable annotated edition of *Frankenstein* with its accompanying essays brings the 'modern Prometheus' flawlessly into our century in a manner sure to inspire scientists and nonscientists in a conversation that Shelley herself might not have foreseen but surely would have encouraged."

Arthur L. Caplan, Drs. William F. and Virginia Connolly Mitty Professor, founding head of the Division of Bioethics at the School of Medicine, New York University

"This wonderful new edition is a happy addition to the critical literature examining the meaning of the tale for our twenty-first-century commitments to heroic science, engineering, and technology."

Rachelle D. Hollander, Director, Center for Engineering Ethics and Society, National Academy of Engineering

"The Promethean tale of *Frankenstein* is a rich source of questions about the price that scientists and the public pay for knowledge. This annotated edition rescues the classic allegory from popular culture's caricature and presents it with a framework for exploring the questions raised. Among the many questions, perhaps the most important is, when scientists either from amoral arrogance or negligent lack of foresight present a discovery society is not prepared to deal with—nuclear weapons, engineered gene lines, climate modification—what is the scientists' responsibility going forward? Is it merely to watch in horror as the knowledge is unleashed on society?"

Rush D. Holt, Chief Executive Officer, American Association for the Advancement of Science; Executive Publisher, *Science* Family of Journals

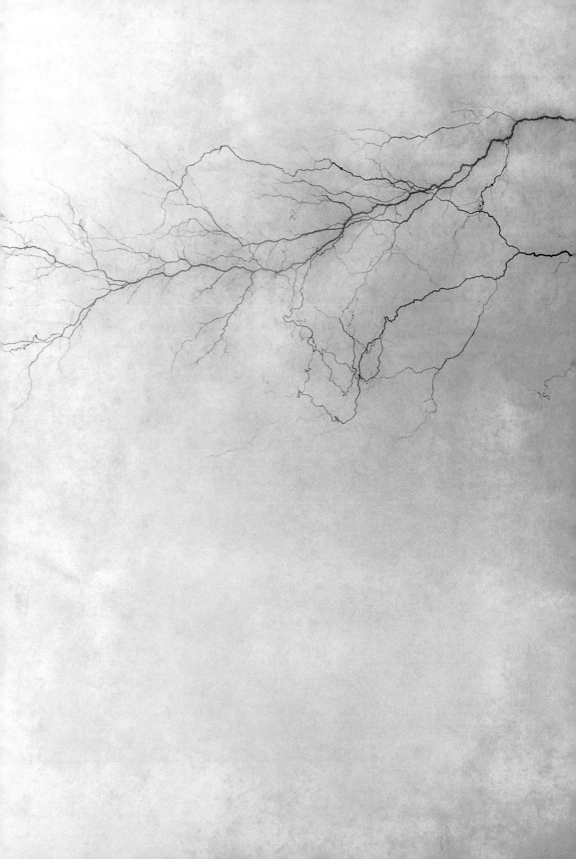

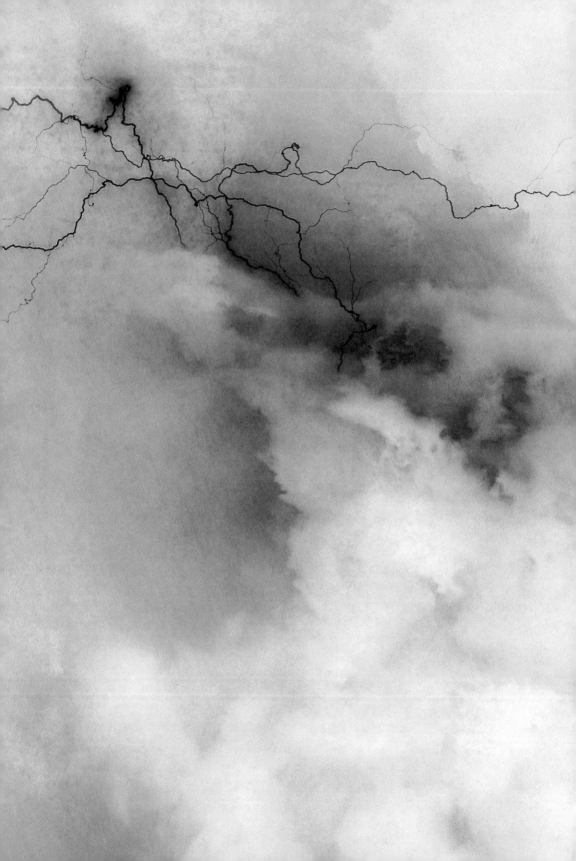